FATAL
JUSTICE

FATAL JUSTICE

FAYE SNOWDEN

KENSINGTON PUBLISHING CORP.
http://www.kensingtonbooks.com

DAFINA BOOKS are published by

Kensington Publishing Corp.
850 Third Avenue
New York, NY 10022

All Kensington titles, imprints and distributed lines are available at special quantity discounts for bulk purchases for sales promotion, premiums, fund-raising, educational or institutional use.

Special book excerpts or customized printings can also be created to fit specific needs. For details, write or phone the office of the Kensington Special Sales Manager: Kensington Publishing Corp., 850 Third Avenue, New York, NY 10022. Attn. Special Sales Department. Phone: 1-800-221-2647.

Dafina Books and the Dafina logo Reg. U.S. Pat. & TM Off.

ISBN 0-7582-0751-4

First Kensington Trade Paperback Printing: October 2005
10 9 8 7 6 5 4 3 2 1

Printed in the United States of America

For Eric

PROLOGUE

The place is beautiful but the two standing under the shimmering green leaves do not notice. They do not see the thriving river or the gray blue water rushing over the rocks. Sunlight sifting through emerald leaves and red flowers tucked at the bases of redwood trees are lost on them. What they do see, however, is each other. How intent each of their faces are, hers with determination and his with equal determination but something else as well. Fear that he is about to lose control yet again.

Maybe he never had control over this woman. Maybe he was a fool to think so. The brown suitcase with the brass buckles, the one she holds in front of her as she listens and does not listen tells him that he has let things get out of hand. The fact that she is packed and ready to go, contrary to what they had agreed—no, what she had promised him—tells him that indeed, he must have been a fool. And things must be set right. But first he has a duty. He must at least try. So he tries to reason with her.

"Debra," he says. "This will not stand. It will never work."

"No," she answers. "It will. I know it will. It has to."

"You can run away all you want but you will never be able to run away from the world."

Her hands, the smooth brown fingers, the painted red nails reach for him. "When running away is all a person has, then running away is the only thing to do. I refuse to rot away doing the right thing."

He stops those reaching hands, places his own hand on her bare arm. He had once thought this woman beautiful. Her smooth dark skin and brown eyes reminded him of Cleopatra. But now he scoffs. The nails greedily clutching at him are chipped. But his job right now is to keep her calm. Her face grows cold as she begins to understand his intent. And as he watches, that face he has loved grows even colder, as cold as the water rushing over the rocks behind them.

He studies her and fully understands how it came to be that he is here in this beautiful wood pleading with this woman to do as he ordered her to do. Here she is, staring at him, her skin as smooth as a ribbon of flowing chocolate, her large brown eyes accentuated by the fake eyelashes, the full mouth now set firm with determination. He had allowed her to catch him like a bear in a trap. He caresses her arm but she jerks away. She stumbles backwards on those ridiculous white go-go boots paired with a miniskirt that only reaches mid-thigh. She had worn that skirt, which revealed her long legs, to enchant him. No, not enchant, to ensnare as she had done on the very first day that they met.

"You have no heart," she tells him. "You have no heart after all that we've been through that you can stand there and look at me like I'm trash."

"Heart?" he counters. "You tell me about heart? How many men have there been besides me, Debra? How many have you gone through before you found the sucker in me?"

The slap stings the side of his face. But she misses the warning in his eyes.

"I did what I had to do to make it," she says. "And you have the nerve to stand here self-righteous with everything handed to you on a silver platter and judge me. If I'm so bad then why in the hell didn't you run the other way? Nothing was stopping you from that."

"I was weak," he says, as if this is explanation enough. In a way, it is. Now, if only she would accept that.

"Not was, are. You are weak. You will always be weak."

He can see how angry she is now. It seems as if the hold she has on the suitcase is the only thing that is keeping her from flying completely out of control. As he watches the determination in her face, he can see that he is about to lose. He cannot lose, he must not.

She is cursing now, words he has never heard, words he didn't even think she knew. She calls him a fairy, a pretender, a worthless piece of flesh and bone. She calls him a worthless piece of shit. As those words fly from her mouth, so do the tears from her eyes. Her mascara draws two black streaks on either side of her face. She is no longer beautiful but uncomely as a woman in hard labor. Revulsion rises in his throat. There must have been something in his face because she hits him with the suitcase.

Before she can strike again he wrenches the suitcase from her. He hurls it out of her reach. She comes at him in a windmill of fists then, shrieking some whore's cry, the cry he should have recognized during those first days of enchantment. The fists surprised him. He never thought she would come at him with bare fists. The first blow catches him full in the face, causing a coughing pain that makes him lose his footing. Doubled over, he raises his arms to protect his head. The second blow lands on his elbow. Stinging pain shoots up his shoulder.

But then something strange happens. She stumbles and falls. He stands still for a moment, his heart as loud as a train whistle, his breath rasping in his throat. When he calms down, he bends to help her up. He stops suddenly. The black, bouffant wig, the one with the red ribbon tucked in front, has fallen off. A brown stocking cap subdues her natural hair. To him, she seems a monster.

The blood does not help. She has hit her head against a rock and her blood flows as freely as the river behind them. She is conscious but groggy, accepting his help by clutching at the sides of his arms to pull her body up. The blood gives him the idea, tells him what to do next. He knows that if she is allowed to leave this place by the river, his life would be over. Worse, he would be saddled with her, this piece of plastic he has mistaken for a real flesh and blood woman.

He pushes her back down, ignoring the smell of the wet riverbank. She has time to look at him with a question in her eyes—not fear yet—but question. The question turns to fear when he picks up a smooth rock and brings it down against her brow.

But he has not hit hard enough. She cries, raises her hand to her face, then claws at him with fake fingernails that do not hurt at all. He drags her to the edge of the river. By the throat, he pushes her head into water. The blue-gray water swirls over her startled face, then closes like a glass door over her open eyes.

And like that, he watches her die, hardly feeling the hands at his wrist. He watches until the light in her eyes dim, until her mouth opens to accept the river into her lungs.

He stares at her a moment or two. Horror at what he has done sinks into him. He scours the area in search of the suitcase but he cannot find it. Finally, he decides securing the body is more important. With the use of fallen logs and vines, he weights it down as best he can and throws the body into the deepest part of the river. He watches with his hands in his pockets. Like the suitcase, the horror over her death at his hand vanishes. He only feels regret at what had to be done.

For years afterwards he dreams of her. He sees her awakening in the place which she has awakened for the last thirty years, beneath a bed of orange leaves and beneath a sun so hot it has had the power to desiccate an entire river. She lies there waiting, eyes tilted toward the blazing sun.

She is patient. One day someone will come to that now dead part of the wood to discover a curve of white bone through the leaves and find the tattered suitcase that he was unable to find. It has been many years, decade upon decade, but he knows that she is patient. Death is always patient.

Anna

Anna hurt. Anna don't like dark, don't like smell, either. Home smells much better even though it's dark most of the time there, too, even in the daylight because Daddy don't let her go outside, pulls the curtains real tight. Outside, not allowed, Daddy says, outside not safe.

That's why Anna locked away, because she went outside when Daddy wasn't home. She went outside when he told her no. But it was the sun's fault, the sun stabbing through the heavy curtains. And when Anna open curtains, she had to pull her eyes back because the sun hurt. But the sun smelled sweet, too, the outside air sweeter.

So Anna went outside—alone—without Daddy, and then it happened. The screaming happened. So noisy out there, so many sounds, people looking at her, her bare feet, her yellow legs without lotion. Hair all messed up because she had been tricked by the sun, so tricked by the sweet smell on the air that she had to go outside right away. No time to comb hair.

Toot sweet like her mother used to say before she went away and didn't come back no more. Mamma never coming back. Anna knew that when she and Daddy left Virginia. Mamma would never find them in this place where it is summer or spring all the time and it never snows and the air never cuts your skin because it has little slivers of ice in it. Mamma wouldn't know how to find them in Dunhill County, California. She wouldn't find the place even if she searched and searched.

So sun tricked Anna and Anna went outside and everybody stared and Anna whimpered, then screamed, and then, and then, the policeman came. The policeman in his black and white car, all shiny, blue and white lights flashing like blue skies and angry clouds fighting one another, trying to figure out who would win that day—clear blue air or clouds.

Clouds, Anna thought now. Clouds won because the policeman took her away, down to a place with shiny floors and bright lights all over the ceiling and people talking and typing, looking at screens of light. Floor cold on Anna's feet and handcuffs hurt her wrists. Policeman sit Anna down, crooned at her like she was a baby. Anna ain't no baby; Anna twenty-five and Daddy say Anna pretty. He say Anna has skin like butter and eyes like a doe-deer.

Then Daddy come, then that lady doctor, she come, too. And she argue with the policeman. She mad, said he should have took Anna to the hospital, but the policeman told her he didn't see no reason for hospital. Didn't see no reason to sit up in no emergency room all day.

Then Daddy and the lady doctor, they brought Anna here, many long days and nights ago and Anna live here now. It smell funny, like Pine-Sol and Mr. Clean. They give Anna pills every day, hard white things that don't taste good, especial' when you chew them. Daddy say it safer than home. He come see Anna all the time, every day when his joints not hurting and his breathing is good. But it ain't safe, especial' not now, it ain't safe when the lights go out. It ain't safe in the dark.

CHAPTER 1

You don't cry. Forget all the horror books, the mysteries, the TV dramas and true crime stories where the victim rests on his or her knees, hands over face, cringing, crying. And remember this. You don't cry. There are no tears, not in that perfect circle of horror, there is only terror—complete, tangible, bone-numbing like a poison terror. And every instinct in your entire body focuses on one thing and one thing only—survival. But you don't cry. There is no time for crying or for grieving. And if you happen to survive, you might cry later. And that is how it was for Kendra Hamilton. And that was what finally ended her relationship with Richard T. Marvel. The crying that would not come, the realization that she could be dead and her lover was at fault.

Kendra had faced danger before but with less terror. She remembered once being trapped in a foxhole hastily and ineffectively dug by the refugees she was there to treat. Bullets screamed overhead, whizzed past her as she hunched over, covering the refugee lying beneath her and praying that the huge red cross on her back would be protection and not a target. But standing between the gun barrels of both Luke Bertrand and Rich Marvel—one wanting to protect her, the other wanting to kill her—that was different. That feeling, that terror was personal.

And Kendra couldn't abandon it, no matter how hard she tried. As she and Rich made love, the terror lingered. When Rich moved inside her she felt the same spinning as she had when she stood between the barrels of Rich and Luke's guns. Every time Rich touched her, Kendra felt the bullet once again slamming into her shoulder.

Rich knew how she felt, how she relived that night every time she was in his arms. She could tell by the way he would search her face when he thought she was not looking and avert his eyes as she moved to return his gaze. She could tell by the way he avoided touching her at the end of their relationship. Their lovemaking became more infrequent, the sessions briefer. But he didn't say anything. He never said anything. He didn't have to.

They never really broke things off. There was no closure. The phone calls just stopped—especially after the trial, after nothing else forced them together. When Luke Bertrand, the man who had killed her mother and many others walked free from the Dunhill County courtroom, Kendra walked away from Rich, from them both to start her life over.

And now here she was walking right back into his life as if she had a right to. She knew that she didn't but she couldn't help herself. Okay, it wasn't because she couldn't help herself; it was because it couldn't be helped. She needed him now, needed him more than she ever had in the past. She just hoped that Richard T. Marvel would have the inclination to help her one more time.

It took her two days to find him. He had quit the Dunhill County Sheriff's Department two years ago. As far as she knew, he hadn't worked since. He left no forwarding address and Beau Blair, his former partner and good friend, would not tell her more than that. She knew from another friend that he had been drinking heavily and that the upright, uptight Richard T. Marvel had reached a crisis point in his life. But the friend didn't know where Rich was and told her in no uncertain terms to stay away from him, to leave him alone and let him put his life back together.

It was finally Rich's brother, Dominic, who relented, who told her where Rich was. Rich was spending the weekend at Dominic's cabin in Tahoe.

"But if he asks, you didn't hear it from me," he had said, wagging his finger at her before going back on stage to finish his set.

Kendra braved the drive to Tahoe in a pink Ford Fiesta she had rented from a place called Rent-A-Wreck. Money had been tight since she lost her medical license. The beat-up Fiesta was all that she could afford. She made the trip in the middle of the day, the air smelling sweet like summer even though it was early February. Brilliant sunlight dazzled through the tall redwoods rising up and piercing the blue sky. Kendra couldn't believe that on a day as beautiful as this that anyone's life could be so utterly out of focus. She had returned to Dunhill County with one purpose in mind, a sick purpose some would say, but a purpose nonetheless. But instead of being able to carry out her plans, she found herself on the road to the past once again.

Following Dominic's instructions, she came to a cabin about twenty miles from the main highway. She walked a pathway strewn with pine needles to the front door of a large cabin. She opened the screen door and knocked. No answer. Feeling no remorse whatsoever, Kendra pulled over a lawn chair near the front door and peered through one of the front door's small windows. There was no movement in the darkened living room.

She stepped down from the chair and walked out into the front yard. The air was motionless around her. Kendra heard nothing, not even birds chirping in the sky. She turned to leave, then stopped suddenly. One more look around couldn't hurt anything. It was when she reached the backside of the cabin that she almost stopped breathing.

Kendra had stumbled onto the most beautiful landscape that she had ever seen. Beyond a small clearing in the backyard, tall redwoods and bushes with red and orange flowers framed a still lake as smooth and quiet as glass. A canoe, looking as serene as a lotus flower, reflected in the lake's surface and floated upon the blue water. Richard T. Marvel, and Kendra knew it was him by his broad shoulders, sat in the canoe, his hands in his lap, the oars resting idly by his sides. The expression on Rich's face seemed as motionless as the lake itself. Even though he was in profile, he looked like a man who had just been told that his life was over or was about to be over.

Kendra began walking toward the lake. Though her tennis shoes crunched along the gravel and rock, Rich did not turn toward her. He just sat there in the canoe, that same bewildered look on his face. She reached the edge of the lake and opened her mouth to speak. But she found that she couldn't. She didn't have the right words. And the ones that she did have stuck like stones in her throat. She looked at the cloudless sky above them. A duck, its long neck stretched out, spread its wings against the sky, arcing gracefully above Rich's head. The duck honked once, disturbing the silence. But Rich still didn't move.

Kendra licked her lips, found her own voice. "Rich," she said.

It sounded small and fragile. She was not surprised that Rich didn't hear. So she tried again, calling his name louder. He still did not move. It was as if someone had painted him and that canoe on the water.

"Rich," Kendra said for the third time.

His head turned slowly toward her and he stared at her for a moment or two. Then he said, "Hey," almost quietly, in a bemused voice. "Are you real?"

Kendra felt her heart knot. Tears stung her eyes. She realized two things in that moment as Rich looked at her, questioningly, wondering if she were real or not. She realized that he was still in love with her and she realized that she had made a mistake coming here. Richard T. Marvel was in no condition to help her. He couldn't even help himself.

Before she could make up her mind to leave, Rich picked up the oars and rowed the canoe to shore. As he dipped the oars in the water they made no sound. It was when he stepped out of the boat that Kendra noticed the extent of his condition. He didn't lift one leg over the side, but instead, he stumbled and fell on the bank. Out of instinct more than anything else, Kendra caught him before he reached the ground.

The smell hit her as she lifted him up. He stank of alcohol. And not just beer. He smelled of tequila, of rum and whiskey. Richard T. Marvel, the man who used to get his hair cut every two weeks like clockwork, the man who would not wear the same clothes the next day if you threatened his life, Richard T. Marvel stank like a broken-down drunk.

Empty bottles of Corona littered the bottom of the canoe. Some were old, dried out, the glass foggy. Others were brand new with a little dribble of foam around the neck. Budweiser cans lay crumpled along the bank. When Kendra took a step back with the weight of a drunken Richard T. Marvel against her, she almost lost her footing against an empty fifth of Jack Daniel's. She stared at the black label before looking back to Rich.

His hair had grown out in uneven patches around his handsome face. He hadn't shaved in what looked like several days and there were bald spots and bumps dotting his beard. He half stumbled and half jerked away from her.

"Well," he said, only slightly slurred, "it seems that you are real, the great Kendra Hamilton deigning to pay me a visit."

He swooped down in a mock bow. This time, when he stumbled, Kendra did not help him. She could see the anger burning in his eyes. Remembering his temper, she stayed away from it.

"And to what do I owe this honor?" he asked.

"Rich," she said. "You are not well, you need some help."

"Ahhh," he stopped, held a finger in front of his face as if trying to make a point. "Even without your medical license, you still know how to play doctor."

She winced but chose not to respond. Perhaps the best thing to do was to let him talk himself out. He would get tired in a moment and maybe then she would be able to reason with him.

"Tell me this, Kendra," he paused. "Oh, excuse me, *Dr.* Hamilton, how did we both end up in these sorry states?"

"I'm not in a sorry state, Rich."

She couldn't help herself. Sure, the last two years had been bad but she was alive and wasn't about to spend her time crying over what was past. Rich chuckled, a nasty chuckle that made Kendra's blood boil. Even drunk to the point of stumbling, he still knew how to push her buttons.

"Still Polly Anna until the end, aren't you?" he chided. "Still thinking the shit you smell is fine because it's fertilizer for the roses."

She felt the tears that had threatened to spill over when she first saw Rich on the lake. She stepped back as if he had hit her and turned toward the house. His voice stopped her.

"Tell me this, Kendra," he said, then stopped.

She turned around to face him again, this time a safe distance away. He would not be able to see her tears from here.

"Tell me, why did everything go so wrong?" he asked. "I did everything right, didn't I? Caught the bad guy, saved the girl, saved the baby for God's sake." He paused again and waved his hands in the air in a helpless gesture. "I even had my fifteen minutes of fame. I was a fucking hero."

He stopped speaking suddenly as if remembering. It was all true. Going against the sheriff's department, his boss and even his friends, Rich had pursued a serial killer who preyed on Dunhill County's weakest, the drug addicts and whores no one cared about. And when it looked like the predator was one of his own, prominent citizen Luke Bertrand, Rich didn't stop. He did not stop until he had put Luke behind bars. Too bad he couldn't keep him there.

Kendra could not stand to see him like this, so bitter. It took all her might to turn her back on him. But she knew that she had to because she couldn't help him. Rich blamed her too much for that. After all, she had ruined his life. If she had never come to him when her mother was killed, he would be chief of homicide right now and married to a judge's daughter.

The sound of him vomiting stopped her. She turned back around. Rich was on his knees, his right hand clutching the bark of a redwood tree as he vomited into the lake. Before she asked herself what she was doing, Kendra walked down to the bank. She held onto him as he emptied the contents of his belly. She ignored both the smell and the bile rising in her own throat. After he finished and wiped his mouth with the back of his hand, she drew him up by the shoulders. He leaned on her as they walked toward the cabin.

In the bedroom, she helped him strip, then turned the water on in the shower. She pushed him in and shut the door. As she stood there listening to the water running, she looked around the room. The bed with the tree-trunk legs and headboard was filled with pizza boxes and beer cans. The sheets were filthy and Rich's clothes lay in a heap on the floor. She searched the closets and the drawers until she found sheets. After piling the debris into a corner, she stripped the bed and made it up with the clean sheets.

"Kendra."

She turned around and found Rich there, naked, dripping wet. He leaned heavily against the door frame. She didn't say anything, just handed him a towel and helped him into bed. Pulling a plaid comforter over his passed out body, she stared at the drunk who used to be her lover and friend. She wanted to weep. She remembered helping her addicted mother Violet in the same way. When Violet had too much to drink, when she was so strung out she that she didn't even know her own name, Kendra had always been there. Now, she couldn't help but wonder if Rich would be her Violet of the future—another person who she would have to take care of.

CHAPTER 2

Kendra left Rich in the bedroom to sleep it off. He snored as if every breath was a struggle. Another blanket lay on the couch. She sniffed it to make sure it was clean, then wrapped it around her shoulders. The cabin was cold inside despite the alluring sunshine and the brightness outside. Rich's cabin was like walking into an icebox. The kitchen was just as much of a mess as Rich's bedroom. Cups and half-empty plates were scattered over the laminated countertops. Kendra gently closed one of the cupboards. Without acknowledging the intention to clean, she idly emptied glasses and coffee cups into the sink, scraped food down the garbage disposal. In the bedroom she separated the dirty clothes from the trash and hung the towel that Rich had thrown on the bathroom floor.

Back in the kitchen, she sat down at a massive, Mission wooden table. She placed her feet up on the hard bench and leaned back against the window. Kendra hadn't realized that she had fallen asleep until she had woken up. Rich stood at the sink splashing cold water on his face. He had turned on the overhead lights and the room stood awash in an artificial yellow glow. Kendra looked out the window she had been leaning against. It was pitch black outside. No stars, no moon to cast giant shadows for the redwoods, just an all-encompassing blackness.

"You cleaned up." Rich's voice was matter-of-fact, sure of himself.

One look at him told her that he would never be the person Violet was. He did not sound like the man she had just cleaned up from his own vomit. She saw that he had shaved and had donned a clean polo shirt and blue jeans. Except for a few bumps on his face, he was as handsome as ever.

Kendra sat up, the blanket slipping from her shoulders. She caught Rich staring at her. She felt her skin warm under his gaze, conscious of how the sweater molded to her body. As usual, Kendra did not get dressed with anything in mind. Now she made a mental note to herself that the next time she paid a visit to an old lover, it would be best to dress as close to a nun as possible without looking ridiculous.

She pulled the blanket over her and returned his gaze. Looking into his brown eyes, she wondered if her first conclusion had been a mistake, the one she had made when he asked her if she were real. She had thought Rich still loved her. But now, the only thing registering in Rich's brown eyes was resentment, maybe even hate.

"What are you doing here?" he asked her.

"I . . ." she started, but he cut her off.

"How did you find me?"

"Your brother . . ."

". . . has a big mouth," he finished for her. He turned off the water and dried his hands on a kitchen towel. "I asked you what are you doing here."

"It was a mistake," was all she could manage to say.

His stare withered her, scared her more than the darkness outside. In the silence, Kendra realized that she did not really know this man. She could not really trust him. After all, he had changed so much from the Rich she knew. Maybe the change had been her fault. Rich lifted a black eyebrow in the face of her silence, his full lips frowning. It was such a classic Rich move that it calmed her for a minute or two. At least until he spoke again.

"So you are going to keep me guessing? You are not going to tell me?"

He leaned his languid body against the sink. Kendra had nothing to say against the bitterness of his words. He stroked his chin, pretended to consider. "Let's see, you can't be pregnant. It's been well over a year."

Kendra rose from the bench and went into the living room to retrieve the keys to the rental. He followed her, a host of ugly words falling from his mouth. She tried not to listen, but in the silence of the room, she had no choice.

"What else could it be? You hard up? You need a lay?"

Light from the kitchen slid meagerly into the living room but at least she could see. She looked on the coffee table for her keys.

"Okay," he said, "if it's not a quick lay, is it a loan? Are you short of money now that you aren't practicing medicine? You working, Doc?"

She whirled around, heart pounding. "Why are you so bitter?" she exploded. "What did I ever do to you that was so horrible?"

The words were out before she could stop them. Kendra averted her eyes. Of course she knew what she had done to him. She didn't need his face or his words to tell her. She didn't wait for him to answer. Keys in hand, she flung open the cabin door and stopped frozen.

The darkness struck against her like a black hurricane. Even the pink Ford Fiesta from Rent-A-Wreck was not visible in this heavy, bleak silence, this thing so like death that it caused Kendra's breath to catch in her throat. She reached for the miniature flashlight on her key ring and realized that she had left the keys to her apartment in the car. The two keys she held were to the rental, no flashlight to save her from this fear. The longer she stared into the blackness, the harder her heart pounded against her chest. Kendra had been afraid of the dark ever since that night two years ago when Luke Bertrand had dragged her and April Hart around Dunhill intent on killing them both.

"Go ahead," Rich said softly, mockingly. "Go on out there."

But she didn't, couldn't go out there. That blackness would swallow her up. Suddenly, she felt him near her. His hands touched her waist lightly.

"Just what I thought," he said. "Still afraid of the dark."

He reached over her and shut the door. It banged with a finality that made Kendra jump. Rich flicked on the overhead lights.

"You're a bastard . . ." she choked, and then stopped.

God, she had not realized how much he had come to hate her.

What a fool she had been to come here. He stared at her, his arms folded across his broad chest, his jaw tight. And then she saw something in his face give way. The anger receded behind his impassive brown eyes.

"Answer my question," he said.

Kendra waited until her heartbeat slowed to normal.

"I need a favor," she said.

Rich laughed then, a real laugh, then sighed. "But not pregnant? No sex? No loan?" he joked.

It wasn't sincere, that joke. He said it in the manner that he would have said it to the clerk at a grocery store, the cab driver, some stranger he would never see again. Despite the insincerity, Kendra felt her own lips twitch into a small smile as she shook her head. At least he was trying. But she still couldn't look at him.

"I'm hungry," he said, walking away. "Tell me about this favor while I eat."

Rich opened a can of Progresso soup—clam chowder. Kendra did not eat, turned away from the bowl offered her. But Rich ate. He ate as if he had never eaten in his life, head down, scooping soup, not looking at her. He acted as if she were not there, as if she were still a figment of his imagination induced by a two-day drunk. Kendra studied him, wondering how much of one—a drunk, that is—Rich Marvel really was. His hands were steady, not shaking, his eyes clear. But he had spent many hours at his brother's cabin. The trash and the mess proved that.

Kendra wanted to speak but her voice had flown away with the daylight. She did not know what to say. Leaning against the stove, she felt steam from the simmering soup caress her back and shoulders. She turned around and shut off the fire. She looked up to see Rich staring at her. He had pushed the bowl away and now studied her with his arms folded across his chest.

"So," he said finally. "How have you been?"

The question startled her. Kendra had not expected small talk from Richard T. Marvel. She expected recriminations, the accusations to continue, not the greasy phrase *how have you been*, not after all that they had been through together. She stuck her hands in the pockets of her jeans, looked down at the wooden floor. Maple, shiny and supple, the wood looked liquid.

"It looks as if your brother has done quite well for himself," she said. "It's a nice place. You come here a lot?"

Rich's expression did not change, "Do you mean do I come here a lot and get drunk off my ass?"

She looked at Rich full in the face. Maybe he hadn't changed much; it seemed as if he still had a low tolerance for bullshit. She answered truthfully. "Yes."

Rich chuckled, a chuckle that was mirthless and told her that he had no intention of answering her. "I don't think," he said, slowly, "that how often I come here is any of your business, not anymore, anyway. Are you going to tell me why you are here or are you going to keep me guessing all night?"

Kendra left the warmth of the stove, walked over to the table. She sat down and looked at her hands and started picking at the dead skin around her thumb. Still reluctant to speak, she lifted the thumb to her mouth but Rich caught her hand. He had always hated her biting her nails. She did it more often now since they had broken up. She pulled her hand away and they stared at each other for a few seconds.

"I'm not going to beg you," he said. "Just tell me why you are here."

"I screwed up again, Rich." There, she said it, the words finally out. He didn't say anything for a couple of minutes, only rose, went to the sink and ran water into a clean glass. When Kendra dared look at him, his face was unreadable. He returned her gaze, then said calmly, "Start from the beginning."

CHAPTER 3

Start from the beginning, Kendra thought before sighing and taking a deep breath. And so she did, telling Rich about Leroy Cotton. Leroy had a slow country way about him. But the man in overalls with the creased cheeks and foamy brown eyes was not the stereotypical country bumpkin. His hair was dotted with gray, his fingernails yellow and big as dinner plates, but his mind was sharp.

He was the handyman in Kendra's apartment, the apartment on the border of one of the poorest neighborhoods in Dunhill County, The Pit. Kendra lived in a one bedroom apartment that smelled of stale smoke, the walls the color of brown piss. Sometimes, it was hard for her to believe that she had ended up right back where she started, that she and Rich didn't ride out into the sunset Rich had found so promising when he left her recovering from gunshot wounds in Doctor's Hospital. She shot Rich a look when she said this last but he didn't respond. Kendra continued.

But she did know one thing—that the horror Luke had created was over. But she did not know that life as she knew it was over as well until the AMA went after her medical license and returned her to a place of limbo, a place she hadn't been since high school. After she and Rich had broken up, she went overseas, practiced in places where knowledge was valued more than a piece of paper with your name on it. She told Rich all of this. But what she did not tell him was the real reason she returned to Dunhill County. That would come soon enough, and he would understand, especially if he agreed to help her.

Leroy Cotton and his twenty-five-year-old developmentally disabled daughter, Anna, came to Kendra when Anna had a cold she could not shake or when Leroy's emphysema flared up to a point that kept him from working. Kendra worked with him, couldn't prescribe anything, but recommended over the counter meds, some herbal treatments that she knew could be effective.

Anna, his daughter, Anna Cotton, was beautiful. She had long brown legs, a face like a model. Her short hair curled around her face like rings of pure, black silk. If she had all of her faculties, if, she was like the rest of us, Leroy would say, then she'd be a beauty. She could have any man that she wanted just by snapping a finger, turning a heel.

But she wasn't like the rest of us, Kendra told Rich now. Anna was diagnosed as moderately retarded when she was five years old. Kendra stopped here, she hated that word. Retarded. She looked around, surprised that she was back in the cabin sitting with Rich, talking with him as if she had done this every day for the past two years. He still had his arms crossed but he listened intently, warm yellow light spilling around him.

"Go on," he prodded.

Retarded, Kendra continued. Anna had the capacity of a seven-year-old, and she was getting worse because Leroy could not give her the care that she needed. When he left for work, he locked Anna in his one bedroom apartment on the second floor.

Anna was always getting into trouble. One day, she almost set the entire apartment building on fire, burning scraps of paper on the old gas stove. If it weren't for Samantha, the girl who lived across the hall, The Liberty Apartments would have been burned to ash and ribbons of stucco and steel. Luckily, it was summer, and Leroy worked out a deal with Samantha's mother to have her stay with Anna in the daytime. But when Samantha returned to school again, Anna was on her own.

"And so you could not help sticking your nose into their business, hmmm?" Rich asked her now.

Kendra sighed; no, she could not help it. It wasn't only that Anna was a danger to herself; she was *in* danger all the time. The Liberty Apartments was not safe for a woman who looked like

Halle Berry but had the capacity of a child. Anna was constantly harassed by pimps who wanted to turn her out. You see, Kendra explained to Rich, Anna did not like it cooped up in that apartment. She and Leroy had come from the country, a small factory community in Virginia. Anna had the run of the place. Everyone knew her there. She felt safe. She had a mother who could watch her constantly and when her mother couldn't watch her, the town just sort of took care of her.

"So why did they leave Virginia?" Rich asked her.

Simple, Kendra explained. Money. The textile factory pulled out, moved to Mexico. No job or money coming in and the added strain of Anna's condition were too much for Leroy's wife. His wife was already sick. Soon after her death, a despondent Leroy left Virginia looking for work. He and Anna arrived in Dunhill, found The Liberty Apartments, and Leroy became the building's janitor and handy man.

"A very sad story," Rich said now, almost impersonally. "But what has it got to do with you?"

Leroy found Anna increasingly hard to care for. After the fire incident, Kendra told Leroy that he should put Anna in a residential care facility, that he could not leave her locked up in an apartment all day like an animal. Anna needed social interaction, education, some sort of self-fulfillment. But Leroy would not budge. He refused, outright at first, but Kendra pushed on. She knew that it would only be the best thing for Anna.

The last straw came several months ago when Anna escaped the apartment. She didn't go out of the locked door but climbed barefoot out of the window and down the fire escape.

"People stared at her, Rich," Kendra explained. "And you remember how it is around Liberty Apartments, right? Drug addicts, whores, kids, too, some good people, but the whores and the addicts frightened Anna."

So she ran, Kendra explained. She ran in fifty degree temperature, a twenty-five-year-old woman in her bare feet wearing a flimsy tank top and a pair of pajama pants. Anna ended up at a Starbucks coffeehouse. People stared at her and Anna started screaming and screaming. When she wouldn't calm down, the police were called. One of the policemen recognized Anna and called Leroy. Anna was taken into custody and put in a holding cell. When Kendra arrived, she told Leroy that it would be best to institutionalize Anna until they could find a residential care facility. Kendra laughed a bitter hard laugh that did not sound like it belonged to her. She called in a few favors and got Anna placed at Brighton House, a mental institution.

Kendra looked at Rich, who was nodding his head, his mouth grim. "You screwed up," he said.

Kendra dropped her eyes, and nodded yes. How could she know that at Brighton House Anna would get care ten times more horrific than the care she had received in her father's home?

"I screwed up," she responded.

After Anna was committed, Kendra and Leroy scoured Dunhill and neighboring counties for a good residential care facility for Anna. The good ones, the ones run by good people with the care of their patients as their topmost priority, those places were all full. The bad ones, those whose primary objective was money, were also full. So full in fact, that they had put beds in the hallways, converted their garages so they would have room to warehouse the mentally ill like inconvenient baggage. The caseworker assigned to Anna could not help, either. Peggy Preston had two hundred cases assigned to her and she barely looked up from her paper-riddled desk to speak to Leroy and Kendra as they sat in her office pleading Anna's case.

"What happened, Kendra?" Rich asked, his voice heavy.

"About a month ago, during a routine examination, the doctor discovered that Anna was pregnant."

"Jeez," Rich said, disgusted. He pushed his chair away from the table and walked back to the counter. "God, Kendra," he swore under his breath. "Didn't anyone ever tell you that the road to hell is paved with good intentions?"

She swallowed, didn't answer for a while. Instead, Kendra blinked back tears. When she felt she could trust her voice she continued.

"That's not the worst of it," she stopped, looked at him. "How do you think she became pregnant, Rich?"

He did not answer for several moments. He took his time, which was new with him. Only two years ago, Rich would have jumped to a conclusion based on what he knew of the world. He would have answered in two seconds; easy, he would have said, someone did her at the hospital, sick bastards.

"How far along is she, Kendra?" he asked instead.

"As far as they could tell when they found out, a little over a month, maybe more."

He nodded, slowly. "What's the hospital saying?" he asked. "Did they find out who did it?"

Kendra shook her head. "Of course they are saying that she was not raped in the facility. They are saying that it happened while she was at Liberty."

"So." He shrugged. "It wouldn't surprise me if she were raped there."

"That's not what they are saying, Rich," Kendra answered.

Rich stops, considers. "They are accusing the father, Leroy Cotton?" It wasn't really a question.

"It's not only them, Rich," Kendra explained. "It's the police, they've arrested him. Leroy Cotton is in jail. And Anna's no help. She just keeps saying that her father hurt her."

Rich looked at her for a moment or two, and then laughed. "What a fucking mess," he said. "But look, DNA testing will tell them who the father is, right? What do you need from me?"

She shook her head from side to side. "You don't understand, Rich," she said. "Anna isn't pregnant anymore."

Rich's eyes narrowed. "What do you mean that she's not pregnant anymore?"

"She had an abortion."

"You mean Leroy aborted the baby?"

Kendra blew out a breath not wanting to get involved in another argument but knew that there was no way around it. An argument was coming. Looking at him square in the face, she said, "It was my decision, Rich."

He jumped at the statement, a bewildered look on his face.

"Your decision?" he said. "How could it be your decision?"

"I told you. Leroy is ill. He appointed me legal guardian during one of his hospital stays. When I found out Anna was pregnant, I told them that it would best if we gave Anna an abortion."

Rich snapped his fingers in her face. "Get rid of it?" he accused. "Just like that? Like swatting a fly for you, huh, Kendra?"

"Rich, please," she said. "I didn't come here to get into an abortion debate with you."

"Then why did you come here, Kendra?" he asked.

Every muscle in his body seemed to tense. She could tell by the vein pulsing in his forehead that he was losing patience. But she bided her time, anyway.

"Have you been watching the news lately, Rich?"

He rolled his eyes. "What do you think?"

"You said it earlier. It's a fucking mess. Every right wing politician in Dunhill has jumped into this feet first. They think that I aborted the baby because I knew about the abuse. There is talk about appointing another guardian for Anna, too. Some are demanding that I be thrown in jail for negligence."

"Look, I don't know what you expect me to do . . ."

But Kendra cut him off. "When I said every right wing politician, I mean every right wing politician, Rich. I mean Luke Bertrand."

When she said his name, the room stopped. It was as if it had been spinning round and round as she told Rich what had happened to Anna, the tragedies that had befallen her family. But when she said that name aloud, the name that had not been spoken between them in a year, the room stopped spinning and the world became still on its axis.

"Dé . . . jà . . . fucking . . . vu," Rich said slowly.

He stood up and dropped his bowl into the sink. It clattered, dangerously close to breaking, the sound accompanying his departure from the kitchen. Kendra sat in the kitchen for a few minutes longer, her hand curled around the cup of tea Rich had insisted she take as she told him Anna's story. She sat still a few seconds longer, then followed him out of the room.

She did not see him in the darkened living room, so walked slowly to the bedroom.

Leaning against the door frame, she said, "Rich."

He stood with his back to her, his hands gripping the front of the massive dresser. If Kendra did not know any better, she would have said that he was about to vomit again. She advanced into the room, placed a hand on his shoulder. His reaction should not have surprised her. She had given up the right to touch Rich long ago. He jerked away from her, violently, as if her hand had scalded him.

When he turned to face her, he folded his arms across his chest. Kendra could see doors slamming, locks clicking shut.

"You know, you tell a good story," he said. "But I still have no fucking idea why you are here."

"Don't you, Rich?" she challenged him, tired of his games. "Don't you at all? Luke had something to do with this, I know it . . ."

"Oh, come on, Kendra," Rich said. "That's crazy."

"What? What?" she questioned, grabbing his arm, not caring that he kept jerking away. "It's not crazy, Rich. He sat on the board at Brighton House . . ."

"But he's not on that board or any other since the trial, Kendra. Even if he did have something to do with this," he stopped and ran his hand across his head. "Even if he did, you don't have shit to link him to that girl."

"You could find it, Rich," Kendra said, unable to keep the desperate note of pleading out of her voice. "This entire case from Anna to the baby is so much like the other one, the names for God's sake. April, Anna. Maybe that triggered something in him . . ."

"How would he even know about this Anna Cotton? You are not making any sense."

"Luke still talks to people in The Pit. Anybody could have said something to him about her, set him off. He's involved, Rich. I know it."

The room quieted as he studied her face. She still had hold of both his arms and he let her hands stay where they were. When he finally spoke, his voice was quiet and low. His next words came slowly, as if he were speaking to a selfish two-year-old.

"You don't really care about Anna, do you?"

She dropped her hands, let him go in surprise. "What? Of course I do."

"No, no, you don't," he said, shaking his head. "It's Luke you want, isn't it? You want at Luke. That's why you aborted the baby, to get at him."

His words stunned and insulted her. "That's not true—" she spat.

But he wouldn't let her finish. "Yes. It is true. It has been and always will be about him, won't it? As long as both of you draw breath."

Kendra held up her hands in a gesture of surrender.

"Okay, okay," she said. "Let's say for argument's sake that you're right," she stopped. "And just for the record, you are not. But let's say that you are. An innocent man is in prison and accused of attacking the one thing he has left in this life to love. And it's nobody's business what happened with the pregnancy except mine, Leroy's, and Anna's."

"Pretty speech," Rich said.

"It's not a speech." Kendra sighed, almost crying now with the knowledge that he was not going to help her or Anna. "It's the truth."

Rich's smile was ugly. "You wouldn't know the truth if it bit you in the ass, lady. This is about Luke, and primarily, it's about you."

Kendra sucked in her breath. "Are you still drunk?" she asked him. "I told you that this isn't about me."

"I know what you told me," Rich said derisively as he headed for the bedroom door.

"Then think about Anna," she said. He stopped and turned around. For a minute, she believed that he was about to bend. "Forget about me. Do it for Anna," she finished.

"So, what am supposed to do?" he asked, his hands spread out. "Drop everything, run back to Dunhill with you and jump into this shit?"

Kendra didn't answer for a while. During the pause, she realized how heavy her breathing was, how fast her heart beat.

"You going to help me or not?" she asked. "Are you going to help find out who took advantage of that girl?"

She raised her head to look at him. Their eyes locked.

"I was a homicide detective, remember?" he finally said. "I don't do rapes."

"Well, if you like, I could kill someone for you," Kendra countered.

He laughed shortly, leaned forward until he was almost touching her. When he spoke she could feel his breath on her face. "Make it Luke Bertrand, and you've got yourself a deal, lady."

Anna

Anna don't like dark, don't like how the lights in this bright place have minds of they own, how they go out before she pulls the switch, every day at the same time. She don't like how they lock her in at night, and how the door opens, creaking, creaking like a monster creaking up them stairs in those scary books her friend used to read at the apartment, in those books called *Goosebumps*. Her friend Samantha used to sit on the stoop with her after she came home from school, and she read them books, them *Goosebumps*. And Anna listened, her eyes got big, her nails poked her hands, and them cuts bled. She missed Samantha, she missed them fake goose bumps.

Because now she had goose bumps for real. Every day when the lights go out, the door creaks louder, and a line of light walks on in the room, and two feet follow it, two feet in white shoes. Door closes fast before Anna can see his hands, see his face. And now she in here with it, with the monster, but she don't scream. She tried screamin' the first time but them white shoes put they hands over her face, pinched her nose shut till she couldn't breathe no more, laid on top of her and hissed like a rattling snake in her ear. *Scream, retard, scream and I'll kill you.*

So Anna didn't scream, just laid there real still like one of them plastic dolls, the dolls where the legs don't bend and the fingers just stay stretched straight out. The monster connected to them white shoes lay on top of her, and he don't take them shoes off and the heels scrape up Anna's shins real bad as he rubs all against her. Then he lifts up her nightgown until it's all the way around her neck and he bunches it up in one hand and sucks her private parts.

Anna wants to scream, but she don't. She wants to scream, but she can't 'cause she know if she screams he will make her not breathing worse. *Retard, I'll kill you.* She just pushes the scream down her throat, and thinks about Sylvia. Sylvia like her, even though Sylvia a pig, even though Sylvia not real. Samantha told her that one day: *Stupid,* she say, *Pigs can't think. Pigs can't talk.* But then her eyes got real big when she said that, when she called

Anna stupid, because she never talk about Anna being stupid, or make fun of Anna.

But Anna wasn't hurt, 'cause Anna retarded, Anna not stupid. Only the monster who came to her room at night made retard and stupid sound like the same thing. Only the monster rubbing her private parts and pulling down his pants and putting his thing in her. And pushing, and pushing and pushing and groaning and licking like he the pig. Only he made her feel like what Samantha said and didn't mean. He made retarded sound like stupid.

Anna hate his smells. He smells like mouthwash, like sweet wood and his face is all scrappy. His smells sting. Pretty soon, he real still in the dark. And he still laid on top of her, breathing real hard, spitting in her neck. Then he let go of her nightgown that had been choking her a little 'cause right 'fore he stopped, he start pushing harder and going faster and making her nightgown go all tight around her neck. He put his head down, and bit her again, real hard. It hurt, Anna whimpers. And he laughs. A real, satisfied monster laugh 'fo getting up. And the last thing he say to Anna, the last thing he say is, *Tell anybody about this, retard, and I'll kill you. I'll kill you and Rosita, all your friends. Keep your mouth shut.*

Then he open the door, and the light walks in a little bit. But when he shuts it again, the light walks out again and Anna left in the dark.

Anna hurt. Anna don't like dark.

CHAPTER 4

"Yo, Rich."

Rich knew that it was Carlyle even before he looked up from his desk to find the man standing in the doorway to his office at Brighton Industries. Jared Carlyle was the sort of man who worked very hard at being cool, and was the only one who Rich knew who thought saying "yo" still was. He was an acquaintance from the academy and he and Rich had known each other for years.

Rich mentally shook himself, realizing with an uncomfortable feeling in his belly that he had driven the long route back from Tahoe, gone home and gotten dressed, and come into the office in a fog of thought. He had become, for a terrible, dangerous instant, lost in the past, a past that could undo him if he let it.

Seeing Kendra Hamilton again was like walking down the road on a day filled with sunshine, whistling, hands in your pockets, then bam, out of nowhere, the sky opens and the heavens empty every wrong thing you ever did in your life right onto the very top of your pointed head. Although Rich would be the first to admit that he wasn't exactly whistling and his hands were not exactly in his pockets, his life had been coming together once again. He had forgotten about Kendra Hamilton, had gotten over her, in fact. At least, that was what he thought when he saw her standing on the bank of the lake as he drifted on water as smooth as glass, drunk off his ass, but having a good time nonetheless.

After Kendra left him—no, that wasn't quite right, was it? She never did leave. She simply drifted away just as he had drifted on that quiet lake both contemplating and running away from everything that had happened in his life since he met her. After she stopped returning his phone calls, stopped responding to his pounding on her door demanding that she open up, and after she heaped on the final insult and left the country, after she had done all that, he was bad for a while. No escaping that fact, Jack. He drank, refused to see old friends, moved out of the apartment that he had shared with his former partner, and went underground for a while. That was how he could best describe it, he just went under. He had grown weary of trying to climb out of the pit into which he was born.

He rented a house, lived on his savings—the savings that he was supposed to use to buy a house with his fiancée Dinah whom he had left brokenhearted in his frenzied pursuit of Kendra Hamilton. And he had enough money, he discovered, enough money to last for years, perhaps forever. It was just him, after all. But he began to piss his money away. He pissed it away on alcohol, on baseball games that summer after she left, on toys, irresponsible things that he would never have dreamed of buying when he was one of Dunhill's responsible citizens. He bought remote control cars and toy airplanes, took a trip to the Caribbean, lounged on the beach until he became tired of endless days watching waves crash like lightning over his brown feet.

When he returned home, he spent nights at his brother's club in San Francisco, watching Dominic blow golden sounds from his sax. When that bored him, he stayed home and lounged in his pajamas from sunup to sundown. And he drank, sometimes, too, starting in the morning and passing out wherever the last, lethal drop of the day felled him. He would not have characterized himself as an alcoholic, still did not as a matter of fact, but he would have characterized himself as a fugitive.

"Yo, Rich," Carlyle said again. "Mind if I come in, man?"

Rich laughed as Carlyle came in anyway without waiting for a reply. Unfortunately, Rich now worked for a living. But the way he still pissed away money, it was probably a good thing.

Rich could have gone on the way he had for months, years maybe. But then Brighton Industries approached him with a job.

The developer, Thomas Brighton, wanted him to work as head of security for the corporate offices. He would eventually take over security at all of Brighton Industries, including Brighton House where Kendra said Anna had been. Eventually.

Thomas Brighton approached Rich with the job because even though he hadn't been working for the past year, Richard T. Marvel was still a hero in the eyes of most in Dunhill. Even though the charges against Luke Bertrand did not stick, the charges against the sheriff did. And April Hart, the girl he had rescued from death at the hands of Bertrand, became a media darling, singing Rich's praises from Washington State to Washington, D.C.

Sometimes, though, he needed those times when he did not have to think, when he could drink himself into a brown fog, and not think of Kendra or Luke or April Hart or the mess his life had become. Dominic did not like it but he allowed Rich to use his cabin whenever he needed it. And knowing his brother like Rich did, he probably sent Kendra up there to embarrass him out of even those occasional weekend binges.

And the reason she had come, Rich thought, her wanting his help, was the most obnoxious, asinine thing he thought that he had ever heard of. She leaves him without giving him a chance to what . . . he thought. What did he want the chance to do? He threw the thought away. That's the best thing to do with thoughts that don't coincide with your view of the world. Throw them away.

"Looks like you had a rough weekend, man," Carlyle said as he propped his feet on Rich's desk.

Carlyle was a short man who wore lifts inside his shoes to make himself look taller. He had red hair cut into a crew cut and wide shoulders that made his body barrel out at the top. Carlyle was fond of dark suits and ties, which he always wore studded with a diamond tie pin. Aside from the dark suits, he capped his teeth, wore green contacts and dyed the gray in his red hair every other Friday at a salon. Carlyle had a stylist—no Klassy Kuts or Fantastic Sam's for him. Everything about Carlyle was contrived, put on, and made up.

Rich trusted Jared Carlyle as much as he trusted the dubious fact that he could leap from tall buildings. Yet, he had hired him as an assistant. After being betrayed by more people than he could count, Rich vowed that he might be better off by dealing with the devil that he knew. Rich would never have to guess if Carlyle were lying to him, nine times out of ten, if it suited the red-haired debonair, Rich knew that he would. Jared Carlyle would lie without compunction if it was to his advantage.

"Boss man wants to see you," Carlyle said.

"You don't say," Rich answered as he checked his watch.

What would Thomas Brighton want at ten-thirty on a Monday morning? Still with Kendra's visit on his mind, Rich touched the crystal with his thumb as if he were trying to rub time away, to return to two years ago before he had the stupidity to listen to Kendra Hamilton. He couldn't believe that she would ask him to do it again.

"What did you do, anyway?" Carlyle asked now. "Spend the weekend pinned under a Mack truck?"

Rich ran his hand across his mouth, then smiled. "Not pinned beneath the wheels," he said. "But it feels like I've been hit by one."

Carlyle ran his clean, white fingers down the crease in his slacks. "Was she worth it?" he asked Rich.

Rich did more than bark a laugh, now, he laughed out loud. "I'm sure she thinks that she was."

"You know what I say you do with old girlfriends, Rich?" Carlyle began, shrugging his barrel-like shoulders. "I say fuck 'em, and when you can't fuck 'em, forget 'em. Plain as that."

Rich sighed. Carlyle knew about Kendra, not because Rich himself confided to the man but because everyone in Dunhill County knew about him and Kendra. They knew when they were together, they knew when they parted. And when Kendra returned to Dunhill, the community knew that, too. Dunhillians prided themselves on knowing each other's business, but more than that, Kendra's return to town warranted a small one paragraph article in the bottom left-hand corner of society pages of the *Dunhill Review*. It wasn't that Kendra was society; it was that she had made the life of one of Dunhill's most well-connected residents hell. It was news, to them at least, when she returned.

"Anything else, Carlyle?" Rich asked, refusing to join him in a discussion about his love life.

"Nope. Just that he wants to see you," Carlyle said. "Saw him in the gym earlier this morning, said he wants you in his office as soon as you came in."

Rich raised an eyebrow. "Everything all right?" he asked.

"Everything's fine. Nobody called in sick, all the security shit you insisted we buy works, everybody's behaving themselves like good boys and girls. Everything is right as rain."

"Did he say what he wanted?" Rich asked.

Carlyle shook his head, "Nope, mentioned something about being a personal matter. He said to just give his secretary a call before you went up."

Rich checked his watch again. "All right," he said matter-of-factly. "Do me a favor and give Phil a call and tell him I'm on my way."

"Will do," Carlyle said before standing up and leaving the office.

Rich went into his office bathroom and threw some water over his face. He looked in the mirror and saw what both Kendra and Carlyle had seen. Rich had always been proud of his looks, and he still wasn't bad-looking. He just wasn't well kempt anymore. He needed a haircut, desperately; his brown eyes were yellow and bloodshot; and because he hadn't been shaving as often as he should have, he had a few bumps along the jawline.

Well, he couldn't do anything about the bumps, the haircut, not now, but he could do something about the red eyes. He opened his medicine cabinet in search of Visine. He found it but also found something else that bothered the hell out of him. On the second shelf, a bottle of brown liquid—some would call it a fifth—with the label rubbed off. But he didn't need to read the label to know that he was staring at a bottle of Jack Daniel's. But that didn't mean anything. He could stop anytime he wanted to, couldn't he? And besides, he didn't drink all the time, only when he wanted to. Only when he needed to.

CHAPTER 5

When billionaire industrialist Thomas Brighton decided to move two of his bicycle factories back to Dunhill County the entire population heaved a collective sigh of relief. Brighton Industries would mean jobs and jobs would mean survival. Rich left his comfortable chair, the one made of metal that made him feel like he was floating on air, to meet the man who had made it all possible. He took the narrow hallway to the elevator that would lead him to the fifteenth floor, to Thomas Brighton's office.

Rich made it his business to know who he worked for. Who could blame him, after Luke Bertrand? Rich thought he knew Luke, thought he could know someone by looking into their eyes, thus into their hearts, to their integrity. He had been lulled by appearances, jumped to conclusions because of outward behavior. So when Thomas Brighton asked Rich to come work for him, Rich did a background check.

Brighton, the CEO of Brighton Industries, was the son of an honest man. But Brighton himself was a man who pushed everything to the very limits of integrity. And if you asked Brighton, he would say that he was not exactly dishonest. But it would always be a technicality that kept Thomas Brighton honest. He could wriggle out of anything. Carlyle once joked that Brighton would wriggle all one hundred and eighty pounds of himself through the eye of the proverbial needle. Thomas Brighton would find a way to get into heaven.

Rich chuckled as he stepped from the elevator on the fifteenth floor of the Brighton building. The entire thing, fifteen floors of glass and steel, reminded Rich of a tornado of ice. He and Carlyle actually nicknamed the tallest building in this county the ice stadium because of the bright steel and shiny glass that bled light and sun all over Dunhill. Across from the elevator were the double doors of Mr. Brighton's office. And that was how Rich thought of him, as Mr. Brighton. No matter how many times the old man asked him to please, call him Thomas, Rich refused. He just didn't want to be that close. He didn't want to be that close to anybody again, outside those in his family. Even then, he noticed that he still had to be wary. Hell, his brother Dominic told Kendra where to find him, didn't he? He couldn't even be trusted. To get away from those thoughts, thoughts of Kendra, Rich pushed through the double doors.

Brighton's secretary, Phil, was about twenty-five, with round, gold wire-rimmed glasses. Phil liked to wear sweater vests with carefully knotted ties and he was extremely proud of his position at Brighton Industries. Phil was especially fond of keeping people waiting. Other people's discomfort made him comfortable. Rich wondered if that was why the man—so stuck on making sure people understood that he was important—was balding even at his age.

He didn't say hello as Rich stepped into the office. But Rich knew that Phillip Grubb was aware of his presence because the man held up one finger, clean as a piece of chalk, indicating to Rich that he was not ready to talk to him just yet. Phil was hunched over a calendar. The gold pen he wrote with scratched furiously as if he were in a race to finish what he was doing and was winning, but only by a hair. Today's sweater vest was cashmere, plaid, maroon and green to match the maroon tie stuck to the skinny collar around Phil's chicken neck.

Rich was tired, his stomach boiled and lurched with the remembered alcohol as if it were going to jump through the starched whiteness of his Brooks Brother's shirt and spill bile all over the ten-thousand-dollar Persian rug covering the shiny wooden floor in the outer office. Without asking, Rich walked to the wet bar and poured water from a crystal pitcher into its matching crystal cup. The water felt like snow in the hot desert of his mouth. He closed his eyes for a minute, savoring it.

"Comfy?" Phil asked.

Phil had an unfortunate voice, a voice of a young boy still going through puberty. It cracked and burbled at the most inopportune times and Rich could tell by the red flush on Phil's face that now was an inopportune time.

"Not yet," Rich said. He sat down on a small love seat and spread both arms over the back. Placing his feet on the coffee table, he said, "Now, I'm comfy."

Phil had hated Rich on sight, had treated him like a stock boy from the moment he had met him. On that first meeting when Rich came to Brighton's office at the old man's request, Phil had kept Rich waiting for Mr. Brighton for an hour. Rich was about to walk out when Brighton emerged from the office, and scolded Phil for not telling him Rich was there. Phil had turned just as red then as he did now.

He threw the gold pen on the calendar, stood up and spun around without speaking. He disappeared though the door leading to Brighton's office. When he emerged, he said without looking directly at Rich, "They will see you now."

Rich lifted an eyebrow. "They?"

"Yes, Mr. Brighton and Mr. Lane. They are both ready for you now."

Though Phil didn't look directly at Rich, Rich looked directly at him and wondered for the umpteenth time what the man was hiding behind those matching ties and sweater vests. Why he cleaned his glasses until the lenses seemed to disappear and magnify his eyes twice their original size. He didn't wonder because he was curious or cared or because he actually gave a rat's ass about Grubb himself. What he did care about was that Phil Grubb was not comfortable with who he was. Phil liked to hide. And a man who had something to hide sometimes did things when alone to make the face he presented in public respect the face that he despised in private. *Like go on weekend drinking binges.* The thought came to Rich unbidden, hateful. He focused his attention on Phil.

"What are you staring at?" Phil snapped, then flamed red as his voice cracked.

Rich shrugged as if to say nothing. He placed the crystal glass down on the counter of the wet bar without a coaster. Phil ran over and picked up the glass as if he were afraid the maple counter would shatter from the resulting ring of water. A vein pulsed in Grubb's temple. As he watched it Rich thought that he must get a background check on Phillip Grubb despite the fact that Mr. Brighton asked him not to. When Rich first started at Brighton Industries as head of security for the corporate offices, he had insisted on a background check of every employee working at the place. He expanded it to everyone who worked for the corporation and wanted to go after the board next.

But Thomas Brighton was furious when he found out about the background checks. He spouted for an hour about privacy policies and trusting those in the Brighton Industry family. And he told Rich to stop. Hands off the board of directors and for that matter, hands off of Phillip Grubb as well. There are some people, Rich, Brighton had said, that we simply have no choice but to trust.

Every time Rich walked into Thomas Brighton's office, he felt as if he had walked into the library of some English country squire. The place was rich, plush. Again, in Brighton's office, hardwood floors peeked up from plush Persian rugs. The furniture—including the extra wide, extra stuffed sofa—was leather, which was oiled on a regular basis and looked worn and shiny. In here there was a wet bar, too, except it wasn't a simple maple cabinet with a sink and a crystal decanter of water. Brighton's wet bar was tall with recessed lights and slender panes of beveled glass. It was fully stocked with decanters of Scottish whiskey, high-end vodka in tall bottles and home brewed beer in the stainless steel fridge tucked below.

Light was low in Brighton's office, softly spilling out from green shaded lamps with brass necks and pull chains. The glass windows of the building, the glass that made Rich and Carlyle call the place the ice stadium, were covered by heavy brocade curtains, maroon with gold fringes. The walls were paneled and on the west wall, Brighton had hung a picture of his two Dalmatians. The frame and portrait itself was huge; one dog lay at the feet of the other, both pairs of their bright eyes painted so true to life that Rich thought on more than one occasion that the dogs would jump from the face of the canvas. God, how he hated dogs.

"Rich," said Brighton, jumping up from his desk and walking quickly to grasp Rich's hands in both of his own. He always greeted Rich this way as if he hadn't seen him in ages. He smiled into Rich's face and shook his hands.

Rich coughed slightly, using it as an excuse to pull his hand away to cover his mouth.

"Mr. Brighton," he said, returning the greeting.

Brighton sighed and returned to the leather chair behind his desk. "I guess I still can't get you to call me Thomas?" he said.

Unlike his secretary's voice, Brighton's voice boomed with warmth and confidence. He was a polished man of about sixty, the color and texture of sea salt. His hard oily scalp shone through the gray strands of his thinning hair. He was not a very tall man and was several heads shorter than Rich.

Rich didn't respond to Brighton's last question. It wasn't expected of him. They went through this same routine every time they met. Brighton greeted him like the returning prodigal son, held on to Rich's hand for far to long and Rich always found some excuse to pull away, calling him Mr. Brighton as he did so. It was ritual, it was a dance, one for some reason Brighton enjoyed.

"You remember Theo, don't you?" Brighton asked, gesturing to the man sitting in the leather armchair opposite Brighton's desk.

Indeed, Rich remembered Theo Lane. How could anybody forget? The old cat was a wild dresser who wore colors so bright that Rich once joked to Carlyle that the man was probably a part of a circus before settling in Dunhill. Today, Lane had draped his slight frame in a pair of tomato red slacks and black patent leather shoes. A sweater, striped with purple, bright green, and white, hung around his stooped shoulders. A white ascot secured with an emerald tie pin was tucked into the neck of the sweater. Rich shook Lane's hands. They felt dry and cool to the touch, like powder. Theo clamped the pipe he was smoking between his yellow teeth and returned to his seat.

"Please, please, sit down." Brighton pointed Rich to a wingback chair, the same maroon brocade as the curtains hiding the glass window.

"Did you have a rough weekend, Rich?" Brighton asked, his blue ice chip eyes boring into him.

Rich shrugged. Of course Brighton knew that he had a rough weekend. Every time he took a Friday off and came into work late on a Monday, Brighton knew what his weekend was about. He had to know because that prick of a Carlyle told him. Rich imagined the meeting that must have taken place between Brighton and Carlyle after Carlyle had first confronted Rich about his drinking. He could see the surreptitious concern in Carlyle's eyes as he let Brighton in on the secret: *I just think you ought to know sir. Please don't tell him that I said anything.* Rich had expected Carlyle to inform his boss, would have been disappointed in his ability to judge character if Carlyle had kept the fact of Rich's drinking to himself. Because Rich's downfall would mean Carlyle's rise—head of security at Brighton Industries, the new vice president.

Brighton had even brought up the fact of the drinking to Rich, told him that he was concerned. Rich convinced him that it was nothing to worry about. He told Brighton that it hadn't affected his work, had it? He challenged him and Brighton left it alone. He wouldn't fire Rich. The former hero cop was part of Brighton's prop, part of his claim to a good-sized chunk of the world. Besides, Rich did a good job and Brighton knew it. Now, he waved his hand as if telling Rich that he was off the hook, no need to reply to his queries about his weekend.

"Can I get you anything to drink?" Brighton asked. "Water, juice perhaps?"

"Water would be good. Cold." Rich said, silently wishing that he would get on with it. What the hell did he want?

As Brighton rose and went to the wet bar, Rich looked at Theo Lane. The old man, his spotted hands folded over the silver horse head of his antique walking stick, returned Rich's appraisal with an absentminded look in his gray eyes and a faint smile on his wrinkled lips.

"Every time I come here, Thomas," Lane threw over his shoulder, "I can't help but stare at the old general." He stuck his chin out to indicate the portrait of Brighton's father Eli over Brighton's desk.

The portrait was done after the father was dead, of course. Eli Brighton would never have sat for a portrait. It had to be painted from a photograph. The old general, as Lane liked to call him, was a legend in Dunhill. He was a watchmaker and made some of the finest watches in the United States. He had a technique he closely guarded and even after the technique and plans for making those fine watches were taken from him in an inter-company spying scandal, Eli kept right on making watches. He kept making watches even when other watchmakers sprung up all over Dunhill. Some customers, those concerned with brand names, like those who might wear designer jeans and carry designer purses while wearing Payless shoes today, kept going to Eli, preferring the original, the real thing. But others, those who couldn't afford the real things, went to the imitators, the fabricators, Thomas called them.

Eli could have diversified, could have used his engineering skills to build motors, bicycles, even. There were plenty of other products that he could have used to stamp his brand of quality on. But Eli Brighton made watches and that is what he continued to do until the day he died. After Eli's death, his son Thomas started making those bicycles, stamping them with the Eli Brighton brand and selling them for a ridiculous amount of money. And he dabbled in development as well, building strip malls all over the western United States. He was lucky enough to obtain government contracts for building roads and highways throughout California. All of this made Thomas Brighton a rich man.

"Yes, the old general," Thomas said as he returned with a bottle of Perrier and a glass filled with ice. "The one who started it all, the one to whom I owe everything."

Rich took the water and ice. Staring at the portrait, he abandoned all hope that this would be a short meeting. The general was in his work clothes, a green visor, and a brown rubber apron. He sat on a barrel of some kind at his worktable. Both wrists rested on his knees and his legs were spread far apart, feet planted square and sure against the splintered wooden floor. He frowned out of the canvas, his bushy eyebrows drawn together over his piercing green eyes. Eli looked like a man who had been surprised by the flash of a camera, surprised and didn't like it one damned bit.

"Looks like a tough man," Rich said.

Thomas Brighton nodded. "He was. He was," he said. "But if he wasn't tough, I wouldn't be where I am today.

I just bet you wouldn't, Rich thought. He didn't say it out loud.

Like everything in Brighton's life, his father was one of his props, one of the things that he kept around to make himself interesting. Rich knew Thomas Brighton would have made it even if he were born in a hole on the side of a mountain and raised by a pack of wild jackasses.

"What can I do for you, sir?" Rich asked, nodding politely at Theo, who listened to all this with his pipe still clamped between his teeth.

Brighton leaned back in his chair, swiveled to the left, then to the right. Rich waited. When Brighton sat up he laced his hands together on the top of his empty but massive desk. Rich knew that he was ready to speak.

"This is not an easy thing that we have to discuss with you this morning, Rich," he said.

"Not easy," Lane agreed. He shook his head sadly. "But very necessary and troubling."

"What is it?" Rich pressed, wanting to get the hell out of there before the stuffy place leeched the soul from his body.

Brighton flung a look over his shoulder at the portrait of his father, then looked back at Rich.

"I guess it's fitting that you were so drawn to my father's portrait today."

Rich wasn't. Theo was. But he let the sentiment stand. Anyway, how could a person help not be drawn to something that was as tall as a man and wide as a small boy? The gilt-frame portrait was huge. You'd have to be a nut not to notice it.

"Yes, sir," Rich said.

"Brighton House, God's Children mental facility, as you know, was built in my father's honor," he said.

And your pocketbook, Rich thought, but kept silent, wondering what this was leading to. That was a government contract, too, and because Brighton had added entire wings, he got to name the place. Lucky him. Eventually when the county threatened to close it down due to budget cuts, Thomas Brighton bought it back from the state and used his own money to run it.

Brighton rubbed his plump chin with his fingers. But it was Lane who spoke.

"Have you been reading the papers, Rich? Are you aware of the problems Brighton House is experiencing?" Lane asked.

"No," Rich said.

Well, it wasn't quite a lie. He had not been reading the papers but he did know what "trouble" the mental institution was going through. But he didn't know the whole story. Because of past experiences with his old girlfriend, he knew that she only told him what suited her.

Thomas looked at the ceiling, which was wallpapered with raised flourishes and rimmed by gold leaf crown molding.

"It will be difficult for me to explain this from the beginning," he said. "To tell you the entire story . . ." He stopped, gripped both arms of his armchair, sighed again, and continued. ". . . this unfortunate business," he said heavily, blinking rapidly.

He couldn't tell if the water floating in those blue ice chip eyes was real or affected, but he didn't want to take a chance if it was.

"Yes, well," Brighton continued briskly, getting himself together. "A patient was raped, a retarded girl. They think the girl's father did it. Probably did, the horrible man is in jail, but . . ."

"But what?" Rich was surprised at how cold his voice sounded.

And apparently, so was Brighton, because he looked up quickly, a splinter of startled surprise in his face. Brighton finally nodded in understanding.

"But Brighton House now carries a stain," Lane broke in.

He had finally taken the pipe out of his mouth. His face looked white as milk against the colors of that ridiculous sweater. His gray eyes watered with pride and indignation. "Our honor, son," he said. "Our honor is at stake. In this day and age, that may not mean much to you but when you reach the age of Thomas and me maybe you'll understand. A stain on the reputation of Brighton House is a stain on both of our personal honors."

Rich choked back a laugh, then looked at Theo Lane to see how serious he was. Looking at his face, the set of his eyes, the purse of his lips, Rich could tell that the old man was as serious as the death about to take him. He knew that three years ago, Lane battled prostate cancer. He was in remission now but it looked like the disease had crippled the old soldier. Maybe Brighton wasn't, but Lane was clearly thinking about the legacy he would leave. He was thinking about mortality. And his legacy would be threatened if he was connected to any scandal. Since Lane was a member of the board at Brighton House, a stain there would mean a stain on his name.

"So I'm guessing she's already contacted you, Rich? Your old girlfriend? She wants to pull you into this matter, am I right? Is that why you had a hard weekend?"

Rich stood up and stuck his hands in his pockets, trying to find a place in this stuffy room to put his eyes. *God, don't let it be,* he thought. *Don't let him ask me to look into this thing, too.*

"She had some concern," Rich confirmed.

Lane, balancing himself on the head of his walking stick, stood up. He hobbled over to Rich, placed a hand on his arm. The hand was surprisingly strong and steady.

"I don't know this Hamilton woman very well, Mr. Marvel," he said. "But I've known Luke for a number of years, though I have not had occasion to know him well, especially since he is no longer associated with Brighton House."

"I'm aware," Rich said, not sure what Lane was getting at.

"He's made some unfortunate accusations," Theo Lane said. "About this Hamilton woman. And she's made some herself. I think all of Dunhill would be better off if we don't bring up the memories of those unfortunate incidents again."

"Those unfortunate incidents, sir," Rich said, "involved Luke poisoning drug addicts, including Kendra's mother. I think she has a bone to pick. And frankly, I don't blame her."

Theo nodded as if understanding. "But both you and I know that bone has already been picked clean at great cost to this county. If you have any influence over Hamilton, keep her out of this. Let sleeping dogs lie."

It was on the tip of Rich's tongue to tell Lane that he hated dogs. Instead, he said, "I have no influence over Kendra Hamilton. Is this what this meeting is about?"

"Not quite," Brighton amended.

"I can't get into this, Mr. Brighton," Rich said.

"I'm not asking you to look into this, Rich," Brighton assured him. "Though I think they could use your talent. Please sit down."

Rich sank back into the chair. He was curious now. Right when the words Brighton House floated from Kendra's mouth, he knew because of his position with the company that he had no choice but to look into the rape. There was liability to worry about and security in general. He had some vague notion who handled security at Brighton House but he wasn't quite sure. He knew that it had fallen well within his purview to investigate and it would take more than an ex-lover to keep him away.

"I believe that they have the man who did this, but I am pleased at your reaction," Brighton brushed imaginary dust from the desk. "I heard about this incident, that Kendra Hamilton was involved and was helping this Leroy fellow. I knew about your connection and that she would ask you to become involved. She's done this before, hasn't she? With that Luke Bertrand business. The girl has a habit of running to you."

"What is this all about, sir?" Rich said, the impatience in his chest wrapped in his voice.

"I need you to stay away from the case and Kendra Hamilton until this is done, which," Brighton stopped, one palm up, he thrust his fingers at Rich, "I believe would not be too hard for you, considering your reaction. As you know, the girl is a trouble-maker."

"What else?" Rich asked. He knew there was something else. With men like Brighton, there always had to be something else.

Brighton let his scrubbed white hand fall to his knee.

"I know that there is no possibility that that poor girl was taken advantage of . . ."

"You mean raped," Rich interrupted.

Brighton bowed his head in concession. "Okay, raped," he said. "Whatever you want to call it. I know that this horrendous thing could not have happened in my facility." A dramatic pause here and a glance passed between Lane and Brighton. The latter puffed out his chest to gear up for a speech. *Note what comes next*, that pause said.

"I built Brighton House with the help of the state and city government as a refuge and haven for those mentally disturbed people whose families are not strong enough to support loved ones with mental illness. Men like Theo have helped me sustain it."

Thomas stood up, thrust his hands into his pockets, turned his back to Rich for effect.

"My own mother, Rich," Thomas said. "After her stroke, was mentally challenged. The world became an unfamiliar place for her, even her body became an unfamiliar place. She no longer knew how to dress herself, did not understand her bodily indications." Turning to Rich, Brighton waved a hand over his stomach. "But my father, who loved her so, took care of all that for her. He washed her, bathed her, brushed her hair nightly until it shone. How I used to watch them. She was so well cared for that you wouldn't guess she was ill. That is, until she opened her mouth."

Brighton stopped, lost in some memory. Rich let out a puff of air, impatient. He didn't care if this memory of Brighton's was real or not. He just wanted him to get to the point. All of this was old history to Rich. Everyone in Dunhill knew this goddamned story. Brighton repeated it every chance he got, every chance he got and when it was useful to him. The entire thing was like a made for television movie, except Rich hoped to God no one would ever be sick enough or greedy enough to make it.

Brighton found his voice again. "And after the stroke, how I would sit and watch my father brush that hair and wonder how it would be to have someone love me as much as he so obviously loved her." He stopped suddenly, and turned to Rich. Rich could see that he would cut the speech short today. Now, the old man's face was all business. His next statement startled and surprised Rich.

"That old bastard worked himself to death taking care of my mother as required, not to mention killing himself over a product that was passed around and cheapened more than a two dollar whore on a Saturday night."

Just as Thomas Brighton's voice had been filled with love and longing just a few minutes before, now it was filled with venom. Rich was sure that Brighton was being honest. He hated his father; he hated the man behind his desk, the man seated on a barrel with a frown so deep it seemed like a cartoon.

"Don't look so surprised Rich, I loved my father, but he had his faults."

This was a lie, the love part, but Rich kept silent.

"He worked himself to death. In a way, he tried to escape his own body. He did not understand his own limitations. He would not bend. He died a year before I graduated from Harvard, leaving both my brother and me orphans."

But what about your mother? Rich wanted to ask him, but didn't. He just wanted to get the hell out of there.

"I built Brighton House to honor the love he had for her, Rich, for my mother," he said. "But I also built it because I don't want other young boys to go through what I and my brother went through."

Brighton looked up at the portrait. For a minute, Rich thought he would shake his fist at it.

"I built it for practical reasons," he said. "Because I wanted people who needed help to have a place to go and be cared for by people who knew what they were doing and loved them in some way. Do you understand? People who loved and respected them as human beings."

This last was not a part of the typical speech. Rich knew for some reason Brighton believed everything he was saying, believed in it with his whole heart, if not with his head.

"And now, I have this, this . . ." He stopped, again boring those blue eyes into Rich's. ". . . scandal." It sounded as if Brighton had pulled the word up from the very bottom of his gut.

Lane joined his outrage by saying, "To think that anyone could take advantage of that beautiful child in such a manner." He walked over to the wet bar and Rich watched as he emptied a can of apple juice into a small glass.

"You knew her, Mr. Lane?" Rich asked.

He sighed before taking a sip of the juice. "I knew of her, saw her once during a tour there." He placed the cup on the bar, shook his head. "I think we were all there, weren't we Thomas? The entire board. Such a beautiful child; such a waste."

"What can I do for you sir?" Rich asked Brighton, tired of the entire discussion, the feigned outrage of both men.

Brighton swallowed, hung his head for a minute. He was a man struggling to get back into character, struggling to become the man who needed props. He raised his white head once he was together again.

"I want you to review the security protocols at Brighton. I should have turned that over to you when you started a year ago, but I really thought Katherine Holder could handle it."

"Sir?" Rich questioned.

"Katherine Holder," Lane explained. "She's the administrator at Brighton House. A director, I believe."

"Regarding the security protocols . . ." Brighton continued, ignoring Lane's explanation.

"I fully intend to look into them," Rich said.

"Don't get me wrong Rich," he said, shaking a finger. "I don't want you to get into this rape thing. In fact, stay as far away from that as you can. But I want you to look into the security protocols and make sure those patients, my patients, are safe."

Rich took this in. He didn't speak, only turned the words over in his mind. He took a deep breath.

"That's not going to be easy," he said.

"Look, Rich," Brighton countered. "I know that you don't want to be mixed up with your old girlfriend again. I'm not asking you to. Stay as far away from her as your desire tells you. All I'm asking you to do is make sure that something like this cannot happen at Brighton House."

"I know that, Mr. Brighton." Rich said. "But how in the hell am I supposed to do that without looking into this rape?"

Brighton smiled now, fully, showing each one of his small, capped white teeth.

"I'm the boss, remember, Rich? Bosses don't care *how*. It's half of your job to figure out *how*. And as long as you stay as far away as possible from this rape while making sure my people are safe, you will be keeping me happy. And that's the other half of your job, Rich. Keeping me happy."

CHAPTER 6

Rich and Carlyle drove to Brighton House in Carlyle's Hummer, on a clear day, a clear day after months of winter rain and chill. The sky was a placid shade of blue and the sun warmed Dunhill to a palatable sixty-five degrees. Not exactly summer weather but welcome after such a dreary winter. And it was after winter, wasn't it? Though officially, they had a month or more of cold weather, an increased frequency of bright blue days heralded the approach of spring.

No back roads led to Brighton House. The freeway was the only route to the facility, that and helicopter. At first, the land seemed populated. Along the freeway, signs tall as trees with evocative proposals told them that Wendy's was open late, the neon sign above Love's gas station told them that gas, diesel, was $1.79 a gallon, do not drink and drive. As the road continued north, these exhortations became fewer and fewer, and the freeway ran silent, stretching like the last living vein on a dying body. The exit, simply Brighton House, took them in a spiral, emptying them out onto a gravel road. An apple orchard, trees stark and gray, braved a few bright pink blossoms. Black crows, shiny wings twittering, pecked at the ground, looking for seed among the cold gravel.

In the front gardens of Brighton House, the grounds keeper had gone so far as to plant pansies. Purple and black spotted yellow petals almost flush with the brown ground, not a leaf in sight.

Too soon, Rich thought. He didn't know much about gardening, but he did know from his mother's garden that February was too soon to plant pansies, no matter how much winter seems to relent to the coming of spring.

Thomas Brighton's arrogance poured the foundation of Brighton House. He had the best consultants in the field on the project. But having the best consultants and listening to them were two different things. They told him that it would be best if he built a single story building with twenty-four beds. He built five stories, a full hundred and twenty bed facility, and a private room for each patient. They told him that he should partner with Doctor's Hospital and build the facility adjacent to the hospital. He chose a barren piece of land just outside of Dunhill. Brighton House was built in isolation surrounded by redwoods and high fences. A canal ran like a clear ribbon of water behind the south end of the property. Thomas said he wanted the residents to have some peace. He wanted them to be able to see and smell the blue sky, be calmed by the glimmering water behind the facility.

The place was laid out like a cross, with most of the administrative offices and entrance in the west quadrant. What Thomas did do is listen when it came to staff. Brighton House employed so many social workers and nurses and certified nursing assistants that Thomas would brag that he had an employee for each guest at the famed Brighton House. But what he didn't brag about was the number of doctors. They had two—a psychiatrist and a general practitioner. That was about it. Shit, doctors were expensive.

Though the building was five stories, it didn't look very tall. Each floor sprawled over several acres. When Rich first saw the place, he thought one thing: prison. Even the palm tree fronds spiraling out like ceiling fans and the fruit trees planted just inside the high fence did not dispel the notion of anguish, of captivity. Rich was only slightly surprised when he learned that the place was actually a bughouse and not a prison.

Carlyle parked the Hummer near the entrance and they walked to the large double doors. He placed a hand on Rich's forearm as he reached for the handle. This morning, Carlyle's hair flamed brilliant orange in the yellow sun.

"Whatever she says, she's lying," Carlyle said.

Rich blinked, not sure if he heard Carlyle correctly. But that's what

Carlyle said. *Whatever she says, she's lying.* He referred to Katherine Holder, the hospital administrator they were going to visit. What was her title again? Rich ticked the rolodex in his head. That's right. Katherine Holder was the director of Brighton House. Phil Grubb, Brighton's secretary, had arranged the meeting between her and Rich the previous day.

"Why do you say that?" Rich asked.

Carlyle spread his hands. "She's lying," he said. "She has to. She has no choice but not to give you the entire story. I have seen places like this—semiprivate, with state contracts, trying like hell to adhere to all the regulations they are supposed to, never having enough money to do what they need. I don't give a fuck how much dough Brighton has. Just remember something when we talk to Katherine Holder, she's in one mode and one mode only."

"What mode is that?" Rich asked.

"Cover-up."

Rich said nothing, just opened the door and walked into what he and Dominic had called the bughouse. Except unlike a bughouse, the place was as clean as an operating room and quiet as prayer during Sunday church. White tile, not linoleum but honest to God marble tile, gleamed under their feet. The walls were covered with soft beige linen. Brass lights illuminated paintings of landscapes in watercolor hanging on the wall. Directly in front of them, two nurses, both female, hair pulled back, black bobby pins holding their starched white caps into place, sat in wheeled chairs behind the nurses' station.

An orderly stood near them. He wore a clean white uniform starched so stiffly that Rich speculated that the thing could probably stand by itself. He wasn't with the other nurses, Rich noticed, but rather he was standing to the side of them, as if he were awaiting some sort of order.

Rich would not have noticed the apple-faced man with the spiked brown hair if he hadn't been staring at the nurses so intently. His lips were the only thing moving on his body as he stared at the two women, waiting, furiously popping the gum in his mouth. Every flag in Rich's perp-o-meter was set. He instantly did not trust—he stopped in mid-thought, looked at the man's name tag—Chadwick.

"May I help you?" one of the nurses asked, laughing slightly at some joke her coworker told her.

"We are here to see Katherine Holder," Rich said.

"Dr. Katherine Holder?" she asked, a little absently.

Rich laughed. "How many Katherine Holders you got?" he asked, returning her smile.

"They only have one, and hopefully, that's all we need."

Both Rich and Carlyle turned at the voice floating over to them. Dr. Katherine Holder walked to them with her hand outstretched. She shook Rich's hand with both of her own, looking into his eyes, her lined face smiling and welcoming. She did the same to Carlyle then, excused herself and walked over to the nurse's station. She put her hand on Chadwick's shoulder and said something to him. Rich couldn't help but notice how Chadwick stepped back, his lip curling before turning away. Talk about your attitude problems, Rich thought.

Katherine Holder was a short woman, about five feet two inches and shaped like a cube. She wore big-rimmed Larry King glasses. Like her nurses, her thin brown hair was pulled back into a bun. But her bun looked like a lump of sliding mud and was streaked with gray. Strands from her untidy hair lay on the striped collar of her blue suit.

She turned back to Rich and Carlyle, waved them both into her office. Even though two chairs faced a blonde wooden desk, clean except for two or three stacks of papers, she guided them toward a table with three chairs in the corner of the large room. Holder sat down only after they did, crossed her legs and leaned forward. She looked earnestly at them.

"Do all your nurses wear white uniforms?" Rich asked.

She sat back and laughed.

"I know." She sighed. "Now it's a little old-fashioned but the board, especially Mr. Brighton, insists. But only those assigned to the reception desk wear the white uniforms. We find those dealing directly with patients get better reactions if the nurses dress more casually."

Rich smiled. To his surprise, he found himself liking Katherine Holder. Her voice had a quality that reminded him of a firm wind.

"Can I get you anything?" she asked suddenly. "How about some water or pop?"

"Water."

"Seven-Up."

Rich and Carlyle spoke at the same time. Holder smiled before going to a small refrigerator in her office. As they waited, Carlyle pointed to the window behind her desk. It was a large window covering most of the wall and looked out on what was probably a recreation area. The patio was made of concrete and populated with metal tables and chairs. Two patients played Ping-Pong. A middle-aged man sat on one of the stone benches, white shirt, dark pants, eyes squeezed shut. He held both hands on either side of his face, clicking his fingers together. At the same time he clicked his teeth and tongue. His shoes were missing and the bottoms of his bare feet were filthy.

Dr. Holder came back with the bottled water and Seven-Up.

"That's Lenny," she said as she sat down. "He's been here practically since they built the place. No one knows what he's doing, haven't been able to figure it out yet, but for the most part he's harmless." She said all of this quickly, still smiling as if her face would break.

"Why doesn't he have shoes on? Isn't he cold?" Carlyle asked.

Dr. Holder craned her neck to see. "Oh," she said, rising. "Oh. I'm sure he had on shoes this morning, but he takes them off, hates shoes." Her skirt shifted high as she drew the curtain closed. A violent scraping sound filled the room as the metal hooks moved along the bar. Her thighs were hard, round, her calves well developed without an ounce of fat on them. Dr. Holder, Rich thought, was a runner. With the curtains closed, she returned to their little circle of chairs.

"Has anyone ever figured out why he does that, at least?" Rich asked with some sarcasm in his voice as she sat down again.

"He just hates wearing shoes." Dr. Holder smiled. Her teeth straight, narrow. "Mr. Marvel, Mr. Carlyle, what can I do for you?"

"I think you know that we are here to look into the Anna Cotton incident," Carlyle said.

She sat back in her chair. Confusion rippled across her square face. "No," she contradicted. "I understood that you were here just to discuss the security protocols?"

"Which involves the rape indirectly," Rich explained, making sure the broad smile on his face reached his eyes. He stared at her hands, noticing that they were short and square like the rest of her, creased, without the adornment of jewelry. She caught him looking, brushed the back of her left hand.

"I see." She laced her hands together. Leaning forward again, she said, "We have a lot of ground to cover so why don't we get started. First, you are probably a little curious about me." Rich wasn't, but did not get a chance to interrupt her before she rushed on. ". . . since the security and safety of the patients ultimately rests with me."

"Actually," Rich twisted the cap from the Arrowhead water, flicked it on the table. It spun. He waited until the cap fell flat. "I was hoping to meet with your head of security."

Dr. Holder smiled. "Of course," she said. "I'll give you his address and contact information."

She stood, briskly, walked to her desk, and flicked open a card holder.

"His address?" Rich asked.

Carlyle smiled, said nothing.

Sliding out two cards, she said, "We contract with a private company. His office is not on the premises."

Rich nodded, not asking the obvious. He ignored the feel of Carlyle's eyes upon him. He could almost hear him—see, told you, one mode and one mode only. Dr. Holder obviously did not tell Phil that the head of security was not on the premises when Phil called to arrange the appointment. Or maybe she did and Phillip Grubb thought a wasted trip to Brighton House would be good for Rich.

Before he could ask another question, Katherine Holder rushed on.

"Believe it or not, I started out my career as a nun," she said as she returned to her seat.

At these words, Rich's eyes snapped to Carlyle. The man was unimpressed. *Whatever she's saying, she's lying.* Carlyle watched Dr. Holder unflinchingly as if he were a predator keeping his eyes on prey.

Rich could see her as a nun, the sexless cube, the square hands doing God's work. Her calling, she said, put her at a Catholic-run mental home. While there, Katherine Holder recognized more than ever the need for highly trained professionals in the field of mental health. She left the order and went to college, specializing in the field, and found herself at Brighton House.

"I've been here for the past fifteen years," she said.

Carlyle scribbled on a notepad. Rich took another drink of water, almost gone now.

"How many incidents have you had since your tenure, Dr. Holder?" Rich asked mildly.

She sat back, not smiling for one of the first times. Carlyle stopped scribbling.

"Why, none," she said, surprise on her face.

"What about the Anna Cotton rape?" Carlyle asked.

Dr. Holder smiled again, exposing her teeth, making Rich think of butter. "I think you understand, gentlemen, that the Anna Cotton rape did not occur on Brighton House grounds."

"How can you be so sure?" Rich asked, curious.

"As you will see from your security evaluation, it's simply impossible for something like that to happen here. There is no way into the facility except for the front entrance."

"What about . . ." Carlyle began but Dr. Holder cut him off.

"Yes, and the entrances to the loading docks. We have two." She held up two fingers to illustrate. "And both of these loading docks are monitored twenty-four seven by motion controlled cameras. Everyone else uses the front entrance. Even employees must log in and out."

"Then it's an inside job," Carlyle challenged.

Holder shook her head. "No. No. Impossible, not one of my employees."

"Is it an automated time card system?" Rich cut in before Carlyle could go on. What did Carlyle expect? For Holder to agree with him?

"No," Dr. Holder shifted in her seat. "I'm afraid we are not there yet. Expenses you know. But they log out manually using a log book. The guard at the front desk monitors this."

"There was no guard when we came in," Rich said, his voice dry.

Another smile flicked across Dr. Holder's face. "He must have been on break."

"And these cameras," Rich asked. "Are these cameras on continuous record or do you have archives?"

Rich noticed that Dr. Holder dug her fingers into the skin on her arms. When she unfolded them, he saw the indentations her fingernails had left behind.

"We have tapes, I believe, or CDs nowadays, you know, that we archive."

"How far back?" Rich asked.

"I don't know; the security company takes care of all that."

Though she said this without hesitation, Rich noticed that she dropped her eyes when she said it. The fluorescent lights glinted off the wide face of her glasses.

"Who do you contract with for security, Dr. Holder?" Rich asked.

"It's on the card." She pointed at the card in his hand with her pencil. "Tower Security Experts."

"How long?" Rich asked.

She shrugged, turned red as the bun finally slipped its banks and slithered down her back. She grabbed it, twisted it again and stuck the pencil in the mess. "Before my time; I'm sure you can get the details from Mr. Hightower."

"But I thought you said you have been here for the last fifteen years," Carlyle said.

"Not always as the director," she admitted. "I've only been director for the last five."

"I see." Carlyle said, still scribbling. "What about the ambulance entrance?"

She pursed her lips together; her red lipstick flaked like dried blood.

"There is that, yes," she said. "An ambulance entrance."

"Camera-monitored?" Rich asked but already knowing the answer.

"Yes.

"Mr. Carlyle, Mr. Marvel." The words pushed out her mouth as if she were forcing herself to relax. "I am so sorry if I seem a little put off with these questions. But you have to understand that I've given my life to Brighton House. And that includes sacrificing my family." She stopped, leaned forward again. "Do you want to know where I was when my grandniece was born, my first grandniece? It may not seem like much to you, but we are a very close family." She waited for a reply, but getting none, she said, "But in spite of that,

I was right here, handling an emergency patient, if I recall, who had a heart attack. So you see, for someone to say that we have failed in some way means more than just failing at a job, for me it's a passion."

"Whatever you say, Dr. Holder," Carlyle said blandly. "We understand. Believe me, all we want to do is get to the bottom of what happened to Anna Cotton."

"But I thought the police had already done that."

"Yes, they have," Rich answered her. "But Mr. Brighton just wants to make sure that nothing of the sort ever has a chance of happening here."

She sat back. "I see." She smiled. "Well, then, let's get on with it. Le Grand Tour."

She stood up and indicated the door. With another smile she ushered them out of the office. Rich stopped at the entryway, turned and looked at Dr. Holder who held the door open. The smile cut lines on either side of her face, creased her broad brow.

"One more thing, Dr. Holder," Rich said.

"Please call me Katherine," she said.

"Katherine," Rich replied. "I have one more request."

"What's that"—still smiling, as if it hurt.

"Carlyle and I will need the background checks on all the employees at Brighton House."

She blinked, "Background checks?"

"Yes," he said.

"I'm afraid I don't have them."

"Then who does?" Carlyle challenged. "You do conduct background checks don't you? You have to."

"Well, of course we do," she said. "We must but it's done by the . . ."

"Tower Security Experts." Rich finished for her, laughing that fake social laugh he hated on anyone else. She joined in his laughter, touched him on the back saying, "Yes, Tower Security."

Dr. Katherine Holder was immensely proud of Brighton House. She swept through the facility showing them the recreation room, the gymnasium and the art room. She showed them the medical facilities, explaining that since they were so far from the hospital, they employed a full time physician. A patient's room was semiprivate, depending on the condition of the patient, she said, turning to them as she opened the door. Anna Cotton was lucky enough to have one of the private rooms.

They entered a room that looked not unlike a hotel room but only a third of the size. Soothing blue paint covered the wall, and in this particular room, white cheerful clouds decorated the ceiling. A small nightstand, empty except for a lamp, stood in between two twin beds with the requisite pillow lumps and cheerful blue bedspread. More paintings, these of simple daises and houses, were hung on the wall. Children's drawing, Rich thought fleetingly.

But he was more interested in the door which he had caught when Dr. Holder walked into the room. She stood there in the middle of the room watching as Rich swung the door between his hands. He looked at the door handle, jiggled it up and down.

"This door can be locked from the inside," he said musingly.

"Why, yes," Dr. Holder admitted, hands clasped in front of her.

"Are there locks like this on all the rooms?" Rich asked.

"Aside from this one," Carlyle interjected, "which is the model one you probably show on tours?"

Dr. Holder sighed. Her eyes sparkled behind her glasses and the lenses glittered as she cocked her head.

"Believe it or not, Mr. Carlyle, this room that we show on tours is not unlike the rooms most of our guests occupy."

"Guests?" Rich cut in.

"Yes, guests," she said. "Patients if you will. But Mr. Brighton and the rest of the board prefer the term guests."

"So all the rooms have these locks on them?"

"Some of them do, yes. Not for the violent, after all. It gives the patients a sense of security and privacy."

"I see," Rich said. "A sense of security. Who has keys?"

Dr. Holder looked at him. A wry smile covered her face. She walked over to the door and guided Rich outside. She pushed in the lock and shut the door. As they stood behind the closed door, Dr. Holder removed an ID card from her pocket and slid it through a terminal beside it. It turned from red to green before clicking open.

Over Carlyle's low whistle, she said in a hard voice, "We are, after all, gentlemen, a mental hospital no matter how like a hotel Mr. Brighton would like to make it. Everyone has access to these rooms through these door strikes. Everyone."

"So, only through the door strikes? What if you have a power outage?" Rich asked.

"We're prepared for that," Dr. Holder said. "We have a back-up generator. But even if that fails, then the doors can also be opened manually with a master key."

"Everybody have a master key?"

She shook her head. "Not everyone. But we do keep one at the nurse's station for emergencies. And of course, I have one."

She ended the tour along the back of Brighton House, near the canal that seemed to stretch from west to east and wind for miles. Chill air had driven away the warm morning. Rich pulled his jacket around him. Dr. Holder thought it would be nice to walk from the back of the facility to the front parking lot so they would get a sense of the entire facility.

"There is one more thing," Rich said, interrupting her explanation of the meticulous care they gave to the gardens, how they used gardening as therapy for some patients.

"What's that?" she asked, drawing her own jacket closer around her. The wind had blown her hair down again. Sleek strands danced across her square face.

"We need to speak to Anna Cotton."

Her shoulder fell at his words. Her face softened a bit and she said with some wonder in her voice, "Oh, I'm afraid that I cannot let that happen."

"I don't understand," Carlyle said, the tips of his ears turning red.

"I can't let you speak with Anna Cotton," she repeated. "It is out of the question."

"Then how am I supposed to get to the bottom of this," Carlyle snapped, "if we can't speak to the victim? Mr. Brighton insists . . ."

"Oh," she said again. "I'm afraid Mr. Brighton has no jurisdiction in that area. We only have to respond to a police subpoena, which we have."

"Who has jurisdiction?" Rich asked, his voice gentling with the cold wind.

"Her legal guardian, of course," she said.

"And that's still Kendra Hamilton?" he asked.

She grabbed the fleeing hair and once again tied it into a sloppy knot at the nape of her neck. Her face full of annoyance, she said simply, "Why, yes, Kendra Hamilton."

"That broad certainly smiles a lot," Carlyle said in the car on the way back to the office. Rich did not answer him. But Carlyle was right. The broad certainly did smile a lot.

"There is something up with that place," Carlyle said.

"How can you be so sure?" Rich asked.

"When you walked into her office, what was the first thing you noticed?"

"The ugly-ass carpet?" Rich laughed, thinking back to the flat industrial carpet, the color of shit, the texture of a Brillo pad.

"No," Carlyle said. "The recreation area."

"Three people, lots of gray cement, crazy ass mother playing with his hands . . ."

"No, no, no," Carlyle said. "You did not notice people, you noticed patients. Now, tell me what you didn't notice."

Rich thought. "You see how fast she pulled those curtains shut . . ." Carlyle continued.

Rich told him to shut up. Carlyle did. Rich wanted to figure out for himself what Carlyle meant. Green Ping-Pong table, lots of cement, stone benches, three crazies but not a . . . he looked over at Carlyle who was smiling at him, smiling and nodding.

"Against state regulations to allow patients in the recreation area without the proper supervision. Them's points buddy."

Rich thought about that. Points. It was more than points and crazy or not, mentally deficient or not, those three people deserved one thing that they were obviously not getting at Brighton House. Protection. Supervision. And if they did not have it, what of Anna?

"You ever heard of this security company?"

Carlyle grunted. "You mean Tower Security? Yes, I have."

"How are they?"

"Not bad," Carlyle admitted, and it was an admission because Rich could see that he hated having to do that. He wondered why

Carlyle gave up his own security business. What made him run to Thomas Brighton? "They started off kinda small. I know the guy who runs it now." Carlyle shrugged. "Not to drink a few beers with but to say hi and how's it going every now and then."

He went on to tell Rich that Tower Security Experts had grown in the last three years to provide security services for half a dozen hospitals, banks, and apartment buildings around the greater Dunhill area. They had diversified. Now, the guy who owned it, Val Hightower, was richer than Midas. Rich chuckled at this and said that it was time for Midas to have a come-to-Jesus meeting.

CHAPTER 7

Rich's brother, Dominic Marvel, did two things magnificently. The first thing he did magnificently was to play the sax. John Coltrane, some would say, reincarnated, in the flesh. But admittedly, those people who said that were Mom, his other brothers, and Rich when he was in a good mood. But hell, Dominic's playing was good enough to buy him a house in Pacific Heights, enough to take care of a wife and two kids—not to mention the hideaway in Tahoe. But the other thing Dominic Marvel did magnificently, no one inside or outside the family would argue. Dominic was a connoisseur at getting to know people—and not only people, but people who knew how to get things done. And Rich had needed something done and done discreetly.

Phillip Grubb had nagged the hell out of him, that wierdo in the sweater vest. And Thomas Brighton's request was a little what? Yes, that was it, it was off key, did not make sense. Stay away from the rape? Why? What did Brighton know, if anything? Or was Rich just letting his suspicion get the better of him?

After work, Rich went to San Francisco. He drove the entire fifty or so miles, his hand dangling from the open window of his rusted Firebird. A cigarette, lit but not smoked, dangled between his fingers. Rich hadn't smoked since his college days, thought smoking was stupid, a tasteless habit that reminded people every day what their bodies would eventually come to—ashes.

But when his career ended in a shambles and Kendra took her long walk, he started buying the goddamned things. Five bucks a pack, Marlboro, Newport, he didn't give a shit. He would buy the things, stuff the cellophane packets in his glove compartment. And occasionally he would light one with his newly purchased Bic lighter. There was something comforting in watching the orange glow, the gray devouring the brown bits of tobacco and the crisp white paper. He didn't smoke, he watched; and watching brought him closer to a peace that he had not had in a long time.

He drove as the sun, orange and fat, sank before him, color like a bloody egg yolk. Rich drove past apple trees shocked through with tiny white and green blossoms, and the occasional rosebush with one brave bloom slowly freezing in the winter chill. The chill whipped in through his open window. He snatched his hand inside the car, cradled the cigarette in the ashtray, occasionally watching as it burned to the filter.

At the nightclub where his brother Dom played most times, he watched him on stage with The Frontier Jazz Band. Dom, as brown as a pecan with a neat goatee drawn around the hard slash of his mouth and the edges of his chin, leaned to one side as he blew, eyes closed, upper body rocking. The gray stripe of his shirt was barely visible in the dark room but the ring on his pinky finger, a lion's head with a diamond in its mouth, twinkled.

The rest of the band, the three people Dom played with, the skinny kid with the dreads on base, the middle-aged spiked-haired woman on keyboards, and the drummer, old with a face as pitted and spotted as a cantaloupe, did not exist to Rich at the moment. His eyes were only for Dom, and he closed them, seeing his brother play, listening to sound beat the air.

And when he opened his eyes again, he saw the alto sax springing from Dom's mouth, curving like a stream of perfectly golden water.

Dom played at a club called The Lost. Rich looked around and saw that the place looked as if it were indeed filled with those lost. The tables were small as dinner plates, the people there dressed eclectically, some in suits and cocktail dresses, and others with torn jeans, hooks in their noses, studs in their eyebrows and ears. The place didn't serve food and the patrons smoked. But nothing seemed to ever happen to the owners, or the patrons—except maybe lung cancer. But no fines. Stepping into The Lost was like stepping into the past, a past which everyone accepted and no one questioned.

Light applause, and Rich knew the song was over. Dom carefully laid his alto sax in its case. When the house lights were turned on, Rich could see the red velvet inside was faded and creased with pink. Rich's brother was not famous but he made a living with his music. He had the same problems as anybody, he and the wife didn't get along and he had two kids, a girl and a boy as wild as wolves. The boy did well in school, but the girl, Stella, was having trouble in math, and smarted off more than Dom liked.

Off stage, Dom seemed distracted, as if he did not know how he got to where he was, what he was doing there, and if he should care. He came straight to Rich's table and sat down in the brown wooden chair. The small round seat and curved back were just right for his small behind. Before speaking to Rich, he lit a cigarette. Unlike Rich, he inhaled, then sputtered, coughing and laughing at the same time.

"That burns," he said. "Man, I should give these damn things up."

Rich didn't answer him. He reached for his drink, took a sip.

"You dry tonight?" Dom asked the question with a lifted eyebrow. Rich would have thought the question casual if it weren't for the telltale lift of the Marvel eyebrow.

Rich touched the side of the glass; it felt smooth and cool beneath his fingers.

"Coke," Rich answered. "Finished for the night?"

"Finished and dog tired," Dom agreed, nodding a little. Then, looking at Rich, he said, "Look, man, she begged me to tell her where you were."

Soft piano music played in the background. It seems as if the piano player didn't want to call the set done. She touched the piano lightly, the keys pressed as if from a caress, the resulting music like melting ice.

"I figured as much." Rich shrugged.

"Look . . ." Dom started.

"You don't have to explain to me," Rich said.

Dom did not answer him so Rich leaned back and pressed his head against the chair back. He listened to the piano player, the soft fall of the music in the room.

"So what are you doing here, man?" Dom asked. "You didn't drive all the way down here to hear me play, did you?"

Rich grinned. "I'd drive hundreds of miles to hear you play, Dom," he said.

Dominic snorted and Rich knew that they were both thinking of the same thing. How Dom had almost blown the siding from the house with his practicing, how Rich and his brothers would run out of the house swearing that blood was coming from their ears.

"Seriously, man," Dom said, his black eyes glittering in the low light.

Rich sighed. "I need a favor. And I need to talk to you about something."

"Yeah?" Dom said, meaning *tell me something I didn't know.*

"You know anybody who can check up on some people for me, man?" Rich asked.

Dominic laughed. "Hell, yeah, I do," he said. "So do you. What do you need me for?"

"The people I know," Rich said, "I don't know so well anymore." Rich referred to his friends at the sheriff's department. They both knew it but neither one of them commented on it. "And besides," Rich continued, "I need someone who can do the checking discreetly."

"Who is it, man?" Dom asked.

Rich reached into his shirt pocket, pulled out a list of Brighton House board members, including that prick Phillip Grubb. Dominic whistled when he saw it, that's all, just whistled.

"One name missing, man," Dom said.

"What name is that?" Rich asked.

"The president of the United States?" Dominic grinned.

"Come on, I'm serious," Rich said.

"What about Thomas Brighton?"

"I already know what I need to about him," Rich said. "These others, though, I don't. Old man told me that they were off limits. He told me that for a reason and I want to know why."

"Okay, okay," Dom said. "I'm down with that. May need some green to back this up. When do you need it by?"

Rich lit his cigarette, and for the first time in a long time, he inhaled deeply and blew out a long stream of smoke. Strange how easy smoking came after all these years. Sitting back in his chair, he said, "Whenever you can get it to me."

"That means yesterday," Dom said.

Rich laughed. "Something like that."

They sat in silence for a while. The soft music had stopped. The broad on the piano had finally given up.

"I need a place to crash tonight," Rich said. "I don't think I can make it back to my place."

Dom tilted a hand toward him. "Always a pleasure." Then, "You know," he said, "I still go to those meetings."

"Good for you," Rich said, knowing that Dom meant those meetings where drunks and addicts sat around talking about how they couldn't stay off the juice without help.

"Every morning before the sun comes up and twice on Sunday," Dom said, grinning. "Why don't you come with me tomorrow morning?"

"Why?" Rich asked. "Forget your way? Need help finding the place?"

"You love being a smart ass, don't you?"

Rich laughed bitterly. "It's what I do," he said.

"I haven't forgotten my way," Dom said. "I'm not lost, Rich, but I think you are."

Rich nodded, smoke stinging his eyes. "She already called you, didn't she?" Rich asked.

"She's worried about you, Rich," Dom said.

Rich leaned forward, placed his elbows on the table. He looked Dom squarely in his deep, black eyes. "That woman," he said. "The only way that woman could be worried about anything is if she is staring in a mirror. She's completely, totally selfish."

"Ah, man," Dom said. "Don't be—"

"It's the truth," Rich said seriously, taking another drag on his cigarette.

"You blame her for everything, don't you?" Dom asked. "Kendra? She's the cause of all your problems?"

"Not everything." Rich shrugged. "Most things. I blame her for most things."

"Including your drinking binges?"

Rich hunched his shoulders, looking across the club at a woman who was giving him the eye. He stabbed out his cigarette into an amber ashtray already brimming with butts. Exasperation lacing his voice, he said, "Okay. Let's review, shall we?"

"Let's," Dom agreed.

"She lied to me the first day we met. And this was no ordinary, little white lie. She lied to me about her mother's death saying that she didn't know where Violet got her dope. And she kept lying for weeks afterwards . . ."

"Rich . . ." Dom tried to interrupt but Rich was on a roll and there was no stopping that train.

"I left Dinah for her, Dom, put my career on hold and lost it because of her," Rich said.

"But you knew about that lie before you let things get serious, Rich. Besides, you weren't exactly a choirboy."

"No, I wasn't. Not at all. But even after all I'd given up for her she dropped me like a hot rock the first chance she got, as a matter of fact, the minute things became uncomfortable for her. She left the fucking country without saying a goddamn word."

Rich took a deep breath wishing that he could separate the oxygen from the thick smoke stinging his eyes.

"You asked me about the drinking. Do I blame her for that? No. Can I stop it anytime? Yes. It's nothing that I can't handle, Dominic."

"Then quit," Dom said. "If you can handle it, quit like you promised me you would."

In the silence that followed, Rich asked, "What do you hear these days about Luke Bertrand? I need the word on the streets, man."

Dom sighed. "So that's what this is all about?" he said. "That other thing you wanted to talk to me about."

"Just tell me," Rich said. "Kendra says that he's mixed up in this Anna Cotton thing."

Dom shook his head. "He's not mixed up in anything. The man's a recluse ever since he got out of prison. He stays in his palace in The Point and has his food delivered. He's dropped off every board he was on. The man is completely out of sight."

"But they said he's making comments . . ."

"No," Dom said. "He's not. Some reporter attributed a couple of comments to him, feeding off the Anna Cotton case just for the sensationalism. But let me tell you, Rich, Luke Bertrand is a ghost. Let him be."

Dom stood up and clamped Rich on the shoulder. He held on to it, squeezed tight. "When you realize that you are killing yourself," he said, "give me a holler." He started back to the stage, opened the case and pulled out the golden sax. While the soft piano music played once again, Dom laid a tune on top of it, a tune with sudden stops, long starts, and high and low notes that sounded as if he were painting swirls of color on the air.

Anna

Before Anna come to this place, her daddy went all funny. He yell all the time, he won't look Anna in the eye. And when Anna ask him about Mamma, he lie. He tell her that Mamma went away and don't come back no more. He say Mamma dead. But Anna don't believe him. He won't look at her. He won't touch her in no kind of a way. He won't touch her like the monster touch her but he won't touch her like he used to when she was little, either. He won't even touch her like a daddy supposed to. No hugs, no hand holding. He tell Anna to keep away. She too big now.

When Anna lived in Virginia with Mamma and Daddy, she would sit in Daddy's lap and they would play word games. They play twenty questions or he would ask her a riddle and give her hints until she got the answer. But then Anna grow up and people change the way they look at her. Even Daddy. He tell Anna that she too big to sit in his lap, and he say things in front of her, mean things just to scare her. The sound taste bitter.

And they argue. Mamma tell Daddy all the time to leave Anna alone. It not Anna fault that she retarded and she growed up. And it not Anna fault that there some things that Anna don't know about. But the girl got to learn, that what he tell Mamma, the girl got to learn. And they would argue more and Mamma face would wrinkle and she say that she don't want to talk about it no more.

Then one day, Daddy tell Anna that Mamma go away and don't come back. He make Anna get all her things, clothes though. He don't let Anna take her puzzles or her dolls or her yo-yos. Those things stay, he say. And he get in the old truck and he drive away. On the way to gone, he tell Anna that Mamma gone away because she dead. She dead and don't come back no more.

But Daddy lie. He lie because if Mamma die everybody would come. The neighbors would come, the rest of Anna's friends, they would come. And they would dig a hole and put her in the ground and they would all stand around and cry and watch. But that don't happen. See, even Daddy think Anna stupid. But Anna not stupid. And Anna know Daddy lies.

CHAPTER 8

Kendra waited at Dunhill County Jail to visit Leroy Cotton. She sat in the waiting room, her heart breaking with the news that she had to tell Leroy. They wouldn't find any help or any sympathy in Richard T. Marvel. She remembered the day at the lake. He wanted to eat her up, chew slowly, and spit her back out. He hated her that much and considered her a stain upon the earth. But was that true? she asked herself, looking down at her brown hands folded on her blue-jean clad lap. Did he hate her that much?

A man sitting in the plastic chair next to her leaned over and sniffed her neck. Kendra stretched back to get away from him and to also get a better look at him. He was a white man, about twenty or twenty-two. His long, brown hair was matted to his head and yellow grass hung from the dirty dread-like strands. The scent of marijuana wafted up from him like a stink cloud. His teeth were yellowed, his breath stank of shit, and his thick plaid shirt looked as if he had spent the better part of the afternoon rolling in mud.

"Got a cigarette, lady?" he asked, holding up his fingers like he was already holding the asked for object, almost lying on her shoulders.

Without hesitation, using two fingers planted squarely in the middle of his dirty head, Kendra pushed him away. After doing so, she wiped her hands vigorously on the legs of her jeans.

"Fine," the man said, his gravelly voice hurt, "be a bitch."

Kendra looked at him in disgust but didn't respond. Only two years ago she would have been all sympathy for him, probably giving him not only a cigarette if she had it but everything she had in her wallet. But she had changed. She wasn't that person anymore.

He had decided to accost the woman sitting on the other side of him, an older black woman in knit slacks and a cotton top. She had an expression on her face which said that she was used to this, used to sitting in the waiting room of the Dunhill County Sheriff's Department to visit someone or bail them out of jail.

"Hey, pal," the cop at the desk said, pointing at the nicotine deprived man. "I told you to cool it. Keep it up and you will be warming the bunk next to whoever it is you dragged your sorry ass down here to see."

The man held up two hands and shrugged as if to say okay, okay, I got it, I'll go on the patch. The cop behind the desk caught Kendra's eye and winked. The gesture would have been friendly if it weren't for the sly smirk on his face. The smirk said *what a sorry pass you have come to, Doc, in a waiting room with a bunch of stiffs waiting to visit a soon-to-be convict.*

They all knew who she was, knew her history and what she tried to do to the sheriff's department. Kendra knew what the young cop was thinking. After all, wasn't she the one who tried to send Sheriff Freehold to the state pen? Wasn't she the one who badmouthed the cops up and down California, badmouthed them so badly that internal affairs came rolling up in their dark four door sedans and wayfarers to conduct an internal investigation?

And Sheriff Freehold, their boss, he escaped by luck. Though the investigation found him horribly negligent and incompetent in the running of the sheriff's office, they let him stay with a reprimand on his record and a promise to retire at the end of his term. They let the bastard stay, Kendra thought, even when his incompetence and negligence allowed a serial killer to operate in Dunhill, for how long was it? For fifteen years. Kendra was surprised, but Rich wasn't.

When they were together, he told her why Freehold was not sent to jail. If you send him to jail for not figuring something out, for not being able to find the killer, then that would make all cops vulnerable. Imagine being sent to jail because you couldn't solve a particular case? Because you missed a clue or weren't quick or wise enough to figure out something before another person got killed? No one wanted to go down that road or open that new avenue of lawsuits and judgments. In fact, not even he wanted to walk that particular path.

She could almost hear Rich's voice in her head. When they discussed Freehold they were lying in bed, the room was dark. His voice was soft, and she lay on his shoulder with his arms around her. His voice came low and intimate in the quiet, still room. It wasn't like the voice which greeted her at that lake of glass. It wasn't like the voice that asked her what in the hell was she doing coming into his life again.

"Kendra Hamilton," the deputy said.

Kendra stood up, her legs aching. They had kept her waiting for two hours; she felt as if it had been forever.

Great drums throbbing through the air. The line from Countee Cullen's poem came to Kendra unbidden. She knew why the line strummed in her head as the sheriff's deputy led her down a short corridor. She was thinking of Cullen because he was one of Leroy's favorites. The deputy told her that they had not put Leroy into the visiting common room because Leroy was sick and might be contagious. He slowed down a little, turned around and grinned at her when he said *might be contagious.*

As she followed the deputy down the corridor leading to the visitor's room, she thought about what Rich had accused her of doing. He said that she was using Anna to get at Luke. That was not true, Kendra thought. She cared about Anna. How could she not? But she cared about Luke more, about his getting away with murdering her mother and scores of others.

But still, she did owe something to Anna and Leroy. Because of Kendra's insistence that they place Anna in Brighton House, Anna's body had been taken from her. And now Anna was a political pawn for people like Luke Bertrand who didn't give a damn about Anna, only the threat she presented to the cause. In the end, Anna Cotton could go hang for all they cared.

The deputy stopped in front of a gray steel door. He opened it onto a room which was empty except for a gray table and three brown folding chairs. Leroy was nowhere in sight, not yet at least.

"You've got thirty minutes," the deputy told her. "A guard will be sitting right over there." He pointed to a folding chair propped against one white wall. "Even though the glass is two-way there won't be anyone watching on the other side." He looked at her again, catching her eye with that stupid yellow-toothed grin. "We're shorthanded. Have a seat."

He indicated one of the folding chairs at the table. Kendra was surprised at how small the room actually was. It was no bigger than a walk-in closet. Her throat squeezed tight as a feeling of claustrophobia washed over her.

As he left, another deputy entered the small room. This one was also white but younger and thank God, without a predisposition to talk. The creased blue uniform shirt stood out starkly against the room's white backdrop. His badge with the Dunhill sheriff department's seal gleamed. Kendra sat at the card table and waited for Leroy Cotton.

About five minutes after the deputy settled himself in his seat, staring straight ahead like a department store dummy, Leroy Cotton walked in. Leroy was a thin man, tall, with long hands and big-knuckled fingers. His eyes, brown and suspended in a sea of yellow, bulged slightly. Raised black moles dotted the loose skin beneath his eyes. He had a full, wide mouth which closed around a perfect set of pearly false teeth. When he wasn't in jail, which was never—Leroy Cotton had never been in jail a day in his life—he wore overalls and a conductor's cap as he worked at The Liberty Apartments. Some took one look at Leroy and labeled him an uneducated simpleton.

But the fact was that Leroy Cotton was neither uneducated or a simple man. In his spare time, Leroy had worked the farm he and his family lived on. He built trains, restored ancient tractors and read the old works of Dubois and Garvey and the poetry of Countee Cullen. What was the other poem Leroy loved to tease Kendra and Anna with? Oh, yes, the one by Dickey with the line *I want you to kill a man for me.* Leroy would say that line, then recite the entire sick poem. Afterward he would cackle before coughing from too much laughter. Anna, who liked poems, did not like that one. She hated it when Leroy got like that, and Kendra wasn't too fond of him, either. It was as if he were trying to punish Anna or maybe punish both himself and Anna for her inability to understand. It was a mood, Kendra recognized, a dark mean mood that would blow in from nowhere and last days.

Kendra wondered if Leroy would have been different if his wife had lived. But Kendra didn't know. Hell, she didn't even know what Anna's mother's name was because in that area of his life, Leroy remained secretive. He also asked her not to mention any of it to Anna because it upset the girl so. As a matter of fact, Anna refused to believe that her mother had passed.

The Leroy Cotton standing with another guard in the doorway was manacled hand and foot. The chains clinked along the floor as he shuffled into the room. An orange jail uniform, stamped with Dunhill County Sheriff's Department on the back, hung on his thin frame. The material made him look like a Halloween pumpkin. Leroy wiped his runny nose with the back of one of his manacled wrists. His hair, like his daughter's, curly and full in spite of his age and the gray throughout it, was wet with whatever fever he was fighting.

"Leroy," Kendra said quietly, swallowing a little. "The guard told me you weren't feeling well."

Leroy gazed at her and smiled. Kendra noticed that he was not wearing his teeth.

"I've been better," he said. "But I'm doing okay. It's just this flu going around."

He coughed and had to wait until the coughing stopped before speaking again.

"At least it gets me a holding cell by myself and a chance to speak with you privately."

Kendra nodded. "Have you gotten a lawyer yet?" she asked.

Leroy suppressed another cough. "A lady friend of mine in Virginia is a lawyer, she's flying out tomorrow, should be here by tomorrow night."

"Is she good?" Kendra asked.

Leroy laughed then, which set off another coughing fit. "She better be, hadn't she? Let's hope she's damned good."

Kendra looked at the guard sitting motionless in the corner. His chest covered by the bright blue cloth of his creased shirt looked as if it were made of steel.

"Can we get him some water?" she asked him, but the asshole didn't answer.

Instead he stared straight ahead, his face expressionless. Leroy glanced over at him and then started laughing, a good-hearted, mirthful laugh, like he meant it.

"He thinks I'm a war criminal and he's at the Nuremberg trials. You know what, Kendra, the first day I set foot in this county I knew one thing, and Robocop sitting over there confirms all my suspicions."

"What's that?" Kendra asked.

"You all take yourselves much too seriously; you all take yourselves much too seriously with a fury."

Kendra said nothing. Perhaps Dunhill County with its three distinct neighborhoods, with its history, with its scandals jealously guarded as if they were precious jewels, perhaps it did take itself much too seriously. But Leroy's assessment annoyed her. He had not been in Dunhill half a year and he was already judging them.

"It seems to me that you had better take what's happening to you seriously, Leroy, and not worry about how we feel about ourselves in Dunhill," she said.

"Oh, I take it serious enough." He raised his hand to show her the chains. He continued, his voice a little rough. "How can I not? I'm accused of doing something so hateful to my own daughter that it makes me want to vomit. I'm accused of fathering my own grandchild, Kendra. I take this as serious as hell."

But he didn't. He was smiling as he said it. Even though he didn't have his false teeth in, he smiled fully. And the smile revealed pink gums so furiously pointed that Kendra was sure he could probably use them as teeth in and of themselves.

"Then why are you smiling?" she said. "Why are you acting like this whole thing is a big joke?"

Leroy made a motion to stand. The guard stood up as well and placed a hand on the butt of his gun.

"So not a statue then," Leroy said, sitting back down. "Relax big fella."

But big fella didn't relax until Leroy's ass actually touched the brown folding chair. Leroy scooted it firmly up to the table.

"All they have to do is the math, Kendra . . ."

Kendra cut him off. She didn't know why but she wanted to make Leroy uncomfortable. He was sitting there with fever probably, a sick old man accused with the hideous crime of raping his own daughter. Yet he sat across from her without . . . her thoughts stopped. Suddenly, a voice came from deep within her. It was Rich's voice. *Without what, Kendra? Without a sufficient amount of despair? Is he not playing according to your script?*

"The math, Leroy," Kendra said to silence the voice. "Is inexact. They are saying that Anna was maybe ten to twelve weeks along. And even if it were proved that she was less than twelve weeks along, they would have said that you abused her during one of your visits."

Leroy stared hard at her. "Let's keep it straight, Kendra," he said. "My daughter wasn't abused. She wasn't taken advantage of. She was raped. A monster raped her against her will and fathered my grandchild against mine. In a way we have both been raped."

She said nothing for a while. Leroy sat in his chair, both hands gripping his knees.

"Maybe this is all my fault," he finally mused.

"What?" Kendra asked.

"You think that this is your fault because you suggested that we lock her up," he said.

Kendra winced at the words, "lock her up." Leroy didn't seem to notice or care.

"But you know I had been thinking about it a long time," he said. "Long before you said anything. Watching that child was like . . ." He sighed and shook his head.

"Like what?" Kendra prodded.

"She is so beautiful, Kendra. So beautiful." He surrendered his laugh to a fit of coughing. "It reminds me of an old joke," he said after he caught his breath and wiped the spit from his chin.

"What old joke?" Kendra asked.

"The joke about the man in hell relaxing in a lounge chair on a beach of white sands. Next to him he has a bottle of wine and a beautiful woman in a string bikini sitting at his feet."

Kendra stared at him, didn't like the nauseating look in his eyes. She could see that he was in one of his moods, the dark ones that scared both her and Anna sometimes.

"I don't get it," she finally said.

His laugh was wet, edged with spite. "Neither did he," he said. "He was in hell, remember? The bottle of wine had a hole in the bottom and the blonde didn't."

Kendra drew back in disgust. She looked at the guard to see if he had heard the same thing she did. She could see by the look on his face that he had.

"And you are comparing your daughter to that blonde?"

He shrugged. "I used to, thought that she would never find anyone who would want anything to do with her because she was dumb as a brick. But let me tell you, someone else noticed that hole before I did."

"You are talking like this because you are ill," she suggested.

"Maybe," he answered.

"And afraid," she went on.

"Could be," he admitted.

"You had nothing to do with the rape, Leroy. What happened to Anna was not your fault and wasn't my fault. Stop punishing yourself for it."

"You first," he said. "You stop punishing yourself first—"

"Leroy," she cut him off. "Please."

"Then if you don't think it's your fault, why are you here?" he countered.

"I wanted to let you know that Rich won't help us. We have to find out what happened to Anna ourselves."

"And how do you propose we do that?" he asked.

Kendra opened her mouth to speak but closed it again. There was simply nothing to say. Leroy leaned back in his chair. The manacles around his wrists clanked with his movements. He sighed before speaking again.

"I know that you feel some guilt about all this, Kendra," he relented. "No matter what you say. But don't feel that you have to take care of me. I've been taking care of myself for close over fifty years and though it may not seem like it now"—he held up his chained hands—"I've done a pretty good job at it."

"But . . ." Kendra protested.

"But nothing," Leroy said. "I know that you feel guilty. I know that you think this is your fault and you are trying to right a wrong that you've committed. But you are going to have to square that with yourself, Kendra. Please leave me out of paying your penance."

Kendra folded her arms across her chest and looked at Leroy. "I don't believe in penance, Leroy Cotton, but I believe in what's right. And it's not right that you are here while the bastard who raped Anna is running around out there and you got people trying to make a symbol out of her."

"You mean people like Luke Bertrand?"

"Him, too," Kendra agreed.

Leroy laughed and leaned across the table. It rocked from side to side on a leg that was shorter than all the others.

"And what are you trying to make out of her?" he asked. Though the question was harsh, his voice was gentle as he said it.

She knew what he was trying to say. Kendra had known Anna and Leroy a short time. Because they had gone through Leroy's worsening illness and Anna's adventures together, it sometimes felt as if they were old friends. Sometimes. Now was not one of those times.

Leroy had managed to keep details about his life private. What little Kendra knew of his life, knew of him migrating to Dunhill in search of work, she pieced together from the stories Anna told her. My God, she didn't even know what illness plagued him, though she had guessed emphysema. And even with the shortness of breath, every time she saw him in the apartment, Leroy always had a lit cigarette dangling from his lips.

"I care about Anna," she told Leroy now. "I'm not trying to make anything out of her, or use her for anything. I just want the person who did this to her to pay."

"I know you do," he responded, but his voice was dry, detached.

She had expected him to say, so do I, but those words did not come from his mouth.

"I'm not letting this go," she said.

She knew he thought she meant Anna. She did. Sort of. But the other thing she meant was the war she and Luke had started. She'd find the connection with or without Leroy Cotton.

Chains clinking, Leroy stood up. The guard's knees unhinged and he stood up as well. Still looking at her, Leroy said, "There is something that you need to do, child."

Kendra did not rise from the chair. She looked up at him, her arms crossed over her chest. "Tell me," she said.

"Listen to me very carefully," he said. "Listen with a passion."

She drew back, not liking the tone in his voice. But he went on as if she hadn't moved, holding her eyes with his own. She could not look away.

"I did it." he said.

"What?"

"I said that I did it," he continued. "Think about Jeffrey Dahmer."

"I don't understand." she said.

"Jeffrey Dahmer. He did something perfectly hideous, almost as perfectly hideous as what they say I did."

"You mean he ate his victims," Kendra said.

"Yes, cannibalism," he confirmed. "Do you know why he did it?"

Kendra shook her head from side to side, watching Leroy's face for signs of a lie. Instead, what she saw there was that same mean look he used to get when he teased Anna and her with the Dickey poem.

"He did it because he said that he wanted to keep his victims close to him, especially the ones who he liked. Do you know some people in other parts of the world practice cannibalism for just that reason? To keep their loved ones with them?"

"What are you saying, Leroy?" Kendra asked now.

"I'm saying that he had a perfectly reasonable, in his eyes anyway, a perfectly reasonable explanation for what he did."

"Are you saying that you had a perfectly reasonable explanation for raping your own daughter?" she spat.

He shrugged. "Maybe I do. Maybe I wanted to start over, try to fix what I had broken. And maybe starting with my own DNA is perfectly reasonable."

She said nothing, just stared at him, revulsion boiling in her chest.

"In a twisted sort of way." He smiled.

"You are one crazy son of a bitch, Leroy Cotton," she said now, seeing him for the first time in a whole new light.

"So, I see we understand each other?" he said.

"All too well," Kendra said, standing up to leave.

He grabbed her arm. She had to jerk hard to pull away. He held her gaze for a few seconds before speaking again.

"What I'm saying is, if I didn't do it, maybe I should have," he said. "Leave me alone, Kendra. Leave me and my daughter alone and get on with your own life. Stay out of it."

CHAPTER 9

Stay out of it, Kendra thought as she drove back to the rundown apartment complex in the pink monstrosity rent-a-car. *Okay, you sick bastard,* Kendra thought, *you did it.* Maybe it was because he knew that he was dying. The emphysema will no doubt one day kill him. His lungs would refuse to expel one more breath and his tissues would swell with the air that refused to leave his body. And he would take his last rattling breath and keel over.

Maybe raping Anna was an act of revenge against the daughter who did not live up to his expectations. On some levels, Leroy Cotton despised his daughter's disability. Kendra saw that today in that white room. She saw the bitterness that he lived with, the disappointment. But even with that, Kendra knew that when Leroy finally did die, the real horror would begin for Anna. She would be alone in the world.

Kendra opened the door to her drafty one bedroom apartment on the fifth floor of The Liberty Apartments. The place had come fully furnished with a hard twin bed, a beat-up pasteboard dresser, the finish bubbled on top, a small rickety kitchen table and one chair. That's right. One lone crooked-legged chair that made Kendra want to cry when she first saw it.

Sometimes Kendra wondered why she returned to Dunhill. What drew her here? Her mother was dead. Her father, well, she simply did not know who that was, and not that it mattered when your mother was a whore. And Rich, well, he didn't want anything to do with her. But those thoughts were pretense because it was clearer with each passing day why she had returned. Kendra Hamilton had unfinished business in Dunhill County—unfinished business that went by the name of Luke Bertrand.

Kendra removed her rain jacket and placed it on the kitchen chair. Rain had threatened the skies of Dunhill for weeks. But when it finally did rain, it was more of an annoyance than anything else. Cold, drifting fog in the morning, brief needles of rain in the afternoon followed by cold nights where the stars provided recessed lighting for the happenings in The Pit.

And looking from her small window down into the streets below, Kendra could see much goings on. A drug dealer with a pit bull by his feet passed crack cocaine to a teenager on a bicycle. Two young boys threw a football to each other in the empty streets only to scurry out of the way at the sight of any car. She watched them for a while, the ball floating in the air then sinking into a pair of gloved hands.

What would Rich call them, those two boys playing in the street, seemingly oblivious to the drug dealer and the pit bull just yards away? Oh, yeah, that's right. Rich would call them perps or soon-to-be perps. Kendra laughed sharply under her breath. Dumping him was probably the smartest thing that she had ever done.

She shut the window and shut out the smell of rain on the air. On her way to the tiny refrigerator, the phone rang. She contemplated not answering it but then decided that it was better than sitting in this tiny cell pouting about what Leroy had said to her. *Stay out of it*, that's what you can do. Sick bastard.

"Yeah," Kendra said into the receiver.

"Yeah?" Rich's voice on the other end of the line was both imposing and annoying. "Is that how you answer the phone? Yeah?"

"What do you want?" Kendra asked.

"I need you to set up a time for me to talk with Anna," he said.

"Why? Thought you weren't interested unless you had a dead body to poke at?" she replied.

Rich chuckled. "Let's just say I'm doing it for you, sweetheart. I'm in, Kendra."

"Well, good for you. I'm out."

"What?" he said. "Not happy that you pulled me into this shit? No confetti? Screams of joy?"

It was her turn to chuckle but the sound held no mirth. "You overestimate yourself, Rich," she said.

"Whatever," he responded. "When can I talk to her?"

"Who?"

"Anna," Rich said. "Who do you think?"

"Don't bother, Rich."

"Why shouldn't I bother?" he asked.

"Because he did it," Kendra said. "The bastard did it. He told me so himself an hour ago. So don't waste your time. I'm through wasting mine."

Long pause. Kendra listened to the silence with the phone pressed hard against her ear. She contemplated hanging up but Rich's sigh stopped her.

"I'm not satisfied," he said. "I still want to talk to her, Kendra."

"Talk to her," Kendra said. "Knock yourself out."

"You glad to get rid of this thing, huh?" he accused.

"Yep," Kendra agreed. "I've wasted too much time on it already."

"What about the Luke connection?"

Kendra kicked off her shoes. Plumping on the threadbare couch, she said, ". . . wrong about that."

"What?"

"I said I was wrong about that," she said it louder so he could hear.

Silence again but she knew that he hadn't hung up because she heard him breathe into the phone.

"Call Katherine Holder and tell her it's okay if I meet with Anna."

"I don't see why you still need to talk with her," Kendra said. "It'll probably just upset her for no reason."

"Please." That one word was all he said.

"Okay." She shrugged. "Anything else, Your Royal Highness?"

"Yes," he said.

"What's that?"

"A head exam for putting up with you," he said.

"Sorry." Kendra smiled sweetly into the phone. "Fresh out."

She hung up before he could respond. Two minutes later, the phone rang again.

"What now?" she said.

"Kendra Hamilton?" The voice on the other end of the telephone sounded breathless and frazzled.

"Yes?" Kendra responded, sitting up.

"This is Nurse Broderick at Brighton House. I need you to come right away."

Kendra's mouth went dry. "Is Anna all right?" she asked.

"No," Nurse Broderick said. "I need you to come right away."

Kendra didn't hang up the phone, simply let it drop. She snatched her rain jacket and her keys and left the apartment. At Brighton House, a nurse in Dr. Seuss scrubs and white whisper shoes ran up to her before she could even get into the door.

"Ms. Hamilton," she said. "Follow me."

Kendra jogged behind Nurse Broderick to the medical offices of Brighton House. As they rounded a corridor, Kendra heard excited voices and screams. She stopped for a moment and put her hands over her ears. She bent double. She felt Nurse Broderick's hands on her back. The screams were not screams; not really, it was just one, just one long incessant scream coming from behind a closed door to one of the rooms in the hallway. And Kendra, who had not only been affected by dark but by sound as well, thought her ears would fall from her head, the sound was so insistent, so piercing.

"Are you all right," the nurse asked her.

Kendra swallowed, tried to slow her breathing. When was the last time she had heard screams like this? Then she remembered— April Hart during that final showdown with Luke. The screams came from April and they had come from Kendra herself.

"I'm fine," Kendra said.

If you call your brain exploding to bits fine, but Kendra kept that part to herself.

"What is she doing here?" Someone shouted over the sounds.

"I thought she could help," the nurse said. "And besides, Anna has been asking for her."

"What happened?" Kendra asked, now realizing the sound was coming from Anna.

The man who had spoken was wearing a white coat and black horn rimmed glasses. His white face was red with anger and his gray hair stood out on either side of his otherwise bald head.

"She has no business here." He pointed at her.

And when he did, Kendra saw by his name tag that his name was Dr. Dawson. She looked at the other people outside the screaming door. An orderly or probably a certified nursing assistant stood plastered against the wall, his shoulders hunched around his chin, eyes the size of silver dollars. Katherine Holder, wearing a striped pantsuit and a pencil in the sliding mess of her brown hair, stuck out one square hand.

"Hello, Dr. Hamilton," she said. "I'm sorry we have to meet again under these circumstances." She leaned in close to Kendra as she spoke and shouted over the din as if they were all having a pleasant cruise out to sea and needed to speak in loud voices to hear each other over the crashing waves. Kendra shook Holder's hand, shook it because there was nothing else to do with it except to leave it flapping in the wind.

"What is happening?" Kendra asked again as she let go of Holder's hand. She wondered how anyone could hold a scream for that long.

"She barricaded herself in there and won't come out," Holder told her.

"Why?" Kendra asked. The screams filled the hallway like smoke.

Dr. Dawson reddened, his horn rimmed glasses looking even blacker against his pink skin. "It was a routine examination . . ."

He stopped at Kendra's widening eyes and then blushed crimson.

"I didn't do anything, I tell you. It was a routine examination and before I knew what was happening, she yanked the speculum out and started running around the room. I went out to get help but she pushed the exam table and God knows what else against the door."

"You stupid bastard," Kendra said. "You tried to give a vaginal exam to a rape victim? Alone?"

"She would not have been alone if I'd been allowed to go in there with her," the nursing assistant said. He had peeled himself from the wall and joined their shouting circle. "She wouldn't let me near her."

"You assholes," Kendra said. "First of all, you are both men. And second, you smell like you went swimming in Old Spice. Two men should not give a vaginal exam to a rape victim. Why wasn't I notified?"

No one spoke. Kendra shook her head, looking with amazement from each face before turning to the door. She pounded on it, but slowly, calmly, as if she were beating a drum. The screaming stopped in a large wet hiccup.

"Anna," Kendra said, trying to make her voice soft. "Open the door."

"No," Anna sobbed. "No hurt Anna no more."

Kendra stopped, turned and gave the doctor a scathing look. He shrank away.

"Anna," Kendra said. "He was not trying to hurt you . . . look, can I come in?"

Silence. Kendra didn't speak, let the silence extend and stretch around them. Then finally, softly, said again, "Please Anna," she said. "Please let me come in."

Kendra heard metal falling through the quiet behind the closed door. It clicked, and a slice of Anna's beautiful face, the brown skin like honey, appeared through the narrow opening. Kendra could see Anna's hair, curly like wet silk.

"You come in," Anna said. "Nobody else. Just you."

Kendra looked behind her. She noticed the nursing assistant take a step forward as if he owned Anna. But the doctor, the man with the horn rimmed glasses, put his hand up as if to say let's not screw this up any further. Kendra watched him for a moment, then turned back to the door.

"Just me, Anna," she promised, wondering for the fifth time why this girl affected her so, why everyone thought they needed to be so gentle with Anna, so gentle that they didn't warn her how life really was, what to watch out for. No one saw fit to tell Anna, no, Pretty Anna, isn't that what everyone called her? No one saw fit to tell her how cruel the world could be. Instead, because of her looks and her disability everyone treated her as a pet. Kendra had forgotten how cruel the world could be herself until about two summers ago, when her own life suddenly bloomed out of control in Luke Bertrand's and Rich Marvel's hands.

Anna opened the door wider. It was not a welcoming gesture. She had opened the door just wide enough for Kendra to slip her body through if she turned sideways. Inside, the exam table was overturned, the wrinkled paper flung on the floor, the stirrups lying on their sides like silver gladiolas.

Kendra stepped around the instruments scattered on the white floor. She picked her way through the mess, the speculum, the cotton swabs, the ripped wrappers until she reached Anna, who sat on the floor. Her back was bent against the far wall, her knees drawn up to her ample chest.

Kendra knew better than to speak. She knew not to ask Anna if she was all right. She couldn't see Anna's deflated belly, but she knew that what had been inside made nothing all right. Nothing would ever be all right again, not for Anna. Kendra shuddered to think what this young girl, this seven-year-old in a woman's body, thought as some monster lay on top of her and violated her until she became pregnant.

Kendra sat on the floor beside Anna. Their shoulders touched as Kendra drew her knees up to her chest. The exam room was too cold. The stupid bastard who decided on this examination did not have the good sense to warm up the room. Kendra stuck her hands into the pockets of her jacket.

"It's cold in here."

Anna's voice was low, soft as if she were speaking in the dark instead of the artificially bright room. Kendra still did not speak, only nodded.

"Winter, you know," Kendra finally said.

"Roses still out, though, some. Anna see them."

Anna was right. Roses still did come but only one or two were brave enough to bloom. And those that did bloom, in the morning their red petals were dusted with a hard white frost. This February must have blown in from the east. The days were cold, frigid, the trees had shed all of their clothes in surrender, maybe, but the chill remained unforgiving. Those roses would not last much longer if the chill worsened.

"Anna don't like cold," Anna said now into her knees, her voice low and soft.

"I know. I hate the cold, too." Kendra said.

Anna brought her face up from in between her knees. She turned her brown eyes to Kendra. For a moment, Kendra thought she recognized a hint of maturity in the smooth, beautiful face. But it was just a flicker, a small deception. The maturity was replaced with a naive light which brightened the flecks of green in Anna's brown eyes. A troubled light, but a childish one just the same. This is what must have driven Leroy crazy. The brief flashes of maturity promised him that Anna would be okay, that she may have been disabled but that she would someday grow up. But too soon, like those roses too near winter, the flash would dissipate. And in its place would be the child he would have to care for until she wrinkled and fell into the grave—hopefully before he did. Kendra swallowed guilt at these thoughts. Anna was nobody's burden. She was a human being and deserved to be treated as such. Didn't she? She was not a bauble.

"I like summer," Anna was telling her now. "Anna hate winter. Winter cold."

"I know, Anna," Kendra said.

She did not know how long she had been sitting here with Anna but her legs had started to cramp and her back hurt. She stretched her legs out in front of her. Anna watched, saw, and did the same. She looked under black eyelashes at Kendra. Kendra smiled.

"What happened, Anna?" she said after a while. "What made you afraid?"

Anna shook her head quickly indicating that she did not want to talk about it. Kendra was at a loss. She did not know how to deal with this childish stubbornness.

"Come on, Anna," she said. "It'll make you feel better if you talk about it."

Anna plucked at her gown, her tongue curled out of her mouth in concentration as she did so. She seemed fascinated with the drop, most likely from the KY Jelly the doctor had used to perform the examination, drying on the gown. Still plucking and rubbing at the spot, she sent Kendra a sidelong glance.

"How?" she asked.

Kendra had forgotten what she had asked as she watched Anna. "How what?"

"How will talk make Anna feel better?"

Kendra thought for a moment. How indeed? She didn't know, not yet. She looked around the artificially bright room, and thought about how white, how white the light spilling around them seemed. If she had it to do over again, if she was ever to get her medical license back, be allowed to open a clinic, she would not put white light in an exam room, impractical or not. Sometimes, waking from a nightmare in her apartment, the first thing Kendra saw when opening her eyes was the white from the lights she had left on pressing against her eyes like silk. When she practiced medicine again, she would choose lights that were yellow, maybe rose colored, low light that lent intimacy, maybe even a little humanity to the situation. And with those thoughts, she understood what had made Anna afraid. The violation of her body was one thing, but . . .

"How talking make it better?" Anna asked again.

Kendra thought for a long while. "Well," she said finally. "Talking is like a storybook you read over and over again."

Anna's eyes brightened, "Like a poem?" she asked

Kendra nodded. "Yes, like a poem, if you want. But when a thing is talked about, it's like . . ."

". . . writing it down on the air," Anna finished for her. Well, it wasn't quite what Kendra had in mind, but she decided to go with it.

"Yes, like writing the words on the air . . ."

They heard a soft knock on the door. She felt Anna stiffen beside her. Anna's neck tensed like a suddenly stretched rope.

"Just a minute," Kendra whipped out and Anna relaxed beside her, turned to her with eyes that demanded that she finish. Kendra didn't quite know how to finish but tried anyway.

"Well, talking is sort of like that, writing words down in the air. Once you do that, and you do it over and over again, it becomes like a storybook." She stopped and looked at Anna, and added before the girl could interrupt her, ". . . or like a poem. It's out somewhere, written down so you can read or listen to it again and again, so you can sort of understand it."

Anna nodded, went back to plucking her gown. Kendra adjusted herself on the floor. Her back ached.

"I know. I read Sylvia over and over again. Anna understand Sylvia."

Kendra didn't know who Sylvia was but understood that it was something that made Anna feel better. It was a comfort, perhaps more than talking.

"Maybe you could read it to me sometime," she said. "In the meantime, can you tell me what happened?"

Anna nodded again, stopped plucking her gown. "Doctor touch Anna. Anna don't have to take that no more."

It was Kendra's turn to nod. Hesitantly, she pushed on. "Just like the man . . ."

Anna shook her head furiously, "No, not like that, not like that at all." Anna's eyes grew as wide as twin moons in her brown face.

"Can you tell me about the man, the man who did this to you in the first place?" Kendra asked, thinking of Leroy.

Anna did not cry, but Kendra could see the tears spring in her eyes. "No, he come in the dark. He a monster."

"Do you know who he was Anna?" Kendra asked. "Can you tell me?" Anna shook her head, still wide-eyed.

"And was the doctor a monster, too, Anna, is that why you got angry?"

"No," Anna said. "He okay, but he made Anna mad."

"How?" Kendra asked.

"Because he didn't ask," Anna said. "He touched Anna like Anna ain't got no feelings. And he didn't even ask."

Kendra could see that Anna had made some sort of decision about her own body. He didn't ask me, she said. It was that bead of maturity that sometimes shone through Anna's eyes like a flashlight in the darkness. In a way, Anna was less afraid of them all, less afraid than Kendra herself was.

Anna told her about the exam, how the nursing assistant had gotten her from her room a couple of hours before and had taken her to the exam room. How the doctor, the one with the thick black glasses and the foggy hair, told her to lie back on the table so he could *have a look*. And then he tried to stick that thing in her and when she scooted back he told her *stop being a child*.

"That make Anna mad," Anna said.

Anna told Kendra about the promises she made to herself. The next time somebody did something to Anna, she would scream and scream like Sylvia should have screamed and screamed. And that's what she did, screamed and used her body to fight and to tear the table down. After a while, she told Kendra that she was right, that talking did make it better.

Kendra nodded. "I saw your father today," she said.

Anna eyes rounded, soft brown. "Is he okay?" she asked.

"He's fine," Kendra answered. Then on impulse, "He misses you."

"Humph," Anna said staring straight ahead. "He don't like Anna no more."

"Did he hurt you, Anna?"

She nodded her head. For a minute, Kendra did not think that Anna would speak, then she said, "Yeah, he hurt Anna. He hurt Anna all the time, just like everyone else."

They were waiting for them when Kendra and Anna emerged from the exam room. Katherine Holder and the nursing assistant were there. There was someone else as well, another certified nursing assistant in a pair of ridiculous SpongeBob SquarePants scrubs. She wore a purple headband to keep her dreadlocks in place.

When Anna saw them she tried to dart back into the exam room. But the assistant in the white scrubs caught her around the waist and pulled her backwards. Anna screamed. But it was not an angry scream and not like the scream Kendra heard when she first arrived. But this was a frightened scream, a squeal like a stuck pig would make.

"What the hell?" Kendra started toward the struggling bodies.

But Katherine Holder pulled her away from the fray.

"It's necessary," she said. "So she won't hurt herself."

"Hurt herself?" Kendra said horrified. "She was fine. What's that?"

The doctor had a syringe and as the nurse in the SpongeBob scrubs and the other assistant in white wrestled Anna onto a vinyl bed, he plunged the needle into her thigh.

"It's only Inapsine, a sedative to help calm her down."

Outrage exploded in Kendra's chest. Anna's legs jimmied up and down. Her body writhed as she tried to escape the leather restraints at her wrists and ankles.

"Look," Holder said. "This is necessary. You don't know how she gets, Dr. Hamilton."

Once they had Anna restrained, they tied her to the bed using a white sheet. Anna's screams had morphed into low whimpers. Tears streaked her face.

"It's all right, it's all right," Holder murmured as she stroked Anna's hair.

Unable to take anymore, Kendra backed away. The sound of her own footsteps running was the only sound in her head now. And for that, she was glad.

CHAPTER 10

Like words written on air. Kendra thought about that as she gazed from her apartment's living room window with the echo of Anna's screams ringing in her ears. Luke Bertrand. The bastard. He had gotten away with it. Just as Leroy would probably get away with it. Just as Luke had used her to get away with murder, Leroy used her to get his daughter out of the way. Luke Bertrand, the name played in her head over and over again.

Kendra could not forgive herself, hadn't forgiven herself since the bastard walked out of the Dunhill court room two years ago wearing the same camel hair coat he liked to sport in The Pit when he was everyone's hero. Luke Bertrand had gotten away with it. And in a way, in some sort of sick way, it was all her fault. Rich knew it. She knew it. But the difference was that she hadn't gotten over it. Rich in some way had.

Kendra knew one thing, though. She had mentally washed her hands of Leroy Cotton. *The old bastard probably did it,* Kendra thought. Anna even said so. They probably had the right man in custody and Kendra could now go on and do what she came here to do. She could turn her thoughts back to Luke Bertrand. Justice had been served. It was time to move on. She would see to Anna later, right after she had straightened her own life out.

When Kendra walked into her apartment earlier that evening, it was so cold that she could see her breath on the air. Indoors and she could see a fog of white emanate from her mouth. This should have made her feel alive. But it had the opposite effect. It made her feel like a ghost lost in the memories of Luke Bertrand's betrayal.

Luke was a wealthy philanthropist in Dunhill County. He had helped Kendra through medical school and had mentored her since she was sixteen years old. He had held Violet's—Kendra's drug addicted mother's—hands until the day she died.

Or so Kendra thought. Luke Bertrand had actually killed Violet Hamilton because he felt that she was pulling Kendra into the hole that she had fallen into and declined to climb out of. He had killed her by giving her the same poisoned dope, heroin tainted with quinine, that he had given countless other addicts. Like the others, Violet had willingly taken it. She died in a rundown hotel room in The Pit, her face bathed in vomit. The landlord found her with the belt still around her arm and foam still bubbling from her mouth.

Kendra pushed for an investigation because she knew that her mother was murdered. Kendra knew because her mother had no need to get her dope from anyone else. She had found a safe heroin supply in Kendra who gave her the drug when it became clear that Violet Hamilton would remain a drug addict for the rest of her sorry days.

The investigation conducted by homicide detective Rich Marvel eventually led to Luke Bertrand. What had followed was an unauthorized wire tap and a string of dead junkies who had sought Luke for an abortion and had paid with their lives. After their babies were born, Luke had them adopted and sent the junkies happily on their way with a dime bag of heroin laced with poison.

When it all exploded, he and Rich Marvel faced each other with guns pointed and Kendra Hamilton standing between them. Rich missed Luke but shot Kendra. The wound left her right shoulder paralyzed for months. Even after physical therapy, she did not regain full use of that shoulder. When the medical community found out that she had supplied her mother with heroin, they snatched away her medical license. Now you see it, now you don't. Just like that. And even after Luke confessed, a rambling passage with religious references, insisting that he saved those children from those women, he walked.

Kendra stood up and turned on the light in her darkening apartment. She heard the clunk of the furnace attempting to warm the cold room. She returned to the window thinking about that terrible time.

When Luke finally went to trial, he arrived with a lawyer whose rumpled suit belied the finesse he used to get the confession thrown out. The confession, the lawyer said, contained the words of a confused old man who had been recently diagnosed with Alzheimer's. He had even pointed to medical records confirming this. And those dead girls? They were a coincidence. And even if Luke knew that the dope was poisoned, they took it of their own free will. Shit, and he actually cursed in court, drawing a warning and a pointed gavel from the judge. One girl even crawled back to Luke's estate in the middle of the night. She crawled through weeds and bramble, which scraped her knees and bloodied her hands, for that dope. And the only reason Luke gave them the drugs was so that those babies would have a full, complete life. Hell, the lawyer said this one too, like his protégés Kendra Hamilton and Rich Marvel; he had helped them in their youth just as he helped those babies. And now, ungrateful, they had the nerve to accuse Luke Bertrand.

Mouth suddenly dry with these memories, Kendra took a long drink of water, felt it stream down her throat. That lawyer, that slick, unprincipled asshole, presented both of them as two ungrateful people who were trying to get back at Luke for some imagined hurt, for some wrong that never took place. And who would believe them anyway? She was a felon, a drug dealer convicted and on probation, and Rich was a grudge-holding loser, fired from his job.

The heartache was that, after all those deaths, Luke Bertrand walked away using thirty-second TV spots and full page ads in the *Dunhill Review* to rebuild his reputation. The only confession he had was that he was sick, suffering from the beginning stages of Alzheimer's. Too bad those he loved could not see it and could not help him through it. Kendra and Rich had decided that instead of helping him they would stand as his accusers. Heartless, the community called Kendra, ruthless, they called Rich.

Like words on the air. Kendra thought of Anna now. That's what talking was like, like writing words on the air. But Kendra could never talk about it, could not face it. She left Rich because staying with him would remind her every day of that ripping bullet, and that ripping betrayal. Luke Bertrand, the man she thought of as a father, killed her mother and many others. And he had gotten away with it.

She stood up and walked over to the sink. Pouring the water down the drain, Kendra thought about Luke. Most killers like him, she knew, rarely started when they were as old as he was. He was what? Sixty-five? She looked up at the pitted ceiling, making a mental calculation in her head. She remembered a birthday party she and her mother gave for Luke. She was sixteen, and Luke had come to the apartment her mother had managed to get for a while—she actually kept it for about a month and a half before the landlord kicked them out. A cake from Safeway, and there were candles, two candles outlined in blue. A fat five and zero. Luke Bertrand was fifty then. Kendra was sixteen. Fifteen years later, when Kendra was thirty-one and the murders were first discovered, Luke Bertrand would have been well over sixty. Sixty-five or six, he was when he walked The Pit in those camel hair coats and cashmere scarves like he owned the streets of The Pit community and everyone in them.

Kendra had a sudden thought. Maybe she could not talk about what happened to her life, what Luke had done to both Rich and herself, what he had done to their relationship. But there was something more powerful than words. It was making someone pay for the pain that they had caused. It was revenge.

CHAPTER 11

Unable to sleep, Kendra found herself two hours later in the Dunhill Cemetery staring at a grave. The weather was lousy. The wind bent the graveyard's thin birches this way and that. Their leaves made a crumbling sound in the dark and Kendra was glad for the circle of light from her flashlight.

It wasn't her mother's grave that she stared at but it could have been. It could have been her mother's grave if she had not decided to burn Violet's body to ashes and bits and scatter her remains in the Sacramento River. When she did that she realized that she had nothing left to hold on to. Every scrap of her mother, every breath she made, every want, every desire, flamed and disappeared at the crematorium. She didn't even keep the urn but left it in her apartment when she fled Dunhill after Luke walked.

The moon over the Dunhill Cemetery was bright and spotted. Kendra looked at the simple headstone she was standing over. The grave drew her. Some grieving soul had placed two glass vases of cut irises on either side of the headstone. The irises were bearded in white and their green stems looked frozen in the clear water. The person who loved this grave must have placed the irises there sometime earlier in the day, maybe even while Kendra sat on the floor of Brighton House explaining to Anna why it was better to talk.

The name on the headstone was Bethany Jones. And Kendra
didn't think the woman would mind standing in for Violet, being
dead and all. As the thought passed into Kendra's head, she wondered if she had lost her mind. Yes, she conceded. She had, and
the fact that she was standing over the grave of a dead woman she
didn't know, pretending that the woman was her mother, confirmed the fact that she was not all there.

As she drove to the cemetery earlier that night, a Smith &
Wesson .357 tucked under her seat, she asked herself over and
over what it was that she wanted. Justice or revenge? The only rea-
son that she stopped by the cemetery was that it was on the way to
Luke's house. She hadn't planned on the stop but as she left Main
Street and went onto the more desolate roads, she saw the head-
stones and crosses emerging like drowning hands in a calm sea.
She parked the car on the side of the cemetery and walked in.

Now as she stood over Bethany Jones's grave she wondered who
loved her so much that they would have put irises on either side of
her headstone knowing that they would not survive the night.
Kendra pulled the strap of her purse higher onto her shoulder.
She could hear the gun, loaded, yes, it was loaded, slide along the
bottom of the purse.

What would Violet do if their positions were switched? What
would she do if Kendra had been the one who died and Violet had
been the one who outlived her daughter? Kendra asked the question of the silent headstones, the almost frozen irises bearded in
white, but they did not answer back. It was a question that Kendra
must ask herself and it was a question that Kendra already knew
the answer to. Violet would do the same thing that she did when
her son, and Kendra's brother, died by a cop's bullet on the streets
of The Pit. She would find another hit and forget about it.

But the fact was, she wasn't Violet and she wasn't a drug addict.
The one thing that she had used for escape, her career, had been
taken away from her. First by Violet, then by Luke. She had nothing to live for but goddammit, she would take Luke Bertrand with
her. She looked at the grave a few minutes longer. And when she
felt her resolve strengthen, she turned her heel and walked back
toward the Ford Fiesta.

* * *

Luke's house was just as she remembered. Wide marbled steps flowed down from a teak door with a lion's head knocker. Kendra had no intention of using it. Instead she opened the door with a key she didn't know she had until she found it among Violet's meager effects after she died. There it was in the bag Violet always kept with her amid the Campbell's soup cans, the wrinkled shirts and worn gloves. The key had a yellow Post-It note wrapped around it. On the note was a code which Kendra took for the code to the alarm in Luke's house.

Even though there was not a name on the key, Kendra knew immediately that it belonged to Luke. Who else's could it have been? Violet's family had disowned her so long ago that Kendra didn't even know where they were anymore. She and Luke were the only people in Violet's life and the key certainly didn't belong to Kendra. As private as Luke Bertrand had always been she knew that he did not give it up willingly. Kendra could see Violet stealing it or blackmailing Luke out of it so she could use his place as a flop house when the streets became too cold. Perhaps when the streets became as chilly as they had become this winter, two years after Violet's ashes were scattered in a river miles away from Dunhill. Kendra didn't tell anyone about the key, not even Rich. She knew now why she didn't, even as she knew why her mother had kept it.

Kendra placed the key in the lock. The door clicked open easily. She heard the telltale beep of the alarm. Luckily, the panel of blinking lights was just to the left of the double doors. Using her flashlight, she punched in the six-digit code that she had memorized from the Post-It wrapped around the key. She waited for the beep to tell her that everything was okay, that the alarm would not sound loud enough to wake the dead and the cops when the sixty second delay was over. But no compliant beep came. Shit. Kendra thought and punched in the numbers again, this time carefully in spite of the intense beat of her heart and the wavering circle of light. This time the alarm beeped, signaling that Luke's alarm system had been disarmed. The sound was low and reassuring in the wide expanse of Luke's living room.

Kendra flashed the light around the room. The sparse furnishings loomed large and shadowy around her. She closed her eyes for a minute. Even though Luke had put her through medical school she had only been in his house a few times. Once when she was twelve, after her mother went to the hospital for a short time, the second when she was seventeen, right before she left for college. And the third time that she had been to his house was when she wore a wiretap to trap Luke into a confession. It was that last time that she remembered best.

Right ahead of her was the kitchen. It had big copper pots hanging from the ceiling like upside down metal plants. Beyond the kitchen and out the back door was the shed where he kept the girls he would later murder. She knew that to the right, the house ended, and that the bedrooms were to the left of the living room. Kendra opened her eyes and looked to her left down a yawning deep hallway. It was so dark she could not see what lay beyond the threshold. It was out of reach for her flashlight. She thought about leaving. If she left, the worst they could do to her was arrest her for breaking and entering. And that was if they even caught her. She could still turn back if she wanted to.

But Kendra knew that was not the worst that could be done to her. Luke Bertrand had done something much worse. He gave her the worst gift of all, the gift of terror. She took a step toward that yawning emptiness, her hands sweating in fear of the dark. The light created a circle beside her as she walked into the hallway toward Luke's room.

Old people sleep light. Kendra tried remembering where she had heard that. She probably heard it from her mother on the occasion while they were staying with Kendra's grandfather and Violet's father. Kendra and Adam had awakened Christmas morning before everyone else in the house. Excited, they squealed at the decorated tree under which were enough presents for all the kids in Dunhill. Or so they thought. Her mother rushed in and had told them to quiet down because old people, they slept light. Kendra remembered that saying. Violet's voice came into her head like a warning from beyond the grave.

But Kendra didn't care if Luke slept light; she didn't care if she sounded like a train coming. She took the Smith & Wesson from her purse and almost dropped it. Her hands felt as if they had been slicked with oil. Just holding that weapon, the heavy weight, feeling heat from the grooved handle made Kendra's guts feel as if they were slipping from her belly.

Old people must like it hot, too, Kendra thought as sweat rolled down the sides of her face. Even though she didn't care if she woke him, she walked slowly, carefully, her flashlight pointed at the ground. A small circle of light walked beside her as if she had stolen a piece of moon from the Dunhill graveyard.

Two double doors, even whiter than the light of her flashlight, stood at the end of the long hallway. As fate would have it the doors were flung open. Gentle snoring floated to her as she neared the room. It wasn't until she heard that deep breathing when the thought of what she was about to do hit her. She meant to stop that breathing, that poison rattle in the air. She meant to put a bullet in Luke's head and then, then what?

But there was no answer to that question. There couldn't be. The room smelled of fresh flowers and something else. Kendra breathed the scent in. Ah, yes, sandalwood. Flickering light radiated from a TV on the dresser. Apparently, Luke needed the low murmur of voices to sleep at night, maybe something to drown out the sound of the voices inside his own head of those he had killed.

Kendra Hamilton studied Luke's sleeping face. Two years ago there hadn't been a wrinkle on that smooth brow. His face had the look of a carved African mask. But during the trial Luke became more wrinkled with each successive day. It was as if before he went to bed at night, he used a carving knife to cut in a new wrinkle. Two deep grooves ran from each side of his nose to the corners of his mouth. Another deep groove lay across the forehead. He wore rings of wrinkles around his hard neck.

He slept with his hands folded across the chest of his silk pajamas, the color of bone. A satin black bedspread was pulled to just beneath his hands. The bedspread was barely wrinkled, as smooth as if he had not moved since laying his head down. *At least you can sleep, you son of a bitch,* Kendra thought as she raised the Smith & Wesson and pointed it at the sleep-shut face.

She did not flinch as she leveled the weapon. Her mind was made up. Justice was about to be served to Luke Bertrand and it would be served by her hand. She could hear the wind howl outside. Her nose closing with the smell of sandalwood, Kendra Hamilton began to squeeze the trigger. She did so slowly, savoring every second.

Anna

Anna ankle and wrist hurt. They tie a sheet across her chest, pin her down so she can't move. They tie her up in the quiet room. Since Anna can't move, Anna think, she think about the woman who tie her up tonight. Not the other woman Holder. Holder nice to Anna. Sometimes she nice 'cept when she tell the other to tie Anna down. For your own good, Anna, that what Holder say. But the one in the purple headband who help tie her up. Anna close her eyes and think about her.

Her like wisteria, lavender. Soft, flowy. She coo like a bird. But her have hard bones and a mean mouth. Her eyes hard when nobody in the dayroom but her and us. And she ain't all flowy. When no doctors around, no nurses, when it's just us coloring on the white paper—green, red sometime purple, but not a lot with purple cause purple make Anna think of African violets, petals burnt and soft leaves yellow from the sun. Mamma tell Anna, don't plant seeds way out in the sun but Anna don't listen. She did anyway. And at first, the flowers looked like snatches of sunset, but after a while, after the sun burnt them, they shrunk, turned all brown edges before dying down to dirt. Anna don't like to color with purple, not too much.

But when nobody around, wisteria lady, she don't coo like a bird. When nobody in the dayroom, when we color, and they leave her there to watch us.

Once before after they let Anna out of the ropes and the leather, they sent her to color, to be in the dayroom with the others. Told her to be good and not hurt nobody with scissors no more, like she did the man who pop and clack his gum, like she did him when he come 'round to get her out of her room.

The dayroom white, the windows high by the top of the ceiling. And sunlight and blue sky fall in like water pumping into Daddy's fields in Virginia. Everything in the room white, the table white, the chairs white, the paper they make us color on white. The only thing colored skin, and the color we use to draw—red, green, sometime purple.

And wisteria lady clothes, though, they ain't white, they not blue like the pajamas they make Anna wear. Anna hate wearing the pajamas and the paper slippers that whisper along the white floors like slithery things, like snakes. Wisteria lady clothes are bright like firecrackers. She wear smock like ours and pants like ours, except her smock all covered with SpongeBob SquarePants. He got a yellow holey body, two big teeth grinning.

Whereever wisteria lady walk, pop follow. She slap somebody. She uses a brown finger, long and wrinkled like a twig to slide somebody paper to the floor. She like stepping on they crayons after they roll off the table. Bits of red and chips of brown under her shoe, ground into the white linoleum floor like soil. Her eyes glitter. Her face full of mean.

Anna don't listen, try not to look. Ever since Anna stomach start growing and her sick, winter wisteria pay more attention to her. Likes walking over and poking her belly. Not hard, but hard enough to hurt. She call Anna thing like whore, like slut, and she take Anna earlobe between her fingers and twist until Anna can't help it anymore and scream.

Anna keep her head down when she walk by. Anna draw a house and steps going straight up the middle. She put two windows, blue square, a cross in the middle. And she use purple to draw lines under the steps. Those be the violets and that be where the violets supposed to be, under the steps, away from the burning.

But when Anna sit back in her chair, lick her lip and hold the paper up to make sure she got the lines right, she see her. Wisteria lady staring at her with her arms folded. Fingernails long like bullets digging into SpongeBob's big white eye like she trying to put it out.

"Well," she said, cocking her head to one side, letting the fuzzy braids fall across her shoulder. "I heard we had ourselves quite a time yesterday."

Anna want to tell her that we didn't have ourselves quite a time, because Anna didn't see her yesterday. Anna want to tell winter wisteria to mind her own business, but instead, the purple crayon Anna holding crumble in Anna hand. The pieces scuttle down her belly that not growing no more.

Winter wisteria did not move, she a statue. But she say, "My, you do have a temper on you, don't you?" Anna say nothing. "Are you a nut case as well as a retard?"

Anna felt fire in her face but kept quiet. Across the room, on the other side, her friend sat crying, tears sprinkle down her face. She hold her cheek. When winter wisteria walks, pops and smacks follow her like she got firecracker in her shoes. We don't know when she mad or why she mad, but when she mad, sometimes those pops and smacks reach out to get you.

CHAPTER 12

Trees were down all over Dunhill. The same wind and rainstorm that Kendra heard howling outside of Luke's window blew shingles from rooftops in Rich's neighborhood. Trash cans blew with abandon across four-lane streets, lids spinning after them. A one-hundred-year-old maple, a tree people would later say on the six o'clock news that they had swung on when children, snapped in two like a wet toothpick in the wind.

The windstorm with reported winds up to seventy miles an hour was rare in Dunhill. No one had seen anything like it in twenty years. On the drive from work that day, the wind blew the Firebird all over the highway. Unable to slice through that gale force with speed, Rich had to slow down to about forty to dodge paraphernalia the wind hurled through the streets. Empty soda cans from displaced trash cans pelted his car. An empty container of Tide flew across his windshield.

Once he arrived at the small clapboard house, painted a cheerful yellow, now with purple petunias planted in new dirt out front, he staggered to keep his footing. The petunias fluttered in the wind, petals shuddering like hummingbird wings. The wind snatched the screen door from his hand when he opened it. Pushing the door open he went inside with thoughts of Kendra Hamilton and the meeting he had asked her to arrange. He had almost finished his first beer when it started to hail.

During the night, the wind howled until Rich awakened from sleep still fully clothed. Except for his shoes. Even drunk, he could not sleep in his shoes. Staggering to the bathroom, he wondered briefly if people were actually buried in their shoes. And if so, for what? He closed his eyes on the thought, drifted into sleep until the light came again.

The next morning, his mouth like cotton, the maple confronted him. In the night, during the howling wind, the tree had weakened until it had snapped and had found his beloved Firebird. That is what he noticed first, the Firebird. He did not see the wet sheen on the air or the gray skies that seemed to threaten but without much heart or conviction. Bright sun was already burning through the gauze of gray clouds. In fact, Rich refused to see the tree. What he did see was a magic show. The Firebird's roof, crumpled as if all by itself, flecks of red paint scattered among chunks of glass from the window shield.

He stood there for a moment, looking at the crushed Firebird. A teasing breeze lifted his tie. He felt the fingers of the wind across his face as if in a caress. It was then that he saw the tree, the old maple that needed to be trimmed, lying on the car, the top-heavy branches straining and groping like angry children away from an abusive mother. His landlady, instead of trimming the tree as she was supposed to, had planted purple petunias in winter, petunias that would certainly die in the cold and frost.

"Fuck," he breathed, tiredness crawling behind his eyes. "Fuck," he said again, this time louder as he snatched his cell phone from the clip on his belt. "Fuck," he said as he and Carlyle drove away from the totaled Firebird.

Carlyle, for his part, was unsympathetic to the death of Rich's car. Rich could see by the glint in Carlyle's beady black eyes that he was actually a little relieved. No more early morning jaunts to pick Rich up when the firebird would not start, no more late afternoons picking Rich up from the auto mechanic.

"Besides," he told Rich, "it's not like you can't afford to buy a new car."

"That's not the point," Rich answered back.

"What's not the point?"

"That."

"What?" Carlyle said, taking his hands from the wheel of the Hummer in exasperation.

"Buying a new car is not the point," Rich said. "That car meant something to me man, you know, sentimental value?" Rich stopped briefly before continuing. "No," he said. "I don't think you do know. So just shut up and drive."

"Are you going to be like this every time you see her?" Carlyle asked.

His knuckles reddened as he gripped the steering wheel of the Hummer. Rich hated Carlyle's choice in vehicles, he hated the DVD player between the passenger and driver seat; he hated the Play-Station in the back. Carlyle did not even have a wife or kids. Why on earth would he need a car like this? But Rich had to admit that Carlyle's Hummer made candy of the wind.

"Where are we going anyway? Back to the office?" Carlyle asked.

"Naw, man," Rich said, wishing the Altoids he pulled from his shirt pocket was a glass of water, if such a thing was possible. The mint was not curiously strong, not this morning. The feel of the alcohol at the back of his throat made the thing taste like baking soda. He reached into his pants pocket and pulled out a folded square of paper.

"Ten-ninety-five Seventh Street," he said. "That's where we are going."

"All the way downtown? But we have an appointment with Val Hightower at nine-thirty A.M. We'll never make it."

"We'll just be a little late," Rich said.

Carlyle rolled his wrist to look at his watch again. "Not a little," he said. "A lot late."

"He's an old buddy of yours, right, Carlyle?" Rich asked. "I'm sure that he will forgive you."

"Hey, I never said any shit about him being a buddy," Carlyle said.

Rich didn't answer but Carlyle was right. Val Hightower wasn't exactly an old friend of Carlyle's, but Carlyle knew him as an ex-Oakland cop who had made it big in the security business after 9/11. And from what Rich could gather from Carlyle's comments, the carefully constructed ones, including things like *I didn't know him that well* or *I hear he's a smart guy*, Carlyle did not like Hightower. But Rich could not tell if the dislike stemmed from jealousy or something deeper. He only knew that at the moment he did not care to find out. His head hurt too much.

"Rich," Carlyle said. "The Val Hightower meeting."

"We'll get there," Rich said.

"So why are we going downtown?" Carlyle asked.

"Tower Security has a satellite office on Seventh."

Carlyle turned to stare at Rich. "But," he said, "we have a meeting with Hightower . . ."

". . . at his home," Rich completed the sentence for him. "I don't give a shit about how he runs his home. I want to see how he runs his business."

Hightower's estate was located in a Dunhill exclusive community called The Point. The ten-thousand-square-foot mansion sprawled behind a wrought iron fence and a security post. But when Rich and Carlyle rang the front doorbell, none other than Val Hightower himself answered, wearing a blue and white striped polo shirt, navy blue pants and white shoes. He apologized to both Rich and Carlyle profusely, all the way from the marble foyer to his office furnished in what Dinah, Rich's ex-fiancée, would have called Tuscan style.

Val Hightower was a short, Black man, thirty, thirty-five at the most. He was handsome enough with clearly drawn eyes and perfectly etched lips. His skin was blemish free and his head was shaved so cleanly that it reminded Rich of a newly laid brown egg. If it weren't for his nose, broken and sloped to one side, his looks would have been perfection.

"I am so sorry that you had to come all the way out here," Hightower was saying as he ushered Rich and Carlyle onto a leather sofa. "I'm golfing today with Judge Webster and I could not cancel on him."

Rich stiffened at the name drop. But he said nothing.

Carlyle said, "We are sorry that we're a little late . . ."

"A little late." Hightower laughed. "You are over forty-five minutes late. But that's all right, man, it's all good. I have a few minutes yet." As he said this, he flipped up the wrist of his diamond encrusted Rolex, and frowned.

"Can I offer you two anything to drink?" He stood up and lifted both his palms. Still in apologizing mode, he explained, "Maid's day off."

Rich thought how ironic it was that every place he went these days, the first thing people offered him was something to drink. But he couldn't give that much thought now, not with Hightower standing there waiting for an answer with his head cocked like a curious bird dog.

Rich lifted an eyebrow. "Maid?" he questioned. "You only have one?"

Hightower moved his head back as if he had been struck, before laughing.

"You got me there, man. Only one maid. I don't need a lot. Just me. Been divorced for a couple of years, you know."

Rich did know, had made it his business to know. Hightower sacrificed his marriage to his career two years ago on the altar of his now very successful business. He had two children, girls, whom he saw on rare occasions even though he paid child support like clockwork, sent gifts for everything from MLK Day to President's Day.

"Drink?" Hightower reminded him.

"Water," Rich said, unsmiling and not moving.

Carlyle did not offer any help either. "I'll have a Seven-Up, if you don't mind."

"I don't mind at all," Hightower said as he moved to the wet bar. "Diet okay?"

"Diet's fine," Carlyle said.

Hightower handed Rich a Perrier and a glass of ice. After he gave Carlyle bottled Seven-Up, he took a seat in a leather wingchair, the fabric purposely distressed to make the chair look ancient, perhaps something in the family that had been handed down through the generations. Hightower crossed one leg over the other, arched the foot up and inspected the tip of his white golf shoe.

"So," he said, not looking at them, "What can I do for you fellas?"

Rich looked over at Carlyle, who had begun peeling the label from the Seven-Up.

Rich noticed that Carlyle was not comfortable with Val Hightower. He could tell by the red splotches crawling up Carlyle's neck. Rich took a long drink of the Perrier and waited. He did not speak, did not say a word until Hightower looked up questioningly.

"We've never met, have we, Hightower?" Rich finally said.

Hightower's mouth tightened, almost imperceptibly. "Please," he said, "call me Val."

Before Rich could answer, Hightower continued, "I suppose you know that Val is short for Valor. My mother, you know," he said.

Rich nodded. He did know but did not want to discuss it just then. Unlike the chair Hightower occupied, it was probably passed down through the generations, a family name from slaves who named their children after character traits. But what Rich did know is how hastily Valor Hightower explained. No, Val isn't short for Valerie, a girl's name, it is short for Valor. Bravery. Courage.

"Mr. Hightower," Rich amended, not quite ready to be on first name basis with Valor Hightower. "Your firm provides security for Brighton House and several other buildings owned by Thomas Brighton, correct?"

Hightower's eyelids fluttered slightly. But he did not say anything. Instead, he checked his watch, sighed impatiently.

"I see you have done your homework. But what has that got to do with anything?"

He did not look at Rich or at Carlyle, who had sunk into the leather sofa so silently that Rich wondered if he had melted right into the cushions.

"I appreciate that you've come prepared." Hightower stood up then, walked over to a desk which sat in front of a paned floor to ceiling glass window. The garden beyond seemed a kaleidoscope of green in Rich's hungover eyes. He had to shake his head to remind himself where he was.

"But I'm in a hurry," Hightower was saying.

He picked up a stack of brown folders with neatly typed tabs. Back in the sitting area, he reached across the wide coffee table to hand them to Rich. When Rich did not reach out to grab them, he gave them to Carlyle.

"That's what you've come for, isn't it?"

No one spoke. Carlyle tried. His lips moved but no sound came out. When Rich did speak it felt as if his voice had come from a long way down, from way under water. He did not know if Hightower heard the uncertain anger. He hoped that he did not.

"Background checks and the sorts..." Hightower added uncomfortably, waving his fingers like spokes in a wheel.

"I have done more than my homework, Mr. Hightower," Rich agreed. "I actually went to your office on Seventh before I came here."

Hightower did not blink. He smiled but did not show any teeth. His eyes remained two brown marbles, barely moving in his face.

"I wish you had let me know," he said. "I would have arranged a visit."

Rich leaned back, took a sip of the Perrier before speaking again.

"You see, that's where I think that we have an issue," he said. "You thinking I have to tell you anything."

Hightower cocked his head questioningly. "I don't follow," he said.

"Well," Rich explained, hearing the anger now taking free rein in his voice. "Let me see if I can help you along. You work for Brighton Industries. They keep you in this house, keep those child support and alimony payments going to the ex and the kids, keep you in those funny ass shoes. I'm head of security for Brighton House. You know what that means, Mr. Hightower?"

"I think I'm beginning to understand."

"Good. But just in case you have any doubt, let me clear things up for you, make it all nice and pretty, something you can relate to. You work for me," Rich touched his chest, then moved his fingers toward Hightower. "Not the other way around. And right now, we both have a major fuck-up on our hands."

"You mean Anna Cotton," Hightower said.

His demeanor surprised Rich somewhat. There was no anger in Hightower's voice though his shoulders bunched almost imperceptibly.

"Yeah," Rich nodded. "Anna Cotton."

Hightower turned to Carlyle. "Is he always like this?" he asked, a slight chuckle in his voice.

"Only when he runs into old girlfriends," he said.

Rich shot him a look. Hightower laughed out loud, took the peeled Seven-Up bottle from Carlyle's hands.

"I thought we and the police determined that the attack did not occur in the facility," Hightower said as he gave Carlyle another Seven-Up.

Rich was feeling a little silly for coming on so strong. Blame it on the wind, the freezing hail and the tree that ate his Firebird. He did not know why he did not like Hightower. But he did not.

"I think we both know better," Rich said.

Hightower nodded. "I guess we do. But what can I do for you?"

"Aside from the background checks, we need to have the archive disks from the security cameras."

"Of course," Hightower said. "For which dates?"

Rich stopped. For some reason, he had not expected Hightower to be so forthcoming.

"Mr. Marvel," Hightower leaned in. "For which dates?"

"Just get me access to all of them," Rich said.

Hightower laughed then. "Those cameras run twenty-four seven three sixty-five. The archives would fill a small room."

"Just give me the tapes during the time Anna Cotton was there," Rich said.

"She's been there for months, that's thousands of hours of tapes. You sure she's worth all the time you are about to put into this? They have the rapist. I heard the man might have even confessed."

"They have a confused old man," Rich said.

Hightower, the bastard, pretended to contemplate the crown molding, pretended to be lost in thought.

"Now, let me see," he said slowly. "Where have I heard that before?"

Rich stared at Hightower hoping that the look on his face would convey how much he would love to kick his ass.

"Don't push me, Hightower," Rich said.

"Of course not," Hightower responded. "What was I thinking?"

"Besides, I don't believe that the sheriff's department could find their asses with both hands, let alone find out what really happened to Anna."

Hightower shrugged, swirled ice in his glass.

"Suit yourself," he said. He stood up. "Gentlemen," he said. "I am really late. Is there anything else?"

"Yes," Rich said, standing up as well. "I noticed something in Anna's files about a security bracelet . . ."

Hightower's nod cut Rich off. "Yes, we usually use that for forensic, violent patients. But Dr. Holder requested one for Anna."

"What's it hooked up to?" Carlyle asked.

"Oh, the security bracelet is connected to the guard station at Brighton House. Anna Cotton can't take a piss without them knowing that she went to the bathroom."

Hightower stroked his chin. "Come to think of it," he said, "It would be really difficult for the rape to occur at the facility."

"Why is that?" Rich asked.

"There is a security camera in her room," Hightower explained.

"What?" Both Rich and Carlyle said at the same time.

"Yes," Hightower responded. "Another request of Katherine's. She thought it would calm Anna down if she knew that someone was watching."

"Did you tell the police any of this?" Rich asked

"I didn't talk to the police," Hightower answered.

"Why not?" Rich asked.

Hightower spread his hands. "They didn't ask, probably didn't feel that it was necessary."

"Because they already had their rapist?" Rich asked.

"Exactly," Hightower answered.

"I'll need access to those videos as well, you know," Rich said.

"But of course."

At the door before they left him to his golf game, Hightower stopped Rich with a question.

"Your office visit," he asked. "I hope everything was in order?"

Rich looked at Val—short for Valor—Hightower for a long time. He looked at the diamond and gold nugget ring on the middle finger of his right hand, the platinum band as thick as a rope, the jewel in it as big as a knot. He thought about Val going to play golf this afternoon with the father of his ex-fiancée, Judge Webster, whose daughter he had dumped because of Kendra Hamilton. Val was what Rich had wanted to be during his ambitious climb to the top at the sheriff's department and still later, even after his inglorious fall into obscurity over the Luke Bertrand fiasco. He, Rich, should have been standing on the other side of that door.

But at that moment, at the genuine worry in Hightower's clean brown eyes, Rich was glad that he was not. He was glad that he did not have the responsibility.

Rich shook his head at Hightower's question, never taking his eyes from his face.

"Naw, man," he said. "It wasn't in order. A pimply faced kid behind a desk, shoes off, let me walk through the place. Rummage through file drawers, walk in the back room. He wouldn't let us in the safe though, said I would have to get a subpoena for that. All I said was that I was police, flashed my ID. He didn't even look at it. Other guy there, older, holster off, feet on the desk." Rich stopped for a moment. "He was asleep."

Hightower nodded. Rich waited for him to speak. But he did not.

"I woke him up," Rich went on. "And when I asked him why he was sleeping he said that it didn't matter because they were not really guarding anything at the office. Said something about that they were just supposed to answer the phones in case of emergencies from the other sites. I guess they also review security tapes looking for problems. Is this where the archives are, Mr. Hightower?"

Hightower nodded, murmured a thank you before closing the door softly behind them.

CHAPTER 13

Thunder awakened Rich. He was back in the house dozing on and off as he remembered the meeting with Val Hightower. Sprawled on his couch idly nursing a beer, he now realized why he didn't like Val Hightower. The man, after all, was dating Rich's ex-fiancée. He chuckled at the thought. God help him, then. After he and Carlyle left Hightower, they went to Brighton House for the first set of scheduled interviews. Some weird ass people worked at Brighton House, Rich thought now. Some good people did too. Unfortunately, they were outnumbered by the weirdos.

Rich and Carlyle conducted the interviews in one of the conference rooms at Brighton House under the auspicious portrait of Thomas Brighton's mother. Rich shivered when he saw the portrait. The woman reminded him of the See's candy lady on a bad day. If Rich's face was like that and he had to look at it in the mirror every morning, he would probably lose his mind, too.

The person whom they interviewed, Rich looked down at the typed name on the file that he had gotten from Val Hightower, her name was Willamena History. She was forty-two years old, had been a Certified Nursing Assistant, or CNA, since she was twenty-three. She had been working at Brighton House for the past ten years. Nurse History was a model employee, had made employee of the month at least six times since she had been at Brighton House. There had been only one reprimand in her record for mishandling a patient while trying to put him in four-point restraint. It was, she told Rich and Carlyle now, a mistake on her part. No one's fault but her own and she accepted complete and full responsibility. She had simply lost her temper and that was that.

Rich looked at the woman sitting across from him. In spite of the full admission of guilt, her appearance and demeanor set off every alarm bell in his head. And he wasn't even remotely hungover anymore. The sound was so loud that if Carlyle bothered to remove the fingers he had plugged against both eyes to tell them that he had just seen a fire engine rush by, Rich would have believed him.

Willamena had not stopped talking since she walked into the room. The gold tooth in her mouth, the front one with the star cut-out, flashed on and off as her black lips moved. She talked fast. Words flew from her mouth like machine gun fire. Her nails flew too, so long that they actually curled under like animal claws. Rich wondered how she could work with those nails. She had a hard meanness to her pointed face. It was unmistakable. How Katherine Holder missed it, if Rich would live to be two hundred he would never know.

"What did you do before you worked here, Ms. History?" Rich asked.

She leaned over the narrow table and craned her neck to get a look at the file open in front of Rich. Rich closed it and moved it out of her reach. He sat up.

"You don't remember?" he asked.

"Of course I remember," she said. "I worked at the state hospital. But I like it here much better."

"Why is that?" Carlyle asked, fingers still plugged over his eyes.

"Well, we are much more of a family here. People care about each other. No one cares about you at State. You are just a number, punch in and punch out and if you are lucky, you'll get a five-dollar gift certificate for a bonus at Christmas . . ."

And that was it. Willamena was off again. Carlyle's fingers had not moved. His flame red head pressed against the back of the chair as if he were trying to sever his neck.

"What did you do before you became a CNA? Ms. History?" Rich asked.

She had kept talking until it dawned on her what Rich had

asked. He could see the realization creep over her face as her brain caught up with her running mouth.

"What? What?" she said, looking at them both.

"What did you do before you became a CNA?" Carlyle repeated.

"I've been a nursing assistant since I was . . ."

"Twenty-three . . ." Rich finished for her. "Five years after high school graduation, right? Where did you say you graduated from?"

She bristled at this, gum popping and echoing in the quiet room.

"I got my GED," she said. Her voice went up an octave, became more strident. "It's just as good."

"What did you do after you got your GED?" Rich asked.

"Worked at McDonald's," she said. "Got tired of that so I went through a program and got my certificate to become a nursing assistant. Why you asking me?" Her eyes narrowed.

"Oh," Rich said and stretched his hands over his head in a yawn. "Wiping people's asses seems like a hard job. I can't imagine anyone wanting to do that for a living."

"I do much more than wipe asses, mister," she said, gum smacking.

Rich folded his hands across his belly. "Oh yeah?" he asked. He inserted a note of curiosity into his voice. "Like what?"

"Like supervise, that's what," she snapped.

She was getting angry. Good. He wanted her angry.

"Oh?" Carlyle jumped in, sitting up. "Who do you supervise?"

"Patients, that's who," she said.

"You mean retards and crazies?" Rich said. "That can't be too hard."

Rich noted that she didn't object to his terminology.

"It's not easy, let me tell you." She curled two fingers toward her black eyes. "You gotta watch 'em, watch 'em like a hawk. They as sneaky as hell."

"Sneaky?" Rich asked. "What do you mean?"

"They manipulate, that's what I mean. Look, I've been doing this a long time. Some are okay but it's the sneaky ones you gotta keep an eye on. The ones who shut down and fall on the floor when they don't want to do something. Or play like they crazy when you catch 'em doing something they ain't supposed to be doing. Like they don't understand." She stopped, breathing heavily. She had a concerned look in her eyes as if she knew that she had said too much.

"Is Anna one of those?" Rich asked.

Willamena blinked. "One of who?"

"A sneaky one." Rich leaned over the table. He planted a conspiratorial smile on his face. "Come on, is she a sneaky one or just a manipulator?"

Not buying his tone, Willamena drew back. "I don't know why you asking me all these questions," she said. "I didn't rape her. I ain't got no thang. What? Ya'll think I got a thang that I could knock her up?"

Carlyle scooted his chair close to Willamena. He crouched around her.

"Nobody's saying that, Willamena," he said. "But did you ever, I dunno, see her with anybody? Maybe she has a boyfriend here . . ."

He stopped at the light in Willamena's eyes.

"Now I see what you saying." Her voice resumed its sure tone.

She looked at Rich and nodded in understanding. She wagged a long brown finger at him. Rich didn't know why she smiled because he had played poker enough to know that his own face was set as stone.

"You can look at Pretty Anna and tell that she a manipulator. Can't nobody look like that and be that dumb," she insisted.

"Who's she manipulating, Ms. History?" Rich said, tired of the conversation and the interview.

"Why, everybody, especially the men. They all sniff around her. And she eat it up."

"Like who?" Rich pressed.

She placed a red fingernail against her cast iron–colored chin. When she looked up Rich saw that she had no intention of giving them a name.

"You seen Petty Anna yet, Mr. Marvel?" she crooned.

"No, I haven't," Rich said, yawning. "I hope to soon, though."

"Well, when you see her you'll know what I mean when I say everybody with a dick. That's who." She leaned back, pleased with herself.

"Anybody more so than others?" Rich asked, not bothering to hide the disgust in his eyes.

"I'll say," Willamena agreed. "Brandon Chadwick has his nose so far up her ass that I'm surprised that when she say something that it ain't his voice that come out."

"What a fucking fruitcake," Carlyle said when Willamena left the room.

Rich didn't answer. Instead, he was too busy flipping through the rest of the files. Carlyle picked up the one on Willamena and put it in a pile for future consideration. They had about four people at whom Rich wanted to take a closer look. Brandon Chadwick was not among them. It turned out that Hightower had only done cursory checks of these people. He did not do an extensive criminal background check even with people like Willamena.

"She should be in the bughouse, not watching it," Rich muttered under his breath.

"What?" Carlyle asked.

Rich didn't answer. Instead he searched through the names on the rest of the files, ticked through the Rolodex in his head to review the list of people he had spoken to that day. Gary Rollins, Michael Cooper, sure, and on and on. But no Brandon Chadwick.

"It's not here," Rich said aloud.

"What's not here?"

"The Chadwick file. You don't remember talking to a Chadwick, do you?"

Carlyle shook his head, then peered under the table. "Maybe it fell," he said.

"No," Rich said. "Nothing fell. Why would it be missing, man?"

"Maybe it slipped through the cracks." Carlyle grinned. "Seems that Hightower lets lots of things slip through the cracks."

Rich stopped, gazed at Carlyle for a moment. "You don't like him, do you?"

"I hate his fucking guts," Carlyle said.

"Well, one day you'll have to tell me why. But for now we need to find the Chadwick file."

They searched for a while to no avail. According to what Hightower had given them, Brandon Chadwick did not exist. Rich flipped open his cell phone and contacted Katherine Holder. She appeared fifteen minutes later with an apple-faced Brandon Chadwick in tow. Rich remembered where he had seen him before. He was the same man that raised all his perp-o-meter flags.

Unlike Willamena in her SpongeBob SquarePants scrubs, Chadwick's were white and starched so stiffly that Rich was sure they hurt. Even his shoes were white. Chadwick folded his hands on the table in front of him. He looked at both Rich and Carlyle with eyes wet with earnest.

And he answered every single one of their questions. Yes, sir, he did know Anna. Yes, sir, he would understand why Nurse History would say that he "sniffed" around Anna but he resented the implication. He didn't "sniff" around Anna for sexual reasons but instead, to protect her. The women were jealous of Anna and the men were, well, you know, men. And for that matter, Willamena was jealous of him. The nursing business was woman's business and many of them openly resented his position at the hospital. Besides, he turned her in for slapping a patient and she was still angry about it.

"Slapping a patient?" Rich questioned.

"Yes, sir," Chadwick responded, his back ramrod straight.

Carlyle riffled through Willamena's file. "Nothing in her file about slapping," he said.

Chadwick's thumb fluttered outward from his hands still folded on the interview table. Rich noticed that the he hadn't moved a muscle since they started the interview. The only things moving were his lips and his darting eyes.

"I wouldn't know about her files, sir," he responded.

"Where is your file, Chadwick?" Rich challenged.

"I . . . I . . ." Chadwick said, seemingly confused at Rich's tone. "It should be there, shouldn't it?"

"Should be," Rich agreed, his voice hard. "But it's not."

"Well." Those thumbs fluttered outward again. "I don't understand why it's not there."

"How long have you worked here?" Rich asked.

"Two years," Chadwick responded.

"Where did you work before Brighton House?"

"A nursing home in San Francisco."

"How long?"

"What?" Brandon asked, confused.

"I said, how long?" Rich repeated.

"Oh. A year," Chadwick responded, shaking his head a little bit.

"Before that?"

"California State Mental, six months I think . . ."

"Before that?" Rich asked.

"A nursing home in Florida, I don't . . ."

Rich sat back and let out a disgusted breath. Carlyle shook his head, snorted in disbelief.

"Why so many positions?" Carlyle asked.

"It was time to move on," Chadwick explained. "And like I said, the women resent me. They've always given me a hard time. It's like reverse sexual discrimination."

"I just bet it is," Carlyle said.

"You ever been arrested or convicted of anything?" Rich asked.

"Arrested? Convicted?" Chadwick's eyes moved between Carlyle and Rich. "No, never. They would never let me work here. Why? Do you think I hurt Anna?"

They didn't answer him but Rich silently considered the question. Did he think Chadwick hurt Anna? Hell, yes, he did.

"Look," Chadwick explained. "I told you that Anna and I are friends. I protect her."

Rich smiled, slapped Chadwick on the shoulder to put him at ease. He didn't realize that Chadwick was holding his breath until he let it out. Some of the color returned to Chadwick's face.

"I guess you have to do these things to be sure," Chadwick said.

"I guess," Rich agreed, smiling and hoping like hell that Chadwick wouldn't spook and fly before they could prove that he was their perp.

"Well, I can assure you . . ." Chadwick started.

"No need to assure," Carlyle said. "We'll contact you if we need to."

"Thank you, sir." Chadwick ducked his head at them.

Before he left, he shook Rich's and Carlyle's hand. Chadwick's palm was as wet as a fish. When he finally walked out of the room, Rich hitched his pants and sat down. He stared a long time at the closed door, would have stared longer if Carlyle hadn't broken the spell. He made a mental note to himself to tell Katherine Holder to change the card access on Anna's door. He didn't want Brandon Chadwick anywhere near her. For that matter, he didn't want Willamena History, but that might be a harder kite to fly.

"If the father didn't do her," Carlyle said, "I'm putting my bets on that crazy fucker. God, if it ain't a case of the inmates running the asylum."

As Rich listened to the storm rage around his little house, instinct told him that he had his perp. He tried calling Kendra several times that night to tell her but she did not answer her phone. Sometimes, caller ID worked against you. He wanted to tell her that there was nothing left to do but to protect Anna, clear the old man and find proof that would make Chadwick good for the rape.

And with this over, so would his relationship finally be over with Kendra. What would she say or do for that matter when she learned that Luke had no part in what happened to Anna Cotton? Would she give up this obsession, forget about Luke and go on with her life? Rich took a long swig of his beer and chuckled. For a minute there, he was almost as nutty as Willamena and Chadwick.

Anna

Anna think about what happened in the dayroom when Rosita cry. Anna look at her friend. She got tan skin and black hair that shine and move like black water. She got a fat body and tan arms and she got bruises near her potty place, same place Anna got bruises. Anna remember Rosita show her the bruises, pulling down her pants and sitting on the ground. She lean back so Anna can see, hole in her like a mouth saying oh.

Monster go see Rosita sometime too but like Anna she can't say nothing. Rosita tell Anna she got slippery fish caught in her throat. No words can come out, so she just cry all the time and have stomachaches and don't want to go to bed when the lights go out.

And sometime Rosita go to the quiet room with the brown leather ties for sticking her tongue down somebody throat, or grabbing at they breast when they say no. She tell Anna fish try to get out but nobody pays her any attention. They don't hear. But Anna hear. Anna knows.

"Anna don't like you," Anna say now to winter wisteria.

"What?" she come closer, put her face right near Anna. Anna see gold teeth, smell onion, see silver fillings in her teeth bones.

"I say," Anna voice still soft, but the words mean the same thing they say before. "I say Anna don't like you."

Onion smell disappear, teeth bones go out of sight. And winter wisteria standing back up, nails like bullets still poking SpongeBob's white eye. Her arms cross and she say, "Why do you talk about yourself like that?" Her voice not mean no more, not hard, but like she really want to know something but Anna don't know what.

"Like what?" Anna ask.

"Like that," she say. "Do you hear me talk about myself like that? Do you hear me say, Nurse don't like that? Or do you hear me say, I don't like that. Don't you ever say I?"

Anna think about it. Ever say I. No. Not anymore. Anna used to say I, sometime, but don't say I no more. I run away when they lock Anna in this place, I run away when Mamma went away. When they lock Anna in Brighton House I run away and don't come back no more.

CHAPTER 14

"Hurry, hurry. Giant clearance sale! Everything must go!"
Kendra jumped at the words, almost dropped the Smith &
Wesson. Still pointing the gun at Luke, she looked over her shoulder at the TV on the dresser. An advertisement for furniture liqui-
dation, lots of yellow letters and red exclamation points. Kendra
turned back to Luke to see if the sound had awakened him. It didn't.
He still lay on his back, mouth open and snoring gently. Sleeping
as if he hadn't a care in the world, sleeping like a baby.

She moved the light along the room, watched it crawl up the
walls, over the headboard looming above Luke's head like a halo.
A small bottle of pills sat on the nightstand next to the bed. She
walked over to the nightstand, light alternately on Luke's face so
she could make sure he didn't wake up and on the carpet so she
could see where she was going. The bottle contained prescription
sleeping pills. Judging by the glass of water next to the pill bottle,
Luke had taken them before going to bed that night.

She shone the light directly on his face and looked at him now.
Light crawled in and out of the wrinkles like an ant. She switched
on the lamp, then switched it off again. When he still didn't move
she switched it on and left it on. She studied Luke's face: nothing.
If he took a dose of those sleeping pills, he would be out for at least
another four hours. He wouldn't hear a nuclear explosion. She
had come here to kill him, dragged the Smith & Wesson out of her

closet, loaded it—it took her almost an hour, her hands were trembling so—and drove over to Luke's place to put a bullet in his head. But, as far as he was concerned, at least, he was already senseless, already dead to the world.

Kendra wondered when Luke started taking sleeping pills. The Luke she knew would not have resorted to medication even though he was once a doctor. She hoped it was because of the trial and his public humiliation, brief though it was. She surveyed the room. Dresser, white trimmed in gilt like the headboard, looked clean as a hospital operating room. No comb, brush, mirror, not even a Bible on the nightstand. Sterile, clean like the lie Luke had been telling the people of Dunhill for all of those years.

The Smith & Wesson weighed Kendra down. All of a sudden, she felt as if she could no longer hold it aloft. Luke should be sleeping in prison; he should be shitting in a hole in the floor and eating his dinner from a plastic tray. But instead, he lay in a bed wrapped in satin sheets, sleeping in a bed with a white headboard like he was already in heaven, the place he so wanted to be. He thought he deserved it because what? Because he saved all of those children from their junkie mothers, *even you, Kendra,* she heard his voice whispering in her head.

She shuddered, and wanting to be rid of him, that voice in her head, the whole goddamn thing, she raised the gun, slowly, dramatically like she'd seen it done in the movies. She thought that deep down she wanted to draw this moment out and savor it. But what she wouldn't admit to herself was that she couldn't do it.

Over the silver barrel she stared at his face again, memorized every line, every crack. She imagined how his forehead would look after she pulled the trigger. In her mind she could see the small hole, the smoke rising above it as if from a dying fire. Thin. She could hear the jolt, the blood flowering on the white satin pillow. What would he feel? Would he know what was happening?

But she knew the answer to that. He would not know what was happening. And if he did, it would only be for a brief moment. He would die in his sleep, might as well be from a heart attack or a sudden stroke or a blood vessel bursting in his head like fireworks on Fourth of July.

But would he feel it? That's what she wanted to know now. Would he feel it and would he know? She lowered the weapon. She studied Luke's fastened eyes. The pupils were not scurrying back and forth. Not even in REM sleep; Luke was out. He wouldn't feel a goddamn thing. As the saying went, he wouldn't know what hit him. He would just wake up in hell wondering how he had gotten there. That did not give Kendra enough satisfaction. She wanted him dead, but most of all, she wanted him to suffer.

She did not know that she would switch off the lamp until the light suddenly went out and plunged the room into darkness. That old familiar fear, that insane fear of the dark came over her. She had a hard time remembering to breathe. Her heart beat in a protest against the dark as if it were trying to use the power of pulse to generate light. Kendra switched on the flashlight, concentrated on the concentric circle on the carpet. She left Luke's bedroom not knowing what to do next. She only knew that she couldn't kill him. Dying—that way would be too easy for him.

She thought that she would leave, but that also would have been too easy. Instead of turning left at the end of the hallway, she turned right, toward the kitchen. Luke must have an office, something that hinted at the monster inside him. But when she found his office, it was almost as clean and scrubbed as his bedroom. A bookshelf with books stacked according to size and then in alphabetical order. Among them, the entire set of Encyclopedia Britannica. The cherry wood desk was clean, polished to a high gloss. Kendra ran her hand over the cool surface and caught sight of her face.

Her hair, the shape of her hair, was chaotic. The corkscrew curls jutted in every direction, sort of like Violet's. Her large dark brown eyes bulged slightly and even in the desk's dark surface she could see that they were filmed shiny with tears. She touched the harsh lines created by the downturn pull of her full lips. She didn't recognize that face, realized that she did not know herself. Luke Bertrand took that away from her. Rich followed him and took the rest of her away while trying to erase the past in a quest for a new future together.

She tore herself from that distorted reflection. *Get a grip, Kendra,* she thought. She studied the room in much the same way that she had studied the bedroom. The office wasn't a very large room but it was opulent with thick white rugs and a Brighton vintage clock on the wall. Kendra could see by the oversize hands and Roman numbers that it was just a little after two in the morning. There

were a few black and white photographs, one with Luke and
Governor Wilson taken ages ago, another with a prominent Black
judge. He had his college picture hanging on one wall in a simple
black frame. She located Luke in the third row. He was smiling.

Luke's face, black and long, looked like a storm cloud buried
among the white faces surrounding him. All the boys wore white
jerseys with numbers on them, white shorts and new socks. She took
the photo down and studied it. The eyes were crinkled at the corner, but empty as hell. Luke went to Cloughton Medical College,
sent there by the man his mother worked for, the man with no family who left Luke his fortune.

But Kendra did not know much about his college days. From the
photograph Kendra could tell that Luke must have been a little
strange with those empty eyes and that knowing smile.

In spite of the smile trying so hard to be friendly, Luke had both
arms crossed over his chest, tight, as if he did not want to accidentally touch the boys on either side of him. The boy next to him had
his head down and leaned away from Luke. Why did the boy lean
away from Luke? Because Luke was Black or was there another reason? From late night TV shows and occasional readings, Kendra
knew that serial killers did not one day, in their late fifties or early
sixties, wake up and just start killing. They usually started much
earlier. When, she wondered, did Luke start?

As she placed the photo back on the wall, she knocked a small
porcelain jewelry box off the table. It clattered to the hardwood
floor and sounded like a bomb falling in the quiet house.

"Oh, shit," Kendra said out loud.

She bent down to pick it up, not knowing why because the entire thing had shattered to pieces. She'd need a broom to clean it
but cleaning it was not her intent as she sifted through the broken
porcelain. The gold band lying among the shards and glinting
under the light of her flashlight was. She picked it up and gazed at
it against her palm. She looked inside and saw an inscription. It
read, *To Debra, forever mine, LB*. Kendra chuckled at this. Most people would have said, forever yours. It takes a Luke Bertrand to say
forever mine.

But Kendra grew serious as she thought about this Debra. Luke
made it known that he had never been married. In fact, he kept
his love life so private that Dunhill residents speculated that he was

a closet homosexual. Who was this Debra? And if she was Luke Bertrand's wife, why wasn't the second finger on her left hand attached to this ring? Divorce? Kendra read the inscription again. *Forever mine.* Luke would not have let anyone walk away from him. And if they tried, he'd probably fix it so they never would walk away from anyone else again.

Kendra closed her fist around the ring. A slow grin spread across her face.

"Bingo, you sick son of a bitch," she said. "Gotcha."

CHAPTER 15

Kendra spun the band of gold on the kitchen table of her apartment. It twirled and danced before clattering to the wooden surface. She picked it up, bounced it in her palm as if she were testing the weight before purchase. To her knowledge, Luke Bertrand had never been married. To anyone's knowledge, for that matter. What was he doing with a wedding ring? The only empty space on the table was the place where she spun the wedding ring. Strewn over the remainder of the table were the elements of a life. A public life, anyway. Luke's life. Newspaper clippings, yellow edged with age; magazine covers, *Ebony, Jet, Essence,* all with Luke's smiling face and his benevolent eyes.

Inside those covers lay stories of his efforts to raise money for boys and girls, sometimes only a remark or two about a national event involving matters of race. About Rodney King; Luke wrote about police brutality, while lamenting King's questionable character, his delight for "finding trouble." He took heat for that, but he took it in his stride. The tabloids ate him up, regurgitated every word. Luke Bertrand's face was well loved by the camera.

Then Luke was arrested for murder. The nation, stunned, especially the Black nation, said nothing at first. It was as if they had been caught and paralyzed in the bright flash of their own cameras. When they recovered, Dunhill became home to news trucks sporting satellite dishes and pretty reporters in high heels and makeup. Luke was big news. He was the fallen son, or, as one creative news reporter put it, the falling sun.

Kendra had the latter articles, the articles of his shame and pictures of those dead girls, including her mother, spread among the rest of the news of his philanthropy. Looking at the table, she felt as if she were seeing both sides of Luke's personality: the side which dedicated every waking moment to helping the Black community and the other side which was capable of killing.

Kendra stood up and stretched. It was five A.M., still dark outside. Her feet were bare against her kitchen linoleum. The heat still wasn't working in the apartment and she couldn't ever remember it working. She wondered now if it was always winter here. Goose bumps on her arms and her fingertips numb with cold, she picked up a magazine with Luke's face on it and put it down again.

She had been collecting these things all day—the articles. Some she already had. Violet, her mother, the woman Luke had been accused of poisoning like a rat; she had kept some of the articles. Even homeless, her belongings in a bag, Violet kept a scrapbook of sorts on Luke. Admiration? Because she was proud to know him? Kendra did not know. But what she did know was that Violet Hamilton, former heroin addict, did not keep a scrapbook on her own children. Instead, she kept one on a man she feared and hated, a man who had exercised the ultimate power over her, the power to kill and get away with it.

What she hadn't discovered among Violet's things, Kendra found at the library. She spent hours copying items she couldn't check out, dropping the papers on a pile on the floor, garnering a raised eyebrow and pursed lips from another library patron. She left with her arms full when the library closed at ten P.M. Then she spent the rest of the night looking through the articles, trying to find some explanation for the wedding ring.

But she couldn't. No mention of a wife, no mention of a lover or a girlfriend. Kendra picked up the ring, looked inside. *Forever mine. Start from the beginning.* The words bubbled in her head. *Start from the beginning.* That was Rich's voice inside her head. And Kendra knew that whatever was wrong with Luke had been going on a long time, perhaps since he was a child.

According to the magazine and newspaper articles strewn over her apartment, Luke's beginning started in 1970 when he returned to Dunhill after medical school. Cloughton Medical College was courtesy of Luke's benefactor, his own savior who paid Luke's way through both college and medical school. His academic career was unimpressive, but he still graduated, barely, specializing in pediatric medicine. He had a soft spot for children, a real soft spot. He still did. To hear him tell it, he killed for children.

After he returned to Dunhill, Luke practiced medicine for a while. And when his benefactor passed away and left him a fortune, Luke quit practicing medicine in lieu of a better career. He took a job as a local hero, a philanthropist, giving away his money as fast as storm clouds raced across the sky in April. He became society's darling, dropping out of grace when addicts started missing and he had been accused of murder.

But no red flags, nothing before the first girl was fed the poison dope after the birth of her baby. Luke's life was clean, freshly washed sheets hanging in the sun. *I am an open book,* he had said in *Jet* when they did an article on him before he was arrested. But the reporter, a tough-minded young man looking for a career maker, contradicted Luke. He pointed out that Luke rarely had visitors to his estate in The Point. No one knew what had become of his family. Kendra scrambled among the papers, remembering, looking for that particular article. Luke answered glibly. His father had a mental condition, hated him. He and Luke did not get along. His mother passed away ten years before the article was written, breast cancer. But she was peaceful in the end. That was it. The children he worked with, they were his family. Someone should have known right then that something was wrong. But they did not and Luke Bertrand went on one of the most infamous killing sprees in Dunhill. His goal was to save the children from mothers who did not deserve them.

An open book. That couldn't be true. Killing did not just start, like a virus, catching a cold. Killing had a beginning. And killing, she knew, had its aftermath, paraphernalia, and souvenirs. The gold ring was a souvenir. That she knew.

She leaned back in her chair. Her shoulders ached, her eyes felt dry as paper. But she convinced herself that she wasn't tired. Since returning to Dunhill, sleep had been elusive, a phantom. Even with the biting cold, the blankets of her bed made the night as hot as an oven. And when she was awake, heat ringed her forehead, and her mouth felt hot and dry. She rubbed her fingers over her eyes, thinking *what next?* But she knew: find the owner of the ring, and she would find a clue into Luke's past and into his evil soul.

Kendra answered the phone on the first ring. Rich's voice on the other end contained surprise, a small hint of worry.

"Kendra?"

"Yes," she answered, confused.

Her heart thumped and she wondered briefly where she was. She looked around at the table covered with articles about Luke. She had fallen asleep with her head on the table. She rubbed her face.

"I'm sorry to call you so early," he said.

"What do you want?" she asked.

"Sounds like you are awake," he said. "A little bit, anyway."

"I am," she responded.

His voice had an element of warmth to it or maybe worry. It was not businesslike. Hers was. Rich got the hint.

"I'm calling about Anna Cotton," Rich said.

Kendra's forehead creased as she struggled to remember. April, she thought, then no, Anna. She was confused and for a moment, she did not know where she was or who she was speaking to. She needed sleep.

"Yes," she repeated, as if to herself. "Anna Cotton."

"Kendra," Rich's voice sounded impatient. "Where have you been? I've been calling you all night."

"I've been doing what most people do at night, Rich. I've been sleeping. What do you think?" she said, the lie coming easily.

"You are a damn liar," he said. "What in the hell have you been up to, Kendra?"

"None of your business," she said.

He sighed into the phone. "I don't have time for this. Look, can we meet?"

"Yes, I mean no." She stopped, suddenly remembering everything. "I mean yes, I am all right and no we cannot meet."

"Don't you even want to know what it's about?" he asked.

She did not answer him. No, she did not want to know what it was about or why he called her. She wanted him emptied from her life. The only thing she wanted was revenge, to see Luke Bertrand behind bars, to expose him for what he had been from the very moment he drew breath. Kendra Hamilton didn't have time for distractions, especially not Richard T. Marvel.

"I would like to be left alone," she said, hearing the drone in her own voice.

Rich chuckled. "Wouldn't we all, sweetheart? But I need to talk to you."

"We are talking now," she said. "What do you want?"

Even through the phone she could sense his confusion. It was only natural. What, only a week ago she had been begging for his help with Anna and Leroy Cotton. But he had refused. And now, when he called, hinting that he might be involved, wanting to talk, she shut him out. How could he know that she had moved onto other things and no longer cared? Besides . . .

"I've thought about what you said at the lake and decided to look into some things at Brighton House," Rich said. "I need to talk to Anna Cotton. I told you that the other morning."

"I don't see why," Kendra said. "They got the man who did it."

Silence. Then Rich said, "Kendra."

"Look, Rich, he did it, okay? He told me so himself."

"You ever thought," Rich said quietly, "that he told you what you wanted to hear to keep you out of it?"

"You don't know Leroy Cotton well enough to say that. You didn't hear him, Rich," she said.

"No, I don't know Leroy Cotton. But unfortunately, I know you. You wouldn't leave this alone just because he asked you to. It's not too far-fetched to think that he wants you out of his business and he thinks that this is the only way to do it."

"Bullshit, Rich," she said. "You didn't see his face. Or hear him. That man is guilty over something."

"I still want to talk to Anna, hear it for myself," Rich said.

Kendra shrugged. "So talk to her," she said.

"The administration at Brighton House won't let me talk to her," he said. "Not without permission and not without a guardian present."

"So why are you calling me?" Kendra had become annoyed. This was taking too much time. She needed to be done with this. There was much to do.

"Kendra." Rich sighed heavily. "I said that I need permission."

"You need to talk to the father," Kendra told him. "Call Leroy Cotton."

"You love playing games with me, don't you?"

"I don't want to do anything with you, Rich," she said. "I would like you to leave me alone. Please."

"You are telling me that you don't know."

"Know what?" she asked. "The only thing I know is that you are bugging the shit out of me right now, Rich. And wasting my time."

"You are Anna Cotton's guardian. I need your permission to speak to her, and you need to be there when I do."

Kendra stopped breathing for a moment. She was not Anna Cotton's guardian. Leroy Cotton wanted nothing to do with her. He would have surely found some way to terminate her guardianship, especially after what had happened at the jail. And she told Rich so.

"Kendra, he hasn't," Rich said. "He's sick right now, in the hospital almost comatose. Besides, after what he's been accused of, he couldn't terminate a light switch."

"No," she said.

"Are you telling me no?" More anger.

"I said no," she repeated. "You are mistaken. I'm not Anna's guardian."

"Come on, Kendra."

Kendra thought harder about it, then remembered. That's right, the rape. Leroy had no power to terminate her guardianship even if he were well enough to do it.

"Oh," her voice was small as a drop of water. "I forgot. It slipped my mind that he can't do anything about the guardianship."

"Forgot?" Rich questioned. "How can you forget something like that?"

"I don't know," she responded. "So much has happened."

"Like what, Kendra?" Rich asked.

"Nothing," she said. "Why do you need to speak with her?"

"Dammit, I told you. I just need to ask her a few questions. That's all."

"I'll call Dr. Holder," Kendra said.

She went to place the phone in its cradle. Rich's voice, small and tinny, stopped her. She placed the phone back to her ear. He breathed hard as if he had been running.

"What in the hell is wrong with you, girl?" he asked.

She hated that, that girl thing, but said nothing. "I'm fine."

"You are not fine," he said. "You sound flaky as hell."

"I'm having trouble sleeping," she answered simply. "What else do you need?"

"A time to meet," he said. "Don't you think that would be good? When you call Dr. Holder, you can give her some times?"

"When do you need to speak with Anna?" she asked.

"Today. That's why I called so early. I need to talk to her today."

"I can't today," she said.

"Why not?"

Yes, why not? Because she had other things to do today. She walked back to the kitchen table. Light from the naked bulb fell onto the articles, the photocopies. She had read them through the night but had found nothing. No hint. She wanted to crash for a few hours, try for sleep and then reread them. There had to be something in these articles.

"I'm busy," she said. "Tomorrow would be better."

"Tomorrow is too late," he said. "I want to talk to her now and get this thing wrapped up. Besides, the longer we wait, the colder this case becomes."

"Tomorrow would be better," she repeated, picking up a photocopied article from *Jet*, the one written by the bulldog reporter. Luke spoke of his college days in that article, about his days at Cloughton Medical College. Luke Bertrand learned much from that college, had carried those lessons throughout the rest of his life.

Kendra picked up the *Jet*, watched the light slide over it like an oil slick. She barely heard Rich's protests becoming smaller and smaller as she placed the phone in its cradle. Her heart slowed, her breathing calmed because she knew that she had found Luke's beginning. It had to have started at Cloughton.

CHAPTER 16

After her conversation with Rich, Kendra fell into bed. Sunlight streaming through the bedroom window finally awakened her. The strength of that yellow light told her that it was late in the day. *Oh, shit,* she thought, grabbing the face of the Big Ben on her nightstand. It was a little after two in the afternoon, about six hours past when she wanted to wake up.

She threw the covers from the bed and walked shivering to the open window. She banged it shut and stood still in the middle of the room for a minute, debating whether or not to take a shower. She lifted an armpit, sniffed, and decided that for all concerned, it would be better to wash first. Holy shit, she thought. Was she losing all connection to reality? Was she becoming obsessed with Luke Bertrand to the point of insanity? Yes, she decided in answer to both questions. Yes.

She put icy hands to her face to suppress horror at the realization that she was losing it. The very fact that she had been standing over Luke Bertrand's bed with a .357 pointed at his lined forehead waiting for the bullet to emerge had proved that she was walking on the edge of sanity. She didn't shoot for any moral reasons, she thought. The only reason that she didn't pull the trigger was because Luke was oblivious. He would not feel it. And that was the point. He had to feel it.

And now, here she stood in her underwear, February frost on

the windowsill because she left the window open when she returned last night, here she was questioning her sanity because she did not want to take time to wash before hunting down Gregory Atfield.

Dressed in jeans and two sweatshirts, Kendra started toward the door. As an afterthought, she grabbed her purse, a brown leather imitation from K-Mart with long white stitches. She threw the *Jet* magazine along with the ring she had stolen from Luke's house into the bag. She threw the Smith & Wesson Rich had given her after the failed trial of Luke Bertrand in the bag last, not quite understanding why but not wanting to be without it.

The hallway of the apartment building was painted a greasy blue-green. Handprints, some of children at the bottom of the wall and others from drunks who used it as support as they tottered to their apartments, covered most of the wall. Kendra walked along a carpet that was a shit brown and as sparse as dirt. She was halfway to the elevator when a voice stopped her, a voice that resounded off the walls and had all the resonance of a veteran opera singer.

"Dr. Hamilton," the voice said, disapproving.

Kendra winced at the title. Every time she heard it the first thought that came to mind was the loss of her medical license. It was a memory that she could do without.

"Yes," Kendra said, keeping her own voice calm as she turned.

The woman standing at the other end of the hallway approached Kendra. Mrs. Buttress was a large Black woman in her mid-fifties with inflexible brown skin as smooth as beaten cake batter. Her fish eyes swimming in her brown face seemed to know nothing and everything at once. Windows to the soul, some like to say, but Mrs. Buttress's eyes seemed like windows to nowhere.

"How are you, Mrs. Buttress?" Kendra said.

The woman folded her arms across her ample chest. "I'm getting along and if you can call getting along fine, I guess I'm fine."

"That's good," Kendra said. She nodded and turned to go.

"But there is a small matter of the rent."

This stopped Kendra in her tracks. It was no small matter, Kendra wanted to say. It was no small matter at all. What little money she had ran out the first few weeks she was back in Dunhill. Most of it went on the security deposit and the first and last month's rent for this hell hole. She worked at a nursing home for

a while, then at the library, but those were only temporary positions and didn't pay much. Now, Kendra wasn't doing much of
anything except hunting Luke.

"You are a good six weeks behind now," said Mrs. Buttress, dark
eyes accusing or understanding. Take your pick.

"I understand, Mrs. Buttress. I can get you the rent."

"How?" the woman challenged. "You are not practicing." Mrs.
Buttress glanced at the red plastic watch encircling her fat wrist.
"It's two in the afternoon; you can't be working unless you have a
night shift somewhere."

Kendra shifted her weight onto her left foot, rubbed both hands
down the sides of her jeans. No, she was not practicing; unless you
could call the odd jobs she did around the apartments practicing.
She diagnosed the flu, helped people decide whether or not to go
to the doctor or stay in bed a day or two longer. She took out
stitches here and there. But no, she did not practice, not for
money, anyway. Not knowing what to say, Kendra repeated her last
statement.

"I can get you the rent," she said.

Mrs. Buttress nodded with a skeptical look on her brown face,
which told Kendra that she did not believe her. She did not believe
her in the least little bit.

"I'm not running a charity, Dr. Hamilton," Mrs. Buttress said,
arms still folded, face as hard as stone. "But I can see that you have
fallen on hard times. You may stay two more weeks. If you don't
have the rent by that time, you may leave."

"... but ..." Kendra protested. Two weeks. How was she to
come up with nine hundred and fifty dollars in two weeks?

Mrs. Buttress lifted her hand, palm up, into Kendra's face.

"I've been running this apartment for a long time, years, Dr.
Hamilton," she said. "I've heard it all. Everything to I'll get a job,
pawn my guitar, sell my left kidney or donate blood just to stay a
little longer. But over the years, those types of people never came
through."

"What type of people?" Kendra asked.

"Those types of people like you, Dr. Hamilton," she answered.
"Those types of people with something else on their mind, something else holding them down so they don't think about nothing
else except what they want."

Anger flickered in Kendra's gut. She tensed, was about to speak when Mrs. Buttress spoke again.

"What is it that you want, Kendra Hamilton?" she said. "What is it that keeps you out until one or two in the morning, makes you so tired that you can't get up before two to look for a job?"

"I don't think that's any of your business," Kendra answered.

"No." Mrs. Buttress shook her head. "It ain't none of my business. The rent is my business. And if I don't have it in two weeks, you may leave."

With that, she planted a square heel on the shit brown carpet as low as dirt and left a dumbfounded Kendra standing in an empty hallway.

The new chief of homicide for the Dunhill County Sheriff's Department was Gregory Atfield. Beau Blair, the hero cop who had taken Rich's place when he left, lasted only two months before asking, yes, asking, for a demotion. The pressure overtook his heart and soon after he was out on medical leave playing cards in the park with old men in straw hats.

To Kendra Hamilton, Gregory Atfield was a friend. Even before she had gone to Luke's intent upon killing him she had called Gregory Atfield for answers. But of course, she had to leave a message. He had gone home by then. Thoughts of Anna had flown from her mind like birds on the wind. Anna would be fine. The rapist, the girl's father, was destined to live the rest of his life in custody. And now Kendra could focus on what she came to Dunhill to do.

"I heard you were back. I was so glad you called," Gregory said as she walked into his office.

Gregory Atfield came from behind his desk and grabbed both of Kendra's hands in his. She could feel the calluses on his farmer hands. Unlike those hands, the chief of homicide at the Sheriff's Department was elegant. Tall, lanky, fair skinned with gray eyes, wispy blonde hair and a quiet voice and attitude that earned him the nickname of "the priest." He used to work for Rich Marvel, back in the day, before Luke Bertrand was arrested for murder. When it looked like Luke was going to be convicted, everyone involved in capturing him became heroes. No one thought that Luke would fight back. Gregory was one of those heroes. Unlike Rich, he knew how to keep his hero status after Luke walked.

"Thank you for seeing me," Kendra said, pulling her hands from his.

"Please, sit down," he said.

He walked back behind his desk and sat in a black leather chair.

"This is a far cry from the hell hole you used to be in," Kendra said, smiling, trying to sound cheerful.

Gregory smiled a lazy smile that placed a small light in his calm gray eyes.

"What can I say," he said. "Homicide is coming up in the world. Some would say it's even sexy. Besides, the new chief couldn't keep the entire department in the basement. Not forever, anyway."

Kendra nodded, removing the purse from her shoulder and placing it on the edge of Gregory's desk. The weight of the Smith & Wesson caused the purse to sit heavily on its bottom. The top of the bag fell over and knocked several papers from Gregory's desk. She bent down to pick them up. But Kendra didn't miss Gregory's eyes flickering to the purse, to the heavy weight at the bottom and back to Kendra's face.

But he said nothing about what might be in it, which would have been perfectly natural since Kendra Hamilton hardly ever carried a purse. She preferred instead to keep a wallet stuck in the back pocket of her jeans.

Under Gregory's intent gaze, she smoothed a spiral curl out of her face and twisted it behind her ear. She swallowed and touched her throat. Besides the chill outside, the office felt warm. Sweat bubbled on her forehead.

"Even though it is good to see you, Kendra, I wish I could say that you looked great," he said.

Kendra smiled. "Don't worry about me."

Her voice sounded too bright. If she had heard that same voice coming from a patient she would have immediately ordered a psych consult. She slumped back in her seat and decided that truth was a better offense.

"Actually," she said quietly, "I'm going through hell."

She lifted a hand and wiped the sweat from her brow, wiped it on the legs of her jeans. She took the water Gregory had placed in front of her. It was warm but wet and tasted good. It helped to ground her, to help her remember why she was here.

"Are you ill?" Gregory asked.

"Yes," then, "no. I don't know."

"Have you seen Rich?" he asked.

She looked up at him, trying to read his face and finding that she was no better at reading his face than reading the landlady's. Finally, she nodded.

"Yes," she said. "I have. I'm afraid it didn't go too well."

He laughed a little and took a sip of his own water. "Did you expect it to?"

Kendra let out a laugh. "Not really. Of course not. I don't know what I was thinking."

"I'd like to think your decision to go see him means that you were thinking rationally," he stopped. "For a change."

Kendra laughed fully now. She knew that Gregory did not approve of her leaving the country or leaving Rich. After she recovered from the gunshot wound, Gregory begged her on more than one occasion to go get help, to talk to someone. But she refused, insisting that she was okay.

"And I thought when you greeted me so warmly that we would have a good visit," she said, still laughing. "Without your nagging."

But the look on his face was serious. "I'm glad you are back, at any rate," he said. "Where have you been?"

"Where have I been today, the last few weeks, or the last year or so, Gregory? Which is it?"

He chuckled. "I was asking about the past two years, Kendra." He held up two fingers. "You've been gone for two years. You've cut yourself off from everyone for two. Not one or one and a half. Don't sugar coat it."

Gregory was right. She had been gone at least two years but it just didn't seem that long. She met his eyes but didn't answer him, not right away, anyway. Instead, lines kept running through her head. *Little girl, little girl where have you been, I've been to London to see the queen.* Where was that from? *The Owl and the Pussycat,* some nursery rhyme that was never recited to her but perhaps something that she recited to other children. Yes, that's it. But she had not been to London to see the queen, not at all. Kendra Hamilton had spent the last eight months in Northern Sudan in a refugee camp. Not having a medical license had not mattered to the people she worked for. They did only the most cursory of checks.

Where have you been, Kendra? She thought about answering Gregory's question, wanted to answer, but just couldn't. She just couldn't tell Gregory where she had been because no matter how far away she was from her hometown, her heart was always in Dunhill. This place would keep pulling her back as long as Luke was free. *Little girl, little girl, where have you been. Gathering roses to give to the queen.* Violet was her queen and the roses she would lay on the bank of the Sacramento River would surround Luke Bertrand's head on a silver platter.

So she tells Gregory, gathering roses to give to the queen. Gregory cocks his head, laughs a little, "What?" he says.

Kendra chuckles, looks at her hands in her lap, and says with a noncommittal shrug of her shoulders, nowhere, everywhere.

Gregory sat quietly, as he had always, and waited. But this time, Kendra would outlast him. She would not tell him where she had been though the place, the refugee camp, crowded, dark, dank lay just beneath the surface of the quiet madness that was her hometown.

"Kendra," Gregory said. "Are you all right?"

She licked her lips. Her mouth was hot and dry. She reached for the water, only to find that Gregory had beaten her to it. He held out the glass. She took it and drank. Gregory slipped a cool hand onto her forehead.

"You are a little warm. You must have a fever of a hundred. You are getting sick, Kendra."

She pushed his wrist away. "I'm fine."

Gregory stared at her for a minute or two. Behind his gaze, Kendra knew that a metronome clicked steadily. She could see that he had not quite decided what to do with her but he would let the matter drop.

"I see," Gregory said finally. "Do you think it was wise of you to come back to Dunhill, considering?"

Kendra shrugged. "Where else was I to go? And besides, this place is like a narcotic. I can't help but keep coming back."

"That it is," Gregory agreed.

Kendra looked at his hands, still ringless. "So, are you seeing anyone, Gregory?"

He shook his head, "Nope. Too busy." Back at his desk, he folded his hands behind his head. "If I didn't think Rich would kick my ass, I'd ask you out."

Kendra laughed. "Yeah, right," she said, still laughing, "Rich's ass-kicking days in regards to me are over."

"Or you'd like to think," Gregory said.

Kendra stood up and paced the floor. "I don't want to talk about Rich, Gregory," she said. "I didn't come here to talk about Rich."

"I know," he said. "I know why you are here."

Kendra's breath caught in her throat. A mental picture flashed in her mind, the one in which she stood beside Luke's bed with a .357 Magnum pointed at his head.

"How could you know?" she breathed.

It was Gregory's turn to shrug.

"It's in all the papers, your involvement with this girl, the family. Luke's involvement and what he said about you. I've heard a couple of things about that. He never could keep his big mouth shut, could he?"

Kendra's beating heart slowed down. She laughed deep in her throat so he wouldn't hear. Of course he would think it was the girl. Weren't hard cases her specialty? It used to be April Hart, now it was Anna Cotton. April, Anna, they all started to sound the same to her. The entire damn world needed saving and she was just on the A's. But what Gregory couldn't know was that she was way past that, she was way past that and had moved from the world to the personal.

Gregory started to say something else but Kendra's twisted smile stopped him.

"Kendra," he said slowly. "This is about the girl, isn't it? This is about Anna Cotton and her father."

With her eyes burned into him, Kendra shook her head. "It has nothing to do with her."

"Then, what is it?" Gregory asked. He stood up.

Kendra could tell by the warlike stance of his body that he knew exactly what it was and was not pleased about it.

"It's about Luke Bertrand," she confirmed.

"What about him?" he asked as his thin lips disappeared in his face, now pasty with wariness.

Kendra leaned forward in her seat. Her forehead felt hot, like it was the middle of summer. The furnace sputtered, singeing the cool air in the office.

"How far back did the DA go when he looked into Luke's past?" Kendra asked him now.

Gregory took a step back. He folded his lanky frame into the leather chair once again and made a church steeple of his fingers.

He pointed at her. "Leave it alone," he warned.

"Come on, Gregory, how far? Ten years, twenty?"

"Far enough," he said.

"How far is far enough, Gregory?" Kendra pressed.

"They could find nothing," Gregory said.

"Or they didn't want to find anything," Kendra said with bitterness in her voice.

"What are you getting at?"

"Did anyone check out where Luke went to college? Talk to his old classmates? Find out if he had a girlfriend."

This time, Gregory laughed. "That had to have been thirty years ago, if not longer. Why does it matter, Kendra?"

"I want to know, Gregory," she said. "I think there is something there."

"And I think you are sick," Gregory answered.

"No . . ." She began to stand up.

He put his hand up to stop her. He got up and once again pressed her back in her seat.

"You are sweating like it's a hundred degrees outside, and it's freezing if not colder. Your eyes are glassy; you can pack a two week cruise in the bags under them."

Kendra sat back down, her chest caving in like Gregory had just punched her. "I'm not sick," she said in a monotone.

He raised an eyebrow, a habit she despised. It reminded her so much of Rich.

"Even if I am," she said, "I think I still have something here."

"What you have," Gregory said, "is a case of desperation. You need to let it go, Kendra. Get on with your life."

"I am getting on with my life!" She didn't realize that she had shouted until she jumped to her feet. Hysterical, but she could not stop herself. "I am getting on with my life and the way I choose to get along with my life is to see that bastard in jail."

"What about Anna Cotton?" Gregory asked. "What's your involvement with that case?"

"Don't change the subject," Kendra snapped.

"I'm not changing the subject, I'm just curious."

Kendra sighed. "Anna is a child who likes me, that's all. She doesn't need any more heroes, she has her father."

"Who has been accused of rape," Gregory reminded her.

"If not her father, then Rich," Kendra said. "She has Rich now."

"What about Leroy Cotton?" he asked her.

"He's made it clear that he doesn't want anything to do with me, Gregory," Kendra answered.

"Never stopped you before," he said.

"What are you saying?" she asked him.

"I'm saying to let go of Luke Bertrand. Find a new obsession, something you can do some good with."

Kendra stood up and grabbed her purse from the desk. With the loaded gun thumping against her side, she stared at Gregory.

"I'm not looking for a new obsession and I'm certainly not looking for anything I can do some good with," she told him.

"Then what are you looking for?" he asked her.

"Payback, Gregory," she said. "I'm looking for payback."

Anna

I was chosen to live without dread of slaughter. Anna remembered the line from Sylvia's poem, her sayings. Anna did not know what dread meant but she knew slaughter; she knew slaughter meant warm blood, death, to be eaten. Way back, when they live in that other place, her father would slaughter the animals, the pig, the chicken, and they would eat, sometime for days depending on what animal he decided to slaughter. Pig, they eat for days, chicken, a day. So, if slaughter mean death, dread must mean fear. Anna feel fear. It crawls, knock against her belly. Fear make certain smells and Anna throw up. It make the nurses, the nice ones even, turn away whisper things they don't think she hear. Pregnant. Rape. Force. Father.

Rape, that what they call it. Anna don't know what that mean either, but she bet, like slaughter, it had something to do with fear. She remembered way back when her mother was alive, before she went away, her father took Anna to slaughter. Hog too old, he told her. Hog got to go. Then she didn't know what it meant. Anna just happy to go somewhere.

They drive to a field, yellow weeds all around the sky as blue as a petunia petal. Anna sit up front in the old truck. Old truck fender bitten off, and rust circles on the hood. And when her daddy drive it, it make hard sounds, sound like an old hog trying to breathe but can't, sound like the old hog he had tied up on the flatbed. Anna scoot close to her daddy 'cause she was afraid of the axe, the axe leaning against the door. Even though the blade point down, Anna did not like the wooden handle scrape against her leg. Anna pull her blue shorts down to cover her leg, push the axe against the door.

Her daddy cover the dangerous part, the part he sharpened till each side of the blade turn silver. He had the two color part wrapped up in an ole house towel, grease stained and 'bout to be throwed away. Later, he tell Anna he wished he had a gun, he wished he had one even though Daddy don't like guns. But a gun would be better.

So they stop nowhere, in a brown field with weak dirt and gravel. Nothing grow here, Daddy tell Anna. This field, this part of their farm fallow. Anna get out of the truck. Daddy get out too, open the gate to the flatbed and lead the hog out. Hog teats scrap ground, she sag and her steps come slow and thumping, remind Anna of an old tired giant. Sleepy-eyed, head lolling. Daddy let the hog go but she don't run away. Just stand in that empty field, gravel and dirt that won't grow nothing. Her hog eyes just looked all around, her tired head just move from side to side.

Daddy got the axe from the side of the truck. He pull it out the truck like he was pulling a weed out of its hole, the ole house towel flapped, still caught around it like them roots that dangle. Axe in his right hand, he went around the back of the truck, took out a sack of feed.

Anna scared now. The axe made Anna scared, but the hog paid no never mind, just took a baby step forward, sniffed the brown ground. But Anna heart thumped, and her eyes watered real bad. She asked Daddy what happening, but Daddy don't answer. His face was all mud hard, like he mad at something, though Anna did not know what.

CHAPTER 17

Flowers bloomed outside the Dunhill County Sheriff's Department. Rich did not usually know the names of flowers but he did know their color. The flowers blooming on bushes of thick green leaves, petals as thick as cabbage leaves, flung reds and pinks against the slate gray sky almost daring the rain to drench that fury of color. But the weather had calmed since the storm, the air wet but not soaking.

Rich did not tell Gregory that he was coming to visit him. He thought that it should be a surprise to Gregory since it was somewhat of a surprise to Rich himself. He had not been back to the Dunhill sheriff's department since he packed a box with the baseball, forged signature and all, a glass framed photograph of his ex-fiancée and a few other desk trinkets not worth mentioning. He'd like to say that he packed his bags without looking back, but looking back he did and that turned out to be a crucial mistake.

Not only did he look back, he went back. But he didn't return with permission or as chief of homicide, but, as the then and now Captain Freehold liked to put it, as chief vigilante. He, Kendra Hamilton and Gregory Atfield pursued Luke Bertrand with the same fury as the flowers blooming against the sky of a dying winter. And they almost got him. Almost. Luke claimed temporary insanity, brain cancer, senility, fucked up childhood, you name it. But in the end, he got away with it and that ended Rich's career as chief of anything, let alone chief of homicide.

But he did not give a damn then, did he? He did not give a damn because he 'got the girl.' He thought he would start his own business, private detective, maybe go into consulting. Being a cop had ceased to mean anything to him after that business. Kendra, though, she had different ideas. She left him and, left to himself, Rich floundered for a while. Still floundering, Dom would say. Who knows, perhaps he was right. And perhaps Kendra Hamilton's reentry into his already complicated existence would send him floundering further down like a leaf on top of a rushing river.

Rich made his way through the front office of the sheriff's department unnoticed. He slipped to the right of the stairway entrance and, once inside the main double glass doors, he started to Gregory's new office. Homicide occupied the east wing of the second floor. Rich entered and saw that his old department looked like a real office, a cube farm with four cubicles—three for the detectives and one—the one at the front with low walls—for the administrative assistant. Beau Blair, like Rich, did not last long once the department moved into the light. Embarrassed by the constant teasing, the sly looks at letting one of the biggest catches of all time go—Beau was acting when it happened, after all—he packed his things in a box, his bolo tie, cowboy boots and left. Last time he talked to Gregory, he said that Beau had given up law enforcement altogether.

The front desk was empty. A man with a pitted face and a big gut glanced at Rich as he walked further into the office. Rich worked a couple of cases with Kramer before he left the sheriff's department. Kramer was an okay guy, but abrupt, with a distaste for small talk and formality.

"Can I help you?" Kramer said around the wad of gum in his mouth.

"Naw, man," Rich said. "I'm here to see Gregory Atfield."

Throwing a thumb over his shoulder, Kramer said, "straight back" and "nice to see you, man, we missed you," before glancing back at the case file on his desk. Rich saw then that the administrative assistant, who had not acknowledged him, was helping Kramer with the file, two white typewritten pages crushed in her small white hands. Her brown hair was frizzled, she had bags under her eyes and a yellow pencil stuck behind her ear. Rich glanced at Kramer's desk. Manila file folders, some thick as dictionaries, others slim, monopolized the entire surround of the cubicle, barely leaving enough room for the flat screen computer. The keyboard was precariously parked against the cubicle wall. Kramer cursed as his feet shifted, knocking over a modest but awkward pile of folders stacked on the floor. Rich swallowed, knowing that each one of the file folders represented a death, a murder. A beginning for some, hopefully, a beginning for a long stay in prison, and an ending for others. Rich saw that it was the same old homicide department that he left, a department trying to care for a county in love with its own demise.

Rich knocked on the door of Gregory's office. Gregory hugged Rich when he saw him, not a polite hug, but a real hug, pulling him inside the office, clearing a space for him to sit down.

"Sorry about this," he said. "If I'd known you were coming, I'd have cleaned the place up for you, old man."

Rich waved a hand at him to indicate that he did not give a damn about how dirty or clean the place was. He sat down, looked around. An oak desk and a coffee table with a blue and white igloo sitting off to one side occupied the room. Gregory sat down as well, put his lanky legs on his disordered desk. Tall, narrow windows let in the late afternoon sun. The tint used on the window grayed the light that fell in rectangular slabs across the desk and across Rich's face.

"Must be a day for visits from old friends," Gregory Atfield said.

"What do you mean?" Rich asked.

Then Gregory told him that Kendra had visited earlier that day. Rich's heart stopped at the sound of her name. He was about to ask for what when Gregory told him that she had some bug up her butt about Luke Bertrand and that she was packing.

"Packing?" Rich asked. "Packing what?"

"She had a weapon with her," Gregory answered.

"But she hates guns," Rich said.

"Until you convinced her to take one after the Luke mess. Didn't you give her one, teach her to use it?"

"Look," Rich said. "I can't think about this now. There is too much other shit going on. Kendra is going to do what she's going to do."

"Aren't you worried?" Gregory asked.

"I don't have time to be worried. What's all this, man?" Rich asked, waving his hand around Gregory's office and desperate to change the subject.

"Some of it's new, a lot of them are cold cases. You know those murders Sheriff Freehold said he would clear in those campaign promises?"

Rich nodded, "Yeah," he said.

"Well, since you left us, Sheriff Freehold's replacement is actually holding us to it."

"How is it going?" Rich asked, making sure he intoned his voice with the right amount of disinterest, which did not fool Gregory Atfield for a minute.

"Lousy," he said. "Could use some help," he said simply.

Rich snorted. "You mean, drop to my knees and beg Sheriff Asshole for my job back?"

Gregory did not crack a smile, his thin lips remained a narrow slit in his face, his gray eyes as watchful as a cat. Instead, he said, "You wouldn't necessarily have to fall to your knees."

Rich studied him. Gregory had dropped his eyes. Blue veins crisscrossed the thin lids. Was he really asking Rich to come back to the sheriff's department? Rich did not know that. He only knew that his old friend looked tired, defeated.

Rich uncrossed his legs. They had begun to ache. He put both hands on his knees, shook his head emphatically. "No," he said. "I have my pride, Gregory."

"Pride," Gregory said, just as emphatically, "is cold and lonely. In the end, it gets you nowhere. I'd thought you would have learned that by now."

Gregory's words did not offend Rich, only made him wonder. He had not seen Gregory Atfield in, what was it, two, maybe three, months. And here they were jumping headlong into the same conversation they had every time they met, including the last time when they chanced upon each other in a downtown Dunhill restaurant. They never began the discussions with the usual niceties. Rich missed the niceties.

"Whatever happened to how are you, how have you been, how is the family?"

Gregory's narrow mouth broke into a grin. "How are you, how have you been, how is Kendra?"

Rich laughed then. "You are an asshole, man," he said.

Gregory shrugged. "I do what I can."

The silence in the room stretched like the silk of a long spider's string. Gregory's eyes were covered by his thin lids again, blue veins, crow's feet a map. Rich could see that Gregory was about to launch into something again. He had something to tell him. For some reason, Rich cut him off, did not want to hear what Gregory had to say. Later, he would tell himself that he didn't want Gregory to go off into the second part of their long-standing conversation, the ones that began with, so when are you and Kendra going to come to your senses?

"How are you?" Rich asked, to show him that no matter what, he still had manners. And to show him that there were no hard feelings, but the last remark, "how's Kendra," caused a twinge in his gut, the onset of heartburn.

Gregory frowned. His head danced back and forth on his slender neck. "All right," he said. "I guess."

"You liking it here?" Rich asked.

"As much as anybody likes it anywhere," he answered.

"I see."

"Though it's great to see you, Rich," Gregory said. "I can't believe that this is primarily a social call."

Rich admitted that it was not. His call was not social but he hardly had the words out of his mouth before Gregory laughed. He stood up before Rich finished speaking, lifted the top of the blue and white igloo. He pushed aside a cellophane wrapped sandwich and took out a bottle of Arrowhead water. He dipped the cap toward Rich who shook his head at the offer. Rich had had enough of water, had ingested enough water since his last hangover that it surprised him that the stuff did not flow from his toes.

"The detectives," Gregory Atfield said, his voice as quiet as the wind blowing through the flowers at his windows, the same wind attempting to coax away a dying winter, "are Bill Thomas and Fred Moore . . ."

Rich's laugh cut him off. Gregory's answer did not surprise him.

He had not expected cooperation, even from an old friend, a former partner and roommate. After all, it was official. Rich was an outsider, relegated to behind the glass doors. So what that he knew about the stairway door tucked just inside the main entrance. He knew how to slip in and out, unnoticed, and maybe was able to get to the new office. But in the end, he did not belong. He would have responded the same way were he in Gregory's big-ass shoes.

Rich raised both his hands, palms up toward the ceiling.

"Come on, man," he said. "Give a brother a break."

Gregory's Adam's apple bobbed up and down as he chugged the Arrowhead straight from the bottle. His hands did not shake. His voice remained steady.

"I can't go there, Rich," he said. "I can tell you who is working on the Anna Cotton case but your firm will have to get the information from the detectives working it."

"Don't you think we tried that?"

Gregory's blonde eyebrow lifted. "We?" he said.

"Well, Carlyle has. They wouldn't tell him shit."

Gregory brought the water back to his desk. Laughing, he said, "You really didn't expect them or anyone to tell that barrel-chested redheaded wonder anything did you? He was about as smooth as a bull in a china shop."

"So he pissed off some people . . ."

Gregory flipped the white cap from the Arrowhead into the garbage can. "He not only pissed off some people, Rich," he said. "He pissed off the wrong people, mainly Bill and Fred."

"How?" Rich asked, though he could guess.

"How do you think?" Gregory read his mind. "Throwing around Thomas Brighton's name, acting like he was the redheaded rooster of the chicken coop."

Rich put his hand over his eyes, briefly believing that Gregory was not going to tell him anything. But only briefly. He knew Gregory too well. He would eventually give in.

"You really don't like him, do you?"

"I do not."

"So he got to you, too, not just the detectives working the case?"

The shadows lengthened with the silence in the room. Gregory regarded Rich, his eyes unblinking and steady. "All I will say is that you will need to watch your back with that one, Rich." He stopped, letting the silence play before going on. "More than you did with Beau Blair."

Rich nodded, wanted to ask what Gregory meant but not wanting to hear the answer. Instead he said, "I'm not Jared Carlyle."

"So you are not." Gregory smiled. "But I still can't tell you anything."

"Because you can't or won't?"

"Can't and shouldn't is more like it."

"How do you mean?"

"First of all I don't know anything. The two detectives on the case are silent as graves. They are keeping their mouths shut."

"Why?" Rich asked.

"Orders, I suppose," Gregory answered.

"To you or everybody?" Rich asked as the room grew darker. Clouds had gathered once again in the Dunhill sky.

"Everyone but especially to me. Because of the history, you know."

"Because of the Luke Bertrand connection?" Rich asked.

"Yes," Gregory confirmed.

Rich nodded, thinking, but not saying, that he understood. He wanted to ask Gregory if had seen Luke Bertrand since he was acquitted and did not know the words were out of his mouth, that he had actually spoken them aloud until Gregory answered him.

"Though he's been kicked off most boards, like Brighton House, as you know, I think he is an ex-officio member on the board at the hospital. But the man has gone underground, Rich. He's like a phantom, hasn't been seen or heard from in months except for those outrageous statements about your ex-girlfriend."

"You keeping an eye on his place?" Rich asked, thinking how Luke had kidnapped young girls, pregnant, imprisoning them among the rusted equipment in his garden shed for months, only letting them go once they had given birth, then poisoning the girls, tempting them with spiked heroin which if they took it, caused them to die.

"Off the record?" Gregory asked.

"Everything is off the record with us, you know that, man," Rich said.

"Then off the record, I am. I send a unit up there every now and then. Had to be careful because he's caught a couple of them sometimes. His lawyer screamed harassment and got an injunction."

Rich grunted. "Crazy ass . . ."

Gregory put up his hand before Rich could continue.

"I hear he always wears white," Rich said.

Gregory laughed, "Don't believe everything you hear, or read. The tabloids are elevating old Luke to cult status. He doesn't always wear white, and contrary to popular belief, black horns do not protrude from his forehead. But he has become somewhat of a celebrity."

Rich sighed, disgusted. "Fan mail," he said.

"Fan mail," Gregory agreed. "Lots of it. He has to send someone to pick it up from the post office in boxes."

"So Dunhill thinks he is some sort of a hero?" Rich asked.

Gregory lifted a finger. "Be careful, Rich," he said. "It's not only Dunhill. He gets fan mail from all over the United States. Some think that he's a hero for what he has done. He saved many children."

"By making murder okay? Palatable?"

". . . Ah, but was it murder? Twelve people disagree with you."

Rich swiveled around to look for a light switch. "You are freaking me out, man. Where are the lights?" It was full dark now. Outside, the wind kicked up, oleander branches scraped against Gregory's window.

"I didn't come here to talk about Luke Bertrand," Rich said as light flooded the room. "I came to talk about Anna Cotton."

Gregory rubbed his eyes, sighed. "I know you did, Rich, knew you did from the moment I saw you. But I don't know anything. You probably know more than I do."

"I doubt that," Rich said.

"Then tell me what you do know," Gregory said. "Anyway, Kendra tells me that Leroy's confessed."

"Come on, man," Rich said.

"Okay, okay. Do you believe that he did it?"

Rich stood up. "I don't know. I didn't get a chance to talk to him before he got really sick." He turned to look at Gregory. "But I have a feeling that he isn't good for it."

"Oh?" Gregory said, the tuna sandwich stopping just short of his mouth. "You have someone else in mind?"

Rich nodded, thinking of Brandon Chadwick. His scrubbed apple-shaped face and his blonde-tipped hair floated in his mind. He told Gregory about him. Wiping his fingers with a napkin, Gregory said, "Job hopping, being clean is not a crime Rich."

"No, no it's not," Rich agreed. "But I can look at this sick fuck and tell that he had something to do with this. Have Moore and Thomas found out anything about him?"

"I can't tell you that, old man. Besides," Gregory said, "it won't do either one of us any good to have you and Carlyle interfering with this investigation. I can't even believe that you, of all people, Rich, are even considering doing that."

"Gregory," Rich said, tired now. "Save the damn lecture, please. I know you said Thomas and Moore have been really quiet about the Cotton rape but you have to have heard some scuttlebutt."

Gregory's face was serious. "I have." He stopped at the statement.

"Well," Rich said. "You going to clue me in?"

"Sit down, Rich," Gregory said.

When Rich sat down Gregory said, "Whatever I'm about to tell you now is just between us. If you tell anyone where you heard it from, I'll deny it. Do you hear me?"

Rich nodded. Yes, he heard him but did not believe him. Gregory Atfield was one of the most honest men that Rich knew. Gregory described the scuttlebutt, as Rich put it. The talk around the water cooler, the chatter at The Courtroom Bar and Grill, the gossiping in the hallway was that Thomas and Moore were not only ordered to keep quiet about the case, they were also ordered to clear it as quickly as possible. The new Sheriff Freehold, or Asshole, whichever name Rich preferred, demanded that they find a rapist. Period. He was getting pressure from somewhere, maybe Luke Bertrand, but more likely Thomas Brighton.

Further, it was rumored that Leroy Cotton, the man who raped his own daughter and fathered his own grandchild, was impotent. No one could get a rise out of him since he was told that Anna, his first and only child, was retarded. It was well documented in Leroy's medical records that his doctor had prescribed Viagra, a prescription for which he never filled. He could no more father a child than a Ken doll. How did they expect to get away with it, Thomas and Moore, how did they expect to get away with a rapist who could not get it up? Easy. Instead of trying to find out who really raped Anna Cotton, they were scouring the country for experts who would testify that perhaps Leroy Cotton could not get it up for his wife because he was saving it for his daughter.

Rich left Gregory's office with a hollow feeling in his stomach as if someone had punched him. It sickened him, what Gregory had told him, even though Rich knew why he was the lucky recipient of such information. By telling him, Gregory wanted him to do something about it. And the fact that he told him and not Carlyle meant that he wanted Rich to do it. Gregory would risk his new position at homicide if he made a stink about the new sheriff's foray into squalor. Rich could see him ponder the alternatives. If Gregory were fired he could not continue to do what he lived to do, catch criminals. But Rich, he was already fired. He had freedom and, as the old saying went, nothing else to lose.

CHAPTER 18

Since Rich started drinking, what was it, about two years ago when he realized that his life would never go back to normal, whatever normal really was, he became quite adept in putting things out of his mind. He simply did not think about them. But ever since he saw Kendra standing on the edge of that crystalline lake in Tahoe, he could not get her out of his mind. No matter how much he tried to drown the image, it was there poking at him like a sharp stick. He told himself many times that he didn't care, but after his meeting with Gregory, after hearing about the heavy object on the bottom of her purse, he had become worried about her. Worried about what she might do or was planning to do. He did still care and that was that. And the more her face floated in his mind, the more he did not want to drown that image in alcohol. Gregory did not even ask him if he wanted the address, simply wrote Kendra's address on a yellow Post-It note and handed to him, his eyes gray and solemn. Rich didn't bother to tell Gregory that he already had the address, had made it his business to know the minute he got back from Tahoe.

But he decided, this time, care or not care, that he would not drop everything and run after her like a dog in heat. He decided that he would be cooler this time. And part of his plan at being cooler was not to drive like a bat out of hell to her apartment to see what in the hell she was up to. Instead, he went back to his office, updated Carlyle and plunged into work. When he looked at his watch several hours later, he saw that it was almost ten P.M. Kendra Hamilton could wait until the morning.

But thirty minutes later, his resolve shredded like so much ribbon, he found himself pulling into the parking lot of The Liberty Apartments. He sat in his car for a minute or two. It was a new car, a tan Monte Carlo with leather interior and a global positioning system in case he got lost. The damn thing talked to him, told him when he was too close to another car and alerted others when he backed up. He missed the Firebird. Drumming his fingers on the steering wheel, he debated starting the car back up and getting the hell out of there. But he couldn't do that. And when the butterflies in his belly quieted, he left the car and walked to her door.

He knocked. She did not answer. He knocked again, pressed his ear against the door but she still did not answer. Taking a deep breath, he knocked again and called her name. She answered wearing an oversize T-shirt and a pair of faded jeans. She did not have any shoes on her feet even though he could feel the chilly air emanate from the apartment. But despite the temperature, Rich saw that Kendra's smooth brown face was moist and her eyes had a fevered look. She peered at him, curious.

"What are you doing here?" she asked. "How did you know where to find me? For that matter, how did you get my number?"

Rich didn't wait to be invited in. He pushed past her into the apartment, demanding to know where she had been.

"I've been calling you all day," he said when she didn't answer. "Where have you been?"

Kendra smiled. "That seems to be the question of the day. How did you find me?"

Rich faced her. His hands rested on his hips inside his sports coat. He wanted to shake her. He was about to say something else but the room stopped him. Slowly he turned around in a circle, his eyes filled with the jumble of magazines, photos, and clippings of newspaper articles around him.

"What the hell . . ." he whispered.

Kendra stared at him with her arms folded across her chest. "I don't remember inviting you in," she said.

He wanted to tell her that he didn't remember inviting her in either, back into his life, that is, but there she was. But he was too distracted by the chaos around him. Papers and magazine articles were strewn on the love seat, across the wooden floor, and covered what he could see of the kitchen table. And light from three lamps and the overhead illuminated the entire mess, setting it all ablaze in white and yellow light.

He walked over to the kitchen table and picked up a *Jet* magazine. A young Luke Bertrand, hardly a wrinkle on his brown face, started at him. The caption read, *Luke Bertrand triumphs in Dunhill County*. Rich flipped through another magazine, his heart thumping. He looked at Kendra. Her eyes were unreadable.

"What the hell are you doing?" he asked.

She walked over to him and reached for the magazine. He snatched it away before she could grab it.

"Answer me, Kendra," he demanded.

"It's none of your business, Rich," she said.

"If it has to do with Luke Bertrand, it is my business." He twirled around again. "Where did you get all this shit?"

"Library, Rich," she said. "You've heard of those, haven't you?"

He didn't answer her, did not take the bait. And she was trying to bait him. He recognized it as an effort to push him away. Even before they became involved, Rich accused Kendra of treating him like a dumb jock. After they got together, the accusation became the basis for many arguments, especially when their relationship started deteriorating. He accused her of not talking to him about the shooting because she didn't think that he was smart enough to handle it.

"Don't play games with me, Kendra," he said.

"I'm not playing games with you," she responded.

She walked over and closed the front door. As she came back into the room, Rich felt a sensation of intense claustrophobia in the tiny apartment, And a sense of more déjà vu. Here they were, once again surrounded by Luke, letting him come between them in the same way that he had since they laid eyes on each other.

"Aren't you playing games?" he asked now, surprised at how tender his voice sounded in the bright room. He could tell by Kendra's widened eyes that she, too, was surprised by the sound of his voice.

"Look, I'm busy," she said. "Tell me what you want and get out."

He scratched the back of his head.

"Tell you what I want?" he responded. "You see, I would love to,

Kendra. But you won't hear it or see it. You are blind as a bat right now, aren't you? So why don't you tell me what you want, instead? Besides seeing me, why did you come back to Dunhill?"

She laughed a sound that seemed to scrape the back of her throat. "Still the same old Rich," she said. "Arrogant to the end."

Treading very carefully, Rich walked around the papers on the floor. He reached out and touched her face with the palm of his hand. She did not push away and seemed trapped by his eyes. Ignoring the pain of the past two years, the pain of her leaving which warned him to stay away if he did not want more of the same, he spoke.

"I let you down, didn't I, Kendra?" he said. "That's why you left."

"If I remember correctly, you shot me. That could really put a damper on any relationship, Rich," she said.

"That was an accident and you know it," he rasped. "I was trying to . . ."

". . . shoot Luke," she responded. "I know."

"And I let you down. You don't blame me for shooting you. You blame me for letting Luke walk. You think that's my fault."

He tried to read her face but it was impenetrable as a wall of steel. He didn't like the determined tilt of her eyes, the set form of her mouth. He especially did not like the words that came next. She pulled her face away from his hand but did not step back. He wondered if she was conscious of how close they really were to each other.

"You see, Rich. I don't blame you," she said. "It wasn't your fight to begin with. It was always mine but I abdicated responsibility. This has nothing to do with you."

"It has everything to do with me, with us," he corrected. "Or else you would have never come to the lake."

"Bullshit."

"Don't bullshit me," he said. "It's the truth. You don't need me to investigate this rape. It would have made more sense for you to go to Gregory than come to me, especially because of the way you left things with us. For once, let's stop playing games and work this thing out. We could put all of this behind us, Kendra. We could put all this behind us, leave Dunhill. This place is poison."

Looking at her now, he saw something that he hadn't seen in her face in a long time. It was a flash of hesitation, of consideration. He could almost see his words turning over on her fevered brain. For a split second, she was going to put it all behind her. But it was his own eagerness that outdid him. If he had only waited. He moved his hand across her back, the other one clutching her upper arm. Her face, as always, her face mesmerized him. Instead of heeding the warning in his head, he bent to kiss her. But that movement broke the spell. She pulled away from him. When she spoke next it was the new Kendra returning, the one whom he did not love and could never have.

"I'm through running, Rich," she said.

He snorted in disgust. "No, you are not. You're running now."

"I don't want to talk about this," she said.

"Yes, you do," he countered. "You do but you don't know how because of this, because of the obsession that you have with Luke."

"So what am I supposed to do?" she asked. "Forget about him?"

"Yes," Rich said. "Forget about him. He's not worth it. If you worry about anything, worry about Anna, about yourself. You are obviously sick."

"So all of a sudden you want to help Anna?" she spat.

"Yes," he said. "As a matter of fact, we both have an appointment to meet with her first thing in the morning."

"And if I choose not to be there?"

He walked to the door without looking at her, this time not treading carefully, this time crunching under his feet the smiling face of the many Luke Bertrands that she had collected.

"Oh, you will be there," he said. "You'll be there if I have to come by here and drag you there kicking and screaming."

Anna

Anna don't know why Daddy mad in that fallow field. She did know it was from this morning. She sat on the floor of the house, on the blue carpet, playing with her Barbie. Daddy sat on one side in a kitchen chair looking at her. Mamma sat on the other side, on the couch, looking at her, too. Both of they eyes look sad. Mamma eyes say she all alone, even though Anna and Daddy still in the room.

Later after Anna finished playing and put her Barbies back in they cases, Daddy come and tell Mamma he taking Anna for a ride. And that was okay with Anna until she see the axe with the two color blade, until she see the old oil-stained house towel Daddy wrapped around it.

Then they got in the old pickup, Daddy led the old hog onto the flatbed, then they rode out to this empty field. Anna went to stand next to the hog. She looked into the hoggy face, the tiny eyes, the hoggy snout that grunted and sniff her. Anna wondered why hog sniffed her when it was the hog that stank. She smell like spoiled grain.

Before she could ask anything, Daddy ask Anna to sit on the truck, to be still. Then he poured the feed on the empty ground, the ground that don't grow nothing. He poured it into a little pile all neat, like he was making a mountain, a tiny one they could all play with. The hog nudged his hand out the way 'fo Daddy could empty the bag out. It began to eat. Honking and squeezing his throat until little hoggy sounds come out. Daddy took a step back, watched the hog for a while.

Anna could not tell what went on with her daddy eyes. They black, like play beads, like lava rocks. Wrinkles deep, like rivers in his face. Anna was about to ask him what was wrong but he raised the axe high, high into the air, until it fell back. He swung it, grunting over his head and hit the hog on the back of the neck. Blood bust out every which way, red, like a red, red fountain. But the head did not come off, the hog head still stay on. And her daddy swore, goddammit, he said, goddammit, I wish I had a goddamn gun.

The hog grunted and the hoggy sounds became big, big and squealy and the hog tried running, but them feet too little. And they don't hold her, so she fall down, still making them big squealy sounds. Daddy walk over to the hog. Blood droplets all on his face, blood squelches on his shirt. His hand leave bloody fingerprints on the axe. He brought the axe up again. Both Anna and the hog, they scream. And the axe came down on the hog's neck. And it scream for just a little while, until the axe went clean through, and the head rolled off.

And screaming, Anna run, she run. Tears spurt from Anna's eyes, and she run zigzag through the brown dirt. Anna heart burst like surely the hog's heart must have been busting, so much blood coming out of the neck hole. Anna did not want to be that way, so she run, she run in the empty field that won't grow nothing no more, especially since it was being made so dirty by all that hog blood.

Daddy yelled, *Anna*, and started running after her. She looked behind her, the bloody thing chase her—bloody hog shirt, bloody hog face, bloody hog hands—so she keep running. *Anna*. He call again. He told her to stop, to calm down, everything all right. But Anna still run, she run until her heart stopped beating, and her stomach swelled up, and everything she ate that morning came streaming out. Not red, though, Anna vomit yellow.

Daddy caught her, put her in the truck. He took the insides out of the hog, turned it over, and it bled more in the dirt. He tied a rope around the neck, heaved the bleeding thing up on a tree, the only tree growing in that empty field. In the pickup, he told her that natural. Hog is food. *Bacon*, he said. *You like bacon, don't you? And fried pork chops?* Anna don't say nothing, she cry, her nose run snot. *Well, where do you think that stuff come from, chile?* he ask. *It's time you knew where that stuff come from. It's her destiny.*

He got her back to the house, clean himself up, clean her up. But they don't tell Mamma. Anna too scared. But Anna look up the word destiny in the dictionary. It wasn't in the one with pictures so she had to go to the big one, the red one with the gold writing, to find it. And in the little words she saw it, *destiny*. But Anna still don't know what it mean, it had words like predestination, conclusion, finality.

So she asked Mamma. Mamma, what's destiny. And Mamma answered without looking at her, like she was hardly paying attention. Destiny means things that are meant to happen, things that have to happen. Then Anna remember another word from the dictionary. Destiny meant doom. Doom she knew from the TV. Doom meant bad, doom meant dread and dread meant fear and fear meant slaughter.

And ever since that day, in the field with that hog that smelled her right before her destiny, Anna always felt funny on the back of her neck when her head was bent down, and she couldn't see her daddy. She couldn't see him, but she knew he was looking at her.

CHAPTER 19

The winter morning was cool but bright as Kendra walked what had to be the equivalent of a block to the front door of Brighton House. The sidewalks looked bleached to powder in the bright winter sun. Kendra passed a worm drying on the hot sidewalk; saw a lone black bird on a telephone wire, beak up, unimpressed by the desiccated worm below her.

"Sorry I'm late," Kendra said as she walked into the waiting room. Rich glanced at her, anger infused his face.

"Are you?" he asked.

"Yes," she confirmed. "I am, very sorry."

Very sorry I ever got involved with you, you asshole, she thought but for obvious reasons didn't say out loud. But she couldn't help but look at him fully, more so than she had ever done since seeing him at the lake. He looked much better. His hair was cut low again, not as low as when she first knew him, but low and edged perfectly. His skin was clear and smooth, brown and rich like sable. Looking at Rich now, it seemed that the tables had turned. When she saw him at the lake, she thought that he had been the hard case, the one who had sunk far below what either one of them thought that he could have, but it seemed that she was the one losing it all.

"Jared Carlyle," the man sitting next to Rich said.

He stood up, jutting a white hand at Kendra. He was a short

man, with shoulders like a barrel and a narrow white face like a bird's. Kendra took his hand, shook it.

"I'm investigating the rape for Mr. Thomas Brighton of Brighton House," he said importantly, sticking his hands in his pockets. Carlyle was well dressed in a designer suit, starched white collar with points as sharp as knives.

"You are investigating the rape?" Kendra asked. "But I thought . . ." she stopped. "So much for doing me a favor, Rich," she said. "You are doing this because you were ordered by Thomas Brighton."

He leaned close to her, to intimidate, and she stepped backward.

"You going all sentimental on me, now?" he said.

"Absolutely not," she countered. "But I'm not the one who mentioned favors."

"Just where the hell were you, anyway? Why were you so late?"

Kendra did not answer him. Instead, she sat a bag on the table, presents for Anna. Inside were a couple of puzzles, coloring books, a Black Barbie doll in a silver dress with a large, hooped skirt, a "diamond" in the slick black hair. Kendra was late because the car, the pink Fiesta that she had been driving since her return from Dunhill, the one from Rent-A-Wreck, had been picked up by the rental car company. She had to borrow Dominic's Miata for transportation and park it around back so Rich would not see her in it. After all, it was none of his business and she was in no mood for more lectures.

"You not answering me today?" Rich asked.

"I'm not answering you any, Rich," Kendra said. "Anyway, I did not come here so you can grill me on where I've been. We are not involved anymore. No need for you to track and trace my every movement."

"Look, folks," Carlyle interjected, and Kendra could hear in his voice an effort, a failed effort by the look on Rich's face, to placate. "Can we just keep the personal out of this?"

"There is nothing personal here," Rich said, his voice grim. "Right, Kendra?"

She looked at him, the seconds ticked by on the clock above the magazine rack in the waiting room. She noticed for the first time how small the room was and she just wanted out of it, wanted the meeting over so she could get on with what she needed to do.

"You are absolutely right, Rich," she said. "Nothing personal here, nothing personal at all."

Rich's features settled into stone. "So you want to tell me where you were?"

"I think we just established that where I've been is none of your business."

"Look you two," Carlyle said. "Can you save it until I'm out of here? I don't have relationships so I can avoid shit like this."

"You don't have relationships because you are too fucking ugly to find a girl," Rich said.

"Shut up," Carlyle answered, half laughing.

Kendra did not laugh, though. She sat on one of the brown sofas, crossed her legs and waited. Her only thought these last few days was finding the owner of that ring. She knew that if she found out that person's identity, she would find the answer to everything. She was sure of it.

"You with us, Kendra?" Rich asked, his voice somewhat gentle.

She didn't look at him. "Sure am," she said. He didn't answer her and finally, she forced herself to face him.

Rich was about to say something else; she could feel it, could see his body tensing, ready to plunge. The door swung open before he could speak. Dr. Katherine Holder walked in, her sensible square pumps scraping against the thin brown carpet. She shook everyone's hand, apologizing for keeping them waiting.

"Pretty Anna was napping, you see," she said.

Kendra winced at the nickname, was surprised that Katherine Holder used it. Color infused Holder's face.

"Oh, dear, I am sorry," she said. "I hate that name, too, but I just finished talking to one of the staff, and I'm afraid that little saying rubbed off. This way, please." She held the door open and the three of them filed out of the waiting area. Holder led them to her office.

"I know that this is a bit unorthodox," she said. "But I thought it would be better if we met in my office. Neutral territory and all."

"Is it?" Rich asked skeptically. "Neutral, I mean?"

Laughter from Holder sounded like a horse neighing. "I hope so," she said. "She's never been in here before."

All four of them had stopped outside of Katherine Holder's office door. Dr. Holder had a hand on the handle.

"And where will you be when we are finished?" Rich asked her in a casual voice.

Dr. Holder stammered. "I . . . I . . . Why I thought I'd join you."

In a way that Kendra remembered, Rich, still smiling, gently moved Dr. Holder aside. At least, Kendra thought, he had not lost most of his arrogance.

"That won't be necessary," he said. "We will contact you when we're done."

Before Katherine Holder could fully react, Rich had opened the door and ushered both Kendra and Carlyle into Dr. Holder's office as if they were entering an office belonging to him, Rich, and not Dr. Holder at all. Instead of following them into the office, Rich asked them to wait inside while he talked to Dr. Holder alone for a moment. Kendra knew that he did this just to keep Dr. Holder distracted about being kicked out of her own office.

Once the door closed behind Dr. Holder and Rich, Kendra looked around the office to avoid a conversation with Carlyle. She decided that she didn't like him. His puffed chest and his rooster strut played on her already fragile nerves.

The office was as bland as Kendra remembered. Aside from the two chairs facing Katherine's desk, there was an area with a love seat and two armchairs, plaid with wooden handrails. Rich returned alone. He didn't speak to her but nodded at Carlyle. When Kendra thought that her mind would explode with the tension in the room, Anna walked in with a CNA dressed all in white, his face cleaned and scrubbed as a new apple. Anna's head was down, her silken curls as dark as oil. She would not look at Chadwick and kept her arms tightly folded over her breast. Anna's mouth was poked out in a pout.

When Anna looked up and noticed them there, she pushed away from Chadwick so hard that he stumbled backward, almost falling.

"Hey," he protested. Kendra could see the man struggling to control the rage in his face.

"Anna don't like you," Anna spat at him.

A curious look came across Rich's face. Chadwick laughed an uneasy laugh as he glanced at Rich.

"She's been like this all day," he said. "Moody as hell."

Rich stayed silent. His eyes didn't leave Chadwick as he walked from the room.

"Hello, Anna," Kendra said. "How have you been?"

Anna's head snapped up. Her eyes looked happy. "Kendra, Kendra," she said, her feet dancing impatiently. "Anna so glad to see you."

Kendra let herself be hugged, wincing when Anna referred to herself in the third person. That did not happen until after she had arrived at Brighton House, probably not until after the rape, or more likely, rapes.

Anna sat on the love seat, her hands folded in her lap and curled beneath her slack belly. After that initial hug and spark of happiness, she kept her head down, eyes focused on her lap, neck bent in supplication and waiting. Kendra didn't know why but the sight of Anna almost brought her to tears. As Kendra watched her, she remembered why she had gone to Rich in the first place, why she was so angry that someone had taken advantage of this girl.

"You don't come for a long time," Anna said, tears in her eyes. "Anna afraid."

Kendra sat down next to Anna, their knees touching. She reminded her that they had talked only a week ago. "Remember?" Kendra asked.

Anna said that she remembered. Her eyes filled with tears and Kendra could tell that she was thinking about what happened afterwards. The Inapsine, the four-point restraint.

"Anna," Kendra said. "I want to introduce you to some friends of mine. Rich and . . ." She stopped, remembering that she had forgotten Carlyle's first name.

"Jared," Carlyle said.

He stared at Anna, his beady eyes shocked. Kendra looked at Anna and understood his surprise. Anna Cotton was beautiful with her close-cropped silky hair and her glimmering brown skin as smooth as a newly paved road. Her eyes were as large and round as a doe's and the perfectly shaped lips were full with promise. Even under the fluorescent lights, it was easy to see that Anna was an extremely beautiful woman. If not for her one flaw, Kendra knew that both of these men probably thought in their narrow chauvinistic world, if she were not retarded, Anna Cotton would own the world.

"Hi," Anna said, her lashes swooping over her liquid eyes.

She did not smile and Kendra knew by Anna's serious face that she did not like both Rich and Jared there. Kendra could tell that Anna wanted both men gone. Her next words confirmed this. "Anna want to talk to Kendra alone," she said.

"I know, Anna," Kendra said. "We will talk alone again, later, I promise, but right now, Jared and Rich would like to ask you a few questions about what happened."

Anna leaned forward, looking at both Rich and Carlyle. "They tie Anna up," she said. "They hurt Anna. That what happened."

"No, no, not about that," Kendra said. "About the other thing, you know, the reason that you had to go to the doctor."

Kendra glanced up and saw Rich looking at her with a glint of disapproval in his brown eyes. The "thing" that Anna had to go see the doctor for was the abortion. *Why don't you just say it,* his eyes challenged? But Kendra ignored him.

Anna gripped Kendra's hands, so hard that pain rippled through them. God, the girl was strong.

"Anna don't want to talk about it no more," she said. "Anna all tired talking about it."

To his credit, Rich did not answer immediately. Carlyle followed Rich's lead. But Kendra could see by the tension in Carlyle's eyes, how they skittered between the three of them, that he was not comfortable and did not want this to be a wasted trip.

"We just need to ask you a few questions . . ." Rich began.

"Look, Anna," Kendra interrupted him. "I brought you some things."

She untangled her fingers from Anna's and lifted the canvas bag on the table. She made a big production of hoisting it up, making it seem heavier than it was. Anna's face erupted with excitement. She clasped her hands together. Kendra heard Carlyle's snort of impatience but ignored him.

"All mine?" Anna asked.

Kendra laughed. "No, not all yours, some are for . . ." She stopped, looked at Rich to stop him from launching into his questions, she continued quickly. "Some are for some other friends, but guess what?"

"What?" Anna said, never taking her eyes from the bag and the puzzle books and crayons and finally, the Black Barbie Kendra pulled out.

"You get first pick." Kendra smiled at her.

Anna sat up, clapped and smiled, spreading her beautiful lips over even white teeth.

"How many Anna get?" she asked.

"Three, how about three . . ."

Anna placed a long finger to her chin, breathing *three, three.*

Rich opened his mouth to speak but Kendra threw him a warning look. That look said: just give her time, all right. But she missed Carlyle.

"Anna, do you know anything about who did this to you?" Carlyle asked, waving his fingers at her crotch. Anna, who had been cradling the black Barbie, pressing her finger to the cut glass in the doll's hair, cringed as if Carlyle had smacked her.

She looked at Kendra, her eyes hurt.

"Anna don't want to talk about it," she said. "Anna don't want to talk about it no more. Anna already talked to the police."

"I know, Anna," Rich said, his voice gentle like a whispering rain. "We know you talked to the police but you know the man that owns Brighton House . . ."

Anna's eyes widened at this and she nodded, stroking the Barbie's silver dress.

"The man who owns Brighton House wants to make sure that no one else is hurt here . . ."

"Lotta people hurt here, hurt everywhere," Anna said, her voice belligerent. "Anna say go talk to them. Anna don't want to talk no more."

Rich's handsome face was drawn in concern. He laced his fingers together again, and bowed his head as if to gather more intellectual reinforcements. Kendra could see his struggle, understood it, tried to help.

"Anna," she said. "It's okay, we don't have to talk about it if you don't want to, not yet . . ."

"What?" Carlyle exploded. "We didn't drive all this way to watch her play with dolls."

Anna stood up. Her hand jutted and the Black Barbie sailed across the distance between herself and Carlyle. Carlyle ducked. Instead of clocking him on his stupid narrow face, it sailed across the room crashing into the pictures on Dr. Holder's desk. They clattered to the floor.

"Anna don't like you," she screamed. "Anna don't like you one bit. Go away. Get out." Tears glinted in her eyes.

Rich looked at Anna. "Please, sit down," he said. "Please."

"Are you asking Anna or telling Anna?" she said, crossing her arms across her chest.

"He's asking you to sit down," Kendra said. "Sit down and pick your other presents."

Anna stuck an index finger at Carlyle. "He go first," she said. "He go away."

"Now just wait . . ." Carlyle started.

"Carlyle," Rich said, without looking at him.

Carlyle stood up angrily, muttering how he could not believe this before storming from the room. After the door closed Anna sat back down, never taking her eyes from it.

"He listening," she insisted and would not let go of the assumption until Rich pulled the door open to show her that no one was on the other side.

On his way back to his seat, Rich picked up the doll and held it out to Anna. She took it from him but her face filled with suspicion. She smoothed the mussed hair, patted down the rumpled silver skirt. Placing the doll in the crook of her arm, like it was an infant, she picked up a puzzle book. Rich did not speak until she began to hum.

"Anna," Rich asked. "Why did you push Chadwick?"

"Anna don't like him," she answered without missing a beat.

"But I thought you were friends," Rich said.

Anna didn't answer this. Instead, she picked up a puzzle book and started mouthing some of the words. "Find the treasure . . ."

"Anna," Rich said with only a hint of impatience in his voice. "Chadwick told me that he was your friend."

"He a liar," Anna answered.

Rich drew back. Kendra caught his eye but he ignored her.

"Has he ever hurt you Anna?" Rich asked.

"No more than he hurt everybody," Anna answered.

As Kendra watched Anna's fingers trace over the words in the puzzle book, she thought of Leroy touching her and hurting her.

She didn't know what Rich was getting at with this Brandon Chadwick but he clearly should have been focusing on Leroy. He didn't hear the way Leroy sounded when he talked about his daughter. Even though Kendra didn't know Leroy well, she simply didn't picture him a pervert. How could she have been so wrong? Suddenly, she was burning with the need to know. Rich opened his mouth to say something else, but Kendra cut him off.

"Anna," she asked. "Did your father hurt you?"

To Kendra's amazement she nodded and began to cry. But it was a silent cry, and all the while her hand moved among the crayons, the puzzles, looking for present number three.

"Anna, are you sure . . ." she began, but the look on Rich's face, the look that said clearly to shut up, stopped her.

"How did he hurt you Anna?" he asked in low quiet tones.

Anna shook her head.

"Did you tell the police that he hurt you?"

She wiped tears away, nodded. "That's why he don't come see Anna no more. That why he mad."

Rich sighed. "Anna, he doesn't come see you because he is in the hospital. At first, he was in jail, though."

Kendra caught Rich's eyes and mouthed shut up but Rich shook her off. He continued.

"Do you know why he was in jail?" Rich asked.

Anna nodded. "Because he hurt Sylvia," she said. "He kill Sylvia. He kill Sylvia real bad."

Kendra could not believe her ears but Rich, on the other hand, did not seem surprised.

"Did he hurt you like Brandon Chadwick?" Rich asked.

Anna shook her head, wide-eyed. "My daddy would never hurt Anna like that," she said.

"Then like Sylvia?" he asked. "Did he try to hurt you like he hurt Sylvia?"

Anna's eyes widened. She shook her head, silken black curls wiggled.

"No, he would never hurt Anna like he hurt Sylvia. Never." Anna grabbed the back of her neck.

"Where is Sylvia, now, Anna?" Kendra asked, her heart thumping.

"Hurting Sylvia is not why he is in jail, Anna. He's in jail because the police think he hurt you like Chadwick hurt you," Rich said before Kendra could get a word out.

"He did hurt Anna," she contradicted. "Daddy hurt Anna when he kill Sylvia, made Anna cry."

Kendra licked her lips, not believing that Rich was letting the Sylvia thing go even though Anna could be making it up. Maybe Sylvia was a stand-in for Anna, maybe another persona Anna created to escape the abuse.

"How did he kill Sylvia, Anna?" she asked.

"For God's sakes, girl," Rich exploded. "Will you shut up?"

Kendra had had enough. She jumped up. "That's it," she said. "Interview over."

Rich stood up, "What?" he said.

"I've had enough of you Richard *T.* Marvel. No more."

"You," Rich started, pointing at her, "You've had enough?" he asked incredulously.

Anna was standing up as well, looking anxiously from one to the other. Anna nervously plucked the head from the Barbie. Kendra flung the door open to Rich. He looked at Anna, then back at Kendra's furious face. He walked to the door. Before they walked out, Anna's voice stopped them.

"He killed her with an axe," she said. They turned. Her face was anxious, her brown hands squeezing the now headless Barbie. "He killed my Sylvie with an axe."

Rich flew down the hallway in a storm of anger, brushing past a surprised Carlyle and bewildered Katherine Holder. Kendra had to run to keep up with him.

"That was wrong, Rich," she said, grabbing at his arm, which he lurched away.

He turned, pointed his finger at her face. "Let me tell you what we just did, lady," he said. "We blew one of our only chances to find out what in the hell is going on in this place."

She knocked his finger away. "Bullshit, Rich," she said. "You were not getting anywhere."

He put his thumb and index finger together. "We were this close, you hear, this close."

She laughed a bitter laugh. "You weren't close to anything. She wasn't about to tell you anything about the rape. Couldn't you see her face every time you brought it up? You were trying to rush her. I'm telling you that you can't do that."

Rich ran his hand over his head, letting out a breath of air. "Get away from me, please," he said tiredly.

"What?" Kendra said. "Didn't you hear her?"

By this time, Carlyle and Katherine had caught up with them. Kendra did not acknowledge them. "What about this Sylvia? She said that her father had killed Sylvia."

Rich stopped pacing. The hand he was moving over his head halted. He turned and stared at her. She withered under that look. He did not call her an idiot, but then again, he did not have to.

"Let me tell you something, Kendra," he said. "While you've been running around Dunhill on your own personal vendetta, I've interviewed everyone in this place, people who obviously know Anna Cotton better than you. Anna lived on a farm. She had a pet." He stopped speaking.

When she couldn't stand the silence anymore, she said, "I don't understand."

"Sylvia," he said quietly. "Sylvia was a pig."

CHAPTER 20

If she stopped for even a split second, Kendra Hamilton would have admitted that she was afraid. Scaring the shit even out of herself. She put away the incident at Brighton House as neatly as she had packed her bags to leave Rich and Dunhill two years ago. She put it out of her mind so that she could get back to the real business at hand, the business of finding the owner of Luke's ring and that inscription. *Always mine.* Years later, she knew that she would look back on how easily she put Anna aside and be ashamed. But for now she had another job to do.

She had tried the phone first. Of course she did. She had tried calling Cloughton Medical College to ask about Luke Bertrand, an alumnus. They had to know all about him, they must know his history. But they weren't proud of him. They didn't want to talk to her about Luke Bertrand. He had become the disgraced son. They accused her of being a reporter at first. She only wanted to find out if Luke had any friends there, did he belong to the alumnae association. But they wouldn't tell her.

When she convinced them that she wasn't a reporter, they accused her of being a thrill seeker, the first one to car accidents, a letter writer to serial killers. She convinced the voice on the phone that she wasn't a thrill seeker. So then they accused her of being from the sheriff's department, a cop who couldn't leave well enough alone, someone with a vendetta against Luke Bertrand.

Kendra hung up, disappointed. Maybe she would have better luck if she called again and talked to a different person. She did, but it was not much. They transferred her to an old man who said that he would be delighted to talk with her. His voice was like gravel with an excited edge that said Luke Bertrand was the best thing that had happened to Cloughton Medical College since the invention of the stethoscope. How refreshing it was, wasn't it, to have a serial killer for once. Albeit a serial killer who had gotten away with murder. He cackled at this, his own joke, and his gravelly voice skidded into a cough. He was a sarcastic old man who would love to talk to Kendra about Luke Bertrand.

But not now. Not right then. He was preparing for a vacation to Europe. He would go to Paris to visit the Louvre, gaze at the lights strung along the Eiffel Tower, eat French food, and be spit at by the rude French for changing the name of French fries to freedom fries. He cackled again, pleased with himself. There was much to do and he had no time to talk to her. He caught the phone on his way out to pick up his new passport. He would leave in two days and be away for several months.

Strike two, Kendra thought as she hung up the phone. She stopped, laughed, that was what Rich would have said. Kendra knew that her thoughts had become tangled like yarn in a tornado. But when she thought about Luke, they straightened, took on shape. Decisions came easily, such as the decision to fly to Virginia to speak with Professor Harold Boggs in person. She would make him take time to see her. But money was a problem. She couldn't pay the rent; a flight across country would be expensive, especially a reservation to fly tonight, today. She had forty-seven dollars in her savings.

She sat on the couch. A pile of mail sat on the TV tray that served as an end table. She turned away from the mail, put both hands over her eyes. When she dropped her hands, she hit the edge of the TV tray. It tottered before eventually toppling to the floor. Mail skidded across the carpet like white leaves falling.

"Oh, shit," she said, getting up.

She sorted through it as she picked it up, thinking that she hadn't sorted through her mail in several weeks. There was a lot of it. Some bills but mostly junk. She hadn't been back in town for six months and already junk mail had found her. An ad for Save Mart,

T-bones four ninety-five a pound, Del Monte corn nibblets three for a dollar, a kid on a postcard, stranger abduction, have you seen me? She straightened the TV tray, tidied the mail in a pile back on the table. Where could she get the money? The plain fact was that she could not. She was flat busted, as her brother Adam used to say.

Thirsty, she turned to the kitchen but something caught her eye. A piece of mail she had missed still lay on the floor. "Capital One," the return address proclaimed. The envelope was an open invitation to Kendra Hamilton for a credit card. Picking it up, she thrilled, singing low in her throat like a bird. The universe had reached out to her. She was on the right track. Surely she was going down the right path.

Cloughton Medical College was a small elite college in Virginia, student population of about a thousand. The buildings were spread out over several acres, the grass in this, the end of winter, brown. Cold wrapped around Kendra like ice. The navy pea coat she wore was no match for this weather. And she had left so quickly and was so excited that she had not packed warm clothes. The only thing warm was the ring of fever around her face. But she convinced herself that it wasn't fever plaguing her but excitement at being so close to Luke's past.

She had left on the same day that she activated the credit card. The cost of the round trip flight with no notice was fifteen hundred dollars. The rental car was two-fifty. At twenty-two percent interest, she could pay it off in twenty, maybe thirty years. But paying her debt was not paramount in her mind. Making someone else pay for theirs was. She flew through storms on the red-eye, forgetting her promise to Rich to call Katherine Holder for another interview with Anna. She was not thinking about tomorrow. She arrived the next morning in the stinging cold.

Professor Boggs didn't know that she was coming. Standing on the tree-lined sidewalk on the campus she realized that she had no idea how to find him. There were no signs on the gray stone buildings. Students rushed around her like she was a stone in a stream. Standing for several minutes, Kendra collected her tangled thoughts, closed her dry eyes. That's right, she thought, Professor Boggs, self-

appointed school historian, was in the alumnae office. All she had
to do was . . .

"Are you all right?"

She opened her eyes to find a young man staring at her, face a
mass of pimples, hair shocking black against his pasty white forehead.

"I'm looking for the alumnae office."

He grunted, pointed south, shifted the books in his arms and
left her standing there. Kendra turned and saw a building with a
pointing roof and stained glass. This one was redbrick and covered
in ivy. Inside, lopsided wooden floors, dark as oil, heavy furniture
and badly done oil paintings greeted her. The paintings were of
landscapes mostly, the perspective all wrong. Kendra held her
breath after asking for Professor Boggs.

The student behind a heavy antique desk was not interested in
Kendra's anxiety. She did not look up. She did not pick up the
phone. Instead, she pointed to a door behind her and grunted in
much the same manner as the other student had.

"Is he in?" Kendra asked.

"Yep," she said. "Wouldn't make much sense for you to go back
there if he wasn't."

Kendra walked back to the mouth of Professor Boggs's office.

"Hello, hello, hello," he called when he saw her standing in the
doorway. "Do I know you, young lady?"

Kendra tried to smile but her mouth would not obey. Tiredness
pressed on her like a blanket of lead. She had tried to sleep on the
plane, did manage a few naps but they were restless, filled with
dreams of Anna and Rich. And when she wasn't dreaming of them,
she dreamed of gunshots, screams, babies crying, saw Luke's face
as serene as blue water. She was so into these dreams that when the
plane landed, she felt as if it had fallen from the sky. The man next
to her patted her arm, told her that they had not crashed, only
landed. The flight was over.

"No," Kendra said, her lips twitching as Professor Boggs regarded her. "You don't know me."

He pulled at the edge of his wire rimmed glasses until they were
low on his nose.

"Was I expecting you?" he asked.

Kendra shook her head.

He laughed, his voice like tires on a gravel road. "Ha, ha, ha. I love it. Rude people have guts, I say. Come in, come in.

Professor Boggs wore a white shirt and a black bow tie with white dots. The tie was full, looked sort of like something a clown would wear. His glasses were thick and the lenses, when he wore them against his eyes instead of wearing them on the tip of his nose as he did now, reminded Kendra of Mr. Magoo. His hair was thin and gray. The careful part precisely in the middle of his head belied his devil-may-care attitude.

When he rose, Kendra could see he was only about five feet tall, maybe a little taller.

"What brings you here?" he asked. "What can poor old Professor Boggs do for you?"

He held out his hands as he said this last and the liver spotted things shook. Kendra saw that one side of his face, skin rumpled like dirty laundry, twitched uncontrollably as well. When he smiled, poor old Professor Boggs's full lips dropped downward in a sneer. The showing of teeth was the only thing that made the smile friendly. She shook his hand, convulsively placed her other hand over his to stop it from shaking.

"Huh?" Professor Boggs said. "Warm, warm even in this cold weather? You sick?"

The statement surprised Kendra. Warm? "No, I'm fine," she said.

"Well, sit, sit, sit," he commanded, still crouched behind his desk in a half sitting and half standing position.

Professor Boggs's office was not only a mess but a fire hazard. Magazines stacked haphazardly on the floor had become end tables, several coffee cups positioned on top. The desk was covered with papers, some stapled together and flipped open to the middle, others closed. About twenty or so human models, the wooden kind with blank oval faces and rubber band joints, danced on sticks about the room. An old-fashioned skeleton with yellow bones stood in the corner. Posters of flayed bodies, small numbers and letters used to map veins and muscles, covered the wall. Professor Boggs had used the poster of a torso as a window covering. Sun filtered through the red muscles, turning them pink.

"Don't stand there looking dazed, I said sit, sit," he barked, impatient. "Cold water, you need some cold water? Cool you down."

"No . . ."

But before she could finish, Professor Boggs was off again, interrupting her, moving like a crab from behind the desk, stopping well short of the mouth to his office.

"Insolent girl!" he shouted. "Get some water. Cold, ice. Now. Earn your keep."

He turned back to Kendra, raised a bushy eyebrow and winked. Shuffling noises came from outside.

"Can't be too easy on 'em, not even a medical student. Goes to an undergrad college nearby. Work study, you know. We try to co-operate but they expect us to just give things away."

He scuttled back to his desk. It took about a year for him to ease back into his brown leather chair.

"Now, where were we," he said. "Ah, yes, what are you doing here?"

"My name is Kendra Hamilton, Professor. We spoke about . . ."

He frowned-smiled again. His eyes lit up. "Ah, yes, our serial killer alumnus, Lucas Cornelius Bertrand."

Kendra began to answer but he interrupted her by slapping a palsied hand on the desk.

"They think I'm wrong up in administration," he said. "But how many medical colleges can boast of that? Harvard may have its surgeon general, a president or two, but we have Luke Bertrand. Nothing ordinary, here, yes, sir . . ."

Kendra did not know whether to be amused or offended by this eccentric old man, but she wanted to shut him up.

"He killed my mother," she said, her voice bland.

Professor Boggs sat back in his chair. He blinked once. The working corner of his mouth drooped into a frown.

"You don't say," he said. Once he spoke, Kendra realized that her effort to shut him up would be unsuccessful. "And you're asking about him, come all this way? Isn't it odd, Dr. Hamilton, that we attach ourselves to the evildoers in the world, that when they hurt our loved ones, we gladly give them pieces of ourselves, as if they haven't taken enough already?"

Kendra felt her face flame at the title. He had called her Dr.

Hamilton, so he knew something about the case. "Ms. Hamilton," she corrected.

But he waved his hand at that, flapping it like a sheet in the wind. "Bah," he said. "You are 'doctor' to me, no matter what some damn board has to say about it. Those boring glasses of milk can't stand a little unorthodoxy, but they'll get new blood, and that new blood will bring them to their senses." He leaned forward when he said this, looked Kendra in the eyes as if to say that he was not just speaking platitudes. "You are young enough to wait."

Kendra stared at him.

"Don't look so surprised," he said. "Someone calling me up asking about one of our most notorious graduates, I'm going to do a little research. You should be flattered. I spent the better part of yesterday morning going through boxes, breathing dust balls." He coughed wetly, then slammed his hand on the desk. "Insolent girl," he shouted. Kendra jumped.

"Coming, Professor," a voice from the outer office answered and was soon followed by the bored girl from the front desk. She did not hurry. Her step was slow and sure, and unaffected by the professor's ranting. She handed Kendra a plastic green Tupperware of water and ice. She walked to the desk and took the professor's smoldering pipe.

"What are you doing?" he cried. "I wasn't done with that."

"Yes, you are." The girl yawned. "Your doctor said no more, your wife called and wanted to make sure you were not smoking. You want to live a long time, don't you?"

"Why, so I can die of boredom?" he shouted. "Bring it back here."

But the girl did not. Just walked out of the office, shutting the door behind her.

"She's worked for you how long? And from what college?" Kendra asked, a faint smile across her face.

"Don't look so smug," he said. "My sister's granddaughter. Been like that since she was a child. She'd yawn through a nuclear explosion."

I guess that's why she's working for you. Kendra thought.

"But she doesn't call you uncle?" Kendra asked.

"Why do you think I call her an insolent girl?" he said. "She walks around here, shows her belly button, piercing all over, thinking it's something new. Did that in Africa thousands of years ago, you know. Calls me Professor because she doesn't want anyone to know that we are related."

"Did you know Luke Bertrand when he went to medical school here?" Kendra asked instead, wanting to get on with it, the reason she flew thousands of miles across country to meet with this strange old man.

Professor Boggs leaned back in his chair, placed a hand on his desk. He pushed his glasses up to his face and spoke.

"You couldn't help but know Luke Bertrand," he said.

She took a sip of the water, warm, ice almost melted to nothing. She had to wait for a second for him to gather himself well enough to speak.

"He was a handsome man, handsome man," he said. "Piercing eyes that could cleave you in two. And somewhat of an anomaly around this place because he was Black, you know. Two Black students at the time, but compared to Luke that other boy was washed out dishwater." He stopped, laughed. "Not surprised that he didn't practice medicine long, though."

"You mean Luke?"

"Of course I mean Luke," he barked. "Who else would I mean?"

"Why is that?" Kendra asked.

"Why is what?"

Kendra sighed. "Why aren't you surprised that he didn't practice medicine for long?"

Professor Boggs lifted his fingers from the desk. "Not very smart, had a lot of trouble with the concepts, if you know what I mean. Barely passed."

Kendra considered this for a moment, surprised. Luke Bertrand seemed so dynamic, so intelligent. She could not see him failing at anything he ever tried or pursued.

"You remember all that?" Kendra asked, doing some mental calculations. It had to be more than thirty years ago.

"That part I do," Professor Boggs confirmed. "I was an associate professor at the time . . ." He stopped, pointed to a black and white photograph on the wall. A man with alabaster skin and shiny black hair, late thirties or early forties, stared off in the distance. His profile was sharp against the canvas.

"Taught some of Luke's classes, stood in for this one professor in particular. The man was a drunk, I tell you. I ended up teaching almost all of his classes. What was his name . . . ?"

He stopped speaking and leaned back again, pushed his glasses all the way up his nose, magnifying his eyes again.

"Professor . . ." Kendra prodded.

"Oh, yes, yes," he said. "Anyway, his name does not matter, I guess." He stopped, seemed still bothered by the forgotten name. Kendra was glad when he finally spoke again. "But Luke was in some of those classes." He held up a finger to Kendra. "The boy struggled, let me tell you."

"Did he struggle because he was Black and you were hard on him?" Kendra asked. "Or did he struggle because of character and intelligence?"

Boggs knotted his lips together as best he could. A line of dribble fell from the corner of his mouth.

"Well," he said. "Some classes, the easier ones, mind you, that might have been true. And maybe I was a little harder on him because he was a Black man. Just like our country, I was young, brash. What, thirty-eight or thirty-nine? I had some ideas and I didn't always engage my brain before opening my mouth . . . or my fist sometimes . . . for that matter. But I gave Luke a fair chance, or I'd like to think I did. He just didn't get it."

They both sat for a while, neither speaking. Kendra gazed at the pink sun filtering through muscle and veins from the poster covering the window and thought about what it must have been like for Luke, one of two Black students, here at Cloughton Medical College. She thought about him walking the campus, ostracized and demoralized because he just didn't get it. She wondered what that would have done to an already fragile psyche, to a boy who had been rejected by his father for simply being too weak and dominated by his mother.

"Had to give him most of the answers, mark him up on most of the tests."

Professor Boggs's words cut into Kendra's thoughts. She shook her head a little to clear the picture of a young Luke forming there.

"What did you say?" she asked.

"I said that I had to give Luke most of the answers and fudge a lot of his grades," Professor Boggs yelled, as if Kendra were heard of hearing.

"Why would you do that?" Kendra asked.

Professor Boggs chuckled, his drooping chin making the clown bow tie wiggle almost comically. "Because," he said. "We had a little problem."

"What problem was that?" Kendra asked.

"We wanted him out of here," Professor Boggs said. "We didn't want to kick him out because that would make us seem less progressive than we were. I mean, we didn't kick him out when about fifteen or twenty of the student population decided not to attend because we admitted Luke and that other Black fella. One thing the administration did not like." He stopped and held a warning finger out to Kendra. "They did not like being blackmailed or told what to do." He grinned again. "You can relate to that, can't you?"

Kendra could indeed relate to that.

"Late 1960s was a volatile time. He needed to graduate; we wanted both of those boys out of here so I had to do some things," he said.

"Were Luke and the other boy friends?"

Boggs frowned. "I don't think so. Luke was a loner. Not surprising considering, but even the other Black boy made some friends. We were not all assholes, you know, Dr. Hamilton."

"So Luke was a loner?"

Professor Boggs nodded. "Yes, pretty much. But he did have one friend, a white boy from someplace or the other . . ." He stopped, looked up at the ceiling. "I don't think he went to the college though, at least I don't remember. Ah, I don't remember his name either. Thomas Lind or Long or something like that."

Kendra scribbled the name down on the back of her ticket envelope. She didn't know if it would do any good but believed that anyone who knew Luke at that time would bring her closer to the owner of that ring. She waited. But the professor let out a long breath, giving up.

"Ah hell," he said. "I can't remember. I should remember but I can't. When you get to be my age, young lady, it's the details that are a bitch. I remember, you know, the landscape, the canvas, but I can't remember details you know, like the name of the flower or the river. Used to," he went on. "But now I can't, especially after the stroke."

"Did Luke have any girlfriends when he was here?" Kendra asked to get Boggs back on track.

Professor Boggs broke out into a full laugh. He looked like a specter when he laughed, ghoulish, one half of his mouth forced up in a laugh, the other half sneering downward. He reached into his pocket and took out a dingy yellow handkerchief to wipe at his eyes. And he finally tackled the line of drool slipping from his mouth.

"And tell me," he grunted, still laughing. "Who is he going to date? Here?" he said. "There was no one."

Kendra thought quickly. Of course not here, but that didn't prevent Luke from finding girlfriends from someplace. He was able to find a friend someplace else. And she told Boggs so.

But Professor Boggs shook his head. "Luke didn't have time to date while he was here. He was up to his ass in alligators just trying to graduate."

Kendra took the ring out of her jeans pocket and handed it to the professor. His hands shook as he took it. He turned it over in his hand, read the inscription on the inside.

"Always, mine," he breathed. "Where did you get this?" he asked. "I don't understand."

"It belongs to Luke," she told him.

"And he just gave it to you?" he said, looking at her over his glasses. She was about to speak but he held up his hand. "Never mind. I don't want to know."

"It's a woman's ring, Professor," she said.

"I can see that."

"I think it must have belonged to Luke's wife," Kendra said.

"But Luke Bertrand didn't marry." Professor Boggs frowned.

"Not in Dunhill," Kendra explained. "But maybe here. Maybe he met someone while he was at college . . ."

Professor Boggs sighed, shook his head again. He reached out the ring to Kendra. She took it. A dead end, she thought.

"I don't know if Luke had any girlfriends but I do know for a fact that he did not have a wife. Not while he was here, anyway. I never saw him wear a ring."

"Maybe after college, then," Kendra said. "Soon after . . ."

He shrugged. "Maybe, but I doubt it. And I didn't know Luke after college. Lost touch and was glad for it."

"What about the other Black boy here? Do you remember his name?" Kendra asked, thinking that Boggs's assessment was probably incorrect. Maybe the other boy remembered a ring. "I'd like to talk to him."

"Why?" he asked. "I don't remember them having much contact with each other."

"But your memory could be incorrect," Kendra suggested. "You said yourself . . ."

Professor Boggs laughed. "I said details, not the canvas. It's the details that I have a problem with. I think I'd remember two Black boys, together, on this campus in 1969. Just what are you hoping to find with all of this, Dr. Hamilton?"

"For all you joke, Professor," she started. "Luke Bertrand did not just start killing people out of the blue. There must have been some hint of the man he would become. I'm hoping . . ."

She stopped when she saw Professor Boggs nod.

"You are hoping," he continued for her, "that you can unearth some other crime he could be punished for. You want to see him imprisoned. Or dead."

"Neither matters to me as long as he gets what he deserves. Isn't that what you want as well?"

He blinked, his eyes like fish eyes behind his thick glasses. For the first time since they had started talking, Kendra could see seriousness creep into Professor's Boggs's twitching but jovial face.

"How do you mean?" he asked.

"I don't think that you've been in mothballs this morning, Professor," she challenged. "I think that you went to the mothballs the minute you heard that Luke Bertrand had gone on a killing spree. Did you suspect something all along? When he was here, did you realize that there was something not quite right about him?"

His face changed, just like that, like a light. He was the eccentric and funny old man with the bow tie again, the man he had been when she entered his office.

"You are smart," he said, wagging a finger at her. "You see, that's why you will eventually get your medical license back. You may not have principles rooted in this society but you are smart as hell."

Kendra did not respond to the insult. She waited. Professor

Boggs removed his glasses and vigorously wiped the lenses. Still laughing, he said, "Of course you are right. If it weren't for my efforts, Luke Bertrand may never have graduated from Cloughton. Never suspected anything, of course I didn't, but I didn't like him. Something wrong and a little spooky about him those days when he was young and unpolished. Couldn't hide it then, you see."

"Hide what?" Kendra asked.

"I don't know," Boggs responded. "*It,* I guess. That little thing that you can't identify intelligently but you know it's there, just as there is fire in a matchstick. But you can't tell until you strike it. And then, by God, you got trouble."

"So how are you guilty?" Kendra asked.

He sighed. "I wonder if he had not graduated, what would have happened? Would his benefactor still have left him all that money? Would he have had time to create that slick veneer, that mask he used to fool and then kill? Yes, yes, I wonder."

Bitter. Kendra felt bitter. She wanted out of this office. She felt as if she were being suffocated by posters, the dancing bodies, and the blood and bone.

"But it was a volatile time and you wanted him out of here," she said.

The professor placed his glasses back on his face but did not raise them any farther than the tip of his fleshy nose.

"Yes, yes, we wanted him out of here. We wanted them both out of here. The sooner the better. I tell you, we had some happy people up in administration in 1969 when they both graduated."

"You mean 1970," Kendra countered.

"Noooo," Professor Boggs said slowly, "I mean 1969. That's when Luke graduated. I remember that. The final year of the decade and all. New things coming."

Kendra searched her memory, frantically recalling the *Jet* article clearly stating that Luke Bertrand came to Dunhill immediately after graduating medical school in 1970. How could they have gotten it wrong? Was it simply a misprint?

"Let's see," Professor Boggs said, his voice muffled.

He had been ruffling through a stack of papers lying on the floor beside his desk. His thin gray hair, stiffened with hair spray, flapped back into place as he straightened up and rolled up to his desk. "It's right here, Luke graduated in 1969." He stopped and looked up, smiling, tiny flames in his eyes. "Two hundred and ninety-fifth out of a class of three hundred. We were kind of small back then, real small. And as you can see, Luke did not distinguish himself."

"But, but," Kendra protested, thinking not only of the *Jet* article, but the society page articles, and what Luke had told her himself. "He graduated in 1970. He has said so himself. Why would he lie?"

Professor Boggs placed the papers on his desk and they became indistinguishable from the rest of the papers. He sighed and Kendra could see that he had become bored with the conversation regardless of his demons and his perceived culpability in the murder of fifteen girls.

"Why does anyone do anything, anymore, Dr. Hamilton," he said. "Why indeed."

The documents in Cloughton Medical College's historical section in the library yielded much more than Boggs's riddled memory. Though she couldn't find any Thomas Lind or Long in the yearbooks, she did find the same class picture that was hanging on the wall in Luke's office. And underneath the picture, she saw names. Luke's other Black classmate's name was Horace Paxton. Kendra took the photograph to the librarian, pointed to Horace and said five words—*I want to find him.*

In the end it was easy to locate Horace Paxton. After giving the librarian some cock and bull story about looking for some long-lost family member, the librarian told her that Paxton was a generous donor to the college. And he took special interest in the library.

"Tell you what," she told Kendra. "I'll call him and see if he's receptive to me giving you his contact information."

She returned later and told Kendra that Mr. Paxton would be happy to speak with her. Without the Capital One credit card in her pocket, Kendra could not have made the call to Washington, D.C., where Horace Paxton lived. When she told the voice at the other end of the phone who was calling and what it was about, Horace Paxton was not happy. He was not happy at all.

"Look," he said. "Are you another reporter?"

"No, I'm not," Kendra said into the phone.

"Then what do you want?"

"Answers, Mr. Paxton. Just answers."

He didn't speak for a minute or two. Then he said, "Okay, I'll give you answers, the same answers I've given every reporter who's knocked at my door for the past two years. Luke Bertrand is a freak. I knew he was a freak the first day I laid eyes on him at Cloughton. Twenty years later I ran into him in Washington, D.C. He was still a freak. How any of you people could have missed it, how anyone could have missed it is beyond me."

"Mr. Paxton," Kendra interrupted. "I'm just interested in his years at Cloughton."

"In particular? What do you want to know?"

"Did he have a girlfriend?"

"I wouldn't know that, Dr. Hamilton."

"Do you remember if he hung out with a Thomas Lind or Long?"

"No." His voice was both unfriendly and uncooperative.

"What year did you graduate?" she asked him.

"Nineteen sixty-nine," he answered without hesitation.

"But Luke said nineteen seventy."

"He's a liar," he said again without missing a beat.

Kendra couldn't think of anything else to say. Her heart sank. Another dead end. Strike three.

"Is there anything else, Dr. Hamilton?" Paxton asked.

Twisting the silver wire of the pay phone, she leaned her head against the base.

"No," she said. "I've already taken up enough of your time."

As she was about to hang up, a thought struck her.

"Wait," she said. At first, she thought that she had lost her chance, that he had hung up. Then, after what seemed like an eternity she heard his voice. It was still cold, but curious now.

"Yes?"

"Did you and Luke do your residency together?"

He laughed. "Are you kidding me? I did my residency in Virginia."

"Do you know where Luke did his?" she asked.

"You bet your sweet Aunt Harriet I do," he said. "How do you think I knew where I wanted to do mine?"

"So where did he go?"

"To a small town. In Oregon, I believe. A nowhere place that had a hard time finding doctors," he paused. "Now that I think of it, that's probably where the confusion over the graduation year is coming up. That place needed doctors so maybe Luke just stayed on after graduating Cloughton."

Kendra's fingers curled around the wire. "Do you remember the name of the town?" she asked, unable to hide the hope in her voice.

He sighed. "I think it was a place called Kettle Creek. Yes, that was it, Kettle Creek, Oregon."

"Thank you," Kendra whispered as she hung up the phone.

She took the ring out of the pocket of her Peacoat and held it up with both hands. Her heart pounding, she knew that Horace Paxton, the man who thought Luke a freak the first time he had laid eyes on him, had led her to Luke's missing year.

CHAPTER 21

She smelled the alcohol on his breath the minute she walked into Richard T. Marvel's office. He had tried to cover it up with mint but she knew. She had been around it all of her life. When Violet did not have enough money for her main addiction, heroin, she turned to alcohol as a substitute. She could smell it because the minute she walked into his office after getting off the plane that afternoon, he grabbed her by the shoulders and looked into her face as if he had never seen her before. Or as if he thought he would never see her again.

"Where the hell have you been, girl?" he asked.

Kendra brushed his hands from her shoulders and took a step back.

"You stink of whiskey," she said. "It's the middle of the day and you smell like you're on the back end of an all night drunk."

He drew back as if she had slapped him. But the curious thing was he didn't seem angry, not at her statements, anyway. Instead, as he looked at her she became aware that maybe it was still up in the air as to who was the biggest mess. She hadn't changed clothes in two days. Her gray sweatshirt was rumpled, sticking to her body as if it were ninety degrees outside instead of the sixty that it was.

"You don't smell so hot yourself," he said, his mouth grim. "I asked you a question, Kendra. Where in the hell have you been? I've been trying to get in touch with you for the last two days."

She stared at him and thought of the man he used to be. She tried to reconcile that man to the one he had become. Here he was, in his office palace filled with the scent of leather, and glass windows as clear as summer air. She could see him floating in his mesh chair looking out of the long windows onto the pointed peaks and roofs of Dunhill. They all imagined, Dunhill did, that Richard T. Marvel was still a hero in spite of what Luke had said and in spite of what Rich himself thought. They imagined him as the prince on the white horse who had ridden in and saved the less fortunate from those who would judge them, men like Luke Bertrand. But Kendra knew what only a handful in Dunhill knew— that the person who watched over them from his perch on the hill was slowly poisoning himself to death.

"You need to get some help, Rich," she told him now.

Incredibly, he laughed at her, right in the face of those serious words.

"You have some nerve, lady," he said.

He went back to his desk and sat down. She followed him.

"You've got a problem," she said. "Trust me, I've seen it . . ."

He slammed his hand against the desk. The sound plunged the room into silence, the only sound the swinging pendulum on the brass clock announcing the time. He locked eyes with hers, and he said, quietly, "Don't tell me what you've seen. I'm quite aware of it, and it does not give you the right to judge me."

"I'm not judging you . . ." she started.

"The hell you are," he countered. "And like I said, you have some nerve."

Kendra rubbed her hands over her face, shocked by the coldness of her fingertips. They felt like ice cubes.

"Rich, I didn't come here to fight."

"No," he said. "I guess you didn't. But you've got one if you want to continue this line of discussion."

"You can't see that you have a problem, middle of the day and you are drinking . . ." She couldn't believe she was saying the words herself and this disbelief reflected on Rich's face.

"You just can't leave it alone, can you?" he said. "Still thinking you can save the world, all goody-two-shoes. I see you fucking up, but do you see me getting in your face, talking about how you need help?"

"I don't know what . . ."

"What do you mean, you 'don't know'?" he said, waving a hand at her. "Look at yourself, will you? When was the last time you looked in the mirror? Combed your hair? Had a bath, even? You look like hell, Kendra. And you have nerve enough to tell me that I need help."

"I've been on a plane all night," she said. "This is not the way I usually am. At least I'm not drinking my way into a stupor."

"Does it look like I'm in any kind of a stupor to you?" he challenged.

He was right, Kendra thought. Richard T. Marvel did not look at all like he was in a stupor. The suit he wore looked as if it were made for him, his silk tie closed in a perfect knot around his throat, his hair cut, his face shaved. If she hadn't smelled the alcohol on him, if she hadn't gotten so close, she would have never known that he had been drinking.

"Let's not get into a debate as to who is the most fucked up," he said, his tired voice indicating that he was done with the conversation. "I'm sure if we pushed it we would both qualify for his and hers padded cells.

"Now," he said, his voice distant. "Would you please have a seat and tell me why you've been on a plane all night? Where have you been?"

He indicated a chair opposite the desk. Kendra sat down and rubbed her chilled thighs with the palms of her hands. "I've been to Virginia," she said.

"Virginia?" he raised an eyebrow.

"Yes," she said. "I went to Luke's alma mater, Cloughton Medical College, where he went to medical school."

She waited for his disapproval. But he gave none. Instead, she saw the same wall in his eyes that she noticed the morning in Tahoe. She could see by his eyes that she would be ice skating in hell before he let Luke, or her, for that matter, in again.

"Rich," she said. "I know you don't want to talk about this . . ."

"You'd be wrong," he said. "I not only don't want to talk about it, I don't want anything more to do with it. It's behind me now, Kendra. Behind both of us. Let it go."

"But Luke . . ."

He waved his hands in the air. "I know, I know," he said.

"Gregory already told me about it, that you've opened all of this up again."

"There you go," Kendra said. "There you go," she said again.

She went to the window and suddenly remembered why she was so uncomfortable in Rich's new office. She was uncomfortable because it reminded her so much of Luke's office in the Trans-America building in San Francisco. Luke's windows, too, were floor to ceiling, his furniture black.

And he used his fancy office to hide the monster who lurked behind his welcoming exterior. And now Rich was using the same trappings of success to hide. But instead of defeating the monster inside himself, he was running from the monster he had exposed in Luke, the man he had locked up and the man who ultimately betrayed him.

She leaned her forehead against the window overlooking Dunhill County.

"All of this," she explained. "It's not all of this, Rich. He killed my mother and he killed God only knows how many others."

"Kendra . . ." Rich breathed.

She felt his hand on her shoulder, gentle now. But she didn't turn around to face him, finding comfort instead in the cold glass against her forehead.

"Listen to me," his voice was quiet. "It's over."

"It's not over," she protested. "You don't understand. It didn't start in Dunhill, the killing didn't. Luke started killing a long time ago while he was in his twenties, in college."

"What makes you so sure?" he asked.

His hand fell from her shoulders when she turned around to face him. She leaned the back of her head against the glass, twisted her body so she could look up at him. He was standing close. She could feel heat from his body. He didn't step back, instead took a step closer so that they were almost touching

"He graduated from Cloughton in 1969 but he tells everyone 1970." She could tell by the small head shake that Rich didn't get it. "He graduated a year earlier than what he says," she explained.

"So?" Rich said.

"What happened during that missing year, Rich? Where was he? Aren't you curious?"

His face impassive, still standing close enough to touch her, he said, "No."

Kendra wanted to slap him, to scream at him to wake up, to feel the same joy that she had felt when she learned that she might have something on Luke, something that could put him away until the end of his miserable life.

"Why?" she asked him now.

"Because," he said quietly, "Luke Bertrand destroyed my life. And every time you and I are together, I am forced to realize that he has destroyed something else as well."

She looked into his brown eyes, his stone face. She knew what he was going to say, knew it with all of her heart, but she had to hear him say it out loud. Suddenly aware of how close they were standing, she asked him anyway.

"What?" she breathed.

"He destroyed us," Rich said. "When you were with me, all you thought about was him. I never said anything, but I could feel him. There. All the time, in between us."

"Rich," Kendra tried to twist away, but he moved closer, wouldn't let her step away.

Their thighs touching, he said, "No. You are going to listen to me this time, Kendra. You don't get to run away. You let Luke Bertrand destroy us. Now you are letting him destroy you."

She felt anger storm over her face, anger and resentment at his words.

"I don't have the energy for this." She didn't realize that she was yelling until he asked her to lower her voice. "Every time we are together, Rich, you bring this shit up. It's over. We're over. We were over before we started."

"Then why didn't you just tell me that? Why did you leave town, running away like you stole something?"

"Why do you think?" she said. "Don't you see? I couldn't stand it anymore, Rich. I couldn't stand being in the same town with him, running into him on the streets after what he did."

"You could have at least come to me and told me it was over," he still insisted.

"It wouldn't have done any good, Rich," she said. "You wouldn't have believed me."

He shook his head slowly. "No, I don't think that's it. I think you ran because you couldn't end it. You were afraid to face me."

"Well, it doesn't matter because I'm ending it now," she told him.

"Are you?" he challenged.

They stared at each other a few minutes, and as their eyes locked, feelings that she had long tried to bury welled up inside her. It took all of her will to ignore the fact that she didn't want to leave him. She just didn't have a choice.

"Don't be ridiculous, Rich," she said.

"Then tell me," he replied. "Tell me now that you don't want anything to do with me and I'll never bring it up again. I promise."

She didn't say anything. He grabbed her shoulders and shook her, stepping closer. She tried pushing him away but he wouldn't budge.

"I've got to deal with Luke," she said. "I can't deal with this right now."

"Let it go," he said, his voice desperate.

"He will not get away with this," she said. "He will not."

"You see, that's what you don't understand," Rich said. "He has, Kendra. He has already gotten away with it. And I will be damned if I'm going to let Luke Bertrand have one second more of my life. I'm done with it."

She felt paralyzed, could not move when he reached out a palm to touch the side of her face. When she felt his cool fingers against her skin she knocked his hand away but it was too late. He had already felt the heat of fever on her face.

"Goddamn it, Kendra," he said with sudden worry in his voice. He placed a hand against her forehead. "You're burning up. I can't believe you're walking around."

He stepped away from her. Swallowing hard, she felt suddenly cold, had not realized how hard she was breathing until Rich had walked away. She heard him rummaging through his desk drawer, cursing under his breath. She started walking toward him.

"Sit down," he said. "Sit down before you fall down."

He slammed his desk shut and went over to the wet bar.

"What are you doing?" she asked him.

"Looking for some Tylenol. You're burning up."

"I don't need any Tylenol," she said.

"Don't tell me what you need. Stay here, I'll see if I can find a first aid kit."

Overreaction, Kendra thought, that was Rich all over. At least some things never changed. In his search, Rich had knocked down a letter opener from the table. It was gold, wickedly pointed, and glinted against the marble granite floor. She picked it up. When she sat it down on his desk she noticed a typed list. The list caught her eye because of a name among the other names on the list, a name that had been crossed out. It was Luke Bertrand's name.

Using her fingertip she swung the list around so she could see it. The list was entitled Brighton House Board Members. And aside from Luke Bertrand's name on the list, she noticed another name, a name that reminded her of her visit to a crazy old man's office full of skeletons.

As she ran her fingertip across the black letters she thought about her college friends. Though she hadn't spoken with some of them in a couple of years, she still exchanged E-mails with them when she could, would go to her mailbox wherever she was staying to find a postcard, a short note, something. *Still thinking of you,* they would say, or *haven't forgotten about you.* And she knew that if she called one of them with real need, they would be there for her. Like her friend was there for her after she and Rich had broken up. Mary had allowed Kendra to stay with her for an entire week even though they hadn't seen each other in years.

She wondered now as she took the list and folded it into a tiny square, she wondered if Luke was still friends with the boy that Professor Boggs could not remember. She wondered if Luke was still friends with Thomas Long, or Lang, or Lind. And she wondered if the name Professor Boggs couldn't remember was Theodore Lane. His name had not been crossed out on the list of Brighton House board members. And it sat directly underneath Luke Bertrand's.

Once again, Kendra felt the universe move for her. This couldn't be a coincidence. She knew that. Theodore Lane was Luke's old college buddy. He had to be. Why? Because it couldn't or wouldn't be any other way. Theodore Lane would tell her if Luke had ever been married, clue her in on what happened during that missing year. Maybe he even knew who owned the ring. Lane knew something. Kendra was sure of it. She was as sure of it as she was sure of her own name.

Anna

Porcelain berry weed grow in Virginia. Leaves shaped like diamonds, fat with itchy white hair. It grow tall, so tall at our house in Virginia that it curl itself around our roof, drop red berries that look like blood drops. Daddy say he chop the weed down. But he don't. Just let it grow up and around our house like he do it on purpose. Ain't nothing stopping it after a while. Nothing. Anna hate weeds 'cause weeds don't ask. They come in, take a seat, and before you know it, that weed don't go away. That what happened to Anna.

Anna like to listen about how Sylvie play in the snow, how it loved her little baby pigs with the soft pink skin as soft as a puppy belly. But Anna don't like the thing that come stay in her. It remind her of a weed, a weed that come in without asking, without finding out if anybody wanted it there. And now, everybody, the doctor, Kendra, and the man that come visit her, everybody try to make Anna talk about it. Anna don't want to talk.

Weeds grow under steps sometimes, big weeds dark and green and standing up like spears. Anna and Mamma chop down weeds. Bottle brush, alligator weed, pull it up or it'll grow wild and tall like tree of heaven, like the mile-a-minute that Daddy showed Anna in Texas. Weed cover road sign, side of highway, poke through the window of a rusty car. Anna hate weeds. She hate how they attach themselves, uninvited, and stick into where you plant your good things and want to stay, not go away.

Sometime even people you like act like weeds. Sometime they don't ask but try to tell Anna what to do. They tell Anna. Dr. Holder say that they come to talk about "what happened to you." But they did just like the weeds, the mile-a-minute. They come, talking not asking. They want to know how that thing crawled into her belly and nestled like one of Sylvie little pig babies with the soft skin like silk.

But some people ask. Some people will look at you and ask a question. They ask if you would like some soda or they ask if you would like something to eat. They ask you to sit down, look you in the face and ask if they can touch you there. Anna like people who ask.

But the other one, the one who used to come in the night. He don't ask. But sometime, he come, and they walk right out of Brighton House, right out into the night. And they ride away with someone who asks. He has diamond for windows and sinky stuff on the floor that make your feet feel soft. And he give presents, lots of presents to make Anna say yes.

CHAPTER 22

Traffic on the ninety-nine sucked. There was no better way to describe it. It was bumper to bumper. And Carlyle drove like a fucking maniac, riding bumpers, screeching on brakes so he wouldn't smash the car in front of him. At one point, Rich asked him if he were under the illusion that the Hummer could actually drive up and over the pickup truck now parked in front of them. Carlyle only grinned and picked up where he had left off.

"Anyway, as I was saying," he replied, "I've got about thirty people looking at the security camera videos and reviewing the card logs."

Carlyle had been telling him where he was on his piece of the investigation. They were on their way to Val Hightower's estate in The Point—unannounced. Rich wanted to know why Hightower hadn't given him Chadwick's background check.

Rich grabbed his sunglasses and put them on against the sun's glare now pouring through the Hummer's front window. After all the rain over the past week or two, the sky poured blue light all over Dunhill. The air was clean of clouds and the heavens stretched out in periwinkle blue everywhere Rich gazed.

"They find anything yet?" Rich asked.

Carlyle sent him a glance. "You been listening to a word I've been saying? We haven't found anything in those logs or the manual logs. The only things we could find were the appointments Anna had at Doctor's."

"What about the video from the security cameras?"

"That's just it," Carlyle said as he abruptly swerved into the adjoining lane.

Speaking over the blaring horn of the blue Nissan behind him, Carlyle said, "Security camera sounds good, right? But the ones Hightower uses in Brighton House are cheap, mainly for show."

They were behind another pickup now, this one a white Mazda. A statue of a plaster Madonna was wrapped in gold carpets in the back. She held up her hands toward the blue heavens. She reminded Rich of Luke, how it was rumored that he always wore white. And thinking of Luke reminded him of who else but Kendra? He thought about how Kendra had looked at him when he told her to dump him to his face. She couldn't do it. Maybe their relationship was not over but he couldn't tell whether that was a good or bad thing. Sunlight flashed on the plaster Madonna.

"For show?" Rich repeated.

"Yeah," Carlyle confirmed. "For show. The pictures from those things are lousy. You can't make out anything. A couple of the people I got looking at the video say the pictures are so fuzzy that they could argue that they saw Sasquatch in Anna's room."

"Anna's room?" Rich grunted. "You say that they saw something in Anna's room?"

He looked over at Carlyle who shook his head. The man's hair flared red against the blue light outside the window.

"No," he said. "Just a flicker of white. It could have been anything from the nightlight to the light from the hallway under her door."

Rich turned around toward the front again and stared at the blank face of the Madonna in back of the Mazda Carlyle was trying to crawl over.

"That fuck Chadwick wears white," Rich muttered. "All the other nurses and CNAs in scrubs and he wears white. That flicker could be him, you know."

"Look," Carlyle said, looking over his shoulder for another escape route. "I know what you're saying about Chadwick but you don't have any proof. Even if Val Hightower does have the background check tucked away somewhere, whatever he did in the past is not proof that he raped Anna. Why are we going to Hightower's place, Rich? Let's order our own background check."

"Because I want to know why he left out the background check on Chadwick. I want to know what he is hiding," Rich said.

Carlyle shrugged. "What if it was just an oversight?"

"Then we'll get the check and go on our way, won't we?"

"I've had enough of this shit," Carlyle breathed.

At first, Rich thought that he was talking about the conversation. But he soon felt gravel spitting underneath the Hummer's tires. Carlyle had decided to flip a U-turn on the freeway. He launched the Hummer into the center divide. Horns blared, not out of fear or warning, because Carlyle had waited until it was safe before heading out the other direction. They blared out of rage.

"Man," Rich breathed. "Easy."

"We'll just get off the next exit and go the back roads. What will you do if Hightower doesn't have the background check on Chadwick?"

Rich grinned at him then. "Let's just say I know of a few back roads of my own."

This time a maid wearing a black and white uniform answered Val Hightower's door.

"May I help you?" she said, looking from Carlyle to Rich.

"How was your day off?" Rich asked, pushing past her and into the foyer. Rich heard laughter drift from the room that Hightower had spoken to them in on that first visit that seemed like eons ago.

"I beg your pardon?" she said. "Was Mr. Hightower expecting you?"

"Not quite."

Val Hightower emerged from the door of the sitting room. The smile on his face was as phony as Chadwick's friendship with Anna. "Gentlemen, I'm afraid I'm engaged. Can we talk some other time?"

"Don't be afraid, Hightower," Rich said. "I just came to pick up what you forgot to give us the last time we were here. I guess you were not as prepared as you thought."

"Pardon?" Hightower said, his forehead wrinkling.

Rich looked from the maid to Hightower and laughed.

"Sarah," Hightower said. "You can go. It's all right."

Sarah sent Rich a look of annoyance before leaving the room.

"Rich, Jared," Hightower protested. "I'm afraid I'm quite busy."

Rich sniffed the air. "I can see that," he stopped, laughed again. "I mean I can smell that. What is it? Rack of lamb? Brussels sprouts?"

Carlyle wrinkled his nose. "I hate Brussels sprouts," he said.

"Then I won't insist that you stay for dinner," Hightower snapped. "To what do I owe this unasked for pleasure?"

"Believe me, Hightower," Rich said, thinking of the cheap ass camera Hightower used for security at Brighton House. "It's nowhere near a pleasure."

Hightower drew back at Rich's response. From the glitter in his black eyes, Rich could see that the man was genuinely pissed off.

"I see," Hightower said. "Perhaps we can discuss this more comfortably in the sitting room?"

He turned on his heel without waiting for them to follow. Rich knew what he would find once he entered the room and he was not disappointed. Draped over the leather chair he himself had occupied earlier was his ex-fiancée Dinah Webster. Her glossy black hair curled against her honeyed shoulders, the skin set off by the white silk halter she wore. Her green eyes registered no surprise when she saw him. She simply picked up her wineglass with her left hand, swirled the ruby liquid in the bottom of the glass so he would be sure to see the rock she had on the ring finger of her left hand. She sipped the wine, making so much of a show of enjoying it that Rich could almost taste it himself.

"Hello, Rich," she said. "Long time no see."

Across from her Judge Webster glared at him. And he was not the sort of man to waste formalities on the man who had broken his daughter's heart.

"I'm going to the patio," he said. "Call me when you've finished taking out the garbage."

No one spoke for a while after the judge left. That is, until Carlyle opened his big mouth. "Why, Val," he said. "We didn't know that you were having leftovers."

"Now that was uncalled for, man," Rich said.

"You just wish you had thought of it first." Carlyle laughed.

Rich did, but he would have never spoken it aloud. Not because of any sense of chivalry but because Dinah was not a woman easily rattled, had never been. And seeing her rise from the chair and float toward them, he realized that she had not changed much. She stopped several inches away from him. And without looking at Carlyle or Hightower, she said, "I can see that you are still not picky about the company you keep."

Rich said nothing. He just waited for the storm to blow over.

"Tell me, how *is* Kendra?" she asked, folding her arms across her chest, letting him see the creamy curve of her breast in the neckline of the halter.

"She's fine," he lied.

"I hear you two had broken things off," she said.

"For now," he answered.

She looked at him a moment longer before speaking. Then she took a small step closer. She still used the same perfume, Channel No. 5. On any other woman, it would have been a cliché, but on Dinah it was a statement.

"Well, work it out," she said. "I would hate to think she busted us up just to shit all over you. That'd be a waste, now Rich, wouldn't it?"

Rich stepped back. What else, he thought, what else could you do with a woman like Dinah Webster but step back.

"I guest it would," he said.

"Val?" she said, her eyes never leaving Rich's face.

"Yes?"

"Call me when your business is over. I'll be with my father."

"I hope this is quick," Val said after Dinah had left.

Rich rubbed the sweat from his forehead. Carlyle let out a low whistle.

"Man," he said, "I don't know who I feel sorrier for, Val. You or her."

"You'll be feeling sorry for yourself if you don't tell me what you want and get the hell out," Hightower replied between his teeth.

But Carlyle would not let the subject go. "I mean, Rich," he said, staring out the patio door. "What the hell were you thinking?"

"Huh?" Rich asked, confused.

"I mean, look at her." He pointed to the patio where Dinah and her father talked. "And then, look at Kendra. Were you blind?"

"Carlyle," Rich said. "Shut up, please."

Faye Snowden

Carlyle was about to say something else but Rich shot him a warning look. Carlyle's mouth closed.

"You mind telling me . . ." Val started, annoyed, and for once Rich couldn't blame him.

Rich let out a breath of air. "No I don't mind," he said. "But first, you want to tell me why you installed pieces-of-shit security cameras at Brighton House?"

Hightower's face filled with shock. "You're asking me that?" he said.

"Who should I be asking?" Rich countered.

"Well, your boy for one," Hightower answered.

"What boy?" Rich asked.

Hightower looked at Carlyle.

"You mean Carlyle?" Rich was confused.

"Where do you think the money comes from for those security cameras, Marvel?" Hightower asked.

Rich knew that he was right to be incredulous. The budget came from Brighton Industries directly and indirectly from Rich himself. Carlyle handled the budgets for all the security outsourcing. And because that was the case, he handled the security budget for Brighton House. Rich looked over at Carlyle, but the little prick said nothing. He knew all along that those security cameras were shit. But that just didn't make sense. Where did the money go?

"I know what the budgets are like, Hightower," Rich said. "And you should have had enough money to buy something that worked."

Hightower shook his head. "Maybe somebody else would have, but not me."

"Why not?" Rich asked both of them. "Jared?" he said, then tried again. "Carlyle?"

Jared grinned. "I thought Superman over there could handle it, right? Just like you handled me out of the McGill contract?"

"Why, I'm not surprised, Jared. It's just what I thought. Still holding a grudge after all these years? Did you just pocket the extra money your sucker of a boss gave you?"

Rich felt anger well in his throat. He wanted to strangle Carlyle and he hoped the look he sent him conveyed that sentiment. But in the meantime, he had Hightower to deal with.

"Look," Rich said. "I don't have time for this right now. Just give me the Chadwick file and we'll let you get on with your dinner."

Hightower blinked. "The Chadwick file?" he asked.

"Yes," Rich said. "The background check for Brandon Chadwick."

Hightower went to the end table and placed a coaster underneath Dinah's abandoned wineglass.

"I gave you all the background checks that I had," he said dryly.

"But there was one missing," Rich said. "Brandon Chadwick, and he's a weird fuck, Val."

"I don't have it. His was a special case," Hightower answered.

"What do you mean, 'special case'?" Rich asked. "Someone did check this guy out, right?"

"Of course they did," Val said. "But I don't have it. I was told hands off Brandon Chadwick."

Hands off, Rich thought about the Brighton House board members and Phillip Grubb. *Some people you simply have to trust, Rich.* That was Brighton's voice playing like a recording in his head.

"If you don't have the check, then who does?" Rich asked.

"Who do you think?" Hightower answered. "Thomas Brighton."

The drive back to Rich's place was a silent one. It was dark by the time Carlyle had reached Rich's house. Rich stepped down from the passenger door. He held it open as he stared at Carlyle's profile.

"Don't fuck with me, Carlyle," he told him.

Carlyle turned then, looked at Rich. His bird beak mouth stretched out into a grin.

"Why would I fuck you, Rich, when you have already been fucked?"

Still grinning, he reached over the passenger seat and pulled the door out of Rich's hand, slamming it shut. Rich watched Carlyle drive away knowing that tomorrow was not going to be a very good day. It was not going to be a very good day at all.

CHAPTER 23

The dog pictures again. Here he was in Brighton's office staring at those two giant spotted dogs. And on the other wall was Brighton's father, eyes drawn together and scowling. Brighton had summoned Rich first thing this morning, through Carlyle again. Rich remembered the smirk on Carlyle's face, the smugness as he stuck his head in Rich's door and said, "Boss man wants to see you."

"This is most unpleasant," Brighton was saying now. He swiveled in his chair and waved his meaty hand to indicate that Rich take the other chair.

"Most," Theo Lane agreed.

Today, the clown of Dunhill, as Rich liked to think of him, had on a cream silk suit which swallowed his slight frame. A bloodred handkerchief bulged from his breast pocket and perfectly matched the red ascot. He had secured the ascot with a gold pin in the shape of a pig, a diamond for an eye.

"As I was saying, Rich," Brighton continued, "I received a call from a very agitated Val Hightower last night."

"That's funny," Rich said. "I was just over there last night, surprised Val didn't mention it."

Brighton sighed. He picked up a snow globe on his desk and shook it. He did not speak again until the fake snow had settled on the bottom.

"You see this, Rich?" he said, pointing to the building hidden behind the curved glass. "It's a model, an exact replica of the building we are in now. Corporate headquarters for Brighton Industries."

Oh, Lord, Rich thought. *Another story.*

"Brighton Industries has been around a long time before you came along, and will be here a long time after you leave. If you get my drift."

"I'm afraid I don't," Rich said, thinking he would eat a brick before he made this easy for Brighton.

"What Mr. Brighton is saying," Lane broke in, his voice high and thin, "is that we have had a relationship with Val for years. It's perfectly natural for him to call us with concern."

"Us?" Rich questioned.

Brighton laughed a little. "Theo is one of my dearest friends. I depend on him for advice."

Brighton stood up and walked to the portrait of his father. Rich watched as he moved his coat aside and placed his hand in his breast pocket, turned his body to the side in a Napoleon pose. He looked young and strong in that low light. Rich knew that was why Brighton kept the maroon curtains drawn tight and the lights dimmed to this level. He did so because he was constantly on stage, constantly performing.

Rich looked from the model of Brighton Industries shut away in the snow globe to Thomas Brighton posed underneath the portrait of his father. Whatever he had called Rich in for was big. Rich searched his thoughts for what it could be, even though he had a suspicion. Brighton had wanted him to stay away from the rape. Rich hated being told what to do and had done just the opposite. Then there were those background checks that he had asked his brother Dom to do. How discreet had Dom been?

Brighton cleared his throat. But Rich interrupted. There was something he needed to know before Brighton got down to business.

"So what was Hightower crying about, Mr. Brighton?"

Laughter scraped the back of Brighton's throat. "I guess I will never get you to call me Thomas," he asked.

"No," Rich answered without hesitation.

"Okay," he said, turning to Rich fully now, facing him square. "He said that you were very rude."

"Extremely rude." Lane nodded.

"Demanding background checks that he had already given to you," Brighton went on.

"The only problem, sir," Rich said, his eyes boring into Brighton, "is that he didn't give me all of them. I'm missing one."

"Ah, yes." Brighton sighed. "Brandon Chadwick."

Rich raised an eyebrow. "You know him?"

Brighton lifted his fingers toward Lane and then rubbed his forehead. "Theo," he said.

Rich turned to Lane and waited for an answer. Theo straightened his already perfectly straight ascot, dabbed at the corner of his mouth with the bloodred handkerchief.

"You know that there is one in every family," Lane said. "Don't you, Rich?"

"I don't understand," Rich said. "Are you saying that Brandon Chadwick is part of your family?"

"No, not my family," Lane said. "His mother is a good friend of my sister's. He needed a job. My sister begged me to help so I did. I recommended him to Katherine Holder."

"So you know him?" Rich said.

"Vaguely," Lane agreed. "I've met him once or twice but my sister knows him very well. She is well acquainted with the entire family."

"So you see, Rich," Brighton said, holding up his hands. "No huge conspiracy, no one is trying to hide anything from you."

"But we still have a problem, don't we Mr. Brighton?" Rich asked.

Lane picked up his pipe and clamped it between his yellow teeth. As Brighton seated himself behind his massive desk, he said, "And what problem is that?"

"We still don't have a background check for Brandon Chadwick."

"Why, we have the best background check in the world." Lane laughed. "The background check by word of mouth."

"Well, word of mouth has it, Mr. Lane, word from Brandon Chadwick's mouth, that he's made the round at mental hospitals across the country."

"Oh, this is ridiculous," Brighton broke in. "Of course we did a background check on Chadwick, a very thorough one. Nothing in the records that would preclude him from working at Brighton House."

"Then you won't mind me taking a look?" Rich asked, but he knew the answer even before Lane spoke.

"Oh, I'm afraid we can't," Lane said. "There is a small matter of privacy for my sister and her family."

"What about the small matter of patient safety?" Rich asked.

"I'm very concerned about patient safety, Rich," Brighton said. "And Brandon Chadwick had been a model employee for the past year he's worked in my facility. Patients are not in danger from him or any other employee at Brighton House."

"I'm afraid Anna Cotton would not agree with you there," Rich said.

The pipe Lane had been playing with clattered to the floor. The sweet smell of tobacco filled the air. Rich tried to study Lane's face in the low light of Brighton's office but could only make out the frown of worry on his face. Lane murmured an apology and placed the pipe in a crystal ashtray.

"So sorry," he said again. "This is most upsetting."

"He did it," Rich said, not taking his eyes from Lane's. "I believe Chadwick raped Anna and fathered that child. Anna hates him."

"Anna Cotton," Thomas Brighton said, "is mentally deficient. You can't trust anything that she has to say. You know that, Rich."

"She's afraid of him," Rich contradicted. "You don't have to have all your mental capacities to know what fear feels like, not the last time I checked, anyway.

"But she's been through an awful trauma," Lane said.

The sonorous tone of Brighton's voice stopped Rich's next words. "Rich . . ." he said.

Rich waited, knowing what would come next. Brighton did not disappoint. He started with praises, mentioning what a great job Rich had done in the past years securing headquarters, what an asset he had been to the Brighton family.

"Your occasional drinking," Brighton said, "I can tolerate, but not your open defiance."

"And what open defiance are you referring to?" Rich asked

"You were supposed to be looking into security protocols at Brighton House, not stirring up the rape again. I told you to stay away, Rich, remember." Brighton paused. "You mean to tell me that there is more than that?"

Rich smiled, thinking of his brother's snooping. "I don't mean to tell you anything, sir."

"You're fired," Brighton said.

"Of course."

"Do you have anything to say, Rich?" Brighton asked.

Rich shrugged. His hands fluttered apart. "Sure I do," he said.

"What's that?"

"So much for the devil you know."

CHAPTER 24

Two days later Rich stood in the produce section at Save Mart supermarket. It was cold outside. The weather, except for a brief respite these last few days when the sun came out, did not let up. Not needing the big cart, he carried the small red basket in front of him. He held onto the wire handles with both hands. He stood very still, knowing he did this, but was unable to move. A profusion of color burst around him, the tomatoes red and fat, celery pale green and sinewy, cilantro—or was it parsley—a darker green. Oranges were out and stacked precariously high. A little girl in streaming blonde pigtails reached up on tiptoes and pulled one down. They all tumbled like river stones to the buffed floor. Cries from the mother but Rich didn't move. He noticed when he walked in that the peaches were out as well, but still small, hard, most likely green inside. And there were strawberries, insanely expensive but there for the taking.

He had not shaved. He wore an open shirt over a gray T-shirt, work boots and a faded blue Anorak. Since he lost his job, he spent most of the time ignoring Carlyle's frantic calls. He called Kendra Hamilton instead who, in turn, ignored his calls. Rich's mind, with the color of the peaches, cilantro, tomatoes so juicy they looked about to split their skins, was a confused jumble. He had forgotten what he had come for and didn't remember how he had ended up in the produce section of Save Mart. Was it because right behind him was the liquor section? But he told himself that it was not so.

Rich had not had a drink in two days, since the meeting with Hightower. It was a conscious decision, a decision that had surprised him. But he later told himself that it was not because he had a problem. Instead, it was because drinking, falling asleep in his clothes with a bottle close to him, waking up with the smell of it all over him, these things had become a liability. He was tired of hearing it from his brother, from Kendra and Brighton.

But what had convinced him most of all was the package waiting for him when he returned to the office soon after his meeting with Brighton and Lane. It was there on his lacquered desk, a heavy black box tied tastefully with white packing ribbon. Rich opened the note first. On heavy linen stationery, Hightower had written, *I feel we have gotten off to the wrong start and also wanted to thank you for informing me about the problems at the office. I do apologize for any misunderstanding last night. Please accept this gift as a token of our lasting relationship.* If he hadn't been canned, Rich wouldn't have thought anything of it. Just another gift from a vendor.

Curious, he opened the box, wondering what game Hightower was playing. The thought left him immediately after he lifted the lid, the second he undid the bubble wrap. Hightower had sent him a bottle of booze. It was an expensive bottle of booze, whiskey on reserve, but a bottle of booze nonetheless.

The insult was clear. Anger at first, then self-doubt, then self-loathing. How had he let himself get so out of control that others noticed it? That they thought they could use it against him? Hightower was sending a message with the liquor. The message he was sending said don't fuck with me Richard T. Marvel. You may know about me, but I know more about you.

Now, as he gazed at the tomatoes, the liquor on the shelves directly behind him pressed against his conscience with such fierceness that the sensation was physical.

"Can I help you, sir?"

The produce man, red apron, slick black hair, wanted to know if he could help him. Yes, Rich wanted to say, where is your vodka? The one in the tall blue bottle, the large size as big as a baseball bat?

"I was looking for romaine lettuce," Rich said.

The man smiled, pointed, and Rich turned back to the front of the produce section, well out of arms reach of the liquor section.

He stopped by Kendra's apartment on the way home. Well, it wasn't actually on the way, but he stopped by anyway.

He did this without asking himself why because deep down, he knew. At first, he convinced himself that he wanted to know why she took the list from his office. What could Kendra possibly want with a list of Brighton House board members? But God help him, the real reason was that he loved her.

As always, his old girlfriend lived on the edge and on the in between of things. The Liberty Apartments should have been in The Pit. It was so close that Rich was sure Kendra could hear the gang-banging from the poorest neighborhood in Dunhill. But the apartment building was considered to be in The View, the okay if not great side of town. Liberty was surrounded by an established neighborhood, clapboard houses sitting right on the new four-lane street busy with all manner of cars and trucks on their way to the freeway. If asked, Rich believed that he would hear the old folks still living there say that it used to be a nice neighborhood before the exhaust of passing cars and before The Pit got so bad.

He knocked several times on Kendra's apartment door but received no answer. He even resorted to pressing his ear to the door. He heard nothing. The apartment had been silent as a grave. His frustration mounted. Goddammit, he knew that she was in there. She had to be. He pounded on the door with his palm. The sounds were hollow. Worry replaced the frustration and anger. He considered breaking down the door but dismissed the idea outright because breaking down the door was not necessary.

Always come prepared, he thought as he pulled out a set of tools from the pocket of his anorak. He inserted the tension wrench into the lock and followed with the pick. While he did this he asked himself again if he had lost his mind. But God had answered in the form of pins falling into place and the lock clicking open. Obviously, he had not.

When he was able to open the door, he realized that Kendra Hamilton could not have been inside. If she was, she would have fastened the dead bolt, hinged the lock chain. But she had not. He considered shutting the door and walking away but his curiosity won out. She would be angry as hell that he had invaded her privacy, but at least he would get a reaction.

The place felt cold. Rich could see his breath on the air. It looked as if she hadn't been home for a couple of days. A red light pulsed on the answering machine as if there were a million messages there. About half were from him. The Luke paraphernalia sat undisturbed on the coffee table.

Rich walked to the middle of the room, turned slowly around and around, wondering what game Kendra was playing at. He wondered if it were a game at all. She had begged him to help her, put her pride aside and drove to Tahoe to ask him to find out who raped Anna Cotton. And after he had agreed, she had chosen to disappear—again.

"Young man." The voice behind him was angry. "I would have you know that I will call the police."

Rich turned around and stared at the woman before him. She was a large woman, black, wearing a synthetic wig askew on her misshapen head. She had on a dress covered in yellow peonies. Her breasts sagged all the way to the matching cloth belt. Her eyes scraped Rich's face.

"Are you the boyfriend, then?" she asked.

Rich ignored the remark and instead asked, "Where is she?"

She continued as if he had not spoken. "If you are the boyfriend then you should be interested in helping her with the rent." She held out her palm.

"What?" Rich asked, confused.

"The key," she said simply, her voice imperious.

"I don't have a key," he said. "Where is she?"

She folded her arms again. Large and meaty at the shoulders, they tapered almost to nothing at the wrists. "I would not know," she said. "I just know that if I don't get the rent she will be evicted."

"Evicted?" Rich asked.

"Yes," she repeated. "Evicted. She has stopped working, has not paid the rent in over a month. Then I hear she flew off to someplace . . ."

"What?" Rich interrupted her, his heart beating at the thought of Kendra gone without telling him.

"Flew off to someplace, called a cab, and flew off to someplace across country."

"Would you mind telling me what in the hell is going on? How do you know this?"

She stepped heavily into the room. "I am trying to. An acquaintance of mine drives a cab. He told me that he had taken her to the airport and she flew off to someplace across country. And when she returned, do you think that she had the rent? No. She did not."

Rich balled his fists into his pockets. He fought for control, realizing that this woman spoke of the trip to Virginia Kendra had already told him about. This woman was not speaking of a new trip. Kendra had not run away again. "Where is she now?" he asked.

"I would not know," she said. "I would not know at all. All I do know is that she has to go. Your girlfriend has not been living up to her responsibilities. I run an apartment building, not a flop house."

Rich started to say more but she pointed to the door as if he were a disobedient dog and she was an owner throwing it out of the house.

"Did she leave an emergency address with her application?" he asked.

"She did not." She still had her arm out, pointing toward the door. When Rich reached it, she said, "And I will have these locks changed, young man. The key that you have will not do you any good."

Rich only nodded as he walked out of the door. It felt as if a back hoe had dug a pit in his stomach. The unmistakable feeling that he still felt for Kendra, that she had the power to worry him, made him feel lost and out of control.

"Did you hear me?" Mrs. Buttress said to his back.

"Loud and clear," Rich answered. But it was more to himself than to the landlady.

Rich sat in his car outside of Kendra's apartment building. The smell of the new leather, the swirling wood on the dashboard, the silver knobs and digital readouts made him feel as if he were piloting a hearse, a soulless piece of machinery driving him to nowhere. As he sat in the car, listening to 91.9, local blues and jazz, he listened for direction from his scooped out gut. None was forthcoming. The rain, driving needles of ice, started to fall all around him. Water slid slantwise into the windshield, pinged against the Monte Carlo's hood.

He called Carlyle, who was happy and not happy to hear from him.

"Rich," he answered the phone before Rich even heard the ring. "You son of a bitch. Where the hell have you been?"

"Have you heard from Kendra Hamilton?" he asked.

"What?"

"I said have you heard from . . ."

"Hell, no, I haven't heard from Kendra Hamilton. I haven't heard from you, Rich. I have been trying to call you for the last two days."

"Why is that? To gloat about how you fucked me over?"

"Look, man," Carlyle said. "I had no idea that the old bastard was going to fire you. I thought you were just going to get your ass chewed."

"You're a fucking liar, Carlyle," Rich said.

Carlyle laughed. "That I am. But why are you getting so mad, man? That wasn't your gig anyway."

"Whatever," Rich said. "Look, have you seen Kendra Hamilton? At Brighton House or anything?" It was a long shot, Rich knew, but worth a try.

"Is that why you're calling me?" Carlyle asked. "Because you can't find your old girlfriend?"

Rich turned the ignition key. Instead of the sputter he expected, the Monte Carlo's motor sprang into life immediately. He pulled away from the curb.

"Why else would I be calling you, asshole?" Rich said.

"I don't know, Rich," Carlyle replied. "How about putting that fuck Chadwick away?"

Rich pulled the phone away from his ear and looked at it in surprise. "Did I hear you right?" he said. "Is this Jared Carlyle? The same man who took kickbacks from Val Hightower?"

"Hey," Carlyle said. "It had nothing to do with the money. It was personal, Rich. That son of a bitch fucked me. I was returning the favor."

"And now what are you doing, Jared?"

"We both have a score to settle with Chadwick. Let's get him."

"I got fired, remember?"

"I'm still around and I need your help," Carlyle replied.

Rich frowned, thinking. Then he said, "Brighton won't let me near Brighton House."

"What he don't know won't hurt 'em, Rich."

Rich laughed. "So you know that you will be standing in line right behind me in the unemployment office?"

"I was looking for a job when I found this one. Chadwick is a sick one. As a matter of fact, that place is full of 'em. I'll put a lot on my conscience, but leaving the inmates in charge of the asylum is not one of them. You with me on this?"

"Is that why you been calling me?"

"Why else?" Carlyle asked.

Rich paused for a minute, then said, "I'm with you, man."

After he hung up the phone, he listened to the wipers against the windshield, wondering if he might not have been a good judge of character after all.

The rain did not stop as Rich drove to San Francisco, except that it became harder, pounding against his windshield. Rain splattered against the asphalt of the freeway, sending up an angry spray of water that almost blinded him. For a moment during that ride Rich was glad the maple had crushed the Firebird.

Dominic Marvel lived in Pacific Heights, a prestigious address for a musician respected but not famous, successful, but not insanely so. Dominic's wife's income was needed to maintain the address. She worked for the county planning office. The three-story Victorian was pale blue with white trim. Elizabeth's mother sometimes used the attic apartment on the third floor.

Rich's brother answered the door in velour lounge pants, a torn beige T-shirt, and house slippers. A navy-blue beret sat on top of short dreadlocks, which framed Dom's dark face. Rich was enveloped in a bear hug but it became immediately clear that Dom was distracted. As he led Rich to the living room furnished with mismatched furniture and poorly lit by a single light on the vaulted ceiling, there was no, *don't you work for a living,* or *what or you doing here,* or *my, what a pleasant surprise.* The only thing Dom asked him was if he wanted a drink. He quickly amended the offer with ice water or soda.

Rich could hear the kids' voices float from the kitchen. They chattered excitedly about something, talking to someone else in the kitchen. Rich thought that Elizabeth must have taken a day off of work. Every now and then Rich heard a bubble of laughter.

"Sorry about that," Dom said. "The kids are out of school, about to drive me crazy."

Rich sat down without saying anything. He was glad that Dom was not asking why he wasn't at work in the middle of the day. A distant whir, like a blender, sounded before stopping suddenly. More laughter from the children. Before Rich could comment, Dominic said, half standing. "Did you eat already; I could fix you a sandwich."

Rich shook his head, then told Dominic that he was sure when he was asked again. Dominic reached over and pressed Rich's knee.

"You look like hell, man, but you look good, you know. How has everything been going?"

"Fine," Rich said.

He knew what Dom referred to, the drinking, the binges. At the start of his career as a musician, Dom had what they referred to as a walk on the wild side. Drinking, drugs. But what distinguished him from his colleagues was that the walk was a brief one. It took one overdose, one time of waking up in the emergency room staring at the silver-domed bright light in his eyes for him to realize that coke was overrated. And not worth his life.

"How long has it been?" Dom asked him now.

Rich held up the peace sign to indicate two days.

"You done, then, man?" Dom asked.

Rich shrugged. "Done as I can be," he said, thinking of the bottle of booze Hightower had sent him.

Rich did not know what he meant, only at this moment that he would never take a drink again with the pure intent of getting drunk or escaping. Because pretty soon, you not only escape from the things you wanted to escape from, you end up escaping from the things you wanted to keep. And right now, no, two days ago when he opened that box and saw that bottle of booze from Val Hightower, he realized that he no longer wanted to escape from his life, not all of it, anyway.

"Was never that bad anyway, man," Rich said. "It wasn't every day. I'm lucky; quitting won't be that hard for me."

"Physically, maybe not," Dom said, but then tapped an index finger to his temple, "But emotionally, giving up that crutch is going to be hell, man."

Rich nodded, but did not say anything. He thought about himself staring at the tomatoes, waiting for them to speak. Dom had started to hum to himself in that distracted way of his. He reached over and picked up some sheet music from an end table. It was then that Rich realized he had interrupted Dom working, and that Dom's mind was already switching from him back to what he was doing before Rich arrived. He was sure of it when Dom picked up an unlit pipe and clamped it between his teeth. The pipe reminded him of Theo Lane and one of the reasons he came to see Dominic. Rich knew that he had to get Dom's mind off his work.

"Dom," he said, "those background checks I asked you for, are you done with them?"

Dom nodded absently. "Yes, yes," he said, and then disappeared.

He returned with a legal tablet scribbled with notes that Rich knew he wouldn't be able to decipher even if he had a Ph.D. in cryptography. That was the only thing about using Dom. His organization skills sucked. Good thing his memory was good.

"You get to the extra name that I gave you?" Rich asked.

Dom nodded. "That was Chadwick, right? I think I did," he said.

"What did you find?"

"Let's get to him later. I'd rather do the easy ones first."

Rich had an idea of what Dom meant by the easy ones but didn't say anything. But his brother went on to say that he didn't find anything out of the ordinary on the board members. A shady deal or two, a few kickbacks.

"Kickbacks?" Rich asked.

"Yeah, yeah, your boy Carlyle, for one."

"I know that, Dom, but his name wasn't on the list."

"No, Rich," Dom agreed. "That's right. But I took that one up by myself. Hope you don't mind."

"I do," Rich said.

"Well, that's too bad, you should know," Dom said.

"Let's leave him out of it. What else do you have?"

"That's about it. Everybody else checked out on the up and up." Dom stopped and laughed. "I guess you don't want to know who has prescriptions for Viagra." Dom picked up his pipe again and clamped it between his teeth. He shook his head.

Rich laughed. "How do you do it? Find all this shit out."

"Talent," Dom said. "And my brother used to be a cop, man. I learned everything I know from him."

Rich snorted. "Yeah, right. So who's on the love juice?"

"Thomas Brighton is," he said. "Well, I guess he has to keep the wife happy. And that weird cat, Lane."

Rich lifted an eyebrow.

"You need to do something about that eyebrow thing," Dom said.

"You're kidding me," Rich challenged. "Theo Lane?"

"Nope, I'm not kidding and yep, Theo Lane."

"Did you find a girlfriend?" Rich asked.

"Not one who he makes mention of. His wife died about a year back." He looked down at his notes. "I meant to say last January."

"So no wife, no girlfriend? What's he doing taking Viagra?"

"Beats the hell out of me," Dom said. "Besides, I didn't say that he was taking it. I said that he had a prescription for it. It may have just been one of those automatic refills. Wife's not been gone that long."

"Did you find out anything else about him?" Rich asked.

"Naw," Dom responded. "He was kind of a hard nut to crack, especially since he's not from Dunhill and keeps pretty much to himself. There was only so much I could do."

"I see," Rich said. "I guess that makes sense. What about Grubb?"

"Now, him, and that Chadwick," Dom said, "are into some weird ass shit."

Rich sat up. "You mean Grubb has a connection to Brandon Chadwick?"

Dom nodded, then looked at Rich. "How do you get mixed up with these people, anyway? You're like some sort of damn freak magnet . . ."

"Dom," Rich said.

"Okay. Grubb and Chadwick are porn buddies."

"What?" Rich said.

"You know, porn buddies."

"No, I don't know," Rich said.

"They swap shit, man. Movies. They go to strip clubs together, share whores. That sort of thing. Chadwick's not too quiet about it, either. Now, him, he's a bragger."

Rich leaned back. So that was what was bugging the hell out of him about Phillip Grubb. That was what he was hiding. But what Rich didn't understand was how Grubb and Chadwick met. Dom's voice interrupted his thoughts.

"I guess they must have met when Chadwick was helping Lane with his wife."

Rich shook his head, disgusted. Theo Lane forgot to mention that little detail. He kept to himself the fact that Chadwick actually worked for him. Friend of the family, my ass, Rich thought.

"That it," Rich asked.

"Isn't that enough?"

More laughter from the kitchen. Rich heard Stella's high-pitched squeal. No, that wasn't exactly enough, Rich thought as the laughter died down. Rich knew that Dom and Kendra had become friends, perhaps closer than she and Rich had, in some ways. If anyone knew where she was then Dom probably had an idea.

"Have you heard from Kendra?" Rich asked him.

Dom removed the pipe from his lips. He stared at Rich.

"She's here, man," Dom said. "I thought you knew that."

Rich sat up. "You mean she's here? Why didn't you tell me? Why didn't you call me?"

"I thought you knew." Dominic said again. "She's in the kitchen with the kids."

Rich had not known he was standing until Dom said this last. Unlike the rest of the house, the kitchen was a large bright room with a black and white tile floor and shiny copper-bottom pots hanging from a black rack suspended from the ceiling. Kendra stood at the sink in a sleeveless T-shirt and faded Levis. They were too big for her and hung on her waist showing the brown skin of her back. Her hair, as always, was a like a train wreck. Curls sprang around her serene face; the rest of her hair was bunched into a clip at the nape of her neck. She wore a mask of calm, her face still and smooth.

She was cutting the tops from strawberries, laying each one on a white dish towel spread out on the counter. She dropped the severed leaves and white tops into the sink. Some of the strawberries were oversize, a gelatinous red like a pulsating blood vessel against the white towel. Others were small, hard, and pink, and probably as bitter as malt vinegar. Several zipper lock freezer bags lay nearby.

The children were not quiet. Stella had the Kitchen-Aid blender on the island beneath the copper pots. Next to it sat a container of Dryer's ice cream. Stella's white turtleneck, too small for her pudgy body, was covered in strawberry stains. She ate ice cream straight from the container with a brown wooden spoon. Ice cream melted into her dirt-rimmed fingernails and down her arms. It had gotten into her hair.

Five-year-old Turner dug the ice cream scoop into the same container before dumping great gobs into the mouth of the blender. The surrounding island and the pots were not spared the mess. They were covered in pink and white globs of ice cream and strawberries. Stella and Turner had been using the blender without the lid, laughing at the resulting storm. Kendra did not seem to notice or care. She just stood there, eyes downcast, cutting away the strawberries' white tops. Rich did not know Dom had followed him into the kitchen until he spoke.

"Kids," he said with an outstretched hand.

Stella turned toward them, crying "Uncle Rich." Before Dom could stop them, Rich felt two sets of very sticky arms around his waist. Stella still had the wooden spoon. The mess had gotten over Rich's T-shirt, the legs of his jeans, the tops of his brown work boots. Dom, unperturbed by the state of the kitchen and less so, if it could be possible, by the state of his children, laughed.

"Sorry about that," he said, peeling Stella and Turner away.

Rich gave them both hugs, returning their hellos, and promised to come play with them later. All the while Kendra stood at the sink, refused to acknowledge his presence. She picked up another strawberry. Rich walked over to her, could see that her fingernails were stained red.

He turned away from the sink, leaned against it and folded his arms across his chest. He stood close enough to her, as close as he could without touching her. If she would turn her head to look at him, he would feel her breath on his face. After the kids and Dom left the room, the silence settled around them like a thick fog. The copper pots had ceased to swing from the assault. The blender's whir had disappeared as if it had never been. It was so quiet, so still for a while, that Rich swore that he could hear the twisting sound of the serrated blade cut into the flesh of the strawberry. Kendra placed it on the white towel where it came to rest with the others, red and glistening from the tap water. She picked up another strawberry, lifted the leaves to prepare it for the cut. They stood that way for a long while, through the next three strawberries. Finally Rich spoke.

"Fancy meeting you here," he said.

She did not reply. He could feel that she was careful not to move because if she did, she might accidentally touch him. Her neck had gone as stiff as a rod. The only movement the twisting of her fingers as she gathered the leaves, the circling of the blade. He knew her well enough from their brief and tense time together that she wanted to be near him but not near enough to touch or be touched.

"Looks like you have a lot on your mind," he said, and his voice was almost as quiet as the room, as if he had become a part of the soft sounds around them.

"I do," she answered.

He cocked an eyebrow. "Is not having a place to stay one of them?"

She dropped the paring knife into the sink.

"That's not a problem for me yet," she said.

"But will be soon, right?"

The moment of intimacy borne from a physical relationship that ended almost two years ago had passed. A step to the left on her part put her out of his reach. Now grabbing a towel, she furiously dried her hands.

Looking at him calmly, she said, "Will be is not is."

And he knew that she was not pretending to not be worried. She and her mother lived on the streets most of her life. When Luke Bertrand came along, she did not live with him but in foster homes all over Dunhill. Rich believed that the longest she spent in any place was at school, first college, then medical school. He was sure that she would find a place to stay. She put the towel on the counter and turned away from him. She picked up the wet container of ice cream and placed it in the sink. Rich watched the sides collapse.

"I've been looking for you," Rich said.

She did not answer. Instead, she ran water into the carton until the contents turned a milky white. She poured the entire stream down the garbage disposal, watching the liquid swirl as the garbage disposal roared. She did not look at Rich. And Rich could tell by the rigid set of her profile that she wanted him to go away, that she wished with all her heart that he was not there.

"Why are you here, anyway?" he asked.

"I got sick," she said matter-of-factly. I asked Dom if I could use the attic apartment for a couple of days until I felt better."

"And do you feel better?" he asked.

"A little," she answered.

He said, "When were you going to tell me about this?"

She turned off the water, turned off the garbage disposal. Silence wrapped the kitchen, once again. "I hadn't planned on it," was all she said.

"How long are you planning to stay here?" he asked. She did not answer him.

He sat down at a wooden kitchen table with matching chairs that were as uncomfortable as they looked. These chairs were not to be sat in. Elizabeth, Dom's wife, put the table there to the left of the nook just to fill the empty space in the cavernous kitchen. Elizabeth believed that every square inch of the house should be filled with something, even if that something was a chair that looked as inviting as the back of a porcupine.

Kendra did not follow him. Not immediately, anyway. She waited, until she had taken all the copper pots and placed them one by one on top of each other into the wide silver sink. Rich listened to them clang against each other. He spoke over the running water, raising his voice so that she could hear him.

"We need to talk," he said.

She was in a mood. He could see that now. When they were together she would get that way sometimes. Long silences, face empty except for the iceberg frost. He knew that it had nothing to do with him. Some demon in the distant past. That's what hurt the most, that she would move him aside, anything aside even if she claimed it meant the world to her, to go demon hunting.

Nonetheless, she turned off the water and walked over to the table carrying a soaked dish towel. She balled the towel into a bunch and placed it on the wooden table. She looked at him for a long time. *Maybe she's ready to talk,* he thought. But then he made a mistake, instead of waiting, he spoke first.

"So you've been here the entire time?" he asked. "Not flying off to any place else?"

At the question, a funny look crossed her frozen face. Her lips curled upward into just the hint of a smile.

"Why, I've been to London to see the queen," she said. "Or in this case, the king."

Her voice was serious. Confusion buzzed around him. He could feel it in the air; he could feel it in the frustrated tickle in his stomach.

"What?" he said.

She laughed, shook her head a little. "Nowhere," she said. "I mean here, like I told you, the whole time. What's up?"

He leaned back in his chair. From confusion to surprise now. He felt that he had stepped into a surreal painting and all around him were melting clocks.

"What's up?" he said. "What in the hell do you think is up? The shit you dragged me into is up. That's what's up."

"I don't recall dragging you into anything, Rich."

Her voice was calm, modulated, like warm cocoa on a cold night. If it weren't for her sitting here and if it weren't for the chair beneath him, a chair that made him feel every bone in his ass, he would say that he was in a dream. Alone. Asleep and oblivious. Kendra had checked out. She was not with him and at that moment, she could not give a damn about Anna or what was going on with him.

He tried again. "What's going on, Kendra?"

Her hands lay against the lighter brown of the faded table. She lifted her fingers, one after the other, and let them drop back to the table.

"Nothing," she said.

And suddenly he knew. But he did not say anything. He was a detective long enough to know that some leads you just needed to move away from. Right now, she was like a two-ton boulder in front of a cave. He would get nothing out of her without a crane and a forklift. Not now, anyway, perhaps not ever.

"I need some help," he said.

"With what?"

He had arrived at Dom's house in the late afternoon. They had spoken for an hour before Rich asked about Kendra. The skylight above the hanging pot rack had begun to darken. He could almost smell the coming night and feel the bright stars pressing down on him.

He leaned his elbows on the table. "You know with what," he said. "This Anna thing."

"What do you mean?"

He sighed, ran his hands over his head. He could feel the stubble where his short hair had started to grow out. The hair felt sharp, like tiny blades growing out of his head. He did not notice these things when drinking. Ever since he stopped he felt everything times three. He saw with the keen eye of a sharpshooter. Except for the dryness in his mouth, the absent ever-present smell of stale alcohol and this feeling, he could barely believe that he had not had a drink in two days.

As he thought about this, he realized that the two of them had never had any real conversation, especially when she was in this stony mood. They fenced, thrust lightly, retreated easily. They parried. Conversation was more of a tool between them than anyone else he knew. They never talked for the sake of talking, for the pleasure of hearing each other's voice.

He was suddenly sick of it all. What he wanted to say was this: *When you stopped returning my phone calls, left the country without telling me, I was angry. But more than angry, I was scared. I started drinking, a lot. But a couple of days ago, I stopped. I think I am done with all that now. It's over. But you know what, I'm still scared. I haven't been as scared since the day I learned that you were gone, and would not be back. And when I couldn't find you I got the same feeling I had two years ago.* That's what he wanted to say.

But instead, he said, "Okay, straight. I've been drinking too much, screwing up." He looked at her. Now, he had her complete attention. "Worse, I got fired the other day. But it wasn't because of the drinking. It was because I was getting too close to finding out who raped Anna."

She smiled a little again. "I thought you said that you didn't do rapes."

"Will you just listen to me?" he asked.

"Okay. Listening."

"Getting too close," he continued, "I think I know who did this, Kendra, but I need some help."

She blinked, eyes hard. "They have the guy who did this, Leroy, remember?"

They stared at each other a long time. "You are wrong about that, Kendra. Anyway, security is tight around Brighton House. They even have a camera in her room."

"A camera in her room, huh? Why?"

"Because they suspected that she had been sneaking out, stealing and hiding things, I guess. And Katherine Holder thought it would make Anna feel better. She even wears a little security bracelet."

"But if there is a camera in her room, that ought to make things easier, right?"

He shook his head. "No," he said, "It's not. I met with Val Hightower. Do you know him?"

"I know of him," she said. "Another pillar of the community."

He knew what she meant by another. Luke Bertrand was the other.

She said, "I hear he's dating a judge's daughter."

He did not wince. But his look said *come on, Kendra*. He went on. "His company provides security for Brighton House. But the cameras are shit. You can't make out anything."

Kendra had not said anything. The night had pressed in on them. The kitchen had grown darker. "Did you look at the video?"

"It's not that easy," he repeated. "I said that the video is practically useless without more evidence."

Her mouth twisted into a smile. "Well, good luck, Rich," she said. "I know you're smart enough to figure it out."

He tried to keep calm. He would not win any other way. "I'm beginning to doubt that, Kendra," he said. "What I need is a goddamn crime scene."

He had lost her. Her face, an iceberg in the fog, retreated. She stood up and walked over to the light switch. He held up his hands to stop her.

"Kendra," he said. "I don't get this. Don't you care about what happens to Anna Cotton?"

"Anna Cotton," she repeated, and looked at him for a long time. It was not a warm look. Her eyes were cold.

"You know, I'm sick of caring. I decided that the other night, believe it or not, in the dark at two in the morning that I'm sick of caring about other people. I'm sick of young girls in trouble. Anna, did you know, she reminds me a lot of April. Their names even sound the same."

"But it is not the same," Rich said this slowly. They were still in the dark because she had not yet turned on the light. She had spoken of April Hart, the girl who had almost lost her life to Luke Bertrand and almost caused Kendra her own life. She was pregnant, too. That's where all similarity stopped.

"But it is the same, in a way it is exactly the same, has been this way since I left medical school and came back to The Pit to practice medicine. Someone, Rich, someone always grabbing at you, wanting little pieces. I decided the other night that this time, I'm looking out for me. It's about what I want now."

"And what is that, Kendra? What is it that you want?" he asked her.

She turned on the lights. Fluorescent light flooded the room.

"What you need to do," she said, her finger still on the light switch, "to find your goddamned crime scene is to review the medical records."

"I don't understand. Whose medical records?'

"Anna Cotton's. Look at the medical records. I've met her doctor. He's sloppy."

"What am I looking for?"

She folded her arms, cocked her head and laughed at him, a throaty laugh that, for the first time tonight, reached her eyes. "You know what you are looking for, Rich. I don't have to tell you that."

CHAPTER 25

And she did not have to tell him what to look for. The next day, Rich was in Carlyle's office reviewing Anna Cotton's medical records. At first, Dr. Holder had refused to bring them over, said that the rape was a police matter that had been reviewed. But Rich insisted, and more importantly, Kendra, the guardian who no longer gave a shit, insisted. He couldn't tell anything from them at first. The doctor was sloppy. Though some notes had been typed, Dr. Dawson had a few stuck on Post-It notes here and there. Rich had tried to get Kendra to come out but she refused, said something about being too busy. Instead, Katherine Holder agreed to help Carlyle and Rich decipher the mess. She sat across from them now in Carlyle's office.

"I see you wasted no time getting my desk in here," Rich said, looking around. "And my chair."

Carlyle grinned. "You didn't seem to have a need for them," he said.

Holder nervously picked up the gold letter opener that had been in Rich's office prior to Carlyle's raid. She twirled it in her hands.

"This looks like the same one I had," she said.

Rich took it from her and ran his finger over the point, so sharp it actually looked like a knife blade.

"Yep," Rich said. "Christmas gift from the board. I think everybody who worked for Brighton Industries got them. You weren't working here then, right Carlyle? This is technically still mine, you know."

Carlyle didn't answer, just offered the file to Rich so they could both look.

"If you have any questions let me know," Holder offered carefully, her hair slipping out of the topknot splashed on her head.

She was not in the suit today but jeans and a shirt covered with tiny flowers. The soft fabric reminded Rich of a pajama shirt. It was her day off, she had announced earlier as she came in with the records.

"Have you seen this?" he asked her, indicating the records.

"I looked through it, of course," she said. "All seems to be in order."

He smiled, thinking of Kendra. Nothing is ever as it seems, he thought. But he did not say this out loud.

"It looks a little bit like a mess," Carlyle said.

Dr. Holder sighed, crossed her well muscled legs.

"I know that it does. I debated cleaning it up before I gave it to you and the police. But I wanted to make sure that things stayed as they were. Dr. Dawson is the only general practitioner doctor we have for the entire facility. Thirty of our patients are forensic which means that they are there by order of the court. Some are very dangerous and disturbed. He sees about twenty a day. Sometimes he runs out of time."

"So the police have seen this?" Rich asked

"Yes, they have a copy," Dr. Holder said.

Rich pulled out a page. He was surprised at the list of medications Anna was on, which included Zoloft and lithium.

"Why all the meds? Lithium is an antidepressant, isn't it?"

"Not really. It's mainly used for bipolar disorders. But I think here, Dr. Dawson was trying to calm her down. She has some emotional problems and gets manic sometimes."

"You mean she's not just a retard?" Carlyle asked.

"Please," Rich said. "Carlyle."

"Yes. She has somewhat of a violent streak, if you haven't noticed," Dr. Holder answered.

"Was she seeing a psychiatrist? Rich asked.

"No," Katherine Holder said. "She wasn't."

"Why not?"

"Brighton House doesn't believe in counseling for the mentally retarded patients. We don't find it effective."

Rich snorted. "That's the dumbest thing I think I ever heard," he said.

She shrugged. "I know. But our board doesn't agree with it. Besides, Dr. Dawson has a counseling license and can prescribe the drugs needed to keep patients calm."

Rich nodded, thinking about how rough Anna had it. He thought about what he had learned about mental retardation. It was a state of intelligence, from what he read, it was not a mental disease. How smart does one have to be before they can benefit from counseling or just talking to someone?

Dr. Dawson saw Anna on a weekly basis since her arrival at Brighton House. He did not suspect that she was pregnant until the fourth exam. He ordered blood tests but the results were not examined for two more weeks. He saw her more afterwards, prescribed prenatal vitamins and took her off the lithium right up until the time the baby was aborted.

"Wait," Rich said. "Dr. Dawson performed the abortion?"

"He's fully qualified," Holder bristled. "I don't see why that's such a shock."

"But," Carlyle said, "she had the abortion at Doctor's. She had those appointments."

Dr. Holder frowned. She pulled a strand of her slippery hair behind her ear. "What do you mean, appointments at Doctor's? She didn't have any."

"But the logs show that Chadwick signed her in and out for appointments at Doctor's," Carlyle protested.

"You're mistaken," Dr. Holder insisted. She sounded tired, as if she wished this entire thing was over so she could go home, back to Brighton House, roll up like a beetle with a hard shell and people would stop poking in an attempt to find the tender spots. One of those tender spots included the lackadaisical doctor.

Carlyle rolled his eyes. "Yeah, Rich," he said. "We must be mistaken."

"Look," she said. "I'm really tired of you poking your nose into this. If it wasn't for Kendra Hamilton I wouldn't even be letting you see these records. You should know that I contacted the court, explained to them that Kendra Hamilton is not fit to be Anna's legal guardian. They are going to look into it."

"Okay," Rich said, not looking at her.

Instead, he was looking at a copy of a Post-It note in the medical records. It was his second time through. At first he had ignored it because he could not make it out but then he noticed a word—bruise or bruised. Yes, the word was bruise. The date at the top of the Post-It was soon after Anna arrived at Brighton house. Bruise, inside upper thigh, quarter inch. Dr. Dawson had drawn a picture, a fat stick figure with a line drawn on the upper thigh near the vagina.

"What is this?" Rich asked, holding the Post-It out to Katherine Holder.

She took it from him, stared at it for a long time. "Looks like Sam's doodles," she said. "I'm surprised that it's even in here."

"That's what I thought at first," Rich said.

He flipped frantically through the folder looking for something else. He couldn't find any more handwritten notes so he looked at the dates at the top of each typed form. He snatched out the one corresponding with the copied sticky note the good doctor was holding in her hand. He circled around the desk, snatched it from her fingers. He ignored her stare.

His eyes raced through the form—nothing about the bruise there. Only a short note about the patient being uncooperative, a new medicine prescribed.

"What's this?" Rich asked.

"What's what?" Dr. Holder said, her eyes watering with confusion.

Rich stabbed at the medical form, "It said he prescribed Zoloft, isn't that used to control depression? Why is she taking both?"

Katherine Holder held her hand toward the form, "May I?" she said.

He gave it to her. She adjusted her glasses on her nose and carefully read the form out loud in a soft whispering voice. Rich could make out some of the words, patient complaining of stomach upset, refuses to bathe. Then, "Oh, I see," she said, speaking in her normal voice. "He did not prescribe Zoloft in addition to lithium, he prescribed it in the place of it."

"Why would he do that?" Rich asked.

Dr. Holder shrugged. "Many different reasons, side effects you know. From what I'm reading, the lithium caused Anna to become somewhat catatonic."

"But she had been taking lithium," Rich reached behind him and took the records off the desk, "for almost a year. Why would it all of a sudden cause such a drastic change?" Rich felt his heart beat faster as he tattooed the date of the prescription change in his head.

"I don't know." Katherine shrugged. "I don't understand why it matters."

"What does he mean by uncooperative?" Rich asked.

"It could mean anything. " she stopped, looked at Dr. Dawson's notes. "Patient did not want to be touched, refused to disrobe, would not answer any questions, seemed anxious," she read.

"And you don't find that strange?" Rich asked.

"Why, of course not," Holder explained. "She was in brand new surroundings, had been taken forcibly from her home, her mother had recently passed away. Of course I don't find it strange that she experienced some anxiety."

Without speaking, Rich held up to her what she thought, and he did too albeit briefly, were Dr. Dawson's doodles. Dawson meant for these notes to be transcribed into the record but they were missed.

"Let me review for you," Rich said to Katherine Holder now. "She was anxious, did not want to talk, take off her clothes. She had bruises in the area near her vagina and she complained of stomach upset. I don't know what that means in your line of work, Doc, but in mine, when we have someone like Anna, say a seven-year-old acting like that, do you know the first thing we think of?"

"Yes, but . . ." Holder started, then stopped.

Rich did not answer her. Instead, he rearranged the records and put the papers back in relative older. There was one paper he kept on top, however, and that was the form with the December dates. Kendra was right, he thought again, Dr. Dawson was one sloppy bastard.

Because Dawson saw Anna every week during the beginning of Anna's stay at Brighton House, Rich knew that the rape had to occur within the seven days of that appointment when Anna started to become uncooperative. He wondered what Chadwick's alibi looked like during that timeframe. Rich would lay bets that he had the night shift.

Anna

Sometime, Anna dream that Mamma still watches. Sometime she hope that the world is not upside down like Daddy try to make it. Mamma would not go down under the ground even if she do die. She would go to the moon where there is light, not darkness that smells musty. Anna dream Mamma looking down on her from the moon, and she up there all wrapped up in light. Like a quilt, a quilt of light, some with dark patches, some with silver patches, and other with patches so bright they make Anna eyes hurt. She want to come down, but she can't. She can't come down because she all tied up with them silver strings of light. They tie her hand, burn her ankles. The moon only look quiet but Anna know Mamma still looking out for her. She told Anna once before she went away, she told Anna if they ever be apart to look up at the moon. She say she always be under the same moon as Anna. Always.

At the apartment Anna sneak out some time late at night when the moon up and round as a china plate. She watch the moon till she tired. Anna go out even though darkness scare her like a monster made up of smoke. Anna go anyway. When they bring Anna back to Brighton House she couldn't go out no more. No more moon watching. At first.

They think Anna dumb, but Anna smart. She watches. Anna learns. They use them credit card things to open the door. Leave them hanging from ropes on their necks. They leave them in their pockets or clip them to they uniforms. And sometime they forget, set them down on the counter. Anna wait and wait, then she take one. She put it in her own pocket.

Anna watch the calendar and look for the dates. When the moon go full she sneak out. She sneak past the guard, he sleeping, and through Dr. Holder office and out to the recreation area. And Anna go outside the back way and Anna sit on the bench and stare up at the silver moon and see if she can feel Mamma watching. Anna don't stay cooped up in that strange place. Anna like to go out. Anna like to watch.

CHAPTER 26

The leaves were yellow and red on the two maples that flank Theo Lane's gray two-story. Kendra didn't notice them as she rang Theo Lane's doorbell. She had one thing and one thing only in her mind—her obsession with Luke Bertrand. Kendra had been itching to talk to Theo Lane ever since she saw his name on the list of Brighton House board members. But ill and fevered, she finally had to admit that she needed rest. Thank God for Dominic Marvel.

It was a long shot; Kendra knew that. But she wanted to find out if the initials, TL, the initials Boggs remembered, had anything to do with the same Theo Lane on Brighton House's board. She wanted to know if it was more than just a coincidence. But in her heart she believed at the moment when she saw the list on Rich's desk it was more than a coincidence. She believed it to be providence. His address was not hard to find, one phone call to his secretary and she had everything she needed—an address and an appointment.

Theo Lane, the man himself, answered the door. He was short with a curved back and long arms and legs like a spider. The only color on his pale washed-out body was the cranberry of his velour jogging suit. He held out his hand to hers and she shook it. His hand felt cold in hers. The first words from Theo's mouth were not, hello or pleased to meet you. Instead, he said, "Why, my dear, your hands are so warm. You are burning up. Come inside quickly, out of this cold."

Inside, the modesty to Theo Lane's house ended. The walls were painted a brilliant white. The corresponding marble floor was the same color except for the thin veins of gold running through it. He ushered her into the living room, all black leather except for the cream colored ottoman in the center and an orchid which drooped purple petals over the surface of a black coffee table.

The couch crumpled when Kendra sat on it. Before she could speak, Theo quieted her and left the room. She sat there alone for a minute, listening to a Brighton clock tick, watching the gold disk swing back and forth to mark off the seconds. He returned with a blue mug in his hand. Smoke drifted from the hot liquid and with it the smell of honey and lemon.

At first she refused but he insisted that she take it, saying that the hot drink was just the thing for her. Wanting to shut him up so she could ask him what she came here to ask him, she sipped the drink. The taste of honey and lemon coated her tongue. She sipped again and could taste something else. Bitter. She held the cup out to him but Theo wouldn't take it.

"No, no," he said. "Only a splash of whiskey. Don't worry. You will still be able to drive. It may not do anything for that cold but it feels better for your throat, no?"

It was better for her throat, yes. She took another sip, then held the steaming cup between her palms.

"Mr. Lane," she started. "Thank you for seeing me."

He smiled. His teeth were yellow but all the same size, even if a little pointed. *Rat teeth*, Kendra thought. For some reason, even with all of his kindness, she did not like Theo Lane. She took another sip of the drink and wondered why. He had not only been kind enough to allow this visit, he had also seemed kind enough to give her something for the cold.

"What can I do for you, my dear?" he said.

She moved to set the mug on the coffee table but did not see a coaster. Theo did not offer one. She held the cup to her lap, drinking it quickly to get rid of the liquid inside.

"I understand that you were on the board at Brighton House the same time as Luke Bertrand," Kendra began. She stopped, waited for him to speak, to say something. He blinked. She continued. "How long have you known him?"

"So this is what this is about. Luke Bertrand. I figured when my secretary said that you wanted to see me. But why do you ask?"

Kendra hadn't considered this. She thought that she would be able to come here and Theo Lane would answer her questions. He would not want to know or care why she asked. She thought about lying but then thought against it. She said, "I'm doing some research on him, Mr. Lane."

"Research?"

"Yes," she continued. "I want to understand how he could do some of the things he did."

"You mean those so-called murders."

"Yes."

"He was acquitted," Lane said. "Luke Bertrand is an innocent man."

Kendra smiled and stared at him unblinkingly.

"Are you working with a reporter? Or one of those offensive money grabbers working on a true-crime?"

"No."

"Because I would never see one of them," he said. "I thought they might have sicced you on me."

He stared at her for a long time. Kendra had no doubt that he recognized her and wondered why he was playing games.

"I see," he said. "I guess you are not. Lawsuit then? Are you preparing for a lawsuit?"

Kendra shook her head. "Of course not," she said. "I'm not interested in Luke's money."

His lips tightened and pulled back from his teeth in a poor imitation of a smile. He placed the palms of his hands on both knees of his velour jogging pants. The backs were covered with russet-colored liver spots. He blinked again. At first Kendra thought he was not going to answer but then he spoke.

"What an unfortunate business this Luke Bertrand thing was." He stopped, pierced her eyes with his own. "I mean is," he said. "It's over now, two years over and this town has just stopped paying the price."

"I don't understand, Mr. Lane."

He waved one hand at her. "Please, please," he said. "Call me Theo." He reached out and touched her knee. She pulled away, disliking the way his fingers seemed to crawl over her. He noticed. He noticed because Kendra saw his smile melt into a smirk that lasted only a split second.

"Theo, please," he repeated, his voice full of concern. "Call me Theo."

When he took the cup from her hands Kendra realized that she had been in danger of dropping it.

"Look," he said. "Like the rest of the town, you need to move on. Let it go."

"Mr. Lane," Kendra said, wondering why the room was spinning. "Mr. Lane, I'm just interested in if you knew Luke before coming to Dunhill."

"Young lady," he answered, laughing. "What an odd question. I've been in Dunhill a little over five years. I don't know Luke that well but I think he has been here most of his life, am I right?"

She shrugged. "Yes," she said. "But there were a couple of years that he was not, when he was in college and medical school. I was wondering if you knew him when he went to Cloughton Medical College."

"I'm afraid I'm struggling to understand," he said. "Now we are talking about his college? Why?"

She stood up, swayed. Theo touched both her shoulders to steady her. The room was indeed spinning, and the orchid's purple petals twittered as if in a light wind.

"What . . ." Kendra asked.

"Oh, God," Theo said.

Kendra felt a desiccated hand touch her forehead. Another hand, a hand that she thought would disintegrate into dust if she squeezed it too hard, this hand gripped her upper arm.

"I'm afraid that you are burning up," he said.

Kendra looked down at Theo. There were two of him now and both men were smiling. "Tell me why," she whispered.

He let a breath out. "I don't know why," he said. "This entire town never knew why he went on his murder spree. No one did. As I've said, you need to let it go, get on with your life."

She felt Theo gently guide her back to the couch. He was still talking about Luke Bertrand. Maybe she was wrong and there was nothing in the drink that he hadn't already told her about. What did he say? Honey, lemon, water and a splash of whiskey?

"He shouldn't be allowed to get way with it," she said.

"But he did," he said. "And that is what we have to face. This town has had two years to get over it, Dr. Hamilton, and we are all healing. It's about time that you do the same."

"But did you know him?" she asked, her voice raspy. She was surprised that he did not hear it. He answered as calmly as if they were having a normal conversation.

"I knew Luke Bertrand when I joined the board at Brighton House," he said blandly. "I did not know him before I came to Dunhill. Not at Cloughton. Not anywhere."

Kendra deflated. In her fog, she wondered what she had hoped to accomplish by coming to see Theo. She had hoped that he could tell her that he went to medical school with Luke, that he had known what happened to him during that missing year. He would open easily like a package and tell her who the wedding ring, the woman's ring with the inscription, *always mine*, who that ring belonged to.

Kendra tried again. "You didn't go to medical school with him?"

He laughed. "I went to Harvard," he said. "I'm sure Luke Bertrand didn't spend much time at Harvard."

Kendra was sure as well. Maybe the initials were just a coincidence. Now as she thought about it, she realized that it wasn't unusual at all that Theo had the same initials as Luke's friend from his medical school days.

Deflated, Kendra stood up.

"Thank you for your time, Mr. Lane."

She reached out to shake his hand. He brought his hand up to meet hers. Once Kendra felt his hand clasp hers, a blackness so complete that she could taste it descended over her eyes. All memory, all thought departed.

Kendra started awake. It was so black in the room that at first she thought she was still unconscious. Then her fevered brain commanded her to kick. Her legs, thank God, her legs obeyed. Her feet, bare now she realized, scraped against something soft. A blanket. She was lying on a bed in a room as black as pitch. Fear scuttled in her belly. The fear had not sent full alarm warning bells but only offered a vague sense of unease at being in the dark. She stifled the scream forming in her throat, the scream that would demand light. Here she goes, she thought, headlong into a full-blown panic attack.

She concentrated on her breathing and the sensations around her. She lay upon a bed under a thin blanket. Someone had removed her shoes and her sweatshirt. She wasn't hurt or tied up. She couldn't imagine someone who wanted to hurt her making sure she was comfortable first by taking off her sweatshirt and shoes before slipping her under the covers.

"Are you all right?"

Kendra jerked upright at the sound of that voice, trying to decide if it were supple as well as deceptive.

"Shh, shh," it said now. "Everything is fine. I thought you were awake."

Kendra heard a click. Light flooded the room. Theo Lane pulled his hand away from the lamp switch. He was smiling.

"What happened?" she asked.

"You fainted. Dead away," he said.

"You drugged me," she accused.

She waited for the indignation but there was none. Instead, Theo sighed. Exasperated, he said, "Now why on earth would I do that? You came to my house running a high fever, asking ridiculous questions about Luke Bertrand. I answered your questions, gave you something hot to drink, and you fainted. Simple as that. You need to be resting, not running around as ill as you are."

"Then why didn't you call an ambulance?" she asked, still suspicious.

"That would have been a waste. In my medical opinion all you needed was rest and quiet. So I simply put you to bed so you could get it."

She stared at him. Theo Lane was a small man and though Kendra was not a large woman, she still couldn't see him struggling with her dead weight up the stairs. He smiled.

"My wife died about a year ago," he explained as if reading her mind. "Of Alzheimer's. In the end she couldn't dress herself or get herself to the toilet. And I managed with her. I had no problem managing with you."

Kendra swung her legs across the bed. The room swayed but not as much as it had swayed earlier.

"How long have I been asleep?" she asked

"About four hours."

He reached out and put the back of his hand against her forehead. It took all of her might not to jerk away again. "At least your fever has gone down somewhat."

She stared at him, still not quite believing him. "I don't know what to say."

He smiled fully with those perfectly pointed teeth. "Thank you seems simple enough."

"Thank you," she said.

"Would you like me to arrange a lift home?"

"No," she said, looking for her shoes. He brought them over to her along with her sweatshirt. She slipped them both on. "I'll be okay."

"I still don't know if I want you driving," he said with what looked like genuine concern in his eyes. "How about if I call someone for you? Is there a friend I could call?"

"No," Kendra said, thinking of Rich and almost hearing his recriminations in her ears from Theo's house all the way to The Liberty Apartments.

"Well, maybe you are feeling better," Lane conceded.

He took her hand and helped her rise from the bed. She felt guilty as he escorted her to the front door. Had she misjudged this man? She was about to apologize but then the overwhelming feeling that something was missing hit her. She felt her back pocket.

"Mr. Lane," she said, looking him square in the eye. "I seemed to have misplaced my wallet."

"Ah, of course," he responded.

He left for a minute and then returned with the wallet she had always carried in her back pocket, the wallet she favored instead of a purse. She only needed the purse when she felt that she needed the Smith & Wesson. And for some reason she didn't think that she would need it when she visited Theo Lane.

"It fell from your pocket when I helped you upstairs. You were quite heavy."

Of course, quite heavy. That had to be it, even heavy for a man used to struggling with someone's dead weight to get them to where did he say? The toilet or to bed. She smiled; she smiled because there was nothing else she could do, nothing else she could accuse him of. She took the wallet from him. In the Miata she had borrowed from Dominic since giving up the rented fiesta, she creased the wallet open, using the light from the street lamp to see. Everything was there, nothing missing. She didn't expect that, did she?

What she did expect was what the wallet proved. That morning she had taken the eviction warning Mrs. Buttress had placed on her door earlier and folded it so the writing was on the inside. She didn't want to be faced with it every time she opened her wallet. But now the notice was folded inside out, the address and apartment number clearly visible. Theo Lane knew where she lived. And what he would do with that information, she did not know. But the unease that she had when she woke up in that darkened room now turned into fear, real fear brought on by more than just her fever.

CHAPTER 27

She had no choice but to take the stairs. The elevator had been broken since the day she moved into The Liberty Apartments. The light in the stairway was not working again. Kendra flicked on her flashlight. A circle of light swam on the ceiling, on the slimy walls and back to the step she stood on. Vaguely, she wondered about the battery power in the flashlight. When was the last time she checked? She pointed the yellow circle of light back to the ceiling again. When she did she knew why the light did not work.

Splintered glass from the light fixture encircled the place where the bulb used to be. Shards of glass lay on the foyer floor. She closed her eyes and saw in the darkness someone swinging a broomstick at the light. She imagined the chandelier shattering, pieces of glass splintering to the ground. Looking toward the door, she wondered briefly if she should turn back. But turn back to what? Kendra knew that she had no choice but to go forward to the top of the stairs to see what, if anything, lay waiting for her.

Usually, the smells did not bother her. But today, tonight, actually, she had lost at least four hours, the place stank. The stench caused her stomach to lurch. Turn around, she thought, turn around and call the police. Yes, but what would she say? The light's busted in the stairway at The Liberty Apartments and I'm afraid of the dark? And oh, by the way, Theo Lane drugged me but simply let me wake up and walk away? They'd cart her to Brighton House and she'd be sharing a bunk with Anna. She knew that.

She inched up the stairs, placing a cautious foot on the entire stair before rising to the next one. She must not hurry. If she hurried she could fall and break the flashlight and a broken flashlight would leave her in total darkness. Breathing a sigh of relief, she reached the door to the fifth floor. The destroyed stairway light had been her only mishap.

The hallway of Liberty was well lit and smelled of fresh paint. Patches of clean new paint obscured the obscene words and the gang tags Mrs. Buttress routinely painted over. Instead of bringing comfort, a sense of order amid the chaos, the new paint made her only more aware of where she was. Some might argue about what side of town The Liberty Apartments were on, but she knew that the place was squarely in The Pit. And if the monsters that lived near her did not cut her down, the ones she invited, the ones like Theo Lane and Luke Bertrand, would. If someone were trying to kill her, if they broke the light in the stairway because of her, then they would not have left the lights on in the hallway. She had let her imagination run amok once again.

She walked the hall quickly, breathing easier as she neared her door. Then her steps slowed, her legs became heavy. Odd. The word popped into her head like a single falling leaf. Simply odd.

A sliver of darkness slid out of her slightly open door. Kendra did not have to ask herself if she locked it because of course she did. In this neighborhood she would have been a fool to leave it open. She approached with what she hoped were silent steps, wishing that she had the ability to levitate. Maybe whoever was in her apartment would not hear her approach. She had hoped that they had already fled.

But it was a vain hope. The person in there was waiting on her. The open door was an invitation. No, not an invitation, her fevered brain thought. A dare. Knowing her fear of the dark, they were daring her to come in. And if she dared to come in, the light she held would make her a target. A big target.

Kendra killed the flashlight.

Using her foot she pushed open the door and with half her body still outside the apartment, she reached inside and ran a forefinger over the light switch. Nothing. The darkness in the stairs was only a preamble, the pre-show. The real draw was going to be inside her apartment. And whatever happened there would happen in the dark. But it wouldn't just be the two of them—the perpetrator and Kendra. After all, Kendra had friends with her. Smith & Wesson. She reached for the purse slung over her shoulder, calmed by the thought of the .357 magnum in a way that she could not be by the flashlight.

But her shoulder felt curiously light. Then she remembered. Shit, she thought. The revolver was in her apartment, hidden beneath the dresser. She had no purse, only a wallet with thirty-two dollars in cash, a license, a credit card and an eviction notice. She hadn't taken the Smith & Wesson with her when she went to see Theo Lane earlier. She had no idea that she would need it. What a fool.

She took a cautious step into the apartment, the open door behind her, her hand still frantically clicking the light switch. Up, down, up, down, her frightened brain not comprehending that nothing was happening. The snap of the switch sounded like a firecracker in the quiescent darkness. She stopped, left the light in the off position. And listened.

At first the only sound in the room was her own breath scraping and catching the back of her throat. She sounded like a wounded animal and could hear nothing beyond that breathing and the blood rushing in her ears. Be still, she thought. Where had she heard that from? The Bible? She did not know. But she swallowed. When her breath steadied, she heard it. A low, easy, rhythmic humming. Someone was in the apartment. And instead of being afraid or agitated as she was, he breathed as if he were asleep. As if he hadn't a care in the world. He could wait all day for her to come into the apartment.

Cautiously, she placed one foot backward. Suddenly, she spun around and bolted for the hallway. One step, one step and she would have been completely in the freshly painted hallway again. But before she could reach it, the door slammed in front of her, sounding like an explosion. The closed door plunged the entire room into complete darkness. Before she had time to be frightened, her attacker grabbed her and shoved her into the living room. She stumbled against the wall.

She could hear him but not see him. His footsteps thudded

against the wooden floor. Maybe with more light she would have been afraid to see whoever it was, ready to beat the shit out of her. The light would have assaulted her with the determination in his eyes and increased her fear. Using the darkness now she slid her hands along the wall and gripped the tapered handle of the baseball bat. The bat had always been her weapon of choice, anyway. When Luke got out of jail, Rich insisted that she buy a gun. At first hating guns she refused, settling instead for an aluminum Louisville Slugger. You could hit a ball farther and harder with an aluminum bat, Rich used to tell her. With an aluminum bat you could do much more damage.

But several weeks after she had gotten the bat, Rich came to her apartment with the Smith & Wesson, no joke in his eyes, and demanding that she learn how to use it. She did. Partly to please him and partly to get him to leave her alone. She had to get out of this, she thought. Because when she did she could tell Rich that when it really came down to life and death, it was the baseball bat that came through in a clutch. Unless . . .

The thought stopped her cold. She only half-believed it. But half is a lot when you are slithering in the darkness on your knees waiting for your life to end. She shook her head, thinking that it must be the fever causing her to think so crazily. When she thought her attacker was close enough, she swung from her position on her knees. The bat arced, whisked through the air silently. At first she thought that she had missed, then she felt the Louisville connect with a heavy thud. The sting went all the way up her arm. Her attacker grunted. Now, his footsteps no longer sure, he staggered backwards cursing.

Kendra did not wait for him to recover. She rose so that now she was only on one knee, and a little recklessly she swung again. Another thud. She heard him fall but she remained where she was. She really didn't know how bad she had hurt him. He could just be pretending. She held the bat in front of her, swinging it back and forth through the air.

"Who are you?" she said now. "What do you want?"

She wished that the man would speak, willed him to speak. She thought that if she heard his voice, she would recognize him. In fact, she was almost sure of it. But he said nothing. She heard him stagger to his feet. She rose the entire way to her feet, intent on running after him. But when she got close she felt a punch connect with her stomach. Kendra sank to her knees, all air gone. She waited for him to attack again.

But all she heard was running feet, a slamming door. She let the bat clang to the floor. As she kneeled on the floor, blind from lack of light, the things she saw existed only in her mind. And those things were faces, faces of the men with reason to kill her.

"What's he doing here?" Kendra asked Gregory Atfield, who stood in her apartment with two uniformed cops, her landlady Mrs. Buttress, and Rich, who twirled around in the middle of the floor looking at the mess around him.

Kendra hadn't realized that a mess had even been made. Her focus had been on surviving the attack. She had not realized that the coffee table had been snapped in two and the floor was now littered with the face of Luke Bertrand, the scrapbook and newspaper articles about him.

"Goddammit, Kendra," Rich said. He ran an open palm over his head in the old way that she remembered. "Goddammit," he said again, looking around the room now flooded by the lights from borrowed lamps.

"Son. Language," the landlady, Mrs. Buttress said.

But she said it half-heartedly. She walked over to the coffee table, her foot falling flatly over Luke Bertrand's smiling faces. She righted an overturned TV tray.

"I'm going to have to ask that you not touch that," Gregory said.

"Ask all you want," Mrs. Buttress responded. "And then I'll ask who is going to pay for all this."

She placed her hands on her ample hips and looked up at the ceiling. The light bulb, thank God that was all, had simply been shattered in the same way the light bulb in the stairway had been shattered. No wires had been cut. Pretty simple, really.

Rich's eyes had found Kendra's again and it took all her will not to flinch under his gaze. She gave him a hard look. With each passing day, with each passing meeting he seemed to become the man she knew. Unlike Gregory who wore navy blue Dockers and a white polo shirt with a blue trim collar, Rich was dressed more like the chief of homicide he had always wanted to be, fully suited, long wool trench coat, black. And his eyes were a clear shade of brown that now burned with a fury.

She turned away from him and back to Gregory.

"What's he doing here?" she asked again. "I called you, not him."

Gregory sighed. "I thought you could use some support."

"I don't need his kind of support," she said.

"What in the hell is that supposed to mean?" Rich asked, holding her gaze.

"I don't know," she explained. "You tell me."

He looked at her a long time and she could tell by his sharp intake of breath that he knew exactly what she meant. He drew back, knotted a fist on his slim hip.

"Come on, Kendra," he said. "You think I had something to do with this?"

She walked up to him, her teeth clenched, her arms folded. "Let me just say that I wouldn't be surprised."

"Hey, hey, hey," Gregory stepped between them. He held up both hands. "I'm sure she doesn't think that." He waited for Kendra to confirm and when she didn't, he said, "Kendra, that's impossible."

"I don't give a flip who did this," Mrs. Buttress broke the silence in the room. "But someone's going to pay for it. The coffee table, that end table," she pointed around the room. "That lamp and that light up there. Somebody better take out their checkbook for this plus the rent."

Kendra barely heard her. It was as if she and Rich were the only ones in the room. She watched a series of emotions pass over his otherwise impassive face. First incredulity, then hurt, and lastly anger. He touched two fingers to the side of his head.

"You are crazy lady," he said. "Cuckoo."

"Am I?"

"As a loon if you think that I . . ."

"Okay, enough," Gregory said.

He motioned to the two uniforms. They came over with perfectly neutral faces, which told Kendra that they had been listening to every word.

"Take Mrs. Buttress to her apartment and get a statement," Gregory ordered. "And I'll meet you outside."

"But," one of them protested.

"Do it," Gregory said without looking at them.

After they left, the room seemed silent as death. Kendra felt the eyes of both men on her and for a minute she imagined that she was on stage, the main attraction for a freak show. She stood up, ignored the muscle ache in her stomach. She began picking up the mess on the floor.

She reached for a *Jet* magazine. Gregory placed one hand on her wrist.

"Why don't we sit for a minute, Kendra," he said. "Tell us what happened."

When she glanced at Rich, her eyes must have held a slim thread of mistrust because Gregory amended his statement. "Tell me what happened."

Kendra sighed and sat on the couch. Rich and Gregory sat down. As she recounted the events of the past weeks, her meeting with the professor and her meeting with Theo Lane, she began to realize how silly it was to suspect Rich. It was obviously Theo who did this. He had something to do with Luke Bertrand and to cover it up, he drugged her . . .

But Gregory did not let her finish. He held up a hand.

"So let me get this straight," Gregory said. "Theo Lane drugged you?"

"Yes," she said. She looked at both of them. Rich's face was back to unreadable, and Gregory's was neutral.

"He told you that?" Rich asked. "That he drugged you?"

"Of course not," she answered.

"Then what makes you think he drugged you?" Rich asked.

"Because no one just passes out, Rich," she said. "And that's what Theo said I did. He lied to cover up the fact that he drugged me."

"You passed out?" Rich said, alarmed.

"He said that I fainted but he's lying. He put something in the hot toddy."

Rich opened his mouth to speak again but Gregory stopped him.

"The hot toddy?" he prodded.

"Yes. He said something about a fever and then came back with some lemon and honey. But I knew there was something else in it. It tasted funny."

"And you drank it anyway?" Rich asked in a dry voice.

She stopped, didn't think about that. "Yes, I guess I did."

"And you want to tell us that you're thinking straight?" Rich said.

Confusion and doubt ripped through her. But the doubt lasted for only a millisecond as if the world had tilted and righted within the same fraction of a second. When she spoke her voice was sure once again.

"Don't be ridiculous," she snapped. "Of course I am thinking straight. I wasn't sure that he had put anything in the drink until after I woke up."

"Look." She leaned forward, her hands balled into fists on her lap. "I don't see what's so hard to understand about all of this. It's obvious that it was Theo all along. At first, I thought . . ." She stopped, swallowed hard, not looking at Rich. "At first I thought it could have been Rich. But now it's obvious to me that it is Theo who did this."

"Obviously," Greg said dryly. "But," he continued, "if he wanted to hurt you why didn't he do it when you were out?"

She frowned. That's right, why not just take care of her then? Then she realized if Theo had gotten rid of her then, he would have been the last person to see her alive. And people had already known that she had an appointment with him. His secretary, for one. Theo had no choice but to wait. She told Gregory this.

She did not like the frown on Rich's face. She could see by the wave of concentration moving over his face that he chose his next words carefully.

"So why would Theo Lane want to hurt you?"

"I already told you," she said.

"Tell me again," he insisted.

She sighed, exasperated. "Luke Bertrand. Theo wants to cover up his relationship with Luke."

"What relationship?" Rich asked.

"Well . . ." she stopped, blinked. "I don't know that yet. But I will find out."

"No doubt?" Rich asked. "Just convinced, huh? What if it's all just a coincidence?"

"It's not a coincidence," she protested.

"Look," Rich said. "I've seen Theo Lane, okay? I ran into him all the time at Brighton. He's a sick man, sometimes he has to use a cane. There is no way that he could have gotten you up a flight of stairs and there is no way that he attacked you tonight. A strong wind could blow Lane over."

"So what are you saying?" Kendra said. "That I'm making the entire thing up?"

"I think that you are sick," Rich said. "And I think it's making you a little delusional and paranoid. Or worse."

"Explain the worse," she gritted out.

"That you are simply lying. Again."

"So I'm lying about the broken light in the stairway?" she asked. "The mess in this apartment?"

He turned away from her, cursing softly. All three of them fell silent. Rich turned to Gregory. "You buying this, man?" he asked.

She looked at Gregory and waited. But if she was waiting for Gregory to tell Rich that he believed her, she would be waiting until the second coming. His next words confirmed it.

"No," he said. "I'm not. Kendra, what happened here tonight?"

She told him about the open door, the bat, the dark. That the person who attacked her had to know about her fear of the dark and that was one of the reasons that she suspected Rich. At first.

"If it wasn't Theo then who could it have been?" she asked.

Gregory shrugged. "Come on, Kendra. In this neighborhood, it could have been anybody."

"Glad someone is finally talking some sense around here," Rich said.

"It could have been Luke Bertrand," Gregory amended.

Kendra sucked in her breath. She hadn't thought of Luke. He hadn't even crossed her mind.

"Luke Bertrand?" Rich asked.

"Yes," Gregory explained. "Luke. Kendra's been rattling his cage. Haven't you, Kendra?"

She stood up, rubbed her hands together. For some reason she did not want to answer but the mess on the floor answered for her.

"I've . . . I've been looking into some things," she admitted, her throat dry and hot. "Rich knows that."

"More than looking I would hazard," Gregory challenged.

"What do you mean?" Rich asked.

"Luke filed a complaint with the sheriff's department. He said someone had broken into his home, hadn't taken anything, but he knew someone was in there uninvited."

"Kendra?" Rich asked.

"He suspects but doesn't know for sure. It had to have been someone who knew the alarm codes. Luke said that only two people had the code and one of them is dead."

"Well." Rich spread his hands out. "There you have it. Kendra doesn't have the alarm codes."

He waited for her to answer. But instead of answering, Kendra wrapped both arms around her waist. Her stomach had started to hurt.

"You have the alarm code," Gregory said, looking straight at her. "The other person who had it was Violet, your mother, right? And you found it."

Kendra looked straight at him but didn't answer.

"God!" Rich exploded. "Of all the dumb ass things . . ."

"He has no proof that it was me," she said, unperturbed. "He's just guessing."

"He's a pretty good guesser, Kendra."

She shrugged.

"Where is the weapon, Kendra?" Gregory asked.

"What weapon?"

"What weapon do you think?" Rich said. "The Smith & Wesson?"

"I don't have it," she lied. "I got rid of it."

Rich shook his head. "If there is one thing you will always excel at," he said, "it's lying your ass off."

"I don't, Rich," she said in a tone that almost convinced even her. "I don't have it."

The baseball bat may have been her weapon of choice but she did not want it to be the only thing standing between her and crazy Luke Bertrand. If she was going to protect herself she needed that revolver and was not about to give it up.

"Look," Gregory said. "I can't afford to have you running around here until I know for sure what you are up to."

Kendra stared at him. "You mean that you are going to have me arrested for this?"

"Of course not," he said.

She sighed in relief until his next words.

"Only if Rich agrees to keep an eye out for you," Gregory said.

Rich laughed. "My days of keeping an eye on her are long gone, man. Forget it."

"I'm serious, Rich," he said. "Either she goes into a holding cell or goes home with you."

"Holding cell," Rich said without hesitation.

"You can't be serious, Gregory," Kendra protested.

"Oh, I'm very serious," Gregory explained. "If you think for a minute that I'm going to let you run around Dunhill on some vendetta, you are mistaken."

"I don't have room at my place, man," Rich said, holding up his hands.

"Make room," Gregory responded.

"Forget the both of you," Kendra said.

She opened the door only to be greeted by two stone-faced officers, their bright blue uniforms cast a bluish glow onto their faces. She slammed the door in their faces, turned around and looked at Rich. He shook his head wearily from side to side.

"Put it out of your mind," he said. "I won't."

Then she did something that she hadn't done in a long time. She crossed her hands across her chest, looked her ex-lover fully in his clear brown eyes. And smiled.

CHAPTER 28

She sat in the dark again but this time in Rich's new Monte Carlo which smelled of leather and new carpet. The street lamp above washed them both in yellow light. The time on Rich's dashboard clock read just after midnight. The gloom around them suggested an intimacy that could no longer be attributed to them. Rich sat in the driver's seat, unmoving. He sat as still as a stone, the curve of his jaw, the line of his neck like a drawing on canvas. She stared at him, trying to read him. As usual the attempt was to no avail.

"I forgot something," she said.

His hands fell from the steering wheel onto the top of his thighs. Though she couldn't quite make out his face she could hear the disgust in his voice.

"What?" he said.

"I said I forgot something."

He turned the key. "Get it in the morning," he ordered as the engine rumbled.

"No," she said. "I need it now."

"You can't go up there, Kendra. It's a crime scene."

"It's not a crime scene. It's my apartment and I need something out of it."

"You can do without it for a night," he said.

"No. I can't."

She reached into the backseat, rummaged in the duffle bag until she found the flashlight. Rich's voice stopped her as she reached for the door handle.

"What's so important that it can't wait until morning? Tell me, Kendra."

"Why are you always in my business?"

His laugh was intimate, quiet in the darkness. "Because your business is going to get us both killed one of these days. And I like life too much. You think that could be it?"

She rolled her eyes. "Look, just cut me a break. Will you? I'll be right back."

"Wait," he said. "I'll go with you."

"No," she answered. "I'll just be a minute."

"Don't be stupid, Kendra," he said. "In this neighborhood, especially after what just happened? Let me go up."

"Dammit, Rich," she said. "Just dammit."

He had always accused her of trying to take care of the world but here he was trying to take care of her, still, after all that they had been through. Suddenly, she didn't want to be taken care of anymore. She wanted independence from those clutching hands.

"Look," she said now. "I've been on my own in this neighborhood since I was sixteen, Rich. I think I can manage my way to my apartment."

He put his hand back on the steering wheel and turned to look at her. There was no amusement lurking in his eyes. His voice was grim when he spoke.

"If you aren't back in five minutes, I'm coming up there," he said.

The car door resounded in the quiet night. She looked back at Rich and saw that he watched her, his hand still curled around the steering wheel. She wondered briefly if he thought about taking off. She laughed. Maybe he wouldn't be there when she got back. Maybe he had finally had enough.

She took the stairs two at a time, the flashlight crawling like a yellow stain on the greasy walls. In her apartment she saw what Rich and Gregory had seen. Shades of Luke all over the place. Earlier that night after the cops had left she had stacked all the papers and articles and old magazines in a corner by the door.

Rich had stood watching her as she packed her things, his eyes never leaving her hands. He watched everything that she put in the duffle bag.

She shut the door behind her now, locked it just in case she would exceed her five minutes. She had no doubt that Rich would be up there if she didn't come down when he told her to. Lying on her belly she waved her hands under the lip of the dresser. She had been clever. Instead of hiding the Smith & Wesson in the drawer under socks or panties as most people would have done, she hid it underneath the dresser. She had pushed it into a corner. The decorative trim on the old dresser hid it from view.

But when she pulled her hand away from underneath the dresser, the most lethal thing she came away with was dust bunnies. Grunting, she shoved her hand further underneath the dresser until she made contact with the entire space. She thought that she had been clever. No one would think of looking underneath the dresser. But someone had. The Smith & Wesson revolver Rich had given her was gone.

Slowly, she got to her feet, dusted her hands on her sweatshirt and jeans. One thing was clear to her. She could not go back to Rich with nothing. She found a grocery bag, stuffed another T-shirt, some jeans she didn't need, into it. She folded it over until it looked like a small briefcase, wondering about the man who was walking around Dunhill County with a weapon registered in her name, wondering what he would do with it.

During the last few days, ever since returning from Dom's, she had felt alternately chills and fever. But the cold feeling washing over her now like water had nothing to do with sickness. She knew that the person who attacked her had to know things about her, at least two things. He had to know that she had become frightened of the dark this last year and he had to know that she had that weapon. How long did it take him to find it? She wondered now. How long had he had to search for it? Whoever did this, they knew her, knew her as well as Rich did. Or so she thought.

He didn't look at her as she climbed back in the Monte Carlo. She stuffed the paper bag into her duffle bag. Rich started the engine. He put the car in gear, placed his hand on her headrest. He twisted around to make sure no one was behind him as he backed out of the parking place. Once the car was in drive again, he let it idle for a few seconds. Then he spoke without looking at her and his words caused her to look up at him and then quickly out the passenger side window into the darkness, into nothingness.

"I hope like hell," he said quietly, "I hope like hell that you remembered to engage the safety on that weapon."

There were flowers in front of Rich's house, pansies, petals like velvet in the light from the porch. He tried to take the duffle bag from her as she stepped from the car but she wouldn't let him near it. One side of her brain told her to trust him, told her that she had no choice but to tell him about the missing revolver. But the other side of her brain said no. He wouldn't believe her and did not trust her. What was that crack earlier about her business getting them both killed?

She trailed him up the walk. She did not know what she had been expecting as she entered his house. She guessed that she had been expecting a bachelor's pad, maybe something reminiscent of what she had seen in Tahoe—beer cans on the floor, empty pizza boxes. But that wasn't the case at Rich's place. His house was clean as a morgue, bare wooden floors made of maple, tan couch sitting at a slant in the middle of a living room, glass coffee table so clean Kendra would have to touch it to make sure the glass top was there. Quiet, too. Rich's living room was quiet, except for the big ass TV placed square in front of the leather couch. A giant, stupid blind eye. Like hers, Rich would say, like hers.

"Couch pulls out," he said as he stopped beside her near the door.

She hated the feelings coursing through her now, tried to deny them. But there could not be any denying the beating of her heart, the lump in her throat as she thought about the last time she and Rich were together at this hour.

He reached above her head and closed the door behind her. It slammed softly. She had not realized that she had not closed it. He stood there for about a minute, one hand on his slim hip, leaning over her against the closed door.

"So," was all he said as he left her by the door and walked into the room. "As I was saying, the couch pulls out. There is a full guest bathroom, first door on your left."

He pointed to a hallway to the left of the front door.

"My room is at the end of the hall." He looked at her. And she couldn't figure out if that look was to tell her to stay out or to tell her that she was welcome any time. "I have a guest room but I use that as my office. However long it takes," he said, spreading his hand over the couch. "Consider *mi casa su casa.*"

She stood there, wouldn't move.

"You can come in, Kendra," he said softly. "I won't bite."

She took a couple of steps forward, set her duffle bag on the couch. Without letting go of the straps she said, "I don't think this is going to work out."

He folded his arms across his chest. "And why not?"

"What do you mean, why not, Rich?" she said. "You hate my guts, you've made that clear. Why would you want me in your house? This is stupid."

Not to mention—she didn't say it, but ashamed, she did think it—not to mention that if he was the man at her apartment, the man who had attacked her, here she would be at his mercy. If only she had the gun, she thought, she would feel safer. In her heart of hearts, did she think that Rich had anything to do with the attack? She didn't know. But one thing that she did know was that she didn't trust him. Not fully, anyway.

The only thing in her favor was that he didn't know that she didn't have the Smith & Wesson anymore. If she could make him think that she had it, he would think twice about attacking her. If he was the one who did so in the first place. But what would be his reason? Spurned lover? No, Rich didn't strike her as the type. But she had never seen him like this. She remembered the pleading in his eyes at Dom's place. She had hurt him when she left him, hurt him bad. She knew that he blamed her for the loss of his career and his fiancée. Maybe like her, he had been out for revenge.

As those thoughts flickered in her mind, on and off, like a strobe light, he walked over to her. She felt his gaze crawl all over her face. He was reading her, but she could tell that he didn't see everything, didn't know of the thoughts racing through her mind.

"Don't tell me," he said in a quiet voice, "how I feel, Kendra."

"I should just go to a hotel," she said.

But she knew immediately how foolish the words sounded the minute they were out of her mouth. Rich's laugh confirmed it.

"With what?" he said. "You think they are going to let you into a hotel on your good looks? You're broke, remember?"

He looked at the duffle bag still on the couch.

"Move that out of the way for a moment please."

She placed the duffle bag against the wall. Together, in silence, they worked. Kendra and Rich pulled out the couch. He left and returned with blankets and sheets. They made the bed. The white sheet billowed out like a cloud between them.

Once again Kendra settled on the couch while Richard T. Marvel slept in another room. He left her in the dark. *Bastard,* she thought as she flicked on the bathroom light. He probably did it on purpose.

The sheets felt cold; he must keep them in a refrigerator. The mattress was thin and hard as a butcher's block. Kendra's eyes hurt when she closed them and her lids felt grainy. She tossed and turned a few minutes wondering why she couldn't get comfortable. Staring toward the ceiling she realized what it was. No pillows. Rich had forgotten pillows. From the hallway she called but there was no answer. His door was open; she could see the lights from the TV flickering on the wooden floors.

She told herself that all she would do was ask for a couple of pillows. He could spare those, even for the likes of her. Ignoring the voice in her head that told her that the only thing she was asking for was trouble, she continued to his room at the end of the hallway.

What she saw caused her to halt in her tracks. She placed cold fingertips to her throat, touched the edge of the door frame to keep herself from falling over. She was unable to take her eyes away from the man standing before her. Rich stood there barechested, black pajama pants slung low on his hips. She hadn't realized that she remembered every single inch of his naked body until she saw him standing there at that moment. She remembered the train-shaped birthmark on the small of his back, the scar on his muscled chest. She swallowed hard. It was as if she were frozen, thoughts had stopped and she could not turn away.

Slowly, Rich brought his hands down. Still looking at her, he spoke.

"See, Kendra," he said. "No bruises. It wasn't me."

She watched as the door swung slowly closed, knowing that he knew exactly what she had been thinking earlier. As she still knew every inch of his body, so he still knew every inch of her, including what and how she thought.

Anna

Sometime, people get what they deserve. Wisteria lady don't come back no more. She gone. Before she left, she came to Anna and got in her face. She say, *I hope you happy, I hope you happy, retard. You cost me my job.* Anna glad. She glad she gone. Everybody got happy when they heard. Even Rosita. She hug Anna and say that nobody gone slap her no more.

But the other one, the other monster who come at night, he still here. And Anna and Rosita watch him. He nervous now. His eyes water all the time and he stay away from Anna. He don't even come at night anymore. Anna see him, she see him running in his mind all the time. They about to find out. They about to know.

Anna thought she be scared. She remember what he tell her. He tell her *if you say anything, retard, I'll kill you. And I kill your friends, too.* But Anna didn't tell nobody, didn't tell nobody, so he can't kill her. But the other, they know. That Rich man know and he gone make him get what he deserve.

But Anna don't know if she can wait for the nice man to put the monster away. Because the monster, he still go after Rosita. Anna know 'cause when he pass Rosita in the dayroom or outside on the patio, Rosita, she run to Anna and she cry. And the other day, Rosita got a black eye. She tell nurses that her head hit a door but Anna know it the monster still messing with her.

And Anna don't know if she can wait no more. She don't know if she can wait till somebody catch him.

CHAPTER 29

After Rich and Carlyle told Gregory all about Brandon
Chadwick, Gregory didn't need anything else. It had helped
that Carlyle had somehow gotten his hands on the background
check and from it they discovered that Brandon Chadwick and his
past employers had been involved in a serious game of pass the
trash. Before coming to Brighton House, Chadwick had been dismissed from four other facilities for "misconduct." That's what
they put in his official record, "misconduct."

But when Carlyle dug deeper and actually talked to the adminis-
trators at the other hospitals, he discovered that the misconduct
had included possible rape and other physical patient abuse. But
rather than get the police involved, his employers simply dismissed
Chadwick, giving him a lukewarm reference letter so he could become somebody else's problem.

And Gregory understood Rich's wish not to involve anybody but
him. Later, they could bring in the rest of the sheriff's department,
but for now, it was Gregory, Rich, and Carlyle speeding toward
Brighton House in Gregory's blue Monte Carlo sedan.

"Hey, girls," Carlyle said from the backseat. "Do they know we're
coming?"

Rich looked over at Gregory who had a wisp of a smile on his
face.

"Just like old times." Rich grinned.

"Unfortunately," he said.

"No," Rich said loud enough for Carlyle to hear.

Dunhill County had been spared the rain for the night but clouds obscured the stars in the night sky.

"How's Kendra?" Gregory asked as he exited the highway.

"I was waiting for that, man," Rich said.

But Rich didn't answer. He hoped Gregory wouldn't press but his hopes would not be realized.

"Well?" Gregory said.

Rich shielded his eyes with his hands. "She's a fucking freak."

"I hope in a good way." Gregory grinned as he pulled into the Brighton House parking lot.

"Please," he said as he peered at Gregory from beneath his fingers. "The woman is as nutty as a goddamn fruitcake."

"Well, as I seem to recall," Gregory said as he shut the lights on the Monte Carlo, "you are somewhat of a fruitcake magnet. So where is she? I hope you're keeping an eye on her."

Rich grinned and saluted Gregory. "Yes, sir, just like you ordered sir. She's been at my place since last night. But she said something about going to see Dominic and the kids."

"Rich," Gregory said, a wary look in his eye.

"Don't worry, man," he said. "I got her to promise me. And I've already checked in with Dom. He's going to call me as soon as she shows up there. Okay?"

Rich reached for the door handle before Gregory could reply. Rich wanted him to know that as far as he was concerned, the conversation was over. Carlyle got out of the car and shut the door with a thud. Gregory followed. As Gregory and Rich started toward the entrance to Brighton House, they heard Carlyle slap the hood of the car.

"Hey, hey," he said. "Open the door man, my jacket's caught."

Gregory turned to Rich. "See what I mean about you being a fruitcake magnet?"

"Very funny," Rich breathed.

The parking lot was filled with cars, expensive ones—Jaguars, Mercedes, BMWs—the parking lot lights reflecting wetly in the slick surfaces. The moon cast a murky glow in the gray sky.

"What's this?" Carlyle said, sticking his barrel chest out. "A party?"

"I don't know," Rich said as he walked to the front door. "I don't care."

Gregory followed saying nothing. The receptionist desk was empty save for a young nurse whom Rich recognized as the pretty brown-haired nurse he had seen a few times before. She looked up at him and smiled.

"Is Dr. Holder in?" Rich asked.

There was no reason that she should be, he thought as he checked his watch. No, she should not be in at this hour at all but the full parking lot gave Rich a sinking feeling in the pit of his stomach.

"Sure is," the nurse said. "With about a hundred other bigwigs."

"For what?" Rich asked, confused.

"It's our annual open house," she said. "It started at six but it's running a little long tonight. I wish they'd all just get the hell out because when they leave I can go home."

"An open house?" Carlyle said. "In a fucking nuthouse?"

"Hey," the nurse said. "Watch your language. We are a mental institution, not a nuthouse, asshole," she said. "Anyway, after this they usually go to some fancy fund-raiser at the Starlight. I wish they wouldn't come here, though. All those sequins and glitter give the patients nightmares for weeks, especially the paranoid ones. Last year we had one patient, Paul, who swore that the sequins in Dr. Holder's dress were transmitters from alien . . ."

"Hey, gorgeous," Carlyle cut her off. "Could you come back to us now?"

The nurse blushed, smoothed back her hair. "Sorry." She laughed. "I guess I'm getting a little punchy. I'm exhausted."

"Is she back there?" Rich asked. "Dr. Holder?"

The nurse shook her head. "She's showing one of the models to Thomas Brighton." She pointed a painted pink fingernail over her shoulder. "You remember where the models are, don't you?"

Rich remembered where the models were and was not the least bit interested in them. But before he could speak, Gregory slid up to the counter. He looked at the nurse and smiled. She smiled back.

"Is Brandon Chadwick working tonight?" he asked in a quiet voice.

The smile turned into a frown the minute he said Chadwick's

name. "Yes," she said. "Everyone is, even that . . ." she stopped.
"Even him. We stay until the board leaves."

"The Brighton House board?" Rich asked.

She nodded.

"Where is Chadwick now?" Rich asked.

Before she could answer laughter floated from the hallway.
Katherine Holder came around the corner flanked on one side by
Thomas Brighton and on the other by Theo Lane. Brighton wore
a black tuxedo but Lane had on a Chinese jacket with a paisley pat-
tern of red, blues and green. He had paired that monstrosity of a
jacket with a pair of black silk pants. Tonight though, he seemed to
be feeling better. He was sans his cane. Dr. Holder wore a long
black shift. The sequins that Paul was afraid of last year were sewn
all around her square collar. Her hair as usual splashed all over her
head. This time, she had tried to hold it together with two narrow
sticks that reminded Rich of chopsticks.

"Jared," Brighton addressed Carlyle. "I hope there is an explanation for this."

Rich watched Carlyle under Brighton's furious stare. He wondered what Carlyle would do, if he would try to save his job.

"There is, Mr. Brighton," Carlyle said. "But you won't like it."

"What he means, Mr. Brighton," Gregory interjected smoothly,
"is that it's a police matter. I asked him to come here with us."

Carlyle said nothing. Dr. Holder left the two men and pointed
toward her office. She looked pointedly at the nurse.

"Can we please go to my office?" Dr. Holder asked. "No need for
there to be a scene out here."

Both Theo and Brighton sat down without being asked in
Holder's office. Holder went behind her desk. The rest of them
stood.

"We need to speak with Brandon Chadwick," Gregory said. "Do
you know where he is now?"

Katherine Holder blinked. "Why, I'm sure he's working."

"Is there some trouble?" Theo asked.

"Like I told you, sir," Carlyle said. "We think he raped Anna
Cotton."

"You told him?" Rich asked incredulously.

"He told us both, Marvel," Brighton said disgustedly. "How else
do you think he got the Chadwick boy's background check?"

"You gave it to him but not me?" Rich asked, a line of anger drawing his mouth tight.

Lane smirked. "Since we were about to fire you we thought it would be a breach of privacy since you would no longer be with the company."

"If you knew what a snake he was," Rich challenged, "how in the hell could you recommend him?"

Brighton stood up, ran his fingers through his gray hair. He went to Holder's refrigerator and pulled out a bottle of Perrier. He looked at the blue label a few minutes before speaking.

"I didn't recommend him," he said finally. "Theo?"

Theo Lane stood up. "Can I have one of those, Thomas?" he asked.

Theo put his trembling lips to the bottle and sipped. He grunted when he brought the bottle down and wiped his mouth with the back of his hand.

"I recommended him because I thought he was a good kid. I didn't see anything in his record that would warrant his not working."

"What about the misconduct?" Rich said.

"It did not specify, and Brandon explained it away."

Gregory pulled his hands out of the pocket of his navy Dockers. "Look," he said. "We can talk about all of this afterwards. For now, I'd like to get this Chadwick in custody."

Katherine Holder gasped. "You mean you are going to arrest him? Here? Now?"

"Well, we're not going to ask him to the prom," Carlyle said dryly.

"For what?" she asked.

"Raping Anna Cotton," Gregory said.

"You have proof?" Brighton asked.

Gregory looked at Brighton with hooded eyes. When he spoke, Rich understood that his old friend had run out of patience.

"Look," he said. "I don't need your permission to arrest a rapist but I desire your cooperation. We think Anna's sexual abuse started around the same time Chadwick started working the night shift at Brighton House. He has a history of aberrant sexual behavior and he took Anna off the premises without cause."

Theo took another long drink of water, burping loudly after he brought the bottle down.

"Sorry," he said to the faces turned toward him. "Carbonation."

Rich saw that he must have spilled a good amount of water on the front of his dinner jacket.

"But we have cameras in Anna's room," Holder was saying. "If he did attack her on the premises we would know. And what about the card logs? If Chadwick had been in Anna's room, we would know."

"Chadwick didn't need his access card to get into Anna's room. As an orderly, he had easy access to the master key kept at the nurses' station," Rich said. "And those cameras aren't worth the hooks they hang from. But right around the time the rapes started, we noticed flickers of white in Anna's room. We think it was Chadwick."

"Or big foot," Carlyle said, then laughed at his own joke. Rich shot him a warning look and he quieted.

"Dr. Holder?" Gregory questioned.

Holder rose from her desk in a cloud of confusion. "Of course, of course," she said. She opened a drawer and pulled out an access card hung on a ribbon necklace. Drawing it over her head, she said, "He's cleaning one of the quiet rooms. We had a patient in there earlier who had an accident."

"Great," Carlyle said as they left Holder's office.

Someone did indeed have an accident in one of the quiet rooms but it wasn't a patient. When Katherine Holder swiped her access card in the terminal by the door she pushed it open to find a prone Brandon Chadwick. He was lying in the middle of the floor on his side, his knees drawn up to his stomach. A river of blood fanned out from the back of his head. Rich couldn't see his face, only the blonde tips of his spiked brown hair. The clean spaces on Brandon Chadwick's starched white uniform seemed garish in comparison to the brilliant red streaks around his neck and on his smock.

"Oh, God," Holder gasped. Shoving Rich out of the way, she ran into the room.

"Careful," Gregory said in a mild voice.

Holder hitched up her long black dress and bent down. She placed two square fingers to Chadwick's wrist. When she pulled her hands back her fingers were covered with blood.

She looked at the three of them, Gregory, Rich, and Carlyle, crowding the door.

"He's dead," she said.

"You think?" Carlyle said.

Rich didn't say anything. No matter how many times he had seen a dead body, the amount of blood contained in one always surprised him. And like Carlyle, Rich knew from the blood spattered on the room's white walls and pooling on the floor that Chadwick was quite dead. Katherine Holder was like any doctor whom Rich had ever met, always thinking that they can change the world, that there was something left to be done. She'd have probably run in and checked Chadwick's pulse if he was missing his head.

"Dr. Holder, please," Gregory said. "Step back."

She hurried out of the room, wiping her bloodstained fingers on her black evening dress. Outside she took Thomas Brighton by the arm and guided him away from the door. Theo was nowhere in sight.

"Mr. Brighton," she started, then stopped. "We must make sure that the rest of the patients are secured . . ."

Rich turned to Thomas Brighton to see why Holder didn't continue. One look at Brighton's face told him why. Purple suffused his usually florid face and his eyes bulged with anger.

"This did not happen here," he said. "This did not happen in my mother's house."

Rich frowned. "I think that dead body over there would beg to differ," Rich said dryly.

"I'm expecting, detective," Brighton said, addressing Gregory, "that we will keep this out of the press."

"Mr. Brighton," Gregory said. "It is much too early to start thinking about damage control. Why don't you go with Dr. Holder to ensure the other patients are safe?"

Katherine Holder's head bobbed up and down in agreement, her mouth open and her eyes still wide with surprise. Rich could see that she was still in shock. He wondered what would happen when the shock wore off and Holder was left with the first major incident since her tenure at Brighton House. She looked at him, caught his eye. And he was sure that she remembered that first meeting. It was not just a job for her but what did she call it? She called it a vocation. Failing at this job would mean that she had failed at a calling.

Holder gulped air and took one more deep breath. She blinked rapidly. Rich saw a measure of calm settle over her face as she took one more look at Chadwick lying on the floor surrounded by all that blood. Once she was in control she led an outraged Mr. Brighton from the crime scene.

"Go with them," Rich told Carlyle to get rid of him. "Keep an eye on them both."

The longer Carlyle stared at the body the more yellow his face had become. Rich saw that he was fresh out of smart-ass comments. Heaving sounds came from the back of his throat. If he was going to blow, Rich didn't want him to do it all over Gregory's crime scene.

Gregory, in the meantime, advanced into the room, careful not to make any footprints in the bloodstains.

"God, what a mess," he said.

"May I?" Rich asked.

Gregory waved him inside as he flipped open his cell phone to call the sheriff's department. The room smelled of blood, a heavy metallic smell that Rich had always associated with death. As he moved closer to Chadwick, Rich understood why Katherine Holder had looked for a pulse in the wrists. Chadwick's throat had been punctured. That explained the amount of blood in the room.

Gregory closed the cell phone and touched the side of Chadwick's pasty face.

"He's fresh," he said.

"Fresh?" Rich said. "Ugh, man."

"I'm serious, looks like he's been dead only about half an hour."

"What's that at the back of his neck?"

Gregory used a pencil to move Chadwick's brown hair from the nape of his neck.

"Looks like a puncture wound right in the cerebellum. That probably dropped him like a load of bricks."

"Then why cut his throat?" Rich questioned.

Gregory looked at Rich, his gray eyes somber. "Somebody was mighty pissed off," he said.

"I can see that," Rich said. From the bruises on his arm someone also must have whacked the shit out of him as he went down.

Rich opened his mouth to ask about the bruises but the sound of heels beating against the tile floor in the hallway cut him off. Rich stood up and went to the door. Katherine Holder rushed toward him, her long dress fluttering around her calves.

If he had not reached out his arms to steady her, she would have knocked him backward.

"Somebody," she gasped. "Somebody's missing."

Rich held her by the elbows. "Slow down," he said. "Slow down."

She balled a fist against his chest. "I can't find her, we've looked everywhere."

"Find who?" Rich asked.

She swallowed a couple of times, then gulped. When she looked at him, her eyes filled with worry.

"Anna," she said. "I can't find Anna. All the other patients are secured in their rooms, but I can't find Anna. She's not anywhere. I can't find her anywhere."

CHAPTER 30

As Kendra sped toward Kettle Creek on Southwest flight 867, she thought about the promise Rich had extracted from her earlier that morning. A promise that she had been destined to break the moment she uttered it. She closed her eyes as guilt played the scene over in her mind.

God, Rich's house was bright. Kendra made this observation as she banged cupboards open and shut, moved soup cans around in Rich's less than organized pantry and peered behind them. She had spent a sleepless night on his sofa unable to get the sight of his body out of her mind. Maybe she still had fever. She put the back of her hand against her forehead to check. A little warm but she would live. And unfortunately, she was coherent. Yep, it could be that she still had a thing for Richard T. Marvel, God help her. And if she was well enough to realize that things may not be completely over between them, she was coherent enough to make the flight to Kettle Creek. But Rich stood in her way. She just had to think of a way to get rid of him. As she was thinking up one lie, dismissing it in favor of another, Rich walked into the room.

Though he wasn't in a suit and tie, the Beretta sticking out of the holster in his waistband told her that he was dressed for business. Her eyes raked over him but she kept her face as still and smooth as she could.

Instead of greeting him she returned to the task at hand. As long as she was here, she might as well check the place out. She bent down and opened the cabinet door beneath the kitchen sink. Nothing there but Clorox, Cascade and a half used bottle of 409. When she stood up she found herself pressed against his hard body. She took a step back to look into his face to see what game he was up to. She didn't see what she expected. What she did see instead was a face set with determination.

"Where is it?" he demanded.

"Where is what?" she answered as she turned on her heel.

She opened a slim door in the kitchen and found herself staring at a water heater above which was a shelf. She stood on her toes but could not see what was on the shelf.

"You know damn well what I'm talking about," he said as he walked over to her. "The Smith & Wesson."

"I got rid of it a long time ago," she said as she dragged a kitchen chair to the water heater closet. "In case you haven't heard, I hate guns."

She ran her hand over the shelf and found nothing there but a couple of terry cloth towels and a can of WD40. But you could never be too sure she thought as she shook out the towels over the kitchen floor. Satisfied when nothing but lint floated to the floor she placed them back on the shelf and closed the door.

"Don't play games with me, Kendra," he said. "I have things to do today and I don't want you running around loose with a loaded weapon."

She glared at him as she jumped from the chair. Dragging it back to the kitchen table, she said, "You are not my keeper, Rich."

She opened the cupboard above the sink. Nothing but cereal boxes turned on their sides. Maybe not the kitchen, then, she thought as she walked out. He followed her with an exasperated sigh.

"Maybe I should have let Gregory put you in a holding cell."

She wheeled around to face him. It startled him so that he took a step back. "Well, maybe you should have!" she yelled.

She sat on the couch and used both hands to pull open the drawer of the coffee table—a TV Guide, the remote control for the monster television. She banged it shut and went into the guest bathroom. Nothing of interest in the medicine cabinet, and under the sink, only Charmin and extra soap. Irish Spring. He still used Irish Spring. That's what she had smelled on him when he stood near her at the sink. Irish Spring and nothing else.

"Kendra," he said. "You need to stop this."

"What?" she muttered as she swept past him.

"This obsession that you have with Luke Bertrand. It's getting dangerous. How long are you going to put your life on hold?"

"My life's not on hold, Rich," she said.

She opened the hall closet and moved the coats aside. It was too dark inside to see anything. She pulled the chain on the light hanging from the ceiling and looked in all four corners. Empty.

He grabbed her arm. "Listen to me," he said.

She jerked away. With each passing moment of not finding anything, an unreasonable anger welled inside her. She knew that it had to be here. In his office she pulled open the file cabinet.

He grabbed her by the shoulders, wouldn't let her pull away.

"What in the hell are you looking for?" he exploded.

"What do you think I'm looking for, Rich?" she said. "Booze. I'm looking for booze."

She stopped, swallowed. She had stunned him into silence. His hands fell away from her shoulders. Without saying a word he snatched her hand and ushered her through the living room.

"Rich," she said. "Wait . . ."

But he wouldn't wait. He slammed through the kitchen screen door and out into the backyard. He tore the lid from the metal garbage can and it clanged on the sidewalk.

Sunlight glinted on the bottles, some empty but most of them full. Kendra picked up a full bottle of Budweiser. It felt heavy and warm in her hands. She looked at Rich in wonder. His face was distant and he looked like a person she had never seen before.

"I'm getting my life together, Kendra," he said. "What about you?"

She didn't say anything. The Budweiser bottle clinked against the other bottles as she dropped it back into the trash can. She picked up a half bottle of Jack.

"Where is it?" he asked softly. "Where is the Smith & Wesson?"

She shook her head, still unable to speak. Finally, when the words came they were choked with tears.

"I don't have it," she repeated. How many times did he want her to say it?

Rich snorted in disgust. He snatched the Jack from her and hurled it into the trash can. The sound of glass breaking, the smell of whiskey filled the air. She watched as he reached down and slammed the lid back on the garbage can. He swung toward her, stopping at the sight of her face.

"Kendra," he breathed, wiping the tears away with the palm of his hand. "Why don't you just tell me where the weapon is? Tell me and put this vendetta you have behind you. Just let it go."

"I told you I don't have the revolver," she cried. "Why don't you believe me?"

"Because believing you has always proven dangerous for me, Kendra."

"Rich—" she started to protest but he held his hand up to stop her.

"Then make a promise to me," he said. "And if you keep it I'll put you on a higher floor in the trust department."

"Anything," she said, wanting him to trust her, wanting him to believe her at that moment when they had shared so much.

"Promise me that you will give this Luke Bertrand thing up, just . . ." He stopped as she took a step backward. He held up a finger to stop her. "Now, wait. I'm saying just until I can put the Anna Cotton case to rest. Then let's tackle this together."

"But—" she said.

He put a hand against her cheek to stop her. "I'm not asking that you walk away from it forever. I know you can't do that." She nodded. Hell, no, she couldn't do that. "But just until I can help," he finished.

She nodded again.

"Is that a yes?" he asked.

"Yes," she said. "I promise."

And he left then, moving his hand away and eventually leaving her alone in the house. She thought of all this as she headed toward Kettle Creek to speak with Carolyn Sutter, the local town historian and a woman Kendra had contact with since finding out about Kettle Creek. She had fully intended on keeping her promise to Rich but then Carolyn called to ask if she were still coming. Once she heard that voice, the promise vaporized like smoke in a magic act. And she knew that she had made another promise to Rich that she couldn't keep.

CHAPTER 31

Holder was right. Anna Cotton was nowhere to be found. They tried her room first and found the red security bracelet that Anna purportedly wore, lying on her bed. Uniformed officers along with employees of Brighton House scoured rooms, the recreational areas, the bathrooms and even the administrative offices. It was as if Anna had walked through one of Brighton House's walls or maybe found a fire escape like the fire escape at The Liberty Apartments which brought her here in the first place.

The boiling feeling in Rich's gut when it became clear that Anna Cotton was not in the facility made him question if it was a good thing that he did stop drinking. Because after this he would crave one in a big way. With each empty room, with each successive call from a uniformed officer telling Gregory that they had just cleared a room, the feeling grew. An hour after the search began, he saw officers draw their weapons and hold them aloft as they searched.

"Come on, Gregory," Rich said as Anna's face floated in his mind. "What's this shit?"

"Rich," Gregory said. "She may be dangerous."

"Dangerous?" Rich said. "Dangerous? Have you ever seen her? Does she look dangerous to you?"

"A man is dead, Rich," Gregory said.

"He deserves to be dead, Gregory," Rich said. "I'm sure Anna wouldn't hurt . . ." he stopped, realizing what he was about to say.

"You mean hurt anyone else?" Gregory finished for him.

Rich picked up a clipboard and threw it back down on the counter. It skidded and fell to the floor. He and Gregory had taken over the reception area of Brighton House. The pretty nurse who had been there earlier that night was with them now, looking from one of them to the other. She picked up the clipboard and sat it back down on the counter.

"If you can't handle this, Rich," Gregory said, "don't feel that you have to stick around."

"I'm sticking around, Gregory, I'm sticking around," he said.

Rich put both hands to his head as he thought about Anna sinking something sharp and wickedly pointed into the back of Chadwick's apple head. He could see her pulling it free, then using it to cut Chadwick's throat from behind like the pig he so obviously was. He tried to put the image out of his mind but he couldn't help but see her in Holder's office squeezing the head of the Barbie doll that Kendra had given her. Not to mention that Anna had taken so many drugs that it may have adversely affected her behavior. *We don't believe in counseling for our mentally retarded patients.*

"Fuck," Rich said, trying to drown the sound of Katherine Holder's soft voice from his head.

"Rich," Gregory warned again.

He slapped the clipboard the nurse had placed on the counter earlier. It went sailing again, this time coming to rest on a dot matrix printer next to the computer terminal. A tattoo of noise rose from the printer as the green and white paper jammed.

"Hey," the nurse said. "Have your temper tantrums someplace else, will you?"

She opened the printer cover and repositioned the paper over the printer tracks. Rich apologized while watching her with his arms folded.

"If you broke this thing, I'll get my ass chewed," she said. "Lord knows where this place would be if Big Brother couldn't trace your every movement."

"Big Brother?" Rich questioned.

She tilted her pretty face to him. "Yeah, that's what we call it."

She tried to smile but it faltered. He could see in her eyes that she too was worried about Anna. "It's the log system that keeps track of the card swipe system. Whenever someone uses a card, the dates and times are printed out here."

Rich looked at Gregory who shook his head. "Anna doesn't have a card, Rich," Gregory said.

"She could have stolen one," Rich said grimly.

"Can you tell who's who?" he asked the nurse.

She nodded. "Let's see," she said, looking at the printout. "That's odd."

"What's odd?" Rich asked, his heart thumping.

She frowned. "Marsha's been on maternity leave for the past three months."

She pulled up more green and white paper. "Looks like someone's using her card."

"When was the last time it was used?" Rich asked.

"Why, tonight, about forty-five minutes ago on the south door near the loading . . ."

But Rich didn't hear the rest. Before she got the words out, he snatched her access card and raced for the south entrance, Gregory right behind him.

Sloppy. Sloppy, Rich thought as he headed for the loading docks. He couldn't believe it but on some levels he couldn't help but believe it. Security at Brighton House was sloppy as hell, just as it seemed everything else was, in spite of Katherine Holder's calling. They reached the loading dock door. Before they opened the door, Gregory pulled his weapon from his holster.

"Come on, Gregory," Rich protested. "You are not going to need that."

But Gregory was having none of it. A uniformed officer approached. His weapon was also drawn.

Rich ignored him but kept his eyes on Gregory.

"You don't think we can take her?" Rich said.

"Protocol, Rich," Gregory said.

"Fuck protocol," Rich said quietly. "Let me talk to her."

They stared at each other a while longer. Rich tried to put in the stare all that they had been through together. Without taking his eyes from him, Gregory holstered his weapon and ordered the uniform to do the same.

"If I get killed out here," Gregory told Rich, "I will haunt your ass."

Rich grinned. "Yeah, sure you will."

They did not burst through the door. Rich knew better than that. Instead, they opened it slowly. The night was still wintry, bitter to almost freezing. The clouds had departed somewhat, making a space for the face of the moon which now shone on the canal running along the back of the property.

Anna Cotton sat on the bank of the canal, her long brown legs tucked beneath her. She had a long black coat around her shoulders. Her back was to them and her glossy black hair shimmered under the moon's light. Rich felt rather than saw Gregory reach for his weapon but Rich held his hand out to him. Anna did not turn around as they approached though she surely most have heard their footsteps crunch against the gravel.

Gregory hung back and waited. Rich stood next to Anna, the night chill biting through his jacket, making it feel like he was wearing only paper.

"Anna," Rich said.

She did not reply, just stared at the water. Rich stooped beside her.

"You've got a lot of stuff here," he said, picking up the headless Barbie.

"They Anna's treasures," she said softly, then turned to him. Her brown face looked bronze in the moonlight. Her eyes were large and sad. "They my treasures," she amended.

Rich looked at Gregory, noticed that his weapon was not drawn but he had his hand on his holster. Rich looked back at Anna. She stared at him so long it put a lump in his throat. He blinked, and after he blinked, she turned back to the water.

"Could you tell me what you have here?" Rich said.

"Anna's doll," she said, taking it from him and clutching it to her breast. "Anna's puzzle book, Anna's pretty paper." She picked up a piece of tinfoil. "And Anna's flashlight." She stopped, clicked it on and off. He used his hands to shield his eyes.

They sat in silence. Then Rich said, "What about that thing you are still holding?" he asked. "What about that?"

Anna gazed at the smeared letter opener, fourteen carat gold with an onyx handle, the letter opener that she had been clutching when he stooped beside her. She gazed at it as if she had never seen it before. It would have been brighter in the moon's yellow light but it was covered with smudges. Rich made out a darker stain near the handle.

"That Anna's, too," she whispered. "It mine."

Rich held out his hand. "May I see it?"

She shook her head.

"Can you tell me where you got it?"

Silence.

"Anna," Rich said. "Did you use that to hurt Chadwick?"

Her eyes widened. "He a bad man," she said. "He hurt Anna and Rosita."

"Do you know that he's dead, Anna?" Rich asked. "Do you know what dead is?"

She nodded, the corners of her mouth twitched into a smile. "Death mean doom and doom mean destiny. He dead because he got his destiny. He got what he deserved."

Rich hung his head, wiped his hand over his eyes. Without looking at Anna, he said, "Yes, Anna. He most likely got what he deserved."

Rich couldn't remember the last time he cried, couldn't remember the last time he had needed to. It took all of his strength not to give in to it now. Anna put a hand under his chin and lifted his face up. Looking at him with those beautiful eyes, she whispered, "You want to play with Anna's treasures?"

Rich nodded and she gave them to him one by one, starting with the puzzle book, the headless doll, the flashlight and finally the letter opener stained with Chadwick's blood. Rich took these things, trying to handle the murder weapon as little as possible. As he handed them to Gregory he thought that they had found both their rapist and murderer all in one night.

CHAPTER 32

Rich couldn't watch them lead Anna away no matter how gently Gregory did so. Dr. Holder went with her, insisting the entire time that it had to be self-defense. It just had to be. She convinced Gregory to let Anna be taken to Doctor's for observation before taking her to the sheriff's department, and Gregory agreed.

Two uniforms tore apart Anna's private room at Brighton. Rich had never been there, in her room, even to check out the camera. He always talked to her in the dayroom or Katherine Holder's office. *We like to give our patients a feeling of privacy.* Holder's voice sounded in his head. The TV camera Hightower installed greeted Rich like a useless eye. It hung over Anna's bed, which was narrow and pushed against the wall. A plastic beanbag chair, bright orange, sat in one corner, along with a long yarn rug and a dresser on which the drawers had no pull knobs.

Rich watched as one of the uniforms, this one with a trimmed goatee and pointed ears like a leprechaun, flipped over a dresser drawer, emptying the contents on the sterile white floors. He sifted through the resulting debris with the toe of a polished boot.

"What are you doing, man?" Rich said as he walked into the room.

The officer hooked his thumbs into his belt loops. "Detective Atfield wanted us to look around. So I'm looking around."

"Well, it looks like you are deliberately trying to make a fucking mess," Rich said.

"The crazy killed someone," the leprechaun man said. "I think she deserves a little mess."

"Get out," Rich ordered.

"Look, I'm just doing my job," the officer responded. "What's it to you, anyway? The last I heard is that you weren't with the department anymore."

Rich's eyebrow lifted. He took several steps toward the smart ass but when he spoke next his voice was calm and sure.

"Get the hell out of here," he said. "Or it won't only be the last thing you heard, it'll be the last thing that you said."

The officer stepped forward to meet him. Before he could speak, Rich heard Gregory's voice.

"Take it easy, both of you," he said.

Rich whirled on him. "Do you think it's okay that he tear up her things? You okay with that?"

"Rich," Gregory said. "You are overreacting. Officer Gold, take your partner and get statements from Holder and Lane. I've already taken care of Brighton."

After they left, Rich stooped. He righted the empty dresser drawer and one by one, started putting Anna's treasures back inside. A book of poems by a woman named Denise Levertov, a fountain pen with Katherine Holder's name engraved in gold, a plate from the cafeteria, a small palm-sized diary covered in pigs, a purple crayon the color of African violets.

"Looks like Anna got around," Gregory said as he watched Rich. "What a little kleptomaniac."

"Yeah," Rich breathed. "That letter opener must have come from Holder's office. I had one just like it. Goddammit."

"Rich," Gregory said.

Rich stopped for a moment, stared hard at the orange beanbag chair, trying to understand how in the world he had gotten it so wrong.

His wrist dangling on his knee, he said, "But what I don't get is the coat. How in the hell did she get Lane's coat?"

Gregory shrugged. "The same as she got most things, I guess. She took it out of Holder's office. She stole it, Rich."

Rich waved a hand over the items in the drawer. "You see anything like a coat in here?" he asked.

Gregory picked up a uniform top from a pair of scrubs. It still had a name tag on it. "She took it, Rich," Gregory said. "Just like she took everything else."

Still bothered, Rich picked up the rest of Anna's junk, wondering why she chose tonight of all nights to dispose of Chadwick, the man who had terrorized her so much. He was about to replace the drawer in the dresser when he noticed something lying on the floor. He picked up a small gold cuff link and shook it against his palm. It looked real.

"What's that, old man?" Gregory asked.

Rich shook his head to clear his thoughts. He recognized it but did not know from where. Just then, Katherine Holder entered the room. She took the cuff link from Rich.

"She must have taken this from my office with the letter opener," she said, her voice curious.

"So this belongs to you?" Rich asked.

"No, no," she said. "The board members are always in and out of my office, especially tonight. It must belong to one of them."

But the card logs didn't show Anna anywhere near Holder's office that night. He was about to say so when Gregory's cell phone rang. As Gregory listened, Rich saw his face pale and his eyes become more silver than Rich ever thought they could. When he hung up the phone he didn't say anything. He just stared at Rich. Rich felt a fear gather in his belly and climb high in his throat.

"Spill it man," he said. "Don't just stand there. What's going on?"

"Where's Kendra, Rich?" Gregory asked.

"I told you earlier, she said something about going to Dom's place. Why?"

"Have you heard from him?"

Rich shook his head.

"Luke Bertrand's been shot," Gregory said.

Rich tried to brave it out but every fiber of his body told him what Gregory would say next. "So you say been shot. That means the bastard's not dead?"

"No, he's not," Gregory confirmed.

"Any suspects?" Rich asked.

"Rich."

"I told you she's at Dom's place. She told me that she was going to hang out over there. I'm watching her or having her watched just—"

"Rich," Gregory repeated, cutting him off. "They found .357 magnum shell casings at the scene.

Rich felt air leave his lungs. "No." The word came out hot and dry.

Still staring at him, Gregory said, "I'll give you twenty-four hours to bring her in. And I mean it, Rich. I want her in."

CHAPTER 33

The doorknob to Kendra Hamilton's hotel room in Kettle Creek quivered. As she watched it twist she wished that she did have the Smith & Wesson instead of the lamp from the bedside table to use as a weapon against the asshole on the other side of the door, picking her lock. She stood just to the left of it, holding the lamp by its wooden base. Whoever came through that door would be greeted with the only weapon she could find when she first heard the hollow shake of the doorknob.

Kendra had found the motel easily enough after her plane landed. It was only two miles from the airport, an L-shaped single story building sitting on a pool of newly paved blacktop. Each door was painted an oily green and locked with a key instead of an access card. The interior of the room was just as disappointing: a double bed covered by a green plaid bedspread, a chair and an ottoman next to a bathroom the size of a shoe box. But Kendra did not really care about the furnishings of her room. Her main concern was getting a full night's sleep so she could meet Carolyn Sutter the following morning. She set her alarm clock and laid down for a good night's sleep.

That was hours ago. It was three A.M. when she first heard someone outside her door. She grabbed the only thing in the room that wasn't nailed down, the only thing that she could use as a weapon, the wood-based lamp with the same patterned squares as the headboard. She raised the lamp above her head and by the light of the neon sign outside her room, watched the door.

The doorknob twisted. She gripped the lamp harder and raised it higher above her head. The door whined as it opened. Sweat drenched her palms and she had to catch the lamp before it fell. The resulting jangle ruined all her chances for a surprise. She had no choice but to strike and strike she did. But it was too late.

A powerful hand tightened around her wrist. The resulting ache caused her to drop the lamp. She tried to scream as it clattered to the floor but she felt a hand press against her mouth. As he reeled her around and pinned the back of her head against his chest she smelled the familiar scent of Irish Spring. And the arm crossed above her breast she had encountered before but never in a circumstance like this.

Panic subsided; her breathing began to return to normal. But the fear she felt from a stranger attack was replaced with something else. She heard Rich's hand slap the light switch next to the door.

"Let me go," she said.

He did just that. She swept her fingers to her throat, remembering how close his arm was to cutting off her breathing.

"Shit, Rich," she said. "Don't you knock?"

"Would you have answered the door if I had?" he asked her as he shut the motel room door.

She sensed anger radiating from him in waves. He placed his hands on his hips, looking at her as if she were a dangerous stranger. She licked her lips, raked a hand through the tangle of hair falling around her shoulders.

"I'm sorry I had to lie to you, Rich," she started.

"No, no, you are not." His words held a note of curiosity, and a more troubling realization that he was beginning to see her for what she was.

"Rich . . ." she tried.

"You knew that it was a lie the minute it came from your mouth, Kendra. I was the only sucker who believed it."

He watched her out of the corner of his eyes as she approached. She stopped inches from him, placed the palm of her hand on his muscled chest. He didn't move, still gazed at her with that look of wonder in his eyes. Kendra understood one thing at that moment, that she was about to lose him, that is, if she hadn't already.

"I can explain," she said.

He was shaking his head, slowly. "No, you can't," he said. "There is no explanation for your behavior. What I didn't realize was that there never was. I just wanted there to be. I gave you too much credit, Kendra."

She pressed closer to him until she could feel herself against him, his belt pressing against her. Staring into her face he placed both his hands on her forearms and pushed her away.

"Don't worry," he said softly, never taking his eyes from her face. "That's not why I'm here."

It was already too late, she had lost him. Suddenly, she felt naked. The pajama bottoms slung low on her hips exposed her stomach and waist, the tank top was much too small. She folded her arms across her chest.

"Then why are you here?" she asked.

She didn't expect an answer. But he gave one anyway, matter-of-fact and devoid of feeling or accusation. "A favor for Gregory," he said.

"A favor? For Gregory? Why?"

"He asked me to bring you in, and that's what I'm doing."

Her laughter was devoid of mirth. Here she was so close to finding out what happened thirty years ago to Luke's mystery woman and Gregory and Rich had conspired together to bring her in for some minor transgression. So what that she had broken into Luke's place? She was about to expose him for what he was, for what he had always been, and here was Richard T. Marvel getting in her way. Again.

"I'm not going anywhere," she told him, her voice hard. "You're crazy to think that I am. I have an appointment with Carolyn Sutter tomorrow, Rich. She knew Luke and his wife. I'm not leaving here until I talk to her."

"So let me get this straight," Rich countered. "It wasn't enough that you shot him, you still want to prove he was a monster from the get go?"

Kendra's mouth dropped open. "Shot him?" she questioned. "Rich, I didn't shoot . . ."

She stopped, remembering a night over two weeks ago when she stood at Luke's bed pointing the Smith & Wesson at his forehead. She remembered now that the only reason she didn't do it was because he wouldn't feel it. Guilt must have settled over her face because suddenly Rich spoke.

"Uh-huh, yeah," he said, his eyes raking over her. "Thought so. Get dressed. We've got a plane to catch in an hour."

Stunned, Kendra sat on the bed. She rubbed her hand along the side of her face, a desperate plea in her eyes. *Please don't let him be dead,* she thought. He can't be dead, not before he knew that she knew about what he did, must have done to the woman who wore that ring. His dying would be like a part of her dying.

She looked at Rich. "Is he dead?" she asked.

He walked over to her, placed his hands on either side of her, and brought his face down to hers until they were almost touching. With a glare in his eyes, he said, "No." He lifted one hand to point to his head. "You are a doctor, Kendra. You'd think you'd know to aim for the head."

He straightened up. "Get dressed," he said again.

"Rich," she said. "I didn't do it. I didn't try to kill Luke . . . I . . ." she stopped, knowing that she did. He didn't miss the lie in her eyes. With disgust he threw her overnight bag on the bed. She grabbed his arm; he jerked away.

"Okay, okay," she said. "Truth. I wanted to kill Luke but I couldn't."

"You wouldn't know truth if it . . ."

"Rich, stop it," she choked out.

He did. She followed him to the bathroom and watched as he picked up her toothbrush and toothpaste.

"I did what I had to do when I came here," she said. "But I didn't shoot Luke."

Ignoring her, he threw both items into her overnight bag.

"Okay," she said. "When was he shot?"

"Please," Rich said in disgust

"No, Rich, tell me. Was it tonight? If it was tonight I was on a plane, Rich. I was on a plane on my way here to Kettle Creek. I was nowhere near Dunhill. If you don't believe me, just think."

He said nothing. She went to the nightstand, rummaged through the drawer. She thrust the plane ticket at him. He let it hang in the air. She waved it at him.

"Take it," she said. "Look at it."

"It's not me you have to convince," he said, his face grim.

"I'm not going with you," she said.

"Yes, you are," he said this without looking at her. He found her Levis in her overnight bag. They thumped against her chest, fell to the floor.

"Get dressed," he ordered.

"No," she answered.

What could he do? For all his bravado Rich wouldn't drag her from this motel room half dressed. She knew that he wouldn't. And she was right. With growing horror, she watched him pick up the phone.

"What are you doing?" she asked.

"There is a warrant out for your arrest. I don't need this shit. The police can deal with it."

She ran to him.

"Rich, please," she said, hearing the frantic plea in her own voice. She didn't know she had touched him until he once again knocked her hands away. She stood there, frozen, as he dialed information.

"All I'm asking for is one night," she said. "Just give me one night."

He turned away from her. "Kettle Creek Sheriff's Department," he said.

She walked to him, got in his face so he had to look at her. "You would do this to me," she asked him, not really convinced that he would.

His brown eyes clear and hard, his mouth set, Rich said, "You did it to yourself, sweetheart."

She snatched the phone from him and threw it on the floor. The sound it made as it crashed to the floor added to the desperation that she felt. Rich's mouth twisted into a smile. He unhooked his cell phone from the clip on his belt and flipped it open.

The silence hung around them thick and heavy as he dialed the sheriff's department. Kendra felt, all at once, that what she had worked so hard for the past week was slipping away. She was here, in Kettle Creek now. She had a scheduled appointment with Carolyn Sutter in the morning. If she did not uncover Luke's past then it would remain buried forever.

"Rich, please," she said again, grabbing the hand with the phone, sliding her body against his.

She placed her hands on both sides of his face, rubbed her lips against his. He dropped the cell phone but only so he could move her away again. But she wouldn't let him. She kissed him again harder, this time drawing her tongue across his lips in a way she knew used to drive him crazy. Used to. When she pulled back to look at him, his face was motionless. He had folded his arms across his chest, reminding Kendra of a stone statue.

"This won't work," he said.

Yes, it will, she thought. She couldn't have been wrong about the way he felt about her. He wouldn't be here if he didn't care. Before she could change her mind, she stroked his arm until he dropped it, kissed him again until she felt his mouth open. But he stopped suddenly and pushed her away again. He bent down to retrieve the cell phone. She kicked it out of his way, bent so she was underneath him, murmuring, "Rich, please" against his lips. He let her kiss him; he had gone still in her arms.

But he came to life, slowly at first, putting his arm around her waist and plunging his hand into the tangle of her hair. She hadn't expected the intensity, his mouth hot against hers, his hands ripping the top from her. And she hadn't expected the intense feelings coursing through her as his hands glided over her.

By the time he had killed the lights she was naked in his arms. His shirt was gone, the neon light from the sign beyond the motel room window washed over his smooth brown skin. Her hands running over his chest, the long fingers, the white nails in the darkness, fascinated her in a way being with him never had in the past. She looked up and found that his eyes were on her face, and she read in them that she would get more than she bargained for. And as he whispered the question in her ear, wondering if she were lying to him yet again, she had no answers. For now, the only thing that meant anything to her was Rich's body pressed against hers.

The next morning he caught her as she emerged from the bathroom. She was fully dressed in a pair of Levis and a quilted plaid shirt with a deep inside pocket. He, on the other hand, was naked, a white sheet wrapped around his waist. He watched her, half kneeling, half sitting as she tied her wild hair into a yellow scrunchie. She did everything she could to ignore both the desperation and the accusation in his eyes. Her plan was to keep quiet, to slip out before he woke up. But there he was, the pressed wood headboard of the motel room bed framing his taut body.

"We can be on the next plane out," he said.

"Not before I see Carolyn Sutter," Kendra replied as she placed her wallet in the inside pocket of the shirt.

He caught her wrist as she reached for the keys to the rental car. "I'm asking you to let go of this, Kendra. Leave it alone. You'll be disappointed."

She jerked away. "How do you know that I'll be disappointed? You can't know that. Besides, I can't let it go and will not until I find out what Luke Bertrand is hiding."

Still staring at her, he asked, "What was last night to you, Kendra?"

"It was everything," she whispered.

He did not seem surprised by her answer. But he took a deep breath before speaking again. "Then I'm asking you to give this up, for you, for us."

"I'm doing this for us, Rich," she said. "You were right. Luke Bertrand has always been there between us. But last night he wasn't. Do you want to know why?" He shook his head. She continued. "Because he's about to get what he deserves. And until he gets what's coming to him we'll never be okay . . ."

He pulled her toward him, pressed his lips to hers and kissed her as if he would never see her again.

"You are so wrong," he said. "You are so wrong and have been from the moment you sat foot back in Dunhill County. Can't you see that?"

She held onto his wrists, looked into his eyes as she replied. "That's your opinion," she said gently. "You told me last night that you found out what happened to Anna Cotton, Rich. You took care of your business. Now let me take care of mine."

The phone rang, the hollow sound of the bell resounded off the walls of the room. It rang two more times while Rich stared at her. She could see by the light in his eyes that he was making up his mind. The phone rang two more times. Kendra swallowed hard as she listened to it. She knew it was Carolyn Sutter asking her about the meeting. The woman was anxious to talk to her. But Kendra was afraid that if she answered it, she would break the spell, force Rich into a decision they would both regret. He watched her through two more full rings. Then, he said, never taking his eyes off her face, "I'm coming with you."

CHAPTER 34

When she wasn't playing local historian, Mrs. Carolyn Sutter ran the fruit and produce store in Kettle Creek, Oregon, population five hundred. Kendra and Rich stood among glassy apples, perfectly formed and big as baseballs. Kendra listened as intently as her scattered mind would allow. But while Kendra listened Rich walked among the barrels of fruits and nuts, sampling each with his eyes and hands. As Mrs. Sutter rattled on about the first body they found at Kettle Creek, Rich scooped up a handful of walnuts, let them fall through his fingers. After they clattered back among themselves he walked to the next one. Mrs. Sutter kept talking, ignoring him. But Kendra glanced over at him to see if he was taking in any of what Carolyn Sutter was saying. He returned her gaze with an absent look, which told her that he did listen, but barely.

On the drive over, he lit into her. Kendra had no place to live, no job. She had bigger problems than Luke Bertrand and what he may or may not have done thirty years ago. Besides, Carolyn Sutter, from what Kendra told him, was a lonely woman. From first contact, Mrs. Sutter had called Kendra over and over again to make sure that Kendra's plans hadn't changed and that she was still coming to Kettle Creek. And the woman wouldn't tell her the entire story over the phone, only fed Kendra little pieces of the story at a time. And finally, she insisted that Kendra come to Kettle Creek to talk to her in person.

But Kendra knew in her heart that there was something to Mrs. Sutter's story. She knew Kettle Creek had to be it. Luke may have always been a private man but he talked freely about the stages of his life. His mother, devout, religious, saved him from his father. After she left him she went to work for the person who would become Luke's benefactor. She died with hands warped into the shape of the scrubbing brush and her knees worn from kneeling. Luke's benefactor taught him everything, how to be gentle, his love for chess and for classical music, his calling to help those less fortunate. Then the benefactor paid for college and medical school. And after Luke's education, it was back to his hometown— not the home he was born into—but the place that he and his mother fled to when he was five. Luke stayed in Dunhill and became the man he was today. All of that was common knowledge.

But Kettle Creek, he lived there for at least six months. He never mentioned it. The marriage, never mentioned, either. And if it were not for the wedding ring with the inscription that Kendra found at Luke's place, she would never have known. Mrs. Sutter would help her find the former and quite possibly dead Mrs. Luke Bertrand. Kendra knew this in the red blood of her heart, down to the depth of her gut. As Kendra watched Mrs. Sutter now and listened to her meandering story, she almost doubted. Almost. Mrs. Sutter suspected something about Luke. She had a story burning inside her that she had wanted to get out for thirty years.

Luke Bertrand lived in Kettle Creek after college, Mrs. Sutter told them. She knew because she had been born in the place, had lived in the small town all her life. Her mother was born here, so was her grandmother. Her father came to live in Kettle Creek when he was sixteen, big hands, barrel chest, and vowed it was the one place he would never leave. Unlike Luke. Mrs. Sutter knew he and the woman he lived with were not destined for this place. They had another look about them.

"What look was that?" Rich said. He stood near a barrel of apples. Tiredness edged his voice—and annoyance.

Kendra felt him looking at her, studying her face, her barely combed hair, the wrinkles etched around her eyes. She sweated. She tried not to, but she could not help it. The sweat beaded on her bare arms and hands. She had thought the quilted plaid shirt would be heavy enough for the cold but she didn't think it would be too heavy. But after five minutes in Mrs. Sutter's produce store, she had thrown it off. She could no longer stand the dampness under her arms, the heat under her collar.

Rich walked over to the shirt. He folded it in half, pressed it close to a barrel of bright yellow lemons. She watched him pick one up, bring it to his nose to smell. He rubbed the thick, pebbled skin with his thumb. Even though he had asked the question about what look Mrs. Sutter referred to, he did not listen to the reply.

"The look," she said, pointing a crooked finger at Kendra as if sensing that she was the only one interested in the reply. "The look of a person all the time thinking of something else, of someplace else. Walked around here like he better than anybody."

Mrs. Sutter sat back in her chair, swiped her knee with the dish rag she held in her hand. The hand, the color of hazel nuts, was covered with darker brown spots, moles, and warts.

"And the woman he lived with, was he married to her?" Kendra asked.

Mrs. Sutter paused, scratched her chin. "Well," she said. "I just assumed that they were married."

"Did she wear a ring?" Kendra asked.

She looked at a point over Kendra's shoulders as if she could find the answer there. She shook her head, gray bangs flopping.

"I don't remember that," she said. "In those days, or at least I was still old-fashioned enough to think so, if a fella was with a woman she was usually his wife."

"But you remember her," Rich asked skeptically.

"How could anyone forget her? She was a real piece of work, let me tell you. Dressed like she was in a circus act, hot pants and high boots. And that white boy they had up here with them. He dressed as crazy as she did. The whole town knew that she had something going on with him . . ."

"White boy?" Rich interrupted.

"Yes," Carolyn said. "They sent two doctors up here that year. Luke and another boy, I think from Harvard. We had a real bad flu that year and asked if the program could assign us two for a while."

"Program?" Rich asked.

"Yes," Mrs. Sutter said. "It was one of those programs that put young doctors in places that not a lot of people wanted to go." She cackled. "And back then, even now maybe, a lot of people didn't want anything to do with our little town. Too small. I ran the program for us then."

"Do you remember his name, the other doctor?" Kendra asked.

Mrs. Sutter tilted her head as she tried to remember.

"Can't say I do," she said. "Long or Lake. Something. First name Tony maybe, name like the hope chest . . ."

"Lane?" Rich said.

"Yeah, that's it, Lane." She stopped, looked at the floor for a while. "Maybe. I think so."

Kendra sent Rich a triumphant look. She didn't know what that meant, the fact that Lane was with Luke and his wife in Kettle Creek, but maybe that explained why Lane sent someone after her.

"So maybe Lane was here," Rich said mildly. "Big deal."

"What happened to Luke and his wife, Mrs. Sutter?" Kendra asked.

Mrs. Sutter got up and plugged in an electric teapot that was on the counter by an old cash register. The pot was grimy around the spout and along the bottom.

"Tea?" she asked them.

Rich groaned. Kendra shook her head.

"Luke and his wife, Mrs. Sutter," Kendra prompted.

"Well," she said. "She left him, that's what happened. Luke came to me a couple of months after he started here and told me that his wife had left him for somebody else."

"Smart lady," Rich breathed.

"Rich," Kendra said.

"The town wasn't surprised that much because people suspected that she and that white boy had a thing going on at the river. Luke left about four months after that without her."

"So what?" Rich said. "She and Luke probably got divorced and now she's spending her retirement in Florida."

He still did not take this seriously.

"I told you," Kendra said. "I told you that *he* left. She never did. I can't find any record of her anywhere. It's like she's a ghost, like she never existed."

Rich nodded. His eyes told her that he did not believe her. She thought that last night would have changed that, that by making love to her he had somehow agreed with her that there might be something in Kettle Creek that they needed to see. Kendra knew in her heart, knew it like she knew blood flowed through her arteries, that Luke killed his wife. This was the place, the place Luke Bertrand decided what he was and what he would become.

"What about Lane, Mrs. Sutter?" Rich asked.

"The other doctor? I think he stuck around for a little bit after Luke left but I'm not too sure," she answered.

"So you remember every detail about Luke but not Lane?" Rich asked.

Smoke rose from the spot of the tea kettle. Mrs. Sutter poured the boiling liquid into a Styrofoam cup and pursed her lips to blow the smoke.

"Though that fella dressed like he was in a circus act, too, he wasn't like Luke. There was something about Luke, I tell you. And Debra, she complained to me all the time, said Luke was starting to scare her. He kept her praying so much that her knees were starting to scab up. He wouldn't touch her unless he was falling down drunk. I'm telling you, the boy had a problem and everyone saw it. People didn't want to bring their children to him for treatment."

Neither one of them said anything for while. Mrs. Sutter blew once more on the tea, took a noisy sip.

"You sure you don't want any?" she said. "Warm you right up."

As if she needed any warming up, Kendra thought. The place was hot as an oven. She rubbed the back of her neck and shook her head. And then, Mrs. Sutter said, "If you asked me, I think she is still up there."

Rich rolled his eyes. But Kendra asked, "Who's up there?"

"Debra," Mrs. Sutter replied before taking another sip. "I think Debra's up there cursing the place. She met that white boy up there all the time. Like I said, everybody knew it. Luke's just the type to kill her and hide her body up there."

She sent Kendra an intent gaze, a gaze that said, *you know what I mean.* And Kendra did know what Mrs. Sutter meant. Luke was a man who needed symbols. In his eyes, every action was fraught with symbolic meaning. Killing his adulterous wife and disposing of her body in the river would be fatal justice to him.

"Where is Kettle River?" Kendra asked.

"You are not going up there," Rich said. "You look like hell. We need to get back, clear this Luke thing up and . . ." Get you checked out, was the rest of what he said but his words did not fully register.

This time Mrs. Sutter agreed with him.

"The place growed up and dried out," she said. "Cursed."

"Cursed," Kendra said, and laughed.

"I wouldn't go up there alone," Mrs. Sutter said.

Not alone, that's what Mrs. Sutter said. Kendra looked at Rich who was slowly shaking his head.

"Don't even think about it," he said. "We don't have time for wild goose chases."

Kendra saw that Mrs. Sutter had become so enamored of her own story that she was oblivious to them. For over thirty years, even before Luke's wife left him, maybe even before Luke came to town, bodies started turning up at the river. First the sheriff found a torn piece of clothing, a time-spotted rag, once blue, now a dim gray, wadded and stained with rust. The sheriff, thinking the rust stains blood, searched the place again but found nothing, only a torn saddle shoe beneath the running water. Kids, he thought. After all, the shoe was small. Or it must have been teenagers, horny bastards, leaving their clothes all over the riverbank. That was about three months before Luke's wife left him, if Mrs. Sutter remembered correctly. That's what she said. "If I 'member correctly, Bill found that torn dress late spring. He was hunting, had chased some doe into the woods."

The trees were green then, Mrs. Sutter continued with her eyes misting over. The trees were so green and thick that the sun had to fight every inch of the way to the forest floor. And the place did not smell then like it smelled now. Then the smells were sweet like running water and redwoods. And everyone in town thought that the sheriff was right. Some horny teenagers forgot themselves and left their clothes near the river, probably on a night when the moon was bright as silver.

At first. Townspeople thought that at first. And then the fire happened. Luke was still here, maybe the other doctor, too. But the wife had been gone for weeks by the time of the fire. Who ever heard of a fire that only burned the top of the trees? But there was a fire that hopped from the tip of one redwood to the other. They crackled and exploded like popcorn, filled the air with sparks raining fire all over the forest floor.

The town of Kettle Creek and the Forest Service put the fire out, all right, she said. But the place was ruined pretty much after that. All the animals left or starved to death. No one heard birds up there anymore. And then, more bodies started to turn up. They found two in the summer of '70, in July, exposed on top of the singed ground. Then another one was found about two years later, this one in a box.

After that, the remaining leaves turned brown, the trees died and didn't come back. And the river where the townspeople would have picnics in the daytime and lovers would meet at night, died. The fish went first; the water turned murky with their floating carcasses. And with their death and the death of the animals came the smell of decay. Dead leaves lay on the ground all year around, even in spring and summer. The place was cursed, Mrs. Sutter repeated again. And Kendra would see it if she went up there.

"Where is this place?" Kendra asked.

The way to the river, or what was left of it, was rough. The last body they pulled out of Kettle Creek, the one in the box, they had to take a helicopter to get it. The only reason it was found was because some biologist had hiked up there doing some research or something or other.

"Then how did the body get up there then?" Rich snapped.

Kendra knew he didn't believe a word. She's feeding you a bunch of bullshit and you're swallowing it hook, line, and sinker. Though he didn't say it out loud, at least Kendra didn't think so. She covered her ears to hush the words she heard all around her.

Mrs. Sutter knotted her hand on her hip. "The body, mister," she said. "Somebody left it years and years ago, before the place had become so wild. They tried to save it you see, kept it real nice at first, so they could get back and forth, understand the damage the fire had caused."

But they gave up, left it alone. Most people caring about what caused the fire died and most people caring about restoring the river either left the town or were kicked out of office. As it should be, the place was cursed.

Kendra listened to the muffled voices. She could see Rich's fingers gently stroke a tomato so ripe it seemed as if it would burst at any minute. Though he yearned to touch her, said with his mouth that he loved her, he thought one thing and one thing only, he didn't agree with her. You are sick, Kendra. You need to see a doctor.

"Are you all right?" he asked.

She opened her eyes. He had not been standing by the tomatoes at all. Instead he stood by the counter, next to the cash register. Both of Kendra's hands were still pressed tight against her ears. She brought her hands down. Mrs. Sutter stared at her with wide eyes.

"Was it something I said?" she asked. Her voice shook with concern.

"No," Kendra said. "My head just hurts, that's all."

Mrs. Sutter sprang up. Her long skirts flapped about her ankles.

"You sure don't look good," she said. "I have just the thing to take care of what you got."

She came back, handed Kendra a narrow glass with a juice the color of blood oranges. Sediment clouded along the bottom of the glass. Rich examined it dubiously.

"It ain't sweet," Miss Carolyn said. "But it'll take care of that headache and that fever."

Kendra took a sip but only to be polite. The drink was not sweet, it was sour, gritty, and tasted of carrots and bad honey.

"You need to get to a doctor," Rich said.

Command was in his voice this time, and worry. His hand pressed into her back. Kendra knew he felt the moist cotton of her turtleneck wet with cold sweat.

"Later," was all she said, and was glad when Mrs. Sutter chimed in.

"It's nothing but a headache and fever. It won't be too long for staying after she drinks that right up." The old woman waved her hand over the glass Kendra held. Kendra took another sip. The fruit or vegetable or whatever was in the glass, the pulp coated her cheeks and settled below her gum line.

Kendra told Mrs. Sutter and Rich that she did not feel good, that Rich was right and that they best get back to Dunhill. A skeptical look crossed Rich's face but he didn't argue. Back at the motel Kendra told Rich that she needed to lie down. He did not believe her, insisted on lying down with her. In the end they compromised. He sat in a chair next to the bed until she had fallen asleep. She pretended at first but pretty soon she was asleep. When she awakened, the room was dark. And empty.

CHAPTER 35

Kendra Hamilton did not believe in curses. She did not believe in old women who had been around since creation, especially those who lured people in with tall tales of bodies, creeks, and curses. But still, Kendra would not rest until she checked out the river. At first, Mrs. Sutter wouldn't tell Kendra how to get to the dry river. But she capitulated when Kendra insisted that she could find out from anybody, not just her. Just save both of them time and tell her now.

Kendra drove the winding road Mrs. Sutter had told her about. The entrance was easy to miss. On one side of the entrance grew a wild thicket of trumpet flowers and honeysuckle, on the other, tall redwoods. And in the middle was an aperture absent of light. Kendra had driven by it three times, had to turn around in a small patch of gravel off the road with her wheels spinning before finally seeing it.

Parking the car off to the side, she stared at the opening. Her heart thumped. She could only imagine what lay on the other side. And as she entered she told herself that it could not be as dark as it looked. The heart that had been thumping a moment before sank when she emerged on the other side. For several seconds, she doubted.

Directly in front of her, the land sheered away. What looked like solid rock formed a bottom that seemed to be streaked with rust.

She took a deep breath in order to calm herself. She closed her eyes and listened to the sound of the forest. She savored not being in Dunhill anymore, to be away from that urban hell. Here the birds still whistled in spite of what Mrs. Sutter had said. But near her right boot, dead leaves whispered. She looked down and saw a black snake hide its body among the leaves and twigs at her feet. Kendra yelped, snatched her foot back. The snake flicked away.

For a moment she thought about walking back out into the sunlight, running to Rich and putting her arms around him. She thought about telling him that she loved him, would do anything for him but just take her away from this, just hide her away from the pain and anguish caused by the longing to see Luke Bertrand punished.

But she couldn't do that. She could no more run away than this place could shake its sorry past. She must see to this. If what she suspected was true, she would find Luke's wife. With this thought, amidst the sounds, she heard water trickling. Yes, she did, it had to be. Faintly, softly like the piano music in the club where Dominic played his sax. She moved toward the sound. Surely this must be the river. "Sick," she heard Rich's voice in her head. "Didn't Mrs. Sutter say the river was dry? You are sick, Kendra."

But they were both wrong. The water trickled to her left, a thin stream where the drop was less steep. Kendra angled her body to the side and stepped down, slow, slow. She looked over the sheer drop, knowing that if she fell, she could lie here for days, for weeks before anyone found her. Rich might know where she was but it would be too late. The drop would kill her and he would find her broken body among the silver- and rust-streaked rocks.

Halfway down the incline, she looked to the bottom again. She stumbled. Immediately she tried to catch her balance but she fell and rolled the rest of the way to the bottom of the clearing. On her back, her head throbbing, she stared up. The trees were less thick here. The sun had concentrated its brightness into a powerful circle. Cylinders of light swirled in Kendra's eyes. Lying on her back, confused, cooled by the lengthening afternoon shadows, Kendra realized that she had actually been unconscious for a while. No thought on how to get back up the incline. Never a thought about that. Her only thought was about going down.

* * *

Rich walked into an empty motel room. He knew the minute he left that she would try to leave before he returned. But he thought he could rush and get back before she woke up. She had been sleeping like a baby when he left. He set the burgers and fries on the nightstand, alternately feeling like an idiot and worrying. What, he wondered, was in his face that said "sucker"? It had to be there but Kendra Hamilton seemed to be the only person who could see it and read it. He grabbed his car keys and headed for the river.

He had tried to remember what that nut Mrs. Sutter had said about where the place was as he drove the car toward the outskirts of Kettle Creek. He still didn't trust her, though, had found out the directions from the owner of Kettle Creek's one and only gas station. How did Kendra find people like her? First Leroy Cotton and now Carolyn Sutter. *"Who's the freak magnet now, Dominic?"* Rich muttered under his breath. When his cell phone rang, he assumed it was Gregory Atfield calling him to ream him about not being back in Dunhill with Kendra Hamilton in tow.

"Don't even say it, Atfield," he said into the phone.

"Ex . . . excuse me," the voice on the other end said. "This is Katherine Holder."

"Yes?" Rich said, his thumb tapping against the steering wheel as he waited for the light in front of him to change to green.

"I would have called Detective Atfield," she said. "But I wanted to run it by you first."

"Run what by me?" Rich asked.

"Rich," she said. "That letter opener we all received from the board for Christmas gifts last year . . ."

"You mean the letter opener that Anna used to kill Chadwick, the one she stole from you?"

"Yes," Holder said. Her voice trembled. "But that's just it. I don't think she stole it from me."

His thumb stopped its drumbeat against the steering wheel. The light changed to green, he pressed the gas pedal. "Come again?" he said.

"I don't keep things like that in my office. Though security is pretty tight at Brighton House," she stopped and sighed. "Okay, even though we thought it was pretty tight, I wouldn't keep that thing around for the very reason you saw last evening. In fact, I gave mine away."

"So you are saying that Anna didn't get the letter opener from you?" Rich asked.

"That's exactly what I'm saying," Holder said.

"Then where did she get it from, Katherine?" Rich asked as he turned left.

"I don't know where, Rich. Where did we get the ones that we had?"

He didn't say anything. Neither did she. He stared at the mountains hulking in the distance, their pointed peaks frosted with snow. *Theo Lane,* Rich thought. They got the letter openers as Christmas gifts from Theo Lane of the Brighton House board.

"Okay," Rich said. "So she must have stolen it from him. You saw the things that she had. Maybe he accidentally left it in your office."

"Could have," she agreed. "But there is something else bugging me."

"What's that?" Rich asked, almost missing his turn.

"Brandon signed Anna in and out for appointments at Doctor's."

"Yeah? So?"

"But there is not any record of his taking any of the Brighton House vehicles."

"So?" Rich said, getting annoyed now. "Maybe he took his own vehicle."

"But Chadwick doesn't, I mean didn't, have a working vehicle. He had to bum rides to work."

"Well, maybe he got a ride when he checked Anna out," Rich said as he pulled behind Kendra's vehicle with a sinking feeling in his gut.

He looked at the opening in the thicket. It was black as pitch. There was no way she would actually go into a place as dark as that. Would she? He twisted around and grabbed the high powered flashlight he had bought at the hardware store after he found out Kendra was missing. He did not know how long it would take to find her and didn't want to be caught in the woods after dark without a light. He didn't realize that the cell phone was still pressed to his ear until Holder spoke again.

"How would he have explained Anna?" she asked. "That's what's been bugging the hell out of me since he was killed. How could he have taken Anna from Brighton House without a vehicle?"

How indeed, Rich thought. But he knew. Phillip Grubb, Chadwick's porn buddy. He told Holder so as he flicked the flashlight on and off to make sure that it was working.

"But what about the letter opener?" Holder asked.

"Look," Rich said. "Maybe Lane accidentally left it lying around like I said and Anna klept it. Call Gregory and have him pick Grubb up. He was probably in on this whole rape thing with Chadwick."

"All right," Holder said.

But she didn't hang up. He could still hear her breathing in the phone. He pointed the flashlight into the gash that served as an entrance to the wood. He could see thick trees beyond. He wondered when or if the place thinned out.

"Is there anything else, Katherine?" Rich asked.

Silence for a few more seconds. Then she spoke again. "The Lane thing bothers me, Rich."

Rich sighed. He didn't want to think about Lane now. Kendra was missing on some crazy hunt for a phantom.

"Katherine," he asked. "Where is Anna now?"

"She's at Doctor's. They had to sedate her and she had a bad reaction to the medication."

Rich stopped. "Is she okay?"

"She's fine but they want to keep her under observation for a few days."

"Guard outside her door?" Rich asked.

"Yes, but . . ."

"Then she's fine," Rich said abruptly. "We can look into this when I get back. In the meantime, give Atfield a call."

"Maybe I should talk to Theo myself . . ."

"No!" Rich cut her off, thinking of Kendra and her suspicions about Lane. He didn't believe for a minute that Lane had drugged her, but he didn't want Holder taking any chances. "Stay away from Theo Lane. If he is involved in this, let the police deal with him."

Rich wouldn't hang up until Holder promised him that she wouldn't call Theo. He swept his flashlight in front of the entrance again and thought, *Kendra, what have you gotten yourself into now?* He stared at it a few minutes longer before returning to the car and driving to the entrance the gas station attendant had told him about, the one that wouldn't send you tumbling ten feet down to sheer rock if you lost your footing.

Kendra bent at her waist, rose. Sitting, she carefully rotated her head to the left then to the right. Seemed okay, but the headache was back. She did not care, ignored it at first. But when the pain wouldn't go away, she convinced her weary mind that it was as it had always been—pain in her head compressed so much that any minute now her brain would burst. Right now, her mission was to ignore it

The thought of finding Luke's secret in the river kept her going. She stood up, no caution in the act. Pain moved from her shoulder and exploded once again in her head. She hoped the path she chose was the one Mrs. Sutter had been thinking about. She had told Kendra that she would smell it first, smell the death in the place. And Kendra did. About half a mile from the clearing where she had fallen, she smelled musk and sweet soil. She smelled death. She pinched her nostrils and breathed behind her hands. Sound had stopped as she went deeper into the wood. A wide band of dead leaves meandered up and away. She followed them, stopped when they dropped down.

There used to be a river here. Water once bubbled and wound through these woods, creating hills and valleys as it went, as it probably had done for thousands of years. But now, as Mrs. Sutter had told her, it was dry. Rocks, some small and others as big as small cars, lay on the edges of the river bed. The leaves crunched under her boots. The place smelled of rot, of death. Dead trees all around, their trunks thin as spider legs. Some trees lived, though. But though they were tall, they were so thin that they leaned over and their stunted, naked branches made them look like long keys.

Kendra could tell the path of the river, could discern its former course. The place it used to occupy was littered with brown leaves. These same leaves from the dead trees leaning to and fro above covered the entire area. And it was as if the water crystallized on its way to the sea into these brown, wasted, dead things.

If a body was dumped when the river was full, which it was in 1969, she imagined that it would be downhill, perhaps right here where she stooped. She held her hands in front of her face, remembering the snake. Ungloved hands, she thought, not smart. She looked around for a stick and found a fallen branch. As she held it up it wobbled from the top. She tried using it to stab at the rotted leaves but the thing broke with one dry snap. Disappointed, she opened her hand and let the rest of the branch fall among the dead leaves.

Rubbing her hand on her jeans she looked for another stick. Everything was buried under dead underbrush and leaves. She did not see anything she could use to poke around with. She felt dampness at the nape of her neck and shrugged out of the peacoat she thought she would need in these woods. She stopped as an idea came to her.

Kendra bunched the peacoat into a long ball. Using both hands to keep the ball from falling open she poked at the leaves. But the coat was not long enough. She took a step forward, tried again, still not enough length. She took another step and then fell for the second time that afternoon. This time she screamed, shrill and short. Leaves crackled and whipped around her. Her jeans felt wet as if she had just fallen into a pile of sludge. A sickening smell filled her nostrils and she held her breath in vain to keep from breathing in the stench of it.

She was up to her waist in dead leaves. Leaves crackling around her, she jerked her arms up in the air and lurched forward to try to get out. Tears stung her checks. She tried to stand but slipped on the sludge again and had to drag herself back to the bank of the dead river. A river used to be here. Mrs. Sutter's voice rang in her head. Kendra lay on her belly this time, too stunned to move.

Finally she scrambled to a kneeling position and thought of giving up again. She thought about making the half mile trek back to the clearing, filthy, hot-cold, mud-streaked and clawing her way up the trench with the trickling water.

She started to sob then. *No,* she shouted to the trees. Not this close, not this far. She beat at the leaves with her fists, jumped back into the mess and scraped and threw the dead leaves out of the river bed. They flew upward as if in a strong wind. They swirled around her head, they fell around her like clumps of brown rain.

She stopped and looked around her. She had emptied places in the river down to its empty bed. Maggots and beetles frantically scampered in the black exposed soil. But nothing human, no body. Mrs. Sutter was wrong on two counts. The river running through Kettle Creek was not dead. It teemed with life. And there was no body to be found. Perhaps there never was.

Red and purple began to streak the sky. The sun was about to set and she would be left in darkness. Knowing that she had failed, again, Kendra stood up, wiped her cheeks with filthy hands. She climbed out of the river bed and began walking back to the trench of slim water. She walked a few steps, not paying attention to her surroundings. Dazed, she changed direction, thinking she was going the wrong way. Leaves crunched beneath her feet. The sound stopped her again. Still not the right way, she thought. The colors of the setting sun confused her even more. How long had she been gone? It must have been hours. She held her hands out as she watched the sun's red shadow move across her hand. Closing her eyes, she listened for the water, the sound of the living forest, and heard it.

She turned southeast, casting one final glance at the dead river. She had not gotten to this part of the river in her earlier frenzy. The dead leaves lay peacefully as if resting in a quiet grave. Light from the dying sun sent a shadow over that piece of the river. Watching it for a while, she thought about how hard it was going to be to return to Rich with nothing. She turned to go, then stopped suddenly. White bone, bleached like marble. She saw it, she was sure. She ran back to the river, tripping, falling, ignoring the explosions of pain rising back up like a buoy on the water. When she reached the river's edge, the white knob of what looked like bone had disappeared. She washed the mud from around her eyes. With every ounce of sight in her body, she ran her gaze over each leaf, taking in the curled edges, the juiceless skin.

Heart sinking, she was about to give up. The dying light made it hard to see. Just before she turned, she saw it again, a white knob like a button sticking out of the surface of this dead river. She did not run this time but walked toward it as if on a tightrope. Kendra Hamilton reached into the dead leaves. When she brought her hand up again, she had hold of a long bone. Not an animal bone, but a human bone, a femur, the longest bone in the human body. She held it in her hands as the sun went down. Calm like warm water washed over her.

"Hello, Mrs. Luke Bertrand," she said.

Reverently she placed the bone back among the leaves and ripped the yellow scrunchie from her hair. She tied it around a fallen tree to mark the spot so she would be able to remember it. Having a former cop for a boyfriend, she knew that she should leave the bone where she found it. That bone was evidence, and she was sure the rest of Mrs. Luke Bertrand would soon follow.

As if taking a stroll in the park on a nice spring evening, Kendra Hamilton walked back, sure footed, to the path that would lead her to what she had wanted ever since returning to Dunhill— Luke's Bertrand's head on a silver platter.

CHAPTER 36

Rich found Kendra an hour later wandering through the woods. She was filthy, her face so covered with mud that he would not have recognized her if he saw her on the streets of Dunhill County. Her eyes glittered; her hair fell around her shoulders in thick coils. And she stuttered when she spoke. He held her for a minute, frightened at how her body trembled against his. He would not let her pull away until she had stilled.

"Co . . . Co . . . Co . . ." she tried.

"Shhh," he said, thinking that she had been trying to tell him that she was cold.

But what she was trying to tell him was "come." He followed her through those strange woods even though she meandered crazily. For what seemed like an hour he was sure that they had walked in circles. It was pitch dark now, the silver moon barely penetrating the tangled bramble overhead.

Even though Rich prided himself on his good sense of direction, he was becoming afraid that he would be lost in this wooded darkness forever, searching for something that was not there.

"We have to go," Rich said. "Now."

"No, no, no," she responded. "It's here, I found it. I should have brought it with me . . . I shouldn't have left it." Her voice rose to a wail and Rich could see that she was working her way into a frenzy.

"Okay," he said. "Stop walking for a minute. Take a deep breath and tell me."

She gulped air. "I found a body, I mean bones," she said. Though calm, her voice was wet with tears.

"Where?" Rich said, fighting the instinct to contradict her. In her condition, that would have been dangerous.

"I don't know," she said. "I . . . I thought . . ."

He reached out and held her shoulders. "Take a deep breath and tell me," he said.

She sent a tentative finger south. "Fine," Rich said. "Then let's go."

They went, sliding down their asses on a small hill. They stood at the bottom as Rich ran his flashlight over the area. His white light found a yellow scrunchie tied to a twig.

"There?" he asked.

She nodded. And it was there. He saw it on top of the leaves.

"Is it human?" he asked her as he picked it up. But even he could see that it was.

"I already told you that it was," she said. "Thigh bone, femur."

He released it and let it fall softly on the bed of leaves.

"Bring your light over here," he said.

She didn't. Instead she had gone farther down the river bed pointing her flashlight away from him. Rich shook his head. For someone afraid of the dark, you'd think she'd have a better flashlight. He poked around the leaves with a stick and found a white plastic boot.

"Rich," Kendra called.

He went over to her and saw her working at the straps of a small suitcase with brass buckles. It was still closed even though the leather had tattered and flaked away in places.

"Kendra, wait," he said. She was trying to pry it open and he didn't think that was such a good idea.

"It's her, don't you see?" she said, her voice wild with delight. "She tried to leave him and he couldn't stand it. *Always mine,* Rich. That's what he put inside her wedding ring, Always mine. And if she refused to be his, she wouldn't be anybody's. He saw to that."

Rich didn't say anything but he wanted to tell her to slow down. They didn't know what they had yet. The body could have belonged to anybody. It could have nothing to do with Luke. From what Mrs. Sutter said, the place had become a dumping ground of sorts for bodies.

The suitcase opened with a pop. A smell so foul rose from the soaked contents that they both put their hands over their noses. Rich ran his light over the open suitcase and saw what looked like a small jewelry pouch and makeup bag. But it was what was on top of the waterlogged clothes that caught his eye. A diary, a plastic affair no bigger than the palm of his hand and decorated with elephants.

"Where did you find this, babe?" Rich asked.

"Over there." She pointed. "Wedged between those rocks."

The clothes, though faded and black and heavy with mildew, still had some of their original color. The woman who owned them must have taken fashion lessons from a peacock. She seemed to favor teeth-rattling neon greens and pinks. Kendra unfolded what looked like a bright red shirt dress, the plastic belt still attached.

"It's her," Kendra whispered. "Remember what Mrs. Sutter said about the way she dressed?"

Rich covered his face with his hands thinking, yes, it's her. They had found the body of Debra Bertrand, Luke's wife. No happy retirement home for her after all. But there was something else, too. Something that Rich knew the minute Kendra popped the latches on the suitcase and he saw those bright colors.

He picked up the diary. He noticed that the elephants on the cover had their trunks up, and their pink tongues lolled out of their wide mouths. Anna Cotton had a diary like this but she used hers to draw pictures. He wondered what Mrs. Bertrand used hers for.

Most of the blue ink had been smeared and turned purple from the water. But the plastic cover had kept some of the writing intact. He was able to make out the date on a couple of the pages. August, 1970 was one of them. That was months after Luke left Kettle Creek and had returned to Dunhill.

"He didn't do it, Kendra," Rich said.

"What?" she said.

She wasn't really listening to him. Instead, she had opened the jewelry pouch. Rich shone his flashlight at her. She squinted in the white light and dropped the pouch. An elephant brooch, gold, rolled out. Two tiny rows of diamonds depicted the elephant's tusks. Rich thought of the only other person he knew who was fond of animal jewelry. He thought about the letter opener and the cuff link in the shape of a pig found among Anna's treasures.

"Luke didn't do this, Kendra," Rich said again.

"What are you talking about?" she said, paused. Then, "No, he did it. We have the body."

Rich thrust the diary at her. She shone her own light on it and read the date at the top. At first Rich thought that Kendra would continue her denial. But then he heard her sob.

"No!" she said. "No, it can't be."

She sobbed next to him. As he held her, Rich realized with growing horror that he had not taken care of the job in Dunhill. He had thought Chadwick raped Anna off the premises. And he had thought that maybe his buddy Grubb helped him. But what if Chadwick had signed Anna out of Brighton House to meet someone? Someone like Theo Lane. When Anna became pregnant, Theo had suspected Chadwick had used her himself and killed him out of what? Outrage? Rich could only speculate but he knew that Theo Lane killed Chadwick and framed Anna Cotton for the murder.

But even before that, when Kendra came around asking questions about Luke, he sent Chadwick after her. The bruises on Chadwick's forearms did not come from Anna but from Kendra's baseball bat. Why didn't he see that? Watching Kendra run her fingers over the torn pages of the diary, Rich knew that Theo had another secret to protect, his relationship with Luke Bertrand and the murder of his lover. Worse, Anna Cotton could still be in danger. And here he was, hundreds of miles away and Anna did not even have the protection of a holding cell, only a lone guard outside her hospital room, a guard that could easily be fooled by the likes of Theo Lane.

CHAPTER 37

Rich and Kendra flew the red-eye back, the only sound the roar of the jet engine in their ears. On the way from the Dunhill airport, Kendra sat beside him in the passenger seat of the Monte Carlo mute as a stone. Ever since finding Debra Bertrand's body and finding out that Luke hadn't been the killer, couldn't have been, she had not said a word. He had seen something in her eyes give way. He told himself that she would eventually heal but there was some part of Rich that didn't buy it.

Rich called Gregory on his way from the Dunhill County airport to tell him about Theo Lane and Katherine Holder's suspicions. He didn't think he had ever heard Gregory curse before. He tried to remember but couldn't come up with a situation where his friend used the words "trust" and "fuck" in the same sentence. He tried to tell him about the body, to call the sheriff's department in Kettle Creek if he didn't believe him. But Gregory did not leave an opening. Frustrated, Rich flipped the phone closed. He held it against his mouth for a few minutes. When he got Gregory back on the line, Gregory was calm but Rich could feel him about to go into another tirade.

"Look," Rich said in the phone. "I know this looks bad but why don't you meet me at Katherine Holder's place? If you don't want to hear what I have to say at least listen to her."

"Is Kendra with you?" Gregory asked.

Rich looked over at Kendra who stared out the window, street-lights illuminating her hair and still face.

"You can say that," he said.

"Then I'll be there. You know where Holder lives?" Gregory asked.

Rich told him no, and Gregory gave him directions to a group of condominiums in The View. Gregory got out of his own Monte Carlo as Rich and Kendra drove up.

"I really hope you have a good explanation for this, Rich. I gave you twenty-four hours; it's been almost two . . ."

"I don't have time to talk about that now," Rich said as he entered the complex.

Gregory jogged behind him and Kendra trailed along, still in the same fog she had been in since they left the airport.

"Lucky number seven, right here, Rich," Gregory said as he rapped on the door.

They stood in the hallway and waited for an answer. None came.

"Should she be here?" Gregory said as he tried the door again.

Rich took a deep breath and placed a hand on the Beretta stuck in the waistband of his jeans.

"She should be," Rich said. "I've called the hospital and she's not there."

"I'm not talking about Katherine, Rich," Gregory said. "I'm talking about Kendra."

Rich spared Kendra a look. He was about to say something but she beat him to it.

"I'm fine," she said.

Rich looked at Gregory. "You heard her, man, she's fine. Try again."

Gregory rapped on the door once more. Still, no answer.

"Would you like to? Or shall I?" Rich asked.

Gregory moved a few blonde strands of hair behind his ears.

"Since I don't know what the hell is going on and don't want my behind in a sling, by all means, be my guest."

Rich didn't bother with picking locks now. Something told him that Katherine Holder was behind that door and that he did not have time to play with locks. He lifted a booted foot and kicked the door with all his might. The frame did not give way until he kicked a third time. An old woman, a pink turban that matched her pink face, stuck her head out of the condo next door.

"Hey, again with all the commotion . . ." she complained.

Gregory flashed his badge before she could finish. She pulled her head back inside and shut the door. Locks clicked into place.

Kendra saw Katherine Holder first and it was the sight of her that released Kendra from her fog. She ran toward Holder who sat stiff as a board on the sofa. Her body looked like a two-by-four someone had left propped against the sofa. Her hips jutted forward, her arms stuck straight out at her sides. She had a small bullet hole in her chest. Rich did not want to know what the exit wound looked like but he could guess. Dr. Holder, too, could probably guess. She was fully conscious, her eyes skating in panic between the three of them. Kendra didn't have to tell them to call an ambulance, Gregory Atfield had already radioed in for help.

"Goddammit," Rich said as he drew his Beretta to clear the apartment. As he emerged from the kitchen, he stuck his weapon into the waistband of his jeans.

"Clear?" Gregory asked.

Rich nodded, ran his hand over his head. "God. Dammit," he breathed.

Gregory reached out and handed something to Rich. Rich found a .357 magnum shell casing in his hand.

"Is she all right?" Rich asked Kendra.

"I don't know," Kendra said.

"Any sign of the weapon?" Gregory asked Rich.

Rich looked over at Kendra as she checked Katherine's airway and listened for a pulse. She grabbed a red blanket lying on the sofa. A flash of white caught Rich's eye.

"What's that?" he asked.

"What's what?" Kendra asked, draping a blanket over Katherine Holder's trembling torso.

"That piece of paper in your hand?"

She looked at the bloody piece of paper she was holding. As if not realizing it was there, she threw it down. "I don't know," she rasped, "It's not important."

"Rich," Gregory interrupted him. "You sure you didn't find any hint of a weapon?"

Rich turned back to Kendra. She didn't hear them. Or pretended not to hear. Rich wasn't sure which and he wouldn't be sure until later. He shook his head in answer to Gregory's question. Katherine Holder's teeth clicked together. Rich felt his heart go into double-time as he watched someone who he thought was about die. He wished that he could make his heart beat for the both of them. Shit, he thought, if only he had made it thirty minutes earlier. Katherine's teeth clicked again.

"Shhh," Kendra said. "Don't try to say anything. Be still."

"No, no, no," Katherine chattered. "An . . . An . . . An . . ."

"Anna," Rich finished for her.

He and Kendra looked at each other. "Go," Kendra said. "I'll stay with her."

"What's going on here?" Gregory asked.

"It's Lane," Rich told him grimly. "He'll probably be after Anna."

"For what?" Gregory asked.

"To shut her up, that's what," Rich replied.

"Go!" Kendra said again. "I'll stay with her."

"I'm not leaving you here . . ." Gregory started.

"Look, Gregory," she said. "We're wasting time. What do you expect me to do? I'm not going to leave her here like this. I'll stay until help arrives. In the meantime, go see about Anna."

Kendra kept her eyes on Katherine's face until the two men had left the condo. The door, she noticed, had been left wide open, probably to allow immediate access for the paramedics. Kendra had already ripped open Katherine's shirt. The bullet wound was nowhere near the heart and Kendra hoped that the very fact that the woman was sitting here looking back at her, still breathing, that the bullet had missed vital organs. She checked Katherine's limbs and body for other gunshot wounds but couldn't find any.

Katherine looked down at the wound herself, and when she saw it she swallowed a sob. Color drained back into her face and Holder's body relaxed on the sofa. Kendra checked her abdomen, sighing with relief when she didn't feel any rigidity. She reached her arms around Katherine's body next as if to hug her and pulled her up so she could get a good look at the exit wound. It was bad, but Katherine Holder would live.

She told Katherine to press the blanket, which she had previously draped around her shoulders to the wound. As sirens whirred outside, Kendra studied Holder, who was calming down. She was more worried about the bullet hole in her torso than anything Kendra Hamilton was doing. With Holder's attention elsewhere, Kendra retrieved the Smith & Wesson she had slid under the couch earlier to hide from both Rich and Gregory. Not taking her eyes off her patient, Kendra slipped the revolver in the inside pocket of her plaid jacket.

The paramedics entered and she gave them the rundown. As they worked, white gurney flashing, jackets crunching, Kendra barely registered the scene in front of her. She was thinking one thing and one thing only. She was thinking that she should have shot Luke Bertrand when she had the chance.

The corridors of Doctor's Hospital smelled of alcohol and reminded Rich of dying carnations. Rich couldn't stand hospitals, would have turned back if he didn't think that Anna Cotton was in danger. Gregory had tried to call ahead but the person on the other end called him a crank and hung up. Doctor's was close to Holder's condominium, about two blocks. Gregory and Rich reached it long before any police unit.

Anna Cotton's room occupied the northeast corner of the ninth floor. The elevators that took them there moved at a snail's speed. When they finally reached Anna's room the guard sitting in front of her door greeted them with a wide smile. He held a *Star* magazine in one hand and an orange lollipop in the other.

"Hiya, Sarge," he said to Gregory as he watched them approach.

"Officer Flounders," Gregory said. "How many times have I told you that I'm not Sarge?"

"Sarge was good enough for me in the army, it's good enough for me now," Flounders answered.

Gregory, at the sight of his officer's comfortable demeanor, had holstered the weapon he had drawn as they approached Anna's room. But Rich, still not comfortable, had his Beretta drawn and pointed toward the ceiling.

"Son," Flounders said. "Put that thing away before you hurt yourself," he said, his orange tongue flapping.

Rich looked at Gregory and rolled his eyes.

"Can't you find anything else to do with assholes this close to retirement?" Rich asked him. He looked at Flounders. "Man, are you drunk?"

"Hey. Now," the man protested.

"Is she in there?" Rich asked.

"Of course she is, smart ass. Where else would she be? She's in there sleeping like a baby."

Rich let out a breath of relief. He holstered his Berretta and wiped sweat from his forehead. He bent double, rested with both hands against his knees. God was that a false alarm that he needed right at that moment.

"I don't want anybody in there tonight," Gregory was saying. "Understand? Nobody but Anna."

At this, Flounders stood up. The *Star* magazine fell from his knees, the pages rustling against the white linoleum floor. He rose, heart-stoppingly slow, to his feet.

"What are you doing, genius?" Rich asked from his kneeling position.

Flounders pointed toward Anna's closed door.

"To tell that gent visiting that it's time to go. He said he was a friend of hers. She didn't seem to mind him coming by."

"What?" Rich asked as the blood of panic filled his ears. "Who?"

"Fella," Flounders said. "Fella in the clown suit . . . Hey . . ."

The words were not out of Flounders's mouth before Rich and Gregory busted through the second door of the night. Theo Lane, wearing a royal blue cashmere sweater and tomato red pants, looked up at them. His lips pulled back from his teeth in a yellow smile. Because she was an accused murderer, one of Anna's wrists was shackled to the bed. The other hand she had knotted in a fist. She used it to beat and claw at Lane, who was pressing a white pillow against her face.

"Let her go," Gregory said.

Though he had his weapon drawn again and pointed toward Lane, Rich's throat had locked. He couldn't get a word out if he tried.

"I loved her," Lane said. "You don't understand. I loved her until that bastard Chadwick ruined her for me. Now she's a whore like the other one."

"Lane," Gregory warned again. "You got three seconds."

"He was supposed to bring her to me," Lane said, while his liver-spotted hand squeezed and pressed the pillow harder against Anna's face.

"Gregory," Rich finally breathed, thinking neither one of them really knew how long Lane had been in there holding a pillow over Anna's face trying to smother the life from her. A brown fist punched Lane's shoulder. He didn't flinch. Anna grunted beneath the pillow.

"One," Gregory said as Rich circled around to the foot of Anna's bed, his Beretta still trained on Lane.

"That's what I paid him to do," Lane said. "To bring her to me." He pressed the pillow harder. "He stole her from me. That's what he did."

"Two," Gregory said.

Anna tried to roll from underneath the pillow. Rich saw her face, how red her eyes were. She gulped a lung full of air before Lane managed to get her face underneath the pillow again.

"And that Hamilton woman," Lane ground out. "He couldn't even do that right. And all the time, he was stealing my treasure, turning my Pretty Anna into a whore."

Rich had no idea what Gregory was thinking and frankly, he no longer gave a shit. He made sure the Beretta was aligned with Lane's face. He pulled the trigger; the gunshot in the tiny room deafened them.

But instead of Lane's face dissolving into a mass of blood and bone, the window behind him shattered. Just as Rich pulled the trigger, Anna had kneed Lane with all her might in the groin. He let go of the pillow, ducked to clutch his testicles. Anna rolled to her side, coughing, sputtering, and sobbing.

"Rich," Gregory said as he rushed toward Lane to cuff him and get him away from Anna. "I almost had him talked down."

"He seemed the one doing all the talking, Gregory," Rich said.

He went to Anna and asked if she was all right. She nodded. The gunshot, the waterfall of broken glass brought running feet. Soon the room was filled with the useless guard and several nurses and doctors. Rich stood in the door of Anna's room watching. As Gregory led a handcuffed Lane past Rich, Lane stopped and looked at him.

"The whole thing's pretty clever, Rich. You have to admit," he said.

"Yeah," Rich breathed. "Pretty clever to rape a mentally retarded girl and frame her for murder."

Lane's silver eyes bored into Rich. "I'm not talking about that," he said. "I loved her. She loved me."

Rich looked back at a sobbing Anna on the hospital bed, the wind billowing the curtains of the shattered glass window.

"I can see that," Rich said. "I saw you loving her when we walked through the door."

"That was unfortunate and unavoidable," Lane said. "I had no choice. She would have started talking. I couldn't take that chance. But you have to admit, the other, shooting Luke, framing that Hamilton woman, that was pretty clever."

"Too bad your aim wasn't better," Rich said. "Is that why you shot him? To frame Kendra?"

He smiled, shook his head. "I shot him to keep him from telling tales out of school. I met Luke in '69 in Kettle Creek." He looked over his shoulder. "His wife was almost as sweet as that one. But she was too smart for her own good. Opposite of my Pretty Anna."

"Lane," Rich said, tired of the conversation. "Where is the Smith & Wesson?"

Lane blinked. "I don't understand," he said. "Where else would the weapon be but with the suicide?"

Rich looked at Gregory. "You tried to make Katherine Holder's death look like a suicide?" Rich asked.

"Yes, I did. Didn't you find the note?" he asked, still smiling. "Pretty clever, huh?"

Kendra knew Doctor's Hospital, had worked there before her mother died and things fell completely apart. Finding where Luke was in that massive building was easy. The nurse at the front desk told Kendra, who played the concerned daughter, that her "father," was in ICU. Luke had been injured by a gunshot wound to the upper torso, just like Katherine Holder. The nurse told Kendra that Luke was in and out but more in than out. And when he was in, he was coherent, could communicate through hand squeezes and eye blinks. When Kendra asked the nurse if Luke would recover, the nurse smiled and said that they were doing everything they could. And in her opinion, just her opinion, Luke would make a full recovery.

She found Luke sharing the ICU with two comatose patients. Luke's breathing machine seemed louder than theirs. She walked to his bedside accompanied by the sucking and plunging noise that for now acted as Luke's wasted lungs. She let the Smith & Wesson dangle toward the floor as she approached his bed. Luke was out of it but she knew that he was only sleeping, most likely sedated. She put the barrel of the Smith & Wesson against his forehead, nudged until the loose skin wrinkled and slipped against the bone of his forehead.

"Wake up, you son of a bitch," she whispered.

His head lolled from side to side. But he did not open his eyes. She pulled at the breathing tube, closed her hand around it. The sputtering startled her. She let go. His eyelids fluttered open.

"That's right," she said. "Look at me you SOB."

She watched as his eyes registered her. When she saw the recognition in his eyes, she stepped back and raised the Smith & Wesson until it was leveled with his face. She licked her lips, pressed the trigger to the back of the weapon. Slowly, telling herself that this time she indeed wanted to savor every second of terror in his eyes.

"Kendra," Rich said.

He saw her shoulders flinch. Good, at least she wasn't so out of it that she wouldn't hear him. He'd just hope that she'd listen. Because Gregory had already lifted his own weapon from his holster. The barrel was trained on Kendra's back.

"Gregory," Rich shouted. "No. Give me a minute or two to talk to her."

"You got thirty seconds, Rich," Gregory answered, his voice so calm that it maddened Rich. "Kendra, I have a weapon pointed at your back . . ."

"Gregory, please!" Rich said again.

He felt as if he had been riding a roller coaster for two days straight. His lurching stomach told him that he was about to take another plunge. He used all the will he had left to calm his own breathing.

"Look at me, Kendra," he said.

She wouldn't turn toward him but at least she answered him. "He deserves it, Rich," she said.

"Yes, yes," Rich soothed. "He does. But Kendra, think what will happen if you pull that trigger."

The revolver wavered in her hands. "Stay away, Rich," she sobbed. "I'll shoot him if you come any closer."

"Rich," Gregory warned in that same mild tone.

"Gregory, please." Rich waved his hands at him. "Just please, okay? I got this."

He turned back to Kendra, inched closer. Sweat broke out on his forehead and the bright lights in Luke's room chilled him. He saw the muscle in her arm tense. My God. She will shoot him, he thought. Gregory saw the same thing. The hammer of his six-shot cocked backward. It sounded like a jackhammer in the room. Rich looked at Luke lying on the bed. His eyes were so wide with terror that Rich could only see the whites of his eyes.

"No, you won't shoot," Rich said, talking to both Gregory and Kendra, but more so to Kendra. "No you won't shoot because you can't. You couldn't shoot Luke when you were in his house, and you can't shoot him now."

Rich moved until he blocked Gregory's gun sight with his own body.

"Rich," Gregory said. "I'm warning you. Move out of the way."

"No," Rich said again. "Gregory, a minute, please."

"Kendra," Rich continued. "If you pull that trigger, you'll be just like him . . ."

"So . . ." she yelled, sobbing now. "I don't care."

"Yes, yes, you do care," Rich said. "You'll be just like him. You'll be playing judge, jury, and executioner just like he did when he killed those girls."

She turned to him then, gazed at him as if she was seeing him for the very first time.

"And someone should be jury for him," she responded. "His jury failed. I'm just cleaning up their slop."

"It's not for you to decide," Rich said. "It wasn't for him to decide when he killed those girls, and it's not for you to decide now. He'll go down, Kendra. One day. But not here. Not now."

"Gregory," Kendra said, not taking her eyes from Rich. "You are going to have to shoot me because I'm not leaving until Luke gets what he deserves."

Rich held his palm to Gregory again who had moved until he had his weapon pointed at Kendra. "Rich, I'm running out of patience," Gregory said, but he still did not shoot.

"What about what you deserve, Kendra?" Rich pleaded. "What I deserve? You pull that trigger, Gregory will pull his. If you don't die, you'll be in jail for the rest of your life. Haven't we both given Luke Bertrand enough? Does he deserve your life? Our life, Kendra?"

He saw the gun waver. He was close enough now to put his hand on her shoulder. He moved his other hand down the length of her arm, stopped when he felt the weapon. Her hand trembled, weakened as Rich untangled her hand from the barrel, her finger from the trigger. He kissed her hair as she sobbed into his shoulder, caressed her neck.

"I'll take that," Gregory said, taking the Smith & Wesson from Rich's hand. "Not bad, old man."

"Did you ever doubt me?" Rich asked.

Gregory glanced at Luke. His lids were closed over his weary eyes. Tears drained from both corners, gathering in his ears. "I didn't," Gregory said. "But it looks like someone else did."

Rich looked at Luke for a long time. Yes, he thought, life was unfair. But Rich was not in the least bit troubled by that fact right now. Once again, Luke Bertrand will be allowed to walk away a free man, that is, if he recovers. But this time he will not take Richard T. Marvel or Kendra Hamilton with him.

EPILOGUE

Finally summer. The sun blazed for more than a few days in a row and the citizens of Dunhill shed their winter coats in favor of bathing suits and flip flops. And so it was with Rich and Kendra when they decided to spend a day at Capitola. Kendra looked over at the woman in the beach chair next to her. At sixty-six, Margaret Cotton knew the damaging effects of the sun. She was swaddled from wrist to ankle in a swimsuit cover-up and the black sunglasses she wore almost covered her entire face. As Kendra watched Mrs. Cotton rub sunscreen on her exposed cheeks only one thought crossed Kendra's mind. And that thought was that Margaret Cotton, Anna's mother, looked very much alive.

Kendra let her eyes skim the beach. Rich tossed a white Frisbee to Anna. But instead of catching it she let it sail in the air and fall swirling to the yellow sands. Anna was too preoccupied with the Labrador puppy Rich had given to her for her twenty-sixth birthday to play Frisbee. Tail wagging, the thing nipped at her hopping heels. When Rich gave the puppy to Anna, he had held it out in front of him as far as he could, as if he was holding a sack of toxic chemicals. Kendra took the puppy from him, laughing, saying that Anna liked pigs, not puppies. But Rich said that while he wasn't too fond of puppies himself, he drew the line at pigs.

Rich saw Kendra watching him and lifted his hand in a wave. She returned the gesture, smiling a little. It had been several months after the incidents at Doctor's hospital. Had Kendra recovered? Yes, she thought that she had, and Anna had recovered, too, for that matter. At first, leaving Luke in that hospital bed, still breathing, was the hardest thing that Kendra had ever done. But afterwards she realized that it wasn't true. The hardest thing that she had ever done was to realize, that for a while, she had gone off the deep end. And the hardest thing after that was to listen, to listen to Anna that her mother had not died and to listen to Rich that she, Kendra, had been sick the entire time.

When Kendra was released from the hospital she launched a search for Margaret Cotton. Leroy had died, and if Kendra had remained shut down, Anna would probably be in a home right now. So with Dominic and Rich's help, she brought Anna's mother home to her. It helped that Mrs. Cotton was searching for her daughter as frantically as Leroy was trying to keep Anna away from her.

Finding Debra Bertrand's family was harder. But she would eventually. In the meantime, she and Rich had lifted that broken body from Kettle River and gave it a proper burial in Kettle Creek after the sheriff's department had finished with it. Debra Bertrand was able to reap revenge against Theo, condemning him with his own gifts, the same gifts he gave to Anna. As Kendra watched Anna frolic with her new pet, she wondered if they would have been able to convict Theo of the rape if Debra had not pointed them in that direction. Kendra didn't think so. God bless you, Mrs. Bertrand, she thought now. Debra had received justice but she had to receive it from the other side of the grave.

Kendra lifted the magazine she had placed on her stomach when those thoughts intruded. Would it be the same for her? Would she have to wait until she died before Luke got what he deserved? She glanced down at the article that she was reading. *Body in a Box,* it read, *Mysterious Discoveries at Kettle Creek.* She looked up at the sun and smiled a little. No, she thought, she wouldn't have to wait until she reached the other side of the grave. Luke Bertrand would get what he deserved. And he would get it while Kendra Hamilton breathed and walked upon this earth.

FATAL JUSTICE

FAYE SNOWDEN

ABOUT THIS GUIDE

The suggested questions are intended to
enhance your group's reading of
this book.

DISCUSSION QUESTIONS

1. Can Anna Cotton ever have a consensual sexual relationship? Why or why not?

2. Do you think Anna Cotton is capable of murder?

3. How did Leroy Cotton feel about his daughter Anna?

4. What was the relationship between Anna and Leroy?

5. How could Anna have been better prepared to protect herself from sexual abuse?

6. How did Leroy contribute to his daughter's vulnerability? What else could he have done to protect Anna?

7. Why do you think that Leroy Cotton confessed to the crime?

8. Is Anna Cotton capable of learning how to live on her own? Why or why not?

9. What was Kendra's motive in asking for Rich's help?

10. Did Kendra have a hidden agenda in her concern to find Anna's rapist?

11. Luke only appears twice in the novel, and both times he is silent. Why do you think that Luke doesn't play a more active role in *Fatal Justice*?

12. How did Kendra's obsession over Luke manifest itself in the story?

13. Did Kendra ever give up trying to make Luke pay for her mother's death?

14. Did Kendra sleep with Rich in Kettle Creek as a delaying tactic, or were 'real' emotions involved?

15. What role did alcohol play in Rich's life, and was he true alcoholic?

16. Why did Rich quit drinking?

17. In your opinion, whose life was most out of control? Rich or Kendra's?

18. Will the relationship between Rich and Kendra last?